THE UNICORN QUEST
THE UNICORN DILEMMA
THE UNICORN SOLUTION

The war on Strand continues . . . and Jarrod Courtak, a young magician growing in strength, is the great hope of the people for victory. For he has found the unicorns, and with their help won the first battles ever in the long, terrible war against the mysterious invaders. But the strange promise of the unicorns has not yet been fulfilled.

This is the tale of that terrible fulfillment.

Tor books by John Lee

The Unicorn Quest
The Unicorn Dilemma
The Unicorn Solution

THE UNICORN SOLUTION

JOHN LEE

TOR
fantasy

A TOM DOHERTY ASSOCIATES BOOK
NEW YORK

THE UNICORN SOLUTION

Copyright © 1991 by John Lee

A Tor Book
Published by Tom Doherty Associates, Inc.
49 West 24th Street
New York, NY 10010

Cover art by Sanjulian
Map by Nancy Westheimer

ISBN: 0-812-50346-5

First edition: February 1991

Printed in the United States of America

0 9 8 7 6 5 4 3 2 1

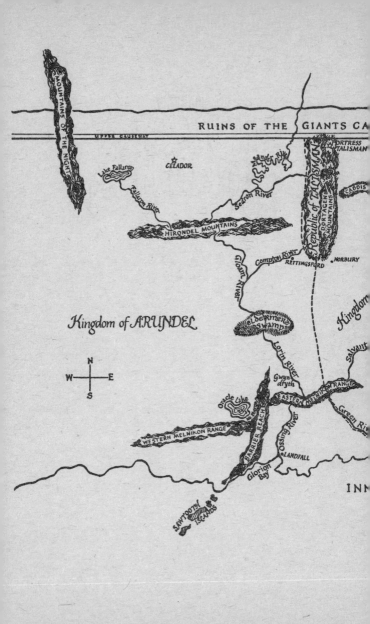

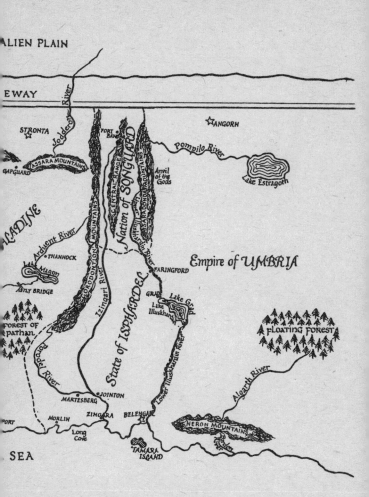

chapter 1

"From Arcage to action made of Polodine greeting," the bunglebird said complacently and shook itself. Half a dozen blue-grey feathers fluttered to the floor of the cote.

"What did it say?" Jarrod Courtak enquired. He was bent forward, more to avoid hitting his head on the roof than to get closer to the bird.

The question was addressed to his friend Tokamo, who was sitting on a stool off to one side. They were the same age, but Tokamo looked much the younger. He was barrel-shaped in his Magician's gown and the stool was invisible.

"From the Archmage to the Acting Mage of Paladine, greeting," he translated. The climb to the top of the building had winded him and he wheezed slightly as he spoke.

"Bloody birds! You'd think the Archmage could afford bunglebirds that could carry a clear message."

"Better take him a couple when you go to Celador," Tokamo replied unsympathetically.

"When I go? You wouldn't, by any chance, know what the rest of the message is?"

"He wants you in Celador and he wants you to take a unicorn with you," Tokamo said obligingly. He nodded towards the bunglebird. "It's wearing a red band, so it's urgent."

"If you already knew what the message said, why did you drag me all the way up here? You know I hate the smell." Jarrod was peevish.

"I thought you might like to hear it for yourself." Tokamo

was unperturbed. "Besides"—the tone sharpened—"it was an opportunity to talk to you without having the Songean guard around."

Jarrod looked at the chubby, seated figure in surprise. He's jealous, he thought. He smiled and went and propped himself against the wall hard by a window. "Sandroz is a little much, isn't he?" he admitted. "But there's nothing I can do about it. He insisted on following me here. He believes that his gods want him to protect me and nothing I say makes any difference."

"What about the other one?" Tokamo wasn't giving an inch.

"Old King Sig? I had to rescue him. He'd been sent off to die in the mountains and he's not ready to die. You've met him, you can see that for yourself. Besides, Marianna was very fond of him. I was there, we had extra cloudsteeds; I couldn't just leave him there to die on the mountain." He heard the defensive note in his voice. "I'm glad I did. He's having the time of his life. He's become the Palace pet." His face softened. "He gets up in the Great Hall after dinner every night and regales them with wonderful stories. He's really good. Every balladmaker at court is scribbling them down on the sly."

"So I've heard," Tokamo said drily.

"What else did the Archmage have to say?" Jarrod asked, reverting to safer ground.

"Nothing. You are to present yourself to him in Celador, accompanied by a unicorn."

"Just one unicorn?"

"Unless the bird got it wrong."

"Marianna isn't going to like that."

"Why should she care, so long as you don't take the big female? She's got enough here to keep her happy. She's got the unicorn, she got a place at Court and her father's here. What more could she want?" It was Tokamo's turn to sound peevish.

"I agree with you, but it isn't going to make any difference." The blue eyes were resigned. "Believe me," he said with a short laugh, "I know the girl all too well. She was furious that she couldn't come to Bandor."

"Then don't tell her. This is a private message after all."

"Wouldn't work. I can't take one of the colts unless Amarine agrees and now that Marianna can talk to her, she's bound to find out."

"That girl's got you on a lead rein," Tokamo observed and shifted his bulk. The stool complained.

"I wouldn't say that."

Tokamo grinned. " 'Course you wouldn't; you're in love with her."

"I am not." The reply was instant and heated.

"Oh, come off it, Jarrod. You don't even see any other girls, you just trot along behind her with blinders on."

"That's just not true."

Tokamo raised his eyebrows and cocked his head.

"Oh, all right," Jarrod said. "I used to think I was in love with her, but now I realize that it was just infatuation. We were alone together for a long time and we were pushed together after we came back, but when I was off by myself at Fort Bandor, I saw things differently."

Tokamo pursed his mouth and nodded judiciously. Even the folds of his robe seemed to convey disbelief. "Ah yes," he said, straight-faced, "Greeningale is coming and the blood is running warm. Now that you're a big hero, appearing at Court to dine with the Queen, you must have all those aristocratic ladies pursuing you." Years of practice had honed his technique in teasing and he was enjoying himself.

"Wisely, the young Sir Jarrod has prepared himself for the onslaught, clearing his decks of romantic baggage. . . ."

"That'll do, Tok," Jarrod said warningly.

"Touchy! Touchy!" Tokamo smiled widely and then became serious. "Are you going to tell me what happened with Marianna?"

"Nothing happened with Marianna. I just grew up a little, that's all."

"Oh, I see. You mean there's someone else."

"I didn't say that, although . . ."

"Come on, Jarrod, you can tell me. Who is it?"

"Well, there's a pretty little blonde lady-in-waiting who keeps looking at me," Jarrod said with a complicitous smile.

"Let me guess. Lettice Greenly."

"I don't know what her name is. I've never even spoken to her. Anyway, I shall be going to Celador and who knows when I'll be back." He shook the subject off. "That reminds me. There's something I've been putting off that I'll have to do before I go."

"Back to Lettice Greenly."

"Stuff a glove in it, Tok, I'm talking about trying to free Greylock. My strength is just about back again and I've put it off too long as it is."

"Yes," Tokamo said, matching his mood instantly, "I can understand why you would think that, but I'm not so sure that this is the best time to do it."

"Tok!"

"Hold on. Hear me out. The thing is that you haven't involved yourself in the day-to-day running of things since you got back." He held up a hand to forestall comment. "I'm not criticising; you've been recovering and Agar Thorden probably wouldn't have thanked you if you'd tried. All I'm saying is that you aren't aware of everything that's been going on. For instance, did you know that our dear Queen Naxania had tried to release Greylock when you were off at Fort Bandor?"

"No, I didn't. She hasn't said anything about it."

"She failed, didn't she? Are you also aware that she plans to withhold this year's Tithe from the Crown lands?"

"She can't do that. She knows that. She's a member of the High Council of Magic."

"That's as may be, but she's doing it. She told Thorden

that the money is needed to rebuild the Royal Forces and without them there will be no Discipline in Paladine, indeed there may be no Paladine.''

Jarrod groaned. ''That old argument.''

''Yes, that old argument, but, as you pointed out, she is a member of the High Council and, as such, she outranks us all. Now, if you were to succeed where she failed . . .'' He let the sentence trail off.

''If I succeed,'' Jarrod said, pushing himself off the wall and ducking his head, ''Greylock will be Mage again and he will deal with her as he always has. If I fail, Agar Thorden's no worse off than he was before.''

The words were terse and decisive and Tokamo knew that the discussion was closed. It hadn't been like that in the past. His friend had changed since he'd gone off to hunt for unicorns. He felt a pang of loss for something he couldn't quite define.

Jarrod took leave of his old friend and made his way to the stable to consult with the colts. That done, he retired to Greylock's tower. He had no time to waste now. He climbed the stairs to the Mage's workroom on the top floor. There was work to be done and all the ingredients he needed would be here. Greylock had waited too long as it was. He took a pestle and mortar off the shelf and put them on the long work table. He went looking for orris root. When he had located what he needed, he pulled out a high stool and settled down to the comfortable and familiar work.

The sound of the door being thrown open froze him in midstroke. He looked round and saw Marianna standing on the threshold. She was out of breath and there were angry spots of red on her cheeks. He saw her through his new-found distance. Tall for an Untalented girl. Pretty, with those big green eyes and pale skin; good figure, even in old riding clothes. One side of the dark red hair had come unbound and covered her right shoulder, the other was still pinned back neatly. The mouth was set in a straight line and the eyes were snapping. There was nothing soft about her. That was why she no longer attracted him, he decided.

The Duty Boy came to a skidding halt behind her. "I'm sorry, sir," he said, panting. "I asked her to wait, but she pushed me aside."

"It's all right," Jarrod said placatingly. "The lady Marianna is an honored guest, but you did well to ask her to wait. You may return to your post now."

"My, we have come up in the world, haven't we?" Marianna was making an effort to keep her temper in. "Since when have we been guarded by little boys?"

"Since Ragnor made me Acting Mage."

"And where's your usual watchdog?" she asked, looking round. "I expected to see Sandroz, or is he too busy packing for Celador?"

Jarrod forced a smile. "I take it that you've been to the stables."

"You didn't think you could sneak out of here without my knowing, did you?"

"Of course not. I only got Ragnor's message an hour ago. I don't even know if Amarine will let one of the colts go."

"Well she won't, not by itself."

"I didn't think she would," Jarrod said easily.

She looked at him suspiciously. "You're taking this very well."

He grinned. He couldn't help it. He so rarely had the upper hand. "My instructions are to take one unicorn, but I knew you would want to come along and I don't suppose that Ragnor will mind having the whole family in Celador."

"Oh. I see. Weeell," she dragged the word out, "I suppose that's all right then." She was clearly disconcerted and that pleased him. "There's a problem though," she added quickly.

"Oh?"

"No unicorn has ever been to Celador. There are no reference points in Northern Arundel."

Jarrod sighed. "I hadn't thought of that. That means we'll have to ride all the way and I suppose that means that we'll have to have an escort."

"Not necessarily." She was back in control again.

"And how do you come to that?"

"Are you going to invite me in and offer me a seat? Greylock didn't seem to mind my being in his workroom."

"I'm sorry," he apologised, scrambling off the stool. "I wasn't thinking. Er, please come in and, er . . ." He gestured toward the chairs by the fire. She always manages to do this to me, he thought.

"Thank you, kind sir." She walked over to the nearest armchair and relaxed into it. "As I was saying, we know that the unicorns can recognise places by looking at a map. They did that in the Anvil of the Gods, remember?"

He took the chair opposite her and folded down into it. "I remember, but that was different. They already had a reference point for the Barrier Reach."

"If you can transmit the image to them, they could use it to break out of Interim at the right place. You'd have to hold the whole map of Arundel in your mind, I suspect, but then you've always boasted about your memory."

Jarrod ignored the thrust. "But I'm unconscious in Interim," he objected.

"The unicorns aren't."

"Are you sure about this, Marianna? It sounds awfully risky. What happens if they come out in the wrong place?"

"You have to have faith. That should be easy enough for you, you're a Magician."

He knew that she was goading him, but he couldn't stop himself. "You know perfectly well that Magic is a science. I've explained all that to you."

She smiled to herself. He was ridiculously easy to manipulate. "And you have faith in it, which may be why it works."

Jarrod started to reply and then caught himself. No, now

that he knew what she was doing, he didn't have to play the game. He took a breath. "And what does Amarine think?" he asked.

"She thinks it would work," Marianna admitted.

"Well, that's settled then. If I can't have faith," he dwelled on the word, "in the unicorns, there's nothing worth believing in."

"I couldn't agree more. When are we leaving?"

"In a couple of days. There's something I have to do before we go."

"That sounds very portentous. Can I ask what it is?"

He glanced across warily. He could stand on his dignity as Acting Mage and tell her that he couldn't discuss it with laics. Not with Marianna, he decided, that would be asking for trouble.

"I'd like to try to free Greylock," he said simply.

"D'you really think that's wise?" Her concern was genuine. "I know that performing Magic takes a lot out of you and so does going through Interim."

Jarrod responded to the emotion behind the words. "I have to try, I really do. I don't know what Ragnor wants me for and I don't know how long I'll be gone. I can't just leave him up there. What if something happens to me? Naxania's tried to release him and she's failed."

She saw the appeal in his eyes and it touched her. "Are you a better Magician than she is?" she asked gently.

He sat back and considered her question. Was he? The Queen was older than he was and had won her place on the High Council of Magic in her own right. And yet . . . deep down he felt that he was a better Magician than she was.

"I don't know," he said honestly. "She's a great incantatrice. My Staff alone is proof of that. My Talents, such as they are, lie elsewhere. It may just be that those are the strengths that are needed for this particular job. All that I'm certain of is that I have to try, and if that means that we have to postpone the trip to Celador, so be it."

"You going to risk offending the Archmage?" She was goading him again.

"Oh no," he replied. "That would never do." He grinned. "It will just be unfortunate that the message arrived too late."

"Well, good luck then," she said and pushed out of the chair. She started towards the doorway and then swung back. "Promise me one thing: you won't try to go through Interim unless you're completely fit. Promise?"

"I promise, but I shan't hold back in the Magic just because of it."

"Agreed. Will you be at Hall tonight? I mean at the Palace?"

"No. I have a purification to go through. I was working on the main potion when you walked in."

"I'll leave you to your work then. Give my regards to Sandroz."

Jarrod got up and took a few steps towards the door. "Give my best to your father, if you see him, and Old Sig."

She nodded, smiled and left. She's so complicated, he thought. You never know what sort of mood she's going to be in from one minute to the next. Nevertheless, her question was a good one. Was he better than Naxania? And if so, why? Probably not, but he had to try anyway. He went back to the worktable and picked up the pestle.

His hands performed the task with the ease of a thousand repetitions and his mind continued to fret. The new Queen was highly gifted, no question about that. She had completed her training, as he had not, and she had more experience, but she had failed to rescue Greylock, despite her advantages. So what made him think that he could do any better? And he did believe that he could.

Well, he wasn't without gifts of his own, had proved it more than once—usually with the help of the colts, his honest side reminded him. Not at Fort Bandor, though; there had been no unicorns there—at least not at the beginning. The internal argument continued as his left hand reached for the next bunch of megswort and fed it under the constantly pounding pestle.

The recapture of Fort Bandor was something that he was proud of and he hadn't even used his Staff for the most difficult part of it. Greylock would have been pleased by the way that he handled it. He smiled gently. Canticles of Correlation into Spell of Unbinding, all accompanied, and topped off by Weatherwarding; not bad. Was he being conceited? He didn't think so.

His restless mind took him back. He was standing on an outcropping of rock halfway down the mountainside. It was night and patches of drifted snow blotched the scarp. He remembered the treacherous climb down and was glad that he wasn't going to relive it. Once was quite enough. He peered out at the blocky darkness, trying to locate the pipe that joined the Outlanders' base camp at the foot of the mountain with the fort up on the plateau above. He was aware, as he had been then, of the silent presence of Sandroz huddled against the cliff behind him and of the uncomfortable fibrillations caused by the pumps far below. He could feel the raw ingredients of the potion, so recently swallowed down with the help of snow, doing their work.

There had been other pressures as well, he recalled. The Outlanders' capture of the supposedly impregnable Fort Bandor had left Songuard and Isphardel undefended. With the enemy's corrosive atmosphere mantling the stronghold, there was no way they could counterattack. If he failed, the expedition would have to retreat ignominiously, and that would not sit well with Darius of Gwyndryth. Jarrod did not want to disappoint the man. Lord Darius was the most famous soldier in the Magical Kingdoms, but he was also Marianna's father, and in those days that had mattered. Oh yes, there had been pressure to succeed, for the Alliance, for the Discipline, for Darius.

He saw again the faint, greenish tinge at the edges of the sky that heralded the coming of the sun. The simples were protecting him from the cold, calming him, buoying him up, but the Jarrod in the workroom knew how bitter the chill of that false dawn must have been. He heard the words of the Canticle of Correlation that he had used to parse the underlying order beneath the seeming incoherence of the surface matter. That is where the skill had come in.

He looked down on the steep fall of crag and dormant vegetation, percieving the rules of the dance that bound them, his instinct for pattern correlating the analogies until the whole came clear. Complexity had been made simple, but he could not control it yet. He gathered his will and froze the inner gyrations of all the solid things. He felt an echo of the thrill he had experienced then. He watched himself unravel the web with cool precision. He selected the weakest point, and the thrust into the fabric of the mountain went true. He severed the fabric and the earth gave and gaped. The rock screamed as it was riven, but the chasm he had made moved swiftly downhill, accompanied by a crushing fall of boulders.

He left the base camp to its doom as he had done before and rose higher still to harness the wind and gather in the storm he had created over Lake Grad. He directed them at the shrouded fort, scouring it, whirling away the poisoned air. He bombarded it with hail to shatter the windows and topple the chimney stacks, to let in the pure and cleansing wind. He felt none of the soaring euphoria that he knew had sustained and elated him then, but he was smiling broadly. It had been a major piece of Spellcasting. Naxania could never have pulled that off.

His eyes refocussed on the mortar. He had ground up far too much of the megswort. He fetched a saucer and emptied the bowl. He moved almost jauntily over to Greylock's trunk and located a vial of powdered cormandel. He shook some out onto the little scale and weighed it carefully. He'd been a little reckless at Bandor, but everything would be done by the book tonight. He wasn't going to take any chances where Greylock was concerned.

He emerged from the ritual feeling clean and strong and confident. There was no room for doubt when he Made the Day and, after that, he had a disgruntled Sandroz to deal with. The Songean, barred from the room during the purification, had spent the night on the landing outside the door. The man's attitude toward Magic was ambivalent at best and Jarrod was conciliatory with him, in good part because he knew that he was going to leave his self-appointed bodyguard behind when he left for Celador. He invited Sandroz to accompany him to the Place of Power. The little man was certain to trail him anyway.

They rode out just after the daymoon rose and two sets of shadows paced them on their left. Jarrod was astride Beldun, his blue robe pulled up to the tops of his thighs. Nastrus and Pellia flanked them and Sandroz brought up the rear on a pony. They rode towards the last remnant of the Place of Power through a thick mist that curled upwards from the damp ground. He shivered. They hadn't been back there since the Battle of the Stronta Gate. The image of maggots squirming through a distant, smoking maw flooded in, causing Beldun to kick up his heels. It was gone as quickly as it had come.

Why had Naxania failed? He intended to use a modification of the Spell of Unbinding. It wasn't difficult technically; surely Naxania was good enough to pull it off? Perhaps he'd just been lucky up until now; perhaps it was all due to the colts. . . .

'*Why do you torment yourself over things you cannot change?*' Pellia's query pushed its way to the forefront of his mind.

'*You know that we know nothing of your Magic,*' Nastrus added.

'*Because I feel I should have done better, done something to prevent it,*' Jarrod answered. '*If I'd had more control perhaps Greylock wouldn't be stuck up there now.*'

'*There is no reasoning attached to this,*' Beldun explained to his kin. *'It is one of the human emotions that we are spared.'*

'What are we going to do when we get there?' Pellia wanted to know.

'Why would you ask that? It's been in my mind all along.'

'She means now that the Force Point is shielded. We can still draw energy from it, but I don't think you can,' Nastrus filled in.

'You're going too fast for me. I don't understand,' Jarrod replied.

'Your Place of Power is a Force Point, a place where your world is attached to a Line of Force,' the colt explained. *'It has been shielded since the battle.'*

'It's odd,' Beldun interjected, *'but the Memory shows that most Force Points are marked by big stones erected by the natives.'*

'Very interesting,' Jarrod said, *'but what's that got to do with me?'*

'Humans are so slow.' Jarrod wasn't sure where that remark came from.

'We draw our special energies from the Lines of Force.' Nastrus was patient with him. *'The closer we are to a Force Point, the easier it is, but I do not think that your Magic works in the same way. When I observed you performing your art at that military camp, we were far from a Force Point.'*

'Well, we'll find out soon enough,' Jarrod said, cutting off the conversation.

The black monolith that was the last remnant of the Place of Power had emerged from the mist. It looked incomplete to Jarrod. Time was, recent time too, when the massive obelisk had been surrounded by a ring of cromlechs. It had also not been alone in the ring. Two other menhirs, one white, one red, had kept it company. They too were gone. As they got closer, the broad circle of bright green grass stood out clearly from the winter silver of the surrounding country.

'Do you people have any taboos about eating that grass?'

Beldun asked. *'It's been a long time since we've had fresh forage.'*

'Not that I know of, though I don't recall anything ever grazing there.'

They pulled up by mutual consent outside the circle. The megalith seemed even taller to Jarrod than it had been when surrounded by its sister stones. Now there were bare patches of earth where the cromlechs had stood.

'We've always ridden round to the front and gone in there,' Jarrod thought, *'but that seems a little silly now. We might as well go straight in, but I'd avoid the bare bits if I were you.'*

He turned to see where Sandroz was and spotted the Songean twenty feet back, a safe distance from the unicorns. He raised his voice.

'We're going in now. You wait for us here, if you will. If anything goes wrong, and I'm not expecting it to, be sure that the colts are all right and then ride for the Outpost and get help. Don't try to help me yourself.''

Sandroz nodded his understanding and Jarrod rode into the Place of Power. The other two unicorns followed in single file. They stopped at the base of the stele. Jarrod craned his neck back and gazed up the black side, festooned now with a latticework of ladders. Up there, on the invisible top, Greylock lay, exposed to the elements. Jarrod had been there when the Mage was stricken, and it was up to him to set his mentor free. He owed him that and more.

'I shall invoke those who dwell here, or at least used to dwell here, and then I shall use Greylock's spell of levitation to get me up there. Once I'm there, I may need your help to complete my spell, so please don't let yourselves get distracted.' He got his leg across Beldun's ample back and slid off.

Jarrod pulled his gown down and shook it into a semblance of order. The effects of the potion were still strong and he felt relaxed and clear-headed. He glanced at the unicorns. Their minds were with him, but they were busy cropping the lush grass. He shook his head and walked to the center of the slab. He squared his shoulders, took a deep breath and then launched into the special words that Greylock had taught him.

They were no more than sounds to him, with carefully learned inflections. The pitch was a little below his normal range because Greylock's voice was deeper than his, but he had a mimic's ear and it wasn't difficult if he concentrated. The words rolled out exactly as he had pronounced them the last time, but there was no accompanying feeling that they were heard. There had been a tension in the air and inside him before: there was nothing now. He came to the end and still felt nothing. A small worm of uneasiness began to move somewhere under his breastbone.

He began the chant that had taken him aloft. Each strophe, note and accent stood clear in his memory and he reproduced them perfectly. The rich sonorities rose and Jarrod's arms rose with them. The prosesong swelled, but he remained firmly rooted. He went on to the finish with as much conviction as he could muster, but he knew that he had missed. His arms hung out there, feeling awkward, and he let them drop to his sides.

'You are affected by the Force Point.' *'What now?'* *'Why don't we boost him up there?'* The thoughts came in a braid, but Jarrod latched onto one strand.

'Could you get me up there?' he asked.

For answer he found himself floating in the air. He had been aware of no transition, but matte-black rock was now sliding downwards. He had the same feeling of unreality as he had had the night of his presentation to the spirits of the Place. Then it had been Greylock who had wafted him upward. The top of the megalith came into view and there was Greylock once again.

The colts deposited him gently on the surface and he stood staring down at the figure at his feet. It had been a long time since he had last seen the Mage—too long. The sun and daymoon were in the East and shone down on the Mage of Paladine, making the runegown glitter. Jarrod had had reports of his master's condition, but the actuality shocked him.

The weather had made no mark on the Mage, or on his clothing. The hair had turned completely white and he now had a neatly trimmed white beard. Greylock had always been a robust man, but this statue's face was thin and seamed. His whole body seemed to have shrunk and the ornate robe looked too big for him. His Staff was lined up neatly by his side and someone had placed his diamond circlet next to his head.

Jarrod knelt and turned back the sleeve. He tried to lift the bony wrist so that he could feel for a pulse, but he could not budge it. He tried to slide his fingers under the arm. It was impossible. He sat back on his heels and stared hard at the chest. He could detect no movement. He touched the hand again, reluctantly. It was no colder than it should have been and the skin was elastic, but those were the only clues that Greylock was alive. The Ring of the Keepers was still on his hand, but there was space between the top side of the finger and the band, emphasizing the loss of weight. The jewel that had blazed so brightly during the battle was dead and dull in its setting.

Jarrod got back up to his feet. The spirits of the Place might have fled or the Force Point might be covered over, but there was no reason why he couldn't call on his own resources to make the Magic. He was going to have to be very careful. He'd used the Spell of Unbinding to good effect at Fort Bandor, but he'd had a mountainside to deal with there. This would require great delicacy and absolute control. There was no margin for error. He ran over the preamble in his mind and reached out for the colts as he did so. They were an instant and reassuring presence.

He began to intone. The words came soft and sonorous and he felt the energy fomenting inside him. It was a relief after the disappointment on the ground. He increased his intensity and began his search for patterns. Flesh and bone, cloth and hair became clear. He concentrated on the rock beneath, but the stele rebuffed him. It remained blank, refusing to yield up its structure. His voice rose as he narrowed his focus. He needed that pattern or he could not pinpoint where the two met.

There was no resulting surge of power, no divulging of mineral secrets. He called on the colts and they obliged him. Power swept into him, heightening his perceptions and warming his body. He stared at the rock, willing it to surrender, but it remained opaque. He toyed with the idea of proceeding without the information, but rejected it. Too dangerous; he could not gamble with what was left of Greylock's life. He cut off the chant abruptly and his hands fell in defeat.

He stood there, shaking from the exertion, allowing the power to drain out of him. The colts withdrew gently and left him feeling empty. There was none of the euphoria that marked the conclusion of Magic making. The only thing that cocooned him from despair was the lingering presence of the potion. He had tried and failed, that's all there was to it. The agonizing would come later.

chapter 2

The Archmage sat at a long table, perched on a stool. He was in his workshop, but he had no work to do. He was in a bad mood and had withdrawn to his lair for solace. The rooftops of Celador could usually be counted on to lift his spirits, but they had failed him today. Oh, the familiar shapes were there, a garden of spires and fanciful stone pavilions, mossy tiles and crazed groupings of chimneys, but there was no life to them.

The roofs were rainswept now. There were no blooms in the pocket gardens, no dallying courtiers preening like cote birds around their females. The vista was grey and drab and forlorn. Ragnor huffed disgruntledly, rubbed his eyes and climbed off the stool to put the kettle on the hob. He arched his shoulders and kneaded the small of his back.

"You're getting old," he said aloud. "That's all that's wrong with you."

He pottered over to the hearth and moved the kettle over a patch of hot coals.

"And if you don't stop talking to yourself, people will think you've gone senile to boot."

Better get yourself a pet, he thought sardonically; talk aloud all you want then. Trouble was, he spent too much time alone. It had been different when Arabella was young and he had a kingdom to run. No time for anything then. But Arabella was a grown woman now and ran the kingdom herself. This was as it should be. He had brought her up to be her own woman, but now that it had happened he felt somehow betrayed.

He tossed a small handful of chai leaves in a pot as the water came to a boil and then filled the pot. The lifting brought a sharp pain to his wrist. That he was, in part, responsible for the pain, having ordered the keen winds and drenching rains to discommode the Outlanders, made it no more bearable. He poured himself a mug of chai and let the rough surface warm his hands. Problems, he thought as he lowered himself gingerly into his chair, nothing but aches and pains and problems.

He had always thrived on solving problems, but he seemed to have run out of answers. He wasn't even sure that he could render the city invisible and he'd have to do that soon, if only to cut down on the flow of refugees. These days, it seemed, he was reduced to gambling on unknown quantities like Courtak and the unicorns. The thought would have galvanized him once; now it depressed him.

Not that Courtak wasn't a major Talent. Greylock had spotted that early and had taken him in hand. He'd done a good job with the boy too. The lad didn't seem overly ambitious, he was respectful and, thus far, he hadn't tried to use the unicorns for his own advantage. Ragnor had read General Gwyndryth's report on the Bandor expedition. Courtak got high marks throughout. No clashes of ego there, evidently. In fact, he thought, if Courtak had a failing, that was probably it. The boy lacked fire.

Strange that, because he obviously had a decent measure of courage. There was a diffidence about the boy. That might change, though. Ragnor thought back. The boy had become harder over the past couple of years, no doubt about that. Part of it was physical, of course. Courtak had filled out, had lost the wild beauty some boys have late in adolescence. The Magic he had performed had added to the maturing process, but he still came across as young. Despite the fame that had attached itself to him, he didn't command a room when he walked into it.

Ragnor snorted to himself and drank some of the chai. The

same couldn't be said about the Gwyndryth girl. Now there was someone worth watching—in all senses of the word. A very powerful young woman, that one. Daughter of a Marches Lord and, more importantly, heir to the Holding. That made her a player on the national scene. Now that her father was commander of the Paladinian armies and, if his information was correct, the Queen's lover, the Lady Marianna had become an international prize.

Mind you, it would take an extremely strong man to control her. She was a discoverer of the unicorns and had made a name for herself at the Battle of Stronta Gate. No matter who was picked for her husband, she would always be more famous than he could ever be. All in all, a formidable young woman.

When you put Marianna of Gwyndryth and Jarrod Courtak together, you had a potentially dangerous alliance. Add Darius of Gwyndryth and you had military expertise. Stir in the unicorns and who knew what could happen. That was never a comforting thought. He'd have to keep a sharp eye on that situation. He shook his head and drank some more of the chai. Problems, nothing but problems.

Jarrod was depressed rather than tired when he met Marianna at the stables. It was not long past the Making of the Day and the dawn was grey and dank. The Outpost looked deserted, it being breakfast time. Both were bundled up against the cold to come.

"Are you sure that you're up to this?" Marianna asked. "Ragnor would never know if we held off a day."

"No; it's all right. I didn't get to do any real Magic. I couldn't make contact with the Dwellers." It was a partial truth and as much as he felt like saying on the subject.

"I'm sorry, Jarrod. I know that it meant a lot to you."

He nodded and gave a tight little smile. He went to the tack room and got his saddle. Nastrus was waiting for him and made no complaint when Jarrod cinched the girthstrap.

Marianna already had Amarine at the mounting block, so Jarrod strapped his saddlebags on Pellia. Beldun was already festooned with Marianna's things.

"How did you manage to give Sandroz the slip?" she called over.

"I didn't," Jarrod replied as he hoisted himself up. "I told him that he could come, but that he would have to ride one of the unicorns through the void. That was too much for him. He worships the unicorns, but I think, at bottom, he's terrified of them."

"Well, you can't really blame him for that," she said as they rode out of the stableyard. "They are pretty remarkable."

Jarrod was aware of the colts' complacent concurrence.

"By the way," she continued, "did you get Naxania's permission to leave Court?"

"I don't have to," Jarrod said. "I'm the Acting Mage. I can come and go as I please." That was true enough, but the fact was that he hadn't thought about it.

"I only asked because I didn't. I don't suppose it'll matter. She'll be glad to have me out of the way so that she can have my father all to herself." There was a note of bitterness in her voice.

"Don't you think you're exaggerating just a bit? I've seen them both at Hall and in the Royal Withdrawing Room afterwards and she hasn't paid him any undue attention—nor he her for that matter."

"Men never notice that kind of thing," she replied, "but I know what I know."

Jarrod let the matter drop. Marianna was touchy to the point of irrationality on the subject of her father.

"I take it you've memorized the map and passed it on," she said, changing the subject, to his relief. "Amarine seems quite clear about where we're going."

"The colts are confident that they can come out of Interim where they want to. It'll be another first for the Memory."

"I'll wager they're as glad to be getting away as I am," she said. "Things were getting a mite dull. Funny, all my life I've wanted to be at Court, and now all I want to do is get away. Mind you, I never counted on the Court being in deep mourning. It'll be a real pleasure to see some bright colors again."

They were clear of the Outpost now. The sun was still hidden behind the clouds, but the Great Maze shimmered of its own accord off to their right. Jarrod swivelled around in the saddle to check how far they had gone.

"Oh, no," he said aloud.

"What's the matter?" Marianna turned her head and caught sight of the Songean. She laughed. "Poor old Sandroz," she said. "He couldn't wait to get rid of us in Songuard and now we can't get rid of him."

"Oh yes we can," Jarrod said firmly. "Let's turn and face west." The colts were already swinging round as he spoke. They pulled up and Marianna waved at Sandroz.

"Hold on tight," Jarrod commanded. "Here we go."

He dug his fingers deep into Nastrus' mane and concentrated on the map of Arundel. He narrowed his focus down to the area just east of Celador, took a deep breath and held it. There was blackness and heart-stopping cold. Jarrod, Marianna and the unicorns vanished. Sandroz was alone on the Paladinian plain.

Hollow darkness, numb and empty; cold like wound-shock. Far away, twin patches of not-quite-black. Jarrod drifted slowly towards the promise of light, light that held out the hope of warmth, light that resolved itself into closed eyelids. With the knowledge came the awareness that his face itched and that breathing was difficult. He lifted his head and opened his eyes, realizing as he did so that he had been face down in Nastrus' mane. He sat up unsteadily and a meadow swam into view. Feeling came back and the chief stimulus was hunger.

They had made it. He sat back woozily in the saddle and looked around. They were all there. The colts were busy eating. The dam was standing somewhat apart with Marianna slumped onto the arching neck. They were in an unfenced pasture. There were trees in the midground and beyond them rose the unmistakable turrets and spires of Celador. He wanted to congratulate the colts, but he couldn't penetrate their preoccupation with food.

He slid off Nastrus and tottered over to Amarine on legs filled with pins and needles. He took off his gloves and reached into the mane, surprised anew by its coarseness. He found a wrist and checked Marianna's pulse. It was strong. She was safe where she was, he decided. They wouldn't be going anywhere until the unicorns had satisfied themselves.

He set off to walk a little authority back into his legs and take his mind off his stomach. The exercise warmed him and his land-legs came back. By the time he had circled around, Marianna was sitting up, and munching on bread and cheese. His stomach twinged.

"How are you feeling?" he asked.

"Cold," she said around a mouthful. "Though it seems to get easier each time we do it."

"I wish I'd thought to bring something to eat. I don't suppose you brought any more of that?"

"No, but you can have some of mine." She tore off a piece and handed it down to him. "There's a waterskin in my saddlebags." He fetched it and they finished the victuals in silence.

"The colts are ready to move on," Jarrod said, wiping away crumbs. "How about Amarine?"

"All set to canter and get the blood stirred up."

"Right then," Jarrod said, regaining his mount and swinging back up into the saddle, "let's get to Celador and dazzle the natives."

The road to Celador was curiously empty, the thin curving tops of the quandry trees that lined it nodding in the wind, but, as they neared the capital, they saw that the fields were full of sheep and kina.

"Looks as if they're having a cattle fair," Marianna remarked.

"Something must be going on. Look at what's coming."

They were close enough now to see the people on the walls and the crowd streaming through the gates towards them. The unicorns slowed down and stopped, responding to the uncertainty that Jarrod felt.

"Did you send advanced notice of our arrival?" Marianna asked.

"No." Jarrod looked around to see if they could get out of the way, but it was either move into the kina in the field to the right or join the sheep on the other side of the road. "Perhaps we should go back a bit."

"Not on your life. What kind of impression would it make if the unicorns were driven off?"

"I'm not suggesting that. I just meant go back until we can find a field to turn into so that we can get out of their way."

"It'll still look as if we were running away. You may do as you please. Amarine and I are staying put." Jarrod knew that tone of voice. There was no use arguing.

Trumpets rang. Horsemen appeared from the south and pulled up in front of the crowd. Their swords were drawn, but they did not use them. They spread out and contained the people without undue coercion.

"What on earth is going on?" Jarrod asked.

"I don't know, but I'd rather be in the open than stuck between these fences. I think we should ride forward." Amarine walked forward as she spoke and the colts followed suit.

They cleared the last enclosed field as a contingent of the Royal Guard pushed its way through the throng. The leader stopped and gave orders to the horsemen and then rode on towards the visitors. He reined in ten paces ahead of them and saluted.

"Welcome to Celador, Excellencies. You took us rather by surprise. There have been rumors that the unicorns were coming, but these days there are rumors about everything. Anyway, someone spotted you from the walls and," he turned and gestured to the scene behind him, "you can see what happened."

"I'm glad you came, Captain," Marianna said before Jarrod had a chance to open his mouth. "Celador has certainly devised a fitting welcome for the unicorns."

"My instructions, my lady, are to escort you to the Archmage. Will you follow me?" The man obviously had no use for pleasantries.

"Gladly, Captain." She looked over to Jarrod and grinned. "Get ready to dazzle them," she said.

The soldiers had cleared a lane through the middle of the crowd and, while the going was close in spots, the people were entirely good-natured. Jarrod and Marianna waved as they rode through and the answering noise was deafening. He expected the noise and the crowd to abate once they were past the gate, but there were even more people inside. Great Court was entirely filled and people hung out of windows.

"This is extraordinary," Jarrod yelled at Marianna, but she pointed to her ear and shook her head.

They rode on, waving until they got through the archway into Magicians' Court. The roar of the crowd diminished abruptly. There were people in the windows here too, but the only person who was totally visible was the Archmage, standing tall and thin at the bottom of the tower steps. The escort swung aside, leaving the unicorns to go on alone. They drew up in front of Ragnor and Jarrod bowed deeply before dismounting. Marianna stayed astride Amarine.

"Welcome, my friends, welcome," Ragnor said, opening his arms in a gesture that embraced the unicorns. "It is good to see you all again."

He came forward beaming and reached up to touch hands with Marianna. "This is indeed a pleasant surprise, my lady." He turned and repeated the gesture with Jarrod.

"We commend you on our promptness, my Lord Mage. Please convey to your friends that we are honored that they have undertaken to visit us." He turned back to help Marianna dismount.

"I take it that you have come through Interim," he said, referring to the number of clothes she was wearing.

"Yes indeed, your Excellency, though I must admit that a second cloak does not come amiss here at this time of year."

"Too true. Even the weather has become a victim of war this year. I am sure that you would all like some rest and some refreshment. I think that, given the present circumstances, it would be better if your friends had a military escort to the stables to protect them from the curious. I have had a special stable prepared."

No wonder there were rumors about the unicorns, Jarrod thought as he unstrapped his bags. *'Will you be all right?'* he asked the colts.

'Of course we shall,' from Nastrus; *'Can we get on with this, I'm thirsty,'* from Beldùn; *'Will you be able to take us for some exercise?'* from Pellia.

'Some time tomorrow, I promise you. Nastrus, no little side trips of your own if you get bored, please.' He rubbed each colt behind the ears and then watched them follow their mother. The muffled sound of cheering rose again.

"Leave your things here," Ragnor said. "I'll have the Duty Boy bring them up. You'll be sleeping in my anteroom I'm afraid, Jarrod. I'm not sure where we'll put you, Lady Marianna." He extended his arm to her and they started up the steps. "I wasn't expecting you," he said as they climbed the stairs, "so I may not be able to secure lodgings suitable to your rank right away. I hope you will bear with me."

"Of course I shall, Archmage, and you mustn't put yourself out on our account. Jarrod and I are accustomed to sleeping rough.''

She's putting on the charm, Jarrod thought as he trailed after them. "Is this a feast day?" he asked.

"Would that that was all it was," Ragnor said over his shoulder. "I'll explain when we are upstairs and you've had a chance to take some of those clothes off."

Food arrived before they had finished changing and that further delayed conversation. When they had finally quenched their appetites, Marianna put her napkin aside. "What exactly is going on at Celador?" she asked bluntly.

Ragnor looked from one to the other. "I take it that the news has not yet spread to Stronta. The Outlanders have launched an invasion from the Unknown Lands and the populace has invoked the age-old privilege of sanctuary." He got up from the table and paced over to the fireplace. "I'm afraid, my dear," he said to Marianna, "that that puts paid to your theory of benign withdrawal."

"I'm afraid I don't agree, Excellency," Marianna countered. "This attack is obviously not benign, but that does not mean that the earlier withdrawal was not sincerely intended. The enemy have, for whatever reasons, changed their minds. One thing has not changed and that is that, at bottom, we are the real aggressors." Her tone had sharpened.

Jarrod closed his eyes and clenched his teeth. She was going to make trouble.

"That's as may be, young lady, but at the moment Arundel, your country, is on the defensive. Her land is being ravaged, her farmers burned out, her families left homeless. This is a time for action, not philosophy." Ragnor was not accustomed to being contradicted, let alone by a girl young enough to be his granddaughter, and he let it show.

"You're quite right, Excellency, but only for the short haul. In the long run, you will have to come to terms with the problem." Marianna, to Jarrod's surprise, was undaunted.

"In the even shorter term," Ragnor said with renewed

urbanity, "I see the Duty Boy hovering and that means that we have found you a room, my lady. I shall be dining in Magicians' Hall this evening and I insist that you both be my guests. We have an excellent cook at the moment." He came away from the fire.

"Boy, do you take the Lady Marianna to her lodgings—her bags are at the bottom of the stairs." He turned to Marianna. "We dine at the tenth hour, my lady. Why don't you join us here for a glass of sherris before the meal?"

He accompanied her to the door and acknowledged her curtsey graciously. When she was out of earshot, he rounded on Jarrod.

"What in perdition possessed you to bring that girl along? I ordered you to come here and bring one unicorn."

"I had no choice, sir," Jarrod said defensively. "Amarine, the dam, would not allow her family to be split up and wherever the dam goes, Lady Gwyndryth goes too. Your message was marked urgent, so I assumed that you would prefer to have four unicorns than none at all."

Ragnor harrumphed and walked back to the fireplace. He subjected Jarrod to a long scrutiny along the way. Let him sweat, he thought. The young pup's come a long way in a very short time. Probably needs a firm hand.

"There's some sack on the sideboard behind you, son," he said at last. "Be a good lad and pour me some. Then come and sit down." He himself selected the righthand chair and settled into it. "Ah, thank you." He waited for Jarrod to sit down. "Now, I asked you to bring a unicorn because I thought it would bolster the morale of the refugees. A lot of them have seen everything they've worked for and everything they own go up in flames. They need something to have hope in and the unicorns should provide that. The other thing they need is a feeling that they are finally safe here and that's where you come in." He paused and gave Jarrod a sharp look.

"Forgive me for interrupting, Archmage," Jarrod said,

taking the bait that the silence offered, "but I really don't know what's going on. When did the Outlanders attack and how did they get past the Upper Causeway?"

"Yes, yes; quite right. You've only just arrived, haven't you." But he took a drink and eyed Jarrod sourly, as if his ignorance was deliberate. "When did it start?" he resumed. "Difficult to say. About the time you recaptured Fort Bandor, perhaps earlier. Perhaps the two were conceived as part of the same strategy.

"First warning we had was the sandcats coming down out of the Mountains of the Night. We should have known then that something was amiss, but no one thought to report it at the time. That answers your second question. The bastards didn't get through the Upper Causeway, they went around it. It's obvious now that the sandcats were driven out of the Unknown lands by the enemy, but at the time the locals put it down to the untamed weather on the far side of the mountains."

Jarrod relaxed as the story unfolded. The Archmage seemed to have forgotten about Marianna's rudeness. The old man cradled his goblet, his eyes far away.

"The appearance of the Outlanders put paid to that theory." He stopped and pursed his lips. "No, that's not right; that's not the way to put it. Nobody's seen an Outlander."

"They were wearing their protective suits were they, sir?" Jarrod put in.

"I don't know, lad. No one does. A pestilential cloud of their atmosphere rolled down the slopes. Big as a tilting yard. Whatever's in it set fire to everything in sight without revealing itself. Bloody unnatural." Ragnor took another drink of sack.

"The Outlanders did the same thing at Bandor," Jarrod supplied. "They brought some method of creating their atmosphere with them. It covered the whole fort, but the Outlanders themselves were wearing suits."

"So I heard. How did you dispel it? Gwyndryth's dispatches weren't entirely clear on that point and since you yourself didn't see fit to send me a report . . .'' Ragnor's voice died away ominously.

"I'm sorry, sir,'' Jarrod said with a sudden feeling of apprehension. "I just assumed that by the time I'd recovered you would have heard all about it. I told the Queen.''

"Don't assume, boy.''

"No, sir. Sorry, sir.'' Jarrod felt like an errant student again.

"Well?''

"Sir?''

"Answer the question. How did you dispel it?''

"Oh, yes, sir. Sorry, sir.''

"For pity's sake stop apologizing and answer the question.'' Ragnor was irritated and Jarrod was beginning to sweat.

He swallowed. "I, ah, I used the Spell of Unbinding to destroy their base camp at the foot of the mountain and the rest was just weather magic.''

"We tried weather spells. Totally ineffective. They just went about their business burning up the countryside. The best we've been able to do is make it harder for them by keeping up a steady rain over the area. There's absolutely nothing that we can do about the trail of poisoned ground they leave behind them.'' Ragnor made a face and took a drink, as if to get rid of a bad taste.

He looked across at Jarrod. "It's a mess, lad,'' he said more kindly. "The army hasn't been able to make the slightest impact on them. They haven't been able to get within bowshot. We've tried fog to shroud the approach, bright sun to dazzle them long enough to let the cloudsteedsmen swoop down and loose their javelins. Didn't do a blind bit of good. We took heavy losses and their cloud kept rolling.

"Once word of that got out, Celador was swamped with families seeking sanctuary. They're still coming. Stupid thing is that most of them abandoned untouched farms, but tradition decrees that they cannot be turned away. Trouble is, the tradition was formed when there weren't nearly so many people." He stopped speaking and sat there, brooding at the fire, his face made mobile by the changing light. The silence stretched.

"And you think that the unicorns and I could be helpful?" Jarrod prompted. The wine, the fire, the food, and the after-effects of Interim were conspiring to make him sleepy. He wished that the old man would get to the point.

Ragnor's head came around slowly and he gave Jarrod a measuring stare. "Yes, I hope so. As I said, the presence of the unicorns should give people a feeling of security. If the situation were truly dangerous, we would never risk bringing the unicorns here, would we?" He looked away again.

"But the unicorns have been involved in battle," Jarrod objected.

"I know they have, but that's not the way people's minds work. They'll believe it because they want to believe it."

"And you want me to take the colts riding around the walls."

"That's part of it. If I thought that the people would follow you, I'd have you lead them away from Celador. No, I need you for something else. Ever heard of the Cloak of Protection, lad?" He shot Jarrod a quick look.

"Of course, sir. It's a unique spell of invisibility known only to the Archmages. In times of peril, the Archmage makes Celador disappear."

"Yes indeed. And this could be deemed a time of peril." Ragnor gave a mirthless little smile. "And if Celador was invisible, only those who were truly desperate would try to find it. Furthermore, since the army is incapable of reassuring the population, it's about time that Magic did."

"I can see that, sir," Jarrod said, not quite truthfully, "but I still don't understand why you need my help."

Ragnor pushed himself upright and took another drink. " 'Cause there's vinegar in the wine, son; vinegar in the wine. The Archmage is supposed to know the spell, but this one doesn't. If my predecessor knew it, he did not see fit to pass it on to me. I have spent the last fortnight in the Arch-magial Archives and I have been able to find no trace of it.'' He paused.

"Now, if you were going to render a city invisible, how would you go about it?" Ragnor sat back and peered over the rim of his cup.

Jarrod stared back owlishly. He wasn't prepared for this. Was it some kind of test? Nothing popped into his mind. He felt slow and stupid.

"Well?"

"I suppose," Jarrod said, playing for time and hoping for inspiration, "that the usual law that one has to be able to see what one is making invisible applies?"

"Correct."

An idea formed, or rather a view. "If one were on a cloud-steed over the city . . ." Jarrod said in a rush.

"Not good enough," Ragnor shot back. "You wouldn't be able to see the outside of all of the walls. You don't want the inside invisible—think of the choas that would cause—you want Celador invisible to anyone approaching it."

"You station Magicians in a circle around the walls and each one makes the area in front of him invisible." Jarrod countered, wakening to the game.

"No good. If that many people had been involved, we'd have heard about it before. Besides, how long d'you think the average Magician can maintain invisibility over a large quadrant that includes not only walls, but towers and spires and chimney stacks? Think again."

Jarrod wracked his brain. He tried to envisage the city from the outside. He had ridden around the walls often enough. He could remember what they looked like, but he couldn't encompass them all in his mind at the same time. He shook his head.

"I'm sorry, sir, I can't think of anything."

He raised his eyes, expecting a sarcastic rebuke, but found that the Archmage was smiling. It looked like a real smile.

"Ever have a toy fort when you were a boy?" Ragnor enquired pleasantly.

"A toy fort?" Jarrod repeated, puzzled. "No. A friend of mine had one and we used to play with it sometimes. Why?"

"Come upstairs with me and I think you'll understand." Ragnor put his cup down and pushed himself out of the chair. "Follow me, young man," he said and moved swiftly towards the door.

Jarrod returned his cup to the sideboard and followed the Archmage out and up the winding stairs to his workroom.

"Steps never used to bother me," Ragnor said morosely, as he made his way to the dull glow of the banked fire.

His robe blotted out the weak light and then there were candles alight all over the room. They revealed a chamber not unlike Greylock's atop his tower at the Outpost, except that here there were glazed doors that led out onto a balcony.

Jarrod turned and looked at the wall behind him, expecting to see shelves of books and instruments and manuscripts. There were shelves, but you could scarcely see them. A solid block of paintings, none of them framed, was hung across them.

"Go and stand over by the doors," Ragnor commanded, "and tell me what you think."

Jarrod hastened to oblige and turned to take in the whole panorama. As he did so, a line of lamps under the pictures flamed into life and burned clearly. The walls and skyline of Celador were spread before him in four long rows.

"Good, aren't they?" Ragnor said. "You can go up close if you like. Every detail's in there. See for yourself." He sounded pleased with himself.

Jarrod walked forward and examined the work. "Quite remarkable," he said.

"Now d'you understand why I asked you if you'd ever had a fort?"

"Yes, I do."

"Think it'll work?" Ragnor asked, surprising Jarrod again.

"I don't see why not. Don't you know?" The moment the question was out of his mouth, he regretted it, but Ragnor didn't seem offended.

"I've no proof. As I told you, there wasn't so much as a hint in the papers. Well," he amplified, "there were entries that said things like, 'raised this day the Cloak of Protection,' or, 'rendered Celador visible again after forty-seven days,' but not one word as to how it was done. I stumbled over these"—he gestured to the paintings—"in a storeroom that looked as if it hadn't been opened in a century." He came over and stood behind Jarrod, looking over his shoulder at the pictures.

"I like the simplicity of the notion," he said. "I find it deeply pleasing. It would also explain why my predecessors didn't bother to write anything down."

"And why the Archmages wanted to keep the secret to themselves," Jarrod agreed.

Ragnor took him by the arm and turned him towards the fireplace. "It goes without saying that not one word of this leaves this room."

"Of course, sir."

"Good. Now sit down and let's discuss this."

"I still don't see why you need me," Jarrod said as he eased down into the chair.

"Well," Ragnor said, leaning forward and poking the fire into life, "you can't just put up the Cloak. The business of government has to go on, the city has to be provisioned. There are preparations to be made. That makes it difficult to keep the matter secret and, at this moment, I cannot afford to raise people's expectations and then fall short. I shan't specify the exact date. That way, if I fail the first time, we shall have another opportunity." He allowed himself a regretful smile. "I'm not as young as I used to be and I'd rather have someone I trust to back me up. That is why I need you."

"I'm very flattered, Archmage."

"So you should be," Ragnor said tartly, "but I shall be grateful for your assistance nevertheless." He glanced at the young man and nodded as if approving what he had said. "Run along now and get some rest. I'll have the Duty Boy wake you in time for Hall."

Jarrod rose. "Thank you, sir. I, ah, appreciate the honor." He hesitated, but Ragnor said nothing. "I'll see you before Hall then, sir."

"Yes, yes indeed. You can tell me all about Fort Bandor. Off you go."

Ragnor turned and watched the Paladinian leave and then turned back to the fire and held his hands out to the blaze. He was taking a chance, but then, what other choice did he have? Under normal circumstances he would have called on Greylock, but Greylock was a captive of his Place of Power. Sumner, if he asked the man, would take it as an assurance that he would be designated as Ragnor's successor and the Archmage had no such intention. Handrom was steady enough and would make an excellent Dean of the Collegium. He was a knowledgeable Magician and a skillful theoretician, but he lacked the power. The royal ladies were out of the question, of course. Membership in the High Council was as close to the center of the Discipline as he intended for them to come. The boy was an unknown quantity, granted, but who else was there? He pulled absently at his beard. No, Courtak it would have to be.

chapter 3

Ragnor was not the only one to see the advantages of having Jarrod, Marianna and the unicorns at Celador. The search for the unicorns had begun from the Arundelian capital, and Marianna of Gwyndryth was the daughter of one of the oldest Holdings in the land. What more fitting than a full-scale celebration of the unicorns? What better distraction for the refugees? A formal banquet and a ball were hastily organized and there was a parade and a Royal proclamation for the unicorns. Bonfires blazed outside the walls, sheep and kina were slaughtered and roasted and the seekers of sanctuary danced and drank toasts to the wondrous creatures. All of which suited Ragnor's purpose admirably.

His summons took Jarrod by surprise, partly because it arrived during the dancing after Hall, but mostly because he had put the Cloak of Protection out of his mind during the sennight-long revelries. He made his farewells, pleading weariness, and hurried over to Magicians' Court.

"Ha! There you are," Ragnor said the moment the Duty Boy ushered him into the workroom. "Took your time, didn't you. Some wench, I'll wager; all bust and bounce and 'come walk with me on the leads.' Well, I'm sorry to have spoiled your fun, but we've work to do. Come on, come on. Don't just stand there gawping. Come in and take your cloak off."

The old boy's in rare form, Jarrod thought as he looked around for somewhere to put his cloak. The room had been cleared and swept. The two chairs by the fire were the only furniture left. He turned back and dropped the cloak in the corner by the door and then stood, not knowing what to do next. The lamps beneath the pictures were lit and he could see their distorted reflections in the door glass. He glanced at the waterclock and saw that it was past the twentieth hour.

The Archmage heaved himself out of his chair. He was wearing a robe of dark silver that seemed molten when he moved. The heavily wrought Chain of the Archmages was draped around his shoulders and winked in the light. It underlined the fact that this was no casual invitation, but then everything about the Mage bespoke ceremony. The long white hair and the beard were combed and the ruby diadem of the Mages of Arundel gleamed above both.

Jarrod felt out of place in his plain blue robe. "You called for me, sir," he said somewhat dimly.

"Yes I did, and I'm sure you can guess why."

"You're going to erect the Cloak of Protection."

"I'm going to try."

"If I'm going to help, shouldn't we wait until I've been purified?" Jarrod suggested.

"Shouldn't be necessary. You'll only be playing a supporting role and you're young enough to get away with it. I've prepared a fast-acting brew for you and that should be sufficient. It's in the hearth. I'd drink if it I were you."

Ragnor pulled back a little and looked Jarrod up and down. "You look a little drab," he remarked, "but I'm wearing enough emblems of power for both of us, so that shouldn't matter."

He waited while Jarrod emptied the bowl and set it on the mantlepiece. "Come over here by me," he said, "and we'll go over the pictures together. Then I'll explain what I intend to do."

Jarrod joined him, feeling rushed and a little resentful. Greylock would never have been this casual about a major spell. As they moved down the lines of pictures, Jarrod concentrated on the areas that were painted in shadow. They would be invisible from the other side of the room. His resentment evaporated, or perhaps it was the brew working, and he began to feel excited about helping the Archmage to recreate one of Celador's most tenacious fables.

"Think you've got it?" Ragnor enquired.

"I think so, sir."

"Good. Let's go and sit down while the concoction does its work. Besides, this gown isn't very warm." He led the way back to the fire and pulled his chair up. Jarrod took the other chair and held his hands out to the flames.

"Now," Ragnor said when he was comfortable, "here's the plan. I'm going to use the standard Spell of Invisibility, with a little more power than usual. I expect you tried it as a boy, everyone does."

"As a matter of fact I used it on a scouting flight at Bandor," Jarrod countered, feeling more secure by the moment.

"So much the better." Ragnor stopped. "Wait a minute, I don't recall your telling me about that."

"That's because I fell off the cloudsteed when we landed. It didn't exactly enhance the dignity of the Discipline." The Archmage's potion was beginning to work and Jarrod was feeling alert and in command of himself.

"Humanizing the Discipline is just as important, but no matter. The good thing is that you're familiar with the spell."

"There is one thing that worries me," Jarrod cut in.

"And what, pray, is that?"

"Well, I was only dealing with a cloudsteed and a couple of riders, but you, Archmage, will be transforming a vast area. I don't know how the eye will react to that."

"What's your point?"

"If there were Magicians stationed in the arrowslits around the walls projecting the illusion of a forest, it would be easier for the mind to accept."

Ragnor leaned back and stroked his beard. "Not a bad thought," he said. "We could use the youngsters at the Collegium. It would be good practise for them and it would give them a sense that they were contributing to the defense of

Celador. Handrom won't like it, of course, it'll disrupt his classes, but these are dangerous times. He'll have to adjust.

"What worries me is whether we can transfer the invisibility from the canvases to the real walls. It works with other kinds of spells, like the one you used at Bandor to incinerate the keep, and I can think of no theoretical reason why it should not work with invisibility, but I certainly haven't tried it before. If it wasn't for the potion, I should be nervous. And speaking of the potion, are you feeling the effects?"

Jarrod grinned at him. "Yes, I am. It's stronger than I'm used to, but I feel in control."

"Excellent. We'll begin in a moment. Of course, if we pull it off, it won't be the final answer to our woes. The Cloak of Protection is only a stop-gap measure, a deception, a way to buy time, but time for what? I have no answers. Your unicorns got any answers?"

"I don't know about answers, but one of the colts, Nastrus, thinks that the Outlanders are mist creatures."

Ragnor snorted. "Mist creatures? They have a remarkably solid impact."

"He made a convincing case," Jarrod said diffidently.

"That's as maybe, but it doesn't help us," the Archmage said flatly. He sat up. "I suppose it's time we got going."

He got to his feet with none of the difficulty he had displayed a sennight before and Jarrod followed suit. The two men walked to the center pair of doors and turned to face the paintings. Jarrod stood slightly behind and to the left side of the Archmage. The candles faded out, leaving the lamps unchallenged. The underlighting and the pointed beard made the face in front of him look demonic. It turned towards him.

"I shall perform the initial spell alone. I want you to summon up your power, but you're to hold it in check. When I transfer the effect from the pictures to the walls, I want you to join me. We must bind the changes onto both the paintings and the stones outside. That clear?"

"Quite clear, sir."

Ragnor took a couple of steps forward and planted his feet. Part of Jarrod's mind was alert and attentive, waiting for the Archmage to begin, preparing to generate as much energy as he could; another part was wondering at what he was doing. How did he get to be assisting the Archmage perform a rare spell, one invoked perhaps once in five lifetimes? He straightened his shoulders and began to breath deeply. No time for that kind of speculation now.

He stared at the pictures, taking them all in without moving his eyes. The light on them seemed to be constant and bright. The details of coign and battlement stood out clearly. He heard the preamble to the spell and immediately experienced a surge of energy. As the Archmage's voice rose and fell with easy authority, the power in him mounted smoothly. The voice turned plangent. It seemed to penetrate Jarrod and make his flesh tingle. Why on earth does he think he needs support? Jarrod wondered.

He concentrated on the paintings and suddenly the layers became plain. Ragnor chanted on and Jarrod was drawn deeper into the dual reality. He could distinguish the structure of the pigment, the weave of the canvas, even the grain of the stretchers. They began to lose substance, became thin, the colors to bleed away. Jarrod pulled back. This was too reminiscent of what had happened to the Place of Power at the climax of the battle.

He was aware of the change in Ragnor's Spellcasting. The lilt had modulated, the pace had quickened. Jarrod knew that what was occurring on the canvases was being transferred to the outer walls. The outside of this very room would disappear. No time to think about that now. The Archmage was calling for him. He felt it rather than heard it, but the compulsion was undeniable.

Views of Celador as he had seen it when riding the unicorns skittered through his head and rearranged themselves into the conformation of the paintings. They too began to fade. Shapes became indistinct, color leached away. Jarrod let the power out, hastening the dissolution, setting the blank canvas, binding the new, eye-defying surface to stone and copper, horn and lead.

His eyes were blank, his stare saw nothing. His ears seemed to be full and he knew that he was swaying. He struggled for control. This is what comes of not being properly prepared, he thought as he damped the flow of power down. When it was contained again, he relaxed and allowed it to drain out of him. He felt hands on his shoulders, shaking him. He opened his eyes and blinked at the Archmage.

"We did it, lad. We did it! I'm the first one in almost two centuries to erect the Cloak of Protection."

"Congratulations, Archmage," Jarrod said, mildly surprised that his voice was working properly. He felt well enough. He wasn't floating on a cloud as he was after the major Magic, but he felt very good. The Archmage, he noticed, didn't seem to have aged.

"Let's go out onto the balcony and survey our handiwork." Ragnor was beaming.

He led the way out and Jarrod noticed immediately that the twisted chimney stacks and the spire atop the Great Hall were gone. There was nothing but blackness there.

"Your theory was absolutely right, sir," he said.

"It's rather impressive, isn't it?" Ragnor said complacently. "Although it's rather unnerving to think that, from beyond the walls, we are standing on nothing."

Jarrod turned and looked at the doors. There was nothing but darkness. He drew his breath in sharply and looked hurriedly at his feet. The stone floor of the balcony was a reassuring sight. He straightened up and found Ragnor smiling at him.

"The doors are straight ahead of you," the Archmage said. "I suggest that we go downstairs and have a drink to celebrate."

"Right you are." Jarrod was relieved by the suggestion and lost no time in pacing forward with his hands out in front of him. The slight step down took him by surprise, but he didn't lose his balance. The workroom was around him, lamps flicking over rows of empty canvases.

"Will the pictures come back?" he asked.

"I don't really know." Jarrod heard the doors being closed and latched. "When I remove the binding, reality will return, but the pictures were never real to begin with." Ragnor patted Jarrod on the shoulder as he moved past him towards the door.

"I have no idea," Ragnor continued as they circled down to the floor below, "if those paintings were the ones used by the last Archmage to perform the spell, or if they were replacements that he provided for whoever needed them next.

"Mull us some wine, lad," Ragnor said to the Duty Boy as he pushed the anteroom door open. "Did you make the fire up?"

"Yes, Excellency."

Ragnor nodded his approval and went through into his chamber.

"Give me a hand with the Chain, will you, son? It's a lot heavier than it looks."

Jarrod hurried over and helped the Archmage to lift it up over the diadem. Ragnor was right. The thing was heavy. He carried it with both hands over to the clothespress and set it down gently on the top.

"Put this with it, if you'd be so kind."

Ragnor was holding out the crownlet, a double circle of rubies, held by two thin bands of red gold. Jarrod took it reverently. It was older and more fragile than he had imagined. Some of the stones were dull and a number were loose in their settings. He laid it carefully between two sweeps of the Chain.

"Come on over and sit you down," the Archmage said. He was bending over, poking the fire. His gown shimmered and ran with his movements. He pushed the end of the poker into the blaze and straightened up. "Nothing like a good bumper of mulled wine to relax one. The boy will be along with the wine in a minute." He settled into his chair and extended his feet towards the fire.

"Mind you," he said, "I don't in the least feel tired. Rather a pleasant change." He smiled across at Jarrod. "I suspect I owe that to you. You were sending out so much energy that I scarcely needed to use any of my own."

Jarrod knew that he was exaggerating, but was grateful for the compliment nevertheless. He turned his head as the Duty Boy brought the pot of wine in and listened as Ragnor gave instructions for the placement of the mulling kettle. He watched as the poker was thrust in, hissing and steaming, and inhaled the rich aroma. He accepted his cup with thanks, holding it gingerly, and listened again as Ragnor, despite the lateness of the hour, ordered food.

The Archmage waited until the Duty Boy was out of the room before he spoke again. "It was a job well done," he said, "and I'm sorry in a way that you won't be able to tell anyone about it. I've stopped looking into the future, as you know, so I have no idea if you'll ever have need of the knowledge. You're a young man and I'm an old one, so the odds are that you won't be Archmage after me. I'd always supposed that it would be Greylock, but now . . ." He let the sentence trail off.

Jarrod sat and sipped the wine cautiously, trying not to let his surprise show. It had never occurred to him that anyone would think of him in terms of the Archmageship. He felt the heat rising in his face and hoped that Ragnor would put it down to the wine.

"If you ever do become Archmage, you can tell the secret to your successor, if you've a mind to, but that's the only person you can tell it to."

"I promise you, sir, I won't tell a soul," Jarrod said quickly. "Although . . ."

"Although what?" The old man's tone was sharp.

"Oh, I just thought, what if there was a direct threat to Celador and the new Archmage couldn't solve the problem?"

"Simple. If he asks you, pretend to have a brainstorm—not too quick a one; let him sweat a little. Better yet, try to make him believe that it was his idea. Let's just hope that the city doesn't fall before then."

"You don't think that could really happen, do you, sir?"

"It's a possibility," the Archmage said judiciously and drank some of his wine. "We've been crouching smugly behind the Upper Causeway for generations, certain that it would save us from our military failings. Well, that's all changed. We've been royally outflanked. I keep on hoping that the bastards will run out of food or fuel, or whatever sustains them, and blow away, but it doesn't seem to be happening. All we have to offer is delaying tactics and we're giving ground steadily. What we did tonight will do more for our morale, I fear, than be an answer to this invasion."

"Has anyone consulted the Oracle?" Jarrod asked as the Duty Boy backed into the room carrying a heavy tray.

"I certainly haven't," Ragnor replied. He turned in his chair. "Put the tray on the table, lad. We'll help ourselves. You run along to bed now." He turned back to Jarrod. "Get me a plate would you, son. A little of everything."

He nodded his thanks when Jarrod brought his platter over. "Interesting thought that, the Oracle. Who knows, it might even do some good."

"Do you not believe in the Oracle?" Jarrod asked.

"I certainly believe that it exists and that it communicates with the priestesses. Do I believe in its pronouncements? Well, that generally depends on the interpretation, doesn't it? The High Priestesses have always been very clever with their wording. If things don't go as expected, they claim that the petitioner misinterpreted the message. Then again, there is absolutely no doubt in my mind that, from time to time, the High Priestesses have made up answers out of whole cloth."

There was a silence while they both tackled the food. It was Jarrod who broke it.

"It's been proved right in the past, surely?"

Ragnor looked up from his plate. "Ha!" He pushed the plate away and emptied his wine cup. "Fill this up for me, would you?" he asked. "Even an Oracle can't be wrong all the time."

"But there's the story of King Garroneth and the Ballad of Sir Wylfryd," Jarrod said, surprised by the cynicism.

"One of the side benefits of my recent delvings into the writings of my predecessors," Ragnor replied, taking back his refilled cup and nodding his thanks, "was finding contemporary accounts of the events that have come down to us through ballads and poetry contests. Take Garroneth for instance. Errathuel was Archmage at the time, I think, and he regarded the man as an astute coward. The way Errathuel tells it, the King couldn't have lost. He was the only direct male heir for one thing, and the coalition that backed him was far stronger than the opposition. However, he had no stomach for a fight, no matter how one-sided, so he used the prophecy to convince the people that the question of the sucession had already been decided by Destiny."

"That's not what they taught us at Dameschool." Jarrod collected the plate and bowl and took them back to the tray.

"Of course not. Garroneth was crowned, wasn't he? And he ruled for a fairly long time. Who d'you think employs the minstrels and the ballad makers? They get to write their verses on parchment. The travelling singers, who can be relied on to give a more satiric version of events, earn the bulk of their living selling broadsheets of their songs, written on flimsy paper, at country fairs for half a farrodpiece. The good melodies have long since acquired other words and the papers crumbled. What we are left with is the official account."

"What about Lord Wylfryd?" Jarrod enquired. "That's always been a favorite of mine."

"Three dozen couplets of falsehood," Ragnor declared promptly.

Jarrod sighed. "No 'fair Lady Janada?' No wicked uncle?"

Ragnor chuckled. "Oh, there was a Janada all right. The Archmage of the day thought she was a trollop. He gets quite heated about it. There was no wicked uncle. What there was was a husband considerably older than she. It was a rich Holding and the Hold itself commanded a bustling harbor." Ragnor had leaned forward as he began the story and now his right hand sketched the fort on the heights and the port below.

"The Lady Janada wanted for nothing. Silks, spices, exotic fruits and birds, all came by sea from Isphardel. The finest wools, leathers and linens in Arundel all passed through the town. Furthermore, Lord Conwellyn derived a moiety from every shipment in or out of the port. He could afford to indulge his young wife and he did. He had exquisite jewelry made for her from rare pearls, and the gowns she wore set the fashions throughout the Marches." Ragnor paused and drank some wine. He was clearly enjoying himself and Jarrod was content to listen. His preconceptions of the past were being shaken, but he was acutely aware of the privilege he was being accorded.

"There are portraits of Janada that survive, you know," Ragnor said conversationally. "I've seen a couple of them. She was a much painted woman. There was, apparently, at least one notorious portrait of her lying on a riverbank with no clothes on. I do not think that my esteemed predecessor actually saw the painting, since he reports that it was kept in Conwellyn's cabinet and that the cabinet was locked unless Conwellyn was working there. The rumor of its existence, however, was enough to generate three pages of denunciation."

"Sir Wylfryd has a vision of her, manacled in a cell atop a tower," Jarrod put in.

"Not exactly; not according to the Archmage. No, the problem seems to have been that despite all this luxury—luxury, by the way, that was unheard of in those times—she was bored. Perhaps her husband was too preoccupied with his business affairs and tried to make up for his neglect with jewels and the things and people that money can buy. However, if the Archmage is to be believed, she sent a copy of the infamous portrait, done as a miniature on ivory, to a lord of a neighboring Holding." Ragnor turned his gaze from the fire and smiled. "I don't have to tell you who that was, do I?"

"Let me guess?" Jarrod said lazily; the wine was doing its work. "Lord Wylfryd was a young, good-looking neighbor, who caught her eye at a wedding."

"The Archmage didn't report that piece of gossip. What he does make clear is that Wylfryd was not an impoverished knight unjustly deprived of his land by Lord Conwellyn. He was of yeoman stock and had married the decidedly ugly heiress of the neighboring Holding. I can't recall the name of it now, but it abutted Conwellyn and was moderately prosperous.

"I don't know if he was covetous of his neighbor's wealth beforehand, let alone his neighbor's wife, but the Archmage is convinced that he conspired with her to poison her husband. His own wife died under mysterious circumstances a month later and, after a suitable period of mourning, the couple was wed. You may draw your own conclusion."

"But he wasn't the King," Jarrod protested. "Didn't you just say that it's the King who employs the ballad makers?"

"Quite right, but this was a special case. Lord Conwellyn had created a court of his own to keep his lovely wife amused. He was a generous patron of the arts. It was a policy that Wylfryd and Janada continued."

Jarrod smiled wryly. "Are all the old tales tainted?"

"Not all of them. Besides, they've survived because they have meaning past their time. Each generation sees them differently, but great poetry, or a story with bridges to the truth, can survive any interpretation.'' He sat back and let the passion fade from his face. The corners of his mouth turned up gently.

''We're tethered to 'em, lad,'' he said quietly. ''We've denied ourselves a history, so we've created our own version. The Archives would be a healthy antidote if they were ever allowed to see the light of day. Mind you, it would make the patient awfully sick before it effected a cure. I have no doubt that there'd be some as would die of it. History's a serious business, son, and don't you forget it.'' He was leaning forward again and shaking his finger at Jarrod. He caught himself in the act and relaxed back into the chair, looking a little sheepish.

''I'm sorry,'' he said. ''I got carried away.'' He ducked his head and made and made a little, circular motion with his left hand. ''It's an affliction that increases in proportion to age. Now, where were we? Oh yes, the Oracle. Have you ever petitioned?''

''No, sir.''

''Well, perhaps this would be a good time for you to do so.'' Ragnor's eyes were twinkling and the smile was growing.

Jarrod felt that he was being included in a warm and wonderful inside joke, elevated to the status of an equal. The only problem was that he couldn't see anything funny.

''I'm afraid I don't understand, sir,'' he said. He took a sip of the now tepid wine.

''I think your idea to consult the Oracle was an excellent one and, if I understood correctly, the unicorns have been to Gwyndryth before and so can go there again. Am I correct?''

''Yes, sir, that's right, but I thought that you wanted the unicorns at Celador.''

''I wanted a unicorn at Celador, but you were thoughtful enough to provide us with four.''

"You want me to take a unicorn through Interim to Gwyndryth and then to petition the Oracle?"

"That's the idea. Oracle Lake is no more than two days' ride from Gwyndryth. Perhaps you should take the Lady Marianna with you. That way you could be assured of hospitality."

"But what am I supposed to ask it?" Jarrod was upright in his chair now; wide awake.

"Oh"—Ragnor waved the question away—"it would be quite improper of me to suggest a question to you. No man has more than two chances to petition the Oracle. To try to dictate the question would be reprehensible." Ragnor paused, hands out, palms out.

"On the other hand"—the long fingers rose and splayed out—"you are aware of the terrible fate that may await Celador, the center of the Discipline, home of the Collegium. . . ."

"I hated my time at the Collegium," Jarrod interjected, reassured by the Archmage's good humor. Now that he knew what was going to happen, he felt entirely comfortable.

"Be that as it may," Ragnor continued, "I cannot think of another topic that could weigh more heavily." He took hold of the arms of his chair and changed his position. He looked back up and his eyes widened into a simulation of innocence. "Who knows, you may be the key to this whole thing. You found the unicorns after all. So, far be it from me to influence your question. You must ask what feels most important to you, or the Oracle might reject your petition. Mind you, I can't think of anything more important to our survival than defeating this invasion, but my only direct advice to you is to keep it simple."

"When would you like me to leave?" Jarrod asked, disappointed with the Archmage's advice.

"The sooner the better. Do you have any investitures or ceremonies left to attend?"

"Not that I'm aware of, I'm happy to say."

"Good. What about the Lady Marianna? I would imagine that her social calendar is somewhat fuller than yours. Pretty women are always in demand." A wicked little smile played around his lips, surprising Jarrod.

"I'm sure her father's senechal will be most hospitable even if she isn't with me. Especially if I'm carrying a letter from you," Jarrod said with pointed pleasantry.

"No you don't, laddie. You brought her here and you're going to take her with you. Besides, it would be a kindness. It must have been a while since the girl saw home."

"As you wish, Archmage." Jarrod acknowledged the inevitable with a graceful bow of the head.

Ragnor smiled back at him. The boy was proving a good choice. "You're a very sensible young man," he said. "You should go far."

"Thank you, Archmage." Jarrod put down his cup. "Where I should really like to go now is bed—with your permission."

"You have my permission and you have my thanks. I shall stay up a little longer and savor my triumph, so do you put another log on the fire before you go."

Jarrod built the fire up and left the Archmage to his reveries. In an odd way, the evening had turned out to be something of a letdown, at least for him, but the old man was obviously delighted with himself.

chapter 4

Gwyndryth was everything that Celador was not. The days were warm and pleasant, the air smelled softly of growing things and there was, above all, a sense of peace and privacy. The lichen on the ancient walls was turning green and the home orchards were a haze of pinks and yellows and white.

Jarrod and Marianna walked beneath the trees in silence. He, a Northerner, was delighted to be able to walk abroad without either jacket or cloak. She, mistress here, looked at the blossom with a proprietary air. Gradually, the silence became oppressive and Jarrod realized that, despite the beauty of the day, Marianna was in one of her moods.

"Is anything the matter?" he ventured.

"What could be the matter?" Marianna answered darkly. "The sun's out, the trees are in bloom and I'm home again."

"I just thought you seemed a little preoccupied," he said, regretting his impulse to break the silence.

"I've got things on my mind," she said dismissively.

"Anything I can do?"

She turned her head briefly and gave him a disdainful look. "Do? Oh, I don't think so. You never have to do anything. Everything just gets handed to you wrapped in cloth-of-gold."

"Oh, I see," Jarrod said, irritation surfacing, "this is about my petitioning the Oracle, isn't it? You think you're the one who should be doing it."

"What do you expect me to say?" she asked, kicking a pile of fallen petals. "I discovered the unicorns, I can talk to

Amarine and I've lived near the temple all my life. I would have thought that that might make me qualified, but apparently not."

"I don't ask for these assignments, you know."

Marianna stopped and blew out a breath. "I know you don't, Jarrod," she said quietly, "and that doesn't make it any better. It's not you that I'm angry with."

"I only got picked because I brought up the idea," Jarrod said, "and I'm probably wasting one of my chances to petition. I don't even know if the Oracle will agree to hear my question."

"It'll agree; have no fear of that." Marianna resumed her walk.

"I wouldn't be so sure." Jarrod fell into step with her. "The priestesses don't know me and they don't know that the Archmage sent me."

"I wouldn't bet on that if I were you, but they don't have to know who you are. Your petition is being delivered by one of our men, and petitioners from Gwyndryth are never refused. The Holding has been the protector of the temple for centuries and that is one of our rewards."

"I didn't know that."

"No reason why you should. We've never felt a need to brag about it. It doesn't guarantee what kind of reception you'll get. That will depend on the kind of gift you sent along with the question."

"Gift?"

"Yes of course." She stopped and turned towards him. "You did send a gift, didn't you?"

"Nobody ever told me anything about having to send a present," Jarrod said, dismayed.

"Typical Paladinian ignorance." Marianna was enjoying his discomfiture. "No sense of style."

"Perhaps I could take something with me," he suggested.

Marianna grinned at him. "Too late, good bird, too late.

Taking it with you is a mark of ostentation and poor breeding.''

"Well, what am I going to do?" he asked, voice rising.

"There's nothing you can do." Her good humor seemed quite restored. "You'll just have to hope that the High Priestess recognises the honor that you are bestowing on the temple by visiting it."

"I can do without the sarcasm, thank you," Jarrod said, turning away and kicking at petals in his turn. "Seriously, now, is there nothing I can do?"

"Not a thing," Marianna said cheerfully. "You may not be made to feel welcome, but at least you know that the Oracle will hear your petition. That's what matters, isn't it?"

"Yes, I suppose so," Jarrod said glumly as the shine seemed to go out of the day. "And I suppose I owe that to you too."

"I expect you can say that."

"And if I don't, you certainly will."

She smiled her most irritating smile by way of reply. "Let's go back and get something to eat, shall we? This walk has given me an appetite."

"Might as well," he said dispiritedly.

They walked back, side by side under the trees. The sun still shone and the quiet breeze wafted scent and petals around them, but the joy he had felt earlier was gone. It occurred to him that she might be teasing him—he'd never heard that the Oracle required a gift. Now that she'd mentioned it, though, it did make sense. Why couldn't she have mentioned it before? This whole trip might be wasted, Ragnor would be disappointed in him and, even if the Oracle granted him an answer this time, it would probably refuse him if he ever wanted to ask something on his own account.

"Have you ever been to the temple?" he asked, more to distract himself than because he wanted to know the answer.

"My father took me when I was a little girl," Marianna replied.

"What was it like?"

"We only went as far as the bridge," she said. "I remember a great black mouth and the monsters."

"What monsters?"

"You'll see them when you get there. They won't harm you, but they gave me nightmares for months."

"Are you making all this up?" he asked suspiciously as they came out from under the trees and through the gate into the meadow where the unicorns were grazing.

"Of course not. Why would I do something like that?

"Out of sheer cussedness," he replied. "I'm not sure that I believe you, but I think I'll take one of the colts with me, just in case."

"It couldn't hurt," she said and smiled the irritating smile.

The return of the herald with the High Priestess' invitation to the temple was an anticlimax, but he was burning to be gone. If he had unwittingly offended by his lapse over an offering, he wasn't going to compound it by being dilatory. Gift or no gift, he rode out on Pellia feeling auspicious. The continued good weather was a tonic. The trees were covered with pale green flowers and fern fronds were beginning to unroll. The day was soft and the air was filled with birdsong and forest scents. He rode alert and contented, in an almost spiritual rapport with his surroundings.

There was one small cloud, the question itself. Had he been right in his choice? Had his inner prompting been a form of prescience or just selfishness? "Keep it simple and unambiguous," the Archmage had said. He'd said it over and over. Well, he'd done that, but he doubted that Ragnor would be happy with the end result. He pushed the thought away. After all, this was his petition, perhaps the only one he would ever make.

They emerged from the woods on the morning of the third day and Oracle Lake lay a sky-borrowed blue at the foot of the hill. Pellia pulled up the moment that it crossed Jarrod's mind. He looked down past the spiral horn at the island that was the temple. It thrust itself up out of the water close to the eastern shore, all black crags and green foliage. The bridge that had so impressed Marianna was clear, but they were too far away to make out details. Petitioners' Way, winding to the bridge along the valley bottom, was empty. He felt uneasy. It was too empty. There should be some movement somewhere.

'I do not understand why you are agitated,' Pellia said as they began the decent. *'It is plain that the island intimidates you, but I can detect no evidence to support that. The lake is beautiful and there is an air of antiquity and calm about the island.'*

'It's difficult to explain,' Jarrod replied. He tightened the grip of his thighs and adjusted his balance as they negotiated a hairpin turn. *"This place is very special to us. An old and powerful spirit dwells there and it is a place of great mystery. The High Priestess is the only one allowed into the presence of the Oracle, the other vestals never leave the temple and ordinary folk may only enter twice in their lifetimes, so very little is known about the place. My petition has been accepted and I've got nothing to fear. I know that, and yet I'm uneasy."*

'I feel no awe, except in your mind, but I do detect the presence of a large number of unmounted females.' She turned her attention away from Jarrod to concentrate on the footing.

They joined the Pilgrims' Way where it began to skirt the shore. A tall border of phragmites undulated to their right as the feathery crests caught the breeze. The bridge ahead was lined with statues. He remembered the engravings of them that he had seen as a child. One side was supposed to be guarded by happy spirits and the other by dismal ones, though he had never been able to tell which was which.

They drew level with the center of the bridge and stopped. Pellia turned and faced the dark cave that was the entrance to the temple. The statues rose on either side of them. Jarrod's eyes were on the level of the heads of the first two guardians, but each statue was bigger than the one in front of it and the two that flanked the portal were veritable giants.

They were not as fearsome as the drawings. Time and moss had softened them and, of course, he was much older now, but it was easy to see how they could have given a twelve-year-old girl nightmares. Some were scaled, some were tusked and some had grotesquely elongated noses and fangs. Some of the creatures wore armor and all sported weapons of some kind.

'Superstition,' Pellia snorted.

'Maybe so, but you can't deny that they're impressive. There are people who believe that they were here before we crossed the Inland Sea.'

'Do they think that this is what your enemies look like?'

'That's always been a popular theory.'

'Shall we proceed?' She was not impressed with his foreboding.

'We might as well. Nobody seems to know that we're here.'

They paced forward between taloned paws and fishes' tails, cloven hooves and round, unarticulated feet.

'D'you sense anything?' Jarrod asked.

'I can smell three unmounted females inside the opening.'

Jarrod could see nothing ahead. He glanced up instinctively at the statue on his left. A broad snout poking out of a winged helmet met his eye and he looked away quickly. Pellia walked on daintily to within a few feet of the entrance. There was silence. Jarrod leaned forward and peered into the gloom. He made out three white spots.

"We have been expecting you, Excellency." The contralto voice sounded clearly. The dots advanced together and resolved themselves into the faces of three women in dark robes with closely wimpled heads. How did they know his title? He had signed Jarrod Courtak. The women stopped as one before the threshold.

"We had not expected the unicorn, but you are doubly welcome for that. We shall prepare suitable quarters for it, if it consents to stay with us while you are here.'' It was the priestess in the center who spoke.

"We thank you and are glad to accept your hospitality,'' Jarrod replied, using the Formal Mode.

"Follow us then.''

The women turned and walked away in unison. Their atramentous skirts moved with the sway peculiar to those who go barefoot. Jarrod wasn't sure whether to dismount or not, but Pellia moved ahead confidently. He was blinded once they were in the cave. There were no links and it took his eyes a while to adjust. There was a feeling of considerable space around them. Pellia's hooves rang on the stone floor. There were no other sounds. He could not make out the priestesses, but Pellia assured him that they were walking ahead.

A point of light appeared and was blotted out again. More sprang up and Jarrod saw that they were in a second cave. Lighted tunnels led out of it. The three priestesses had halted and were waiting, so he dismounted and walked towards them.

"There are stables at the end of that passageway,'' the contralto said. "Since you are the only petitioner and you have no entourage, there is plenty of room. If it is agreeable to you, your friend will be well taken care of there.''

"We have no objection, providing that I can visit her.''

"Whenever your Excellency desires. One of my sisters will take her there. We shall see to it that she has everything that she could want. You will doubtless wish to rest after your journey. There will be time to refresh yourself before you are presented to the High Priestess.''

"And when will that be?'' Jarrod asked as he unstrapped his saddlebags.

"Not before the midday meal. We are not permitted to mingle with our visitors, so your meals will be served in your chamber. Ours is a cloistered life.''

One of the vestals came and led Pellia away, the other

beckoned to him and walked towards an opening on the other side of the cave. Jarrod slung the bags over his shoulder and bowed to the remaining priestess before he followed.

chapter 5

Jarrod walked behind the priestess down one of the lighted tunnels, trying to keep his stride short so as not to overtake her. He had expected to see lamps or links, but there were none. The rock glowed of its own accord. He brushed his fingertips along the wall. It was cool and dry and his hand left no traces on it. He found it eerie to be walking in a world without shadows. His senses were all on edge, probing around for clues and warnings. His eyes saw nothing but a long, gently sloping corridor with identical wooden doors set along it at regular intervals. Guest chambers no doubt. The woman stopped in front of one of the featureless doors. She opened it with a black-gloved hand and gestured for him to enter.

He walked in and eased the saddlebags to the floor. The rock was alight here too, but it was not as bright as in the corridor. He turned to ask a question, but the door had been closed. He opened it and peered up and down the corridor. It was empty. He closed the door again and turned to inspect his new quarters.

He was in a square room, though the ceiling curved. The side walls were hung with tapestries, which accounted for the lower intensity of light. There was an alcove on the far right that he guessed held the jaques, a bed against the left wall, a clothespress, a desk with a plain wooden chair and an armchair with a footstool, but the most remarkable feature of the room was by the back wall. He went over to investigate.

There was a deep, polished depression in the floor. Water flowed through an opening at one end and drained out through a slit at the other. He squatted down and tested the temperature. It was pleasantly warm. There was a cake of soap and a rough cloth beside the basin, making its use obvious. Ingenious, he thought, and, after two days on the road, most welcoming. He turned back and started to unpack. That done, he looked for a bolt on the door before he took his clothes off, but to no avail. He propped the wooden chair under the latch and proceeded to take his bath.

He luxuriated as long as he dared and then rubbed himself down with a towel he had found in the press. He donned one of the two clean robes he had brought and wished for the umpteenth time that dark blue didn't collect so much lint. The gown was wrinkled after two and a half days in a saddlebag, but there was nothing he could do about that. He shook it out as best he could and then propped the lid of the clothespress open so that he could bring some kind of order to his damp, curling hair by means of the piece of polished tin affixed to the inside.

He unblocked the door and then sat in the armchair and waited for something to happen. It had been about two hours until midday when he had arrived at the bridge, so the noon meal should be due. There was no waterclock and, without a sight of the sun, it was difficult to judge what the hour was, but his stomach was a fairly reliable guide and it was ready for food. None came. After what he judged to be a wait of about half an hour, he went and looked into the corridor again. There was no one in sight.

Time seemed a sluggard here, buried under a crag, with no reference points. The room was filled with the sound of quietly flowing water, but there was no way to measure it. There was not even a tallow to notch. He felt the loss of the sky keenly. The light was too even, too constant. He began to feel cut off, unmoored and adrift.

A knocking at the door made him jump. He hurried over and opened it to find two priestesses waiting. They looked to be the same ones who had originally escorted him, but he wasn't entirely sure.

"Have you come to take me to the High Priestess?" he asked.

Neither woman spoke, but one of them motioned to him before they turned and moved off up the tunnel. Jarrod followed them and began counting the doorways in case he should need to find his room again alone. He passed twenty-one of them before they reemerged into the central cavern. They crossed it and took the passage directly opposite. Jarrod reached out for Pellia with his mind, but could feel no trace of her. A slight uneasiness took hold. It's probably nothing more than the effect of all this rock, he told himself. He found it disconcerting nevertheless.

The priestesses stopped before another door. This one, in contrast to all the others, had embossed panels. A black hand emerged from a sleeve and opened it. The priestess gestured for him to go in. Jarrod smoothed his hair and straightened his shoulders. He had to duck under the lintel, but managed to enter with more confidence in his gait than he felt in his belly.

The chamber was more than twice the size of the one he had quitted, but the ceiling was the same height. The walls were hung with deep red velvet and there were Isphardi carpets on the floor. A brazier burned with bright patterns in the center. With the rocklight restricted to the ceiling, the room had a warm and comfortable glow to it. The door behind him closed and the latch click was loud.

There were three women standing, waiting, at the far side of the room. Two were robed and wimpled, but the one in the center, manifestly younger than her companions, was bare of head and hands. She too was dressed in black, but it was close-fitting. He bowed deeply.

"Be welcome, my Lord Mage. It always pleases us when those of the Talent have need of our Master's advice." It was the youngest who spoke. Her Common betrayed no trace of origin and though the words were friendly, the tone was ironic.

"It is accounted a privilege to be admitted into the precincts of the Oracle," Jarrod replied equally correctly. "May I know to whom I have the honor of addressing myself?"

"I am Zena, High Priestess of the Immortal Oracle, and these are Cleantha," the slender, white hand moved to the right, "and Chrysippa," the hand arced gracefully to the left, "my most trusted advisors. We three," she added enigmatically, "are always so named."

Jarrod bowed to each in turn. Cleantha was stout, but that was about the extent of the information to be gained. The robes hid the bodies and the hands were tucked into the sleeves. Cleantha and Chrysippa were of a height. The faces were immobile and unsmiling. Both pairs of eyes were observant and measuring. Their composure was as absolute as a principle. The High Priestess was half a head taller, though still short to Jarrod. She had the kind of face that, in someone older, would be called handsome. The hair was straight and brown and disappeared behind her shoulders. The eyes were a little too large for the rest of her features and the gaze was direct. She wore certainty like chain mail. The mutual scrutiny continued and the silence stretched under it until Zena ended it once more.

"We have seen your request of our Master. It is an offering more than an asking and we commend you for it, but are you sure that there is nothing closer to your heart?"

The question took Jarrod aback. He hadn't expected his petition to be questioned once it had been accepted and, despite the High Priestess' stated approbation, he thought he sensed disapproval behind the words.

"There are many things in my heart," he said slowly, "but should we fail to stem the Outland tide, what benefits it a man to uncover his own secrets?"

"As you will." The voice was cool and indifferent and it stung him. "And what have you brought us," the High

Priestess continued, "that we should jeopardize our person in your behalf? To confront the Oracle is to invite peril. We never know, when we submit ourself to Him, if we shall be able to escape from His embrace. The Oracle is puissant and His favor dangerous. We do not open ourself to Him lightly.

"It is for that that we insist upon knowing the content of the question in advance, for we must weigh the need for an answer. That need must be true and great. For the answer to be valued, it must be costly. So, we ask you once again, what have you brought to us?"

Jarrod's mind was racing. Marianna had said that to bring something with him would be taken badly; besides, he didn't own anything they could want. Should he lie and promise them something? He did not fancy trying to lie to these three self-possessed women.

"Come, my Lord Mage," she was impatient, "you have seen that we have no fields, no kina. Think you that we feast on rock?"

He had to say something. "You spoke, High Priestess, of need. My life, as a member of the Discipline, is dedicated to the good of Strand. I can think of no greater need than to free our countries from the constant peril of invasion. There must be peace and I am dedicated to finding a way to it." He had no need to try to be convincing, he believed in what he was saying. If the worst comes to the worst, he thought, I could use the Voice on her. He reached out to Pellia, but still felt nothing. Except an idea. Enough of being on the defensive, he decided.

"You spoke, Great Lady, of payment, though I would have thought that the need of Strand would have no price; you spoke of nourishment. I have brought you nothing that will fill your bellies or adorn your walls, but I have brought you satisfaction of spirit and the chance for greater satisfaction still." He said it ringingly and noted the stiffening in the postures of Cleantha and Chrysippa. Whatever they had expected, they had not anticipated that answer.

"How so, Excellency?" If Zena was surprised, she did not show it.

Jarrod assembled his sentence before he spoke. He felt sweat began to trickle down his sides. "I bring to you, and through you to the Oracle, the astonishment and delight afforded by the sight of a living unicorn. I bring to you, and through you to the Oracle, the chance to preserve our world and hence yourselves."

He waited, aware that he was under intense scrutiny. The room felt close and he suddenly found himself longing for the open air.

"You make the mistake common to most outsiders, my lord," the High Priestess said. "You think of our Master as if He were a man, but the Oracle cares nothing for our puny race. He was here before us and He will be here long after we are gone. As to those of us who tend His will, there is no satisfaction save in serving Him. Where then is that satisfaction of which you speak?"

"You rate yourself too lightly, lady," he replied, aware that this was the crux of the interview. "You, and those who follow after you, if there be any, are the mouth of the Oracle. Without you he is dumb, pent beneath this island in impotence." His eyes darted across the three women and he was relieved to see faint shiftings in the folds of the robes. "Without the hallowed succession of High Priestesses, he may endure, but he will not live," he concluded. There was a long silence. No one moved. The brazier groaned softly as coals crumbled and settled.

"The unicorn, in truth, is a wonder that we had not hoped to see," the High Priestess admitted. "It does us honor by consenting to be among us. You may be assured that we shall do all in our power to see to its contentment while it is with us." She paused and, for the first time, she smiled, allowing Jarrod to see the young woman behind the demeanor of the High Priestess. "We shall visit it just before we present your petition to the Oracle."

Jarrod smiled back in relief. "If I may be so bold, Sacerdotal Lady, when will that be?"

"You will make known your petition to us in person tomorrow in the Whispering Gallery."

"May I take the unicorn out for some exercise before then, lady? I promise we shall not go far."

"Whatever the unicorn desires," the High Priestess said. "We shall meet upon the morrow. Until then, my Lord Mage." The three women bowed in unison. The interview was over.

He returned the gesture and decided against backing out of their presence. He felt as if he had just won a contest of wills, and there was a lurking resentment at the way he had been treated. The priestesses who had brought him here were waiting for him in the corridor and he told them, curtly, that he wished to see the unicorn. There was much that he wanted to discuss with her.

He kept probing out for Pellia as they returned to the central cave and took yet another tunnel out of it, but it was as if he had gone mentally blind. The new tunnel opened out into a broad, high gallery and he felt her presence instantly. He had not allowed himself to think that something might have happened to her, but now the relief was palpable. She was flattered, amused and soothing all at once.

There were stalls hewn out of the rock down both sides and in front of them water ran through channels in the floor. Hay was stacked against the back wall. Pellia emerged from one of the stalls and came whickering towards him. He ran forward and threw his arms around her neck.

'You know perfectly well that I can take care of myself,' she admonished gently. *'They are most respectful and they have taken good care of me. See? They've combed out my mane and tail and polished my hooves.'*

'Do you mind being down here, stabled underground?' he asked anxiously.

'Not really. It's a lot more pleasant than the cellars of

Gwyndryth. There's plenty to eat, fresh water, good ventilation, and you know I have an affinity for unmounted human females. But that is not what is troubling you. Let me see what has happened.'

Jarrod felt a delicate pressure and then found himself remembering everything that had happened since he had left Pellia.

'They are trying to keep you off-balance,' she said.

'Why?'

'Human reasoning is not my strong point. Even with you, I know what you are feeling and why you think you are feeling it, but I seldom understand how the one leads to the other. You would be better at the why than I. If you know what they are trying to do you may be able to perceive a pattern.'

'What I'd like to do now is get out of here and into the open air. The High Priestess said that I could exercise you.'

'What you mean,' Pellia replied, *'is that you want me to exercise you. It would be easier for you if you had no need for clothing. You will find it difficult to get astride in that wrapping.'*

'You're right, and I suppose I have some kind of dignity to maintain. I wouldn't want to shock the vestals with the sight of naked legs. I'll get a bite to eat and change and then we'll go out.'

'I would rather do it when it was light.'

Jarrod smiled. *'I'm not going to take that long,'* he thought back.

'The sun is already down.'

'It can't be. We haven't been here that long. It's no more than the seventeenth hour,' he objected.

'I cannot measure in your fashion, but I know that the sun went down some time before you came here. I already feel the urge to sleep.'

'No wonder I feel so hungry. I'll see you in the morning then. Sleep well.' He rubbed her nose fondly and went back to the waiting priestesses.

* * *

He came awake with a familiar sensation. The need to Make the Day was upon him and it was welcome. At least that marker of the passage of time was still functioning. He got out of bed and performed his ablutions under the relentless light from above and then put on his riding clothes. The feeling was stronger now and he knew that it was time to perform the ritual. He looked around bewildered. Which way was east? Well, no matter; performing the ritual was what was important. It would be strange doing it in this light, but, if he went deeply enough into himself, it would make no difference.

He sat down, cross-legged, on the floor, and began his silent litany of concentration. He shut out his surroundings and began to descend into himself. He went through his body, muscle by muscle, willing it to relax. He emptied his mind, letting the preoccupations and the pressures drain away. He thought of the sun, only the sun, and of the immense, joined force that it took every single morning to raise it above the horizon and bring light and growth to the world. He joined his will to the effort. When it was over he had no way of knowing if the sun was really up or not, but the pressure within him was gone.

He had just finished shaving when there was a knock on the door. He opened it to a priestess bearing a tray. He thanked her and helped her set it down.

"I shall be taking the unicorn for a ride when I've finished this," he said. "Will there be somebody to guide me to the stables?" She shook her head. "Then could you come back in about a quarter of an hour and take me there? I shouldn't like to get lost." She shook her head again.

"Now look here, the High Priestess herself said that I could exercise the unicorn any time I pleased. All I'm asking for is a little help."

"No, my lord, you don't understand." She was clearly flustered. "The ceremony of Petitioning begins soon. I am to come back and get you for that. You have three parts of an hour at best.''

"I see. Then I suppose I ought to get changed." He said it sarcastically, but she just dropped him a curtsey and left.

Jarrod tucked into his breakfast glumly but hungrily. First they kept you waiting and then they hurried you. They gave you no warning. If he hadn't told that girl that he was going riding, she wouldn't have said a word. She would just have come back as he finished eating and led him away to another ordeal. What did he know of this Ceremony anyway? All the High Priestess had said was that he was to present his petition in person in the Whispering Gallery, whatever that was.

He pushed the tray away, got up and went over to his saddlebags. He rummaged around briefly and came up with a fair copy of his petition. Then he changed into his gown and tucked the scroll into the sleeve pocket. He wound the rope belt twice around his waist and tied it. He straightened his gown and checked his hair. He was ready and waiting when the knock came.

They took a new tunnel this time. Unlike the others, this one was doorless. It curved and twisted with a spontaneity that the ones he had seen so far lacked, and the rock underfoot was less worn. It ended abruptly in an arch. The priestess stood aside to let him enter, but Jarrod hesitated, unwilling to commit himself. The hitherto quiescent knot in his stomach began to tighten. He had no reason to feel uneasy. The High Priestess had seemed pleasant at the last. If the interview had been a test, he had surely passed it. And yet . . . Stop maundering, he told himself sharply. He took a deep breath and walked on.

He was in a huge cave, though there was nothing natural about it. It was as if he was standing inside an enormous cupola. He looked around slowly. There was a lot to take in. The cavern seemed a perfect circle, broken only by the gap behind him. The whole was smoothly polished. It must have taken generations of labor to bring it to its present perfection.

The walls gleamed, but something was different. It took a beat before he realized that light was reflecting off the walls, not coming from them. There were rows of shielded links all around so that, at first glance, the light seemed to be emanating from the walls as usual. Only a faint flickering gave them away.

In the middle of the wall to his left was a backless throne, or rather a throne whose back was the wall. The multicolored facets of jewels winked from it. About twenty feet in front of it, a column grew from the floor and was topped by a massive candle. In the middle of the righthand wall was a smaller version of the throne, this one devoid of ornamentation. It was toward that one that he was now led.

He bowed to the acolyte and turned and faced into the circle. Inky clusters of priestesses lined the walls, like little flocks of white-beaked daws. A group of them was wheeling a slab of rock across the floor. Despite its size, it moved easily and with only an occasional squeak. All else was silence. The priestesses maneuvered it into the archway and sealed up the entrance. When they moved away it was as if the opening had never been there.

A soft chanting began on one side of the space and was taken up by the other. The antiphony overlapped and multiplied as the complex web of echoes came into play. It was as if a thousand voices were crooning the same threnody, but separately. The miasma of sound was complemented by the fact that the priestesses were reflected dimly in the polished floor. The Gallery seemed peopled by ghosts, all sealed up under the dome.

The singing continued, but the containment of the circle was broken when a curving section of wall slid back. Zena, High Priestess of the Oracle, stood framed in the opening. At least Jarrod assumed that it was she: the figure was too far away for certainty. She wore a black cape with a high-standing collar and the long hair was swept up on top of her head. She paced forward into the weave of harmony, followed by a double file of dark vestals. Her carriage was more regal than Naxania of Paladine at her haughtiest.

She came towards him, her blurred and foreshortened twin advancing before the hem of her cape. The vestals swung away and took up positions on either side of the throne. She glided to the center of the chamber and, with the unhurried pace of ritual, inclined toward him. Jarrod bowed low in response. As his head came up, she turned, the cape flaring briefly behind her, and made her way past the pricket to the throne. She swung around and seated herself. After a pause, Jarrod did likewise.

The acolyte who had accompanied him to the chair approached him again. She reached out and pressed his shoulder firmly against the wall. Jarrod tensed, not knowing what was going on, not knowing what he was supposed to do. She placed her gloved hands on either side of his face and turned his head gently to the left until his cheek was almost touching the stone.

"We bid you welcome, Jarrod Courtak, Mage of Paladine and Keeper of the Place of Power." The words were quiet and close and the voice belonged to the High Priestess.

Jarrod glanced round instinctively and the acolyte turned his head back. She raised an admonitory finger and withdrew.

"Do not be alarmed, my lord, we practise no witchcraft here. It is an entirely natural phenomenon of this chamber. That is why we call it the Whispering Gallery. Our voice cleaves tightly to the stone so that, should you take your ear away, you would not hear us." There was a note of friendliness in the voice, almost of conspiracy.

Jarrod cleared his throat and instantly wished that he had turned his head before he did it. "The Acting Mage of Paladine and future Keeper of the Place of Power greets you, Sacerdotal Lady." He felt ridiculous talking to the wall. "Can you hear me?" he asked.

"More than well, Excellency. It would be better if you spoke more softly."

"What am I supposed to do in this ceremony?" He pitched his voice just above a whisper.

"For the moment, what we are doing now. In a while we shall ask you to tell us what it is that you wish us to ask our Master." She dropped the Formal Mode. "But, before then, I should like to converse a while. No one else can hear us. It is the only time that I can speak with you privily. The Cleantha and the Chrysippa are always with me." There was a wistfulness in the words.

"Willingly."

"There is much I would know about the unicorn."

"Have you seen her today? Is she well?" Jarrod cut in.

"I have seen her and she is magnificent. I was with her just before I came here. Tell me, is it true that you can talk with her?"

"What gave you that idea?" Jarrod said cautiously.

"Your messenger was susceptible to the flattery of attention and spoke freely." There was a hint of amusement in the statement.

"Well, it's true up to a point. We don't actually speak, the unicorns can't understand spoken words, but they can read the thoughts in my mind."

"As my Master does with me." She was clearly delighted. "I must tell you that I am much comforted by having met you. The power of divination, the favor of my Master, can render one lonely, even when one is not alone."

"I know what you mean," Jarrod replied. "I've found that having the Talent makes friendships difficult. Finding the unicorns made things worse in a way, but that mental bond, the sense of total acceptance, makes up for it."

"You are indeed fortunate among men, my lord. I would that we had more time to speak together, but I must continue with the ceremony, or they will get suspicious. We shall have one more opportunity to talk when I return with your answer. Is your petition still the same?"

"It is."

"You must repeat it and then you can sit back and relax while I prepare myself for the Oracle. You will wait here until I return with His counsel."

"Repeat my question?"

"Yes, unless you have forgotten it. There is no shame in that. Many are overcome by their proximity to my Master, and I have your petition in my memory. I shall bear it and the image of the unicorn into the presence of the Oracle." The slightly artificial cadences of the Formal Mode had crept back in.

"As the High Priestess of the Oracle desires," Jarrod responded in kind. "My question of your master is this: How may I best serve Strand?"

"As it is said, so let it be presented."

There was a ritual finality to the phrase and he turned his head to the front again. He found that he had been gripping the stone arms of the chair tightly and he made himself relax. The chanting began anew, but the melody was different. He could not see the High Priestess because the candle hid her seated figure. He stared at the flame as the hymn surged and ebbed. The skeins of voices wove in and out until he was cocooned in the mellow suggestion of the sound. Drowsiness stroked him.

"I am ready!" The cry cut through the music and jerked Jarrod alert. The singing stopped but the harmonies rang on around the roof.

The High Priestess emerged above the candle and flung up her arms. The cape fell away and the high-piled hair tumbled down. She was robed in scarlet and seemed to have erupted from the flame. The dark shapes on either side of her closed in as if bent on extinguishing her. They surrounded her and her vividness was snuffed out by the black habits. No part of her was visible as they bore her to the opening and away into the darkness.

Jarrod found himself on his feet, but the wall was sliding back into place. He was locked in with the daws again. The last suspicion of an echo, stubborn vestige of a long-gone chord, died quite away. The priestesses stood immobile in the silence and Jarrod sat down. He made himself as comfortable as he could on the stone seat. There was nothing to do but wait.

chapter 6

He seemed to have been sitting for an eternity. He shifted position again, but it afforded him no relief. He felt that he was built of knobs. Nothing had happened for hours; no one had moved. The only things that had changed were the candle and the links. All were burning low and there was a faint haze in the air. The High Priestess is taking her waiting games past the point of patience, he thought. Unless, of course, there was some trouble with the Oracle, or with the petition. He wished he knew more about the process. He had asked a perfectly simple question. Ragnor had told him to be specific and he had been specific, so it shouldn't take this long. On the other hand, if the Oracle had refused to provide an answer, they should have been back by now.

There was a scraping noise behind him and he turned quickly. He could see nothing that would account for the noise and them remembered his conversation with the High Priestess. Sure enough, a gap had appeared to the right of the throne. One of the sisterhood slipped through it and passed across the floor to the group that stood where the archway had been. She spoke with them, though Jarrod could catch nothing of what was said, and they turned to the wall behind them.

The newcomer made her way back along the circumference, gathering priestesses in her wake. The group to Jarrod's left had unblocked the archway and now they rolled the slab of stone to one side. That done, they left through the exit they had created. Jarrod looked around. There was no one left except the acolyte.

"What's going on?" he demanded.

The woman was silent for a beat, as if deciding whether to answer the question, or trying to summon her voice from the distance of disuse.

"Our Master has favored the Zena too highly. She will not be able to convey His answer to you today. You must return to your room. I shall lead you."

"How do you know that? No one came near you?"

"I know what I know," she replied cryptically. "You must follow me now. You will be summoned again when the Zena is ready for you."

Was this another of their tricks? he wondered. If it was, it would be better if he pretended that it didn't bother him. "In that case," he said as he got to his feet, "I shall take the unicorn outside for some excercise. She hasn't been out in two days and that's not healthy. If you will take me back to my room and wait for me while I change, you can take me to the stables."

"As your Excellency desires." She turned and led the way.

Twenty minutes later he was astride Pellia, riding back across the bridge. It seemed months since they had crossed it and the bars of shadow thrown by the statues enforced his feeling of escaping from a prison. Pellia was as pleased to be out as he was; he felt her eagerness to canter, but for her the escape was from boredom. They clattered off the bridge and she turned north along the lake. She eased into a trot and then smoothly changed the gait to a canter. Jarrod refreshed himself in her physical enjoyment of motion.

She did not pull up until they were clear round the other side of the lake. Jarrod slid off and let her wade into the water to take a drink.

'You are feeling better than you were in the temple,' she remarked, *'but you're still agitated.'*

'I found the ceremony daunting,' he admitted. *'In fact the*

whole place is daunting, but I suppose not knowing what's going on bothers me most.'

'*The atmosphere is deliberate. The girls who tend me are affectionate and playful, both with me and among themselves. I should not like to live underground, but they give off the feeling of happiness.'*

'*I suppose they do it to impress me with the power and mystery of the Oracle.'*

'*In part,'* she replied. She shook her head, sending a rainbow of droplets flying, and waded ashore. '*I think that they also want to impress you because they believe you to be an important man.'*

'*I'm a Magician who didn't even graduate from the Collegium. Any importance I have is because of you,'* he corrected.

'*Nevertheless, people do not treat you as they did at first. I hear it in their tone of voice, I see it in the postures of their bodies and I can smell it.'*

Jarrod swung up into the saddle again and Pellia ambled forward, browsing on the new grass. Jarrod looked across the lake at the crag that was the temple. There were trees on this side and they softened the outline. The sun and the day-moon were high, a breeze ruffled the water's surface, insects hummed and the waterfowl were courting. It was a beautiful day and it made the prospect of returning even more distasteful.

'*You must complete this task,'* Pellia said in his head. '*Danger may be run from, but a challenge should always be met.'*

'*You're right and there's nothing for me to be afraid of. I just wish I knew the reason for this latest delay. Do you suppose that the Oracle refused to answer me?'*

'*I know nothing of Oracles, but it may be that the High Priestess has fallen ill. Did she not say that concourse with the Oracle was dangerous? It could have nothing to do with your petition.'* Amusement intruded. *'You humans always seem to think that you are the cause of everything.'*

'I suppose there's nothing for it but to wait and see. D'you favor a bit of a gallop on the way back? I love the way it feels to you.'

His room had been spacious enough when he was first shown in, but now, after an all too brief stint outside, it seemed cramped and oppressive. There was food waiting for him when he got back and he found that the exercise had put a fine edge on his appetite. He lazed around afterwards. He had a fix on the time again and was pleased to note that supper arrived when he thought it ought to. He tried to question the priestess who brought it, but she would not be drawn.

Once supper was over there was nothing to do. There was nothing to read, no one to talk to, no window to look out of, not even a fire to watch. He treated himself to a very long bath, luxuriating in the stream of warm water. He towelled off and was preparing for bed when he heard a knocking. "Just a moment," he called, thinking that the priestess had returned for the supper things. He struggled into his long, leather riding trews and the insistent rapping came again. "Coming, coming." He tied the last lace and opened the door. A small, dark shape brushed past him.

"Shut the door. Quickly!" It was said in an urgent hiss and he obeyed, all the old questions crowding back into his mind.

He turned and looked at his visitor. She pushed back the hood of her cloak and stood, chin thrust forward, looking like a little girl doing something on a dare. The light from the ceiling filled the hollows of her cheeks with shadows. Though the cloak was anonymous, there was no mistaking the big eyes and the strong features.

"I see you are recovered, High Priestess," he said for want of anything better to say.

"I'm still a little shaky," she replied informally. "May I sit down?"

"Please do." Jarrod indicated the armchair and went and got a clean shirt from the press. "Please forgive my lack of apparel. I was not expecting visitors." He put the shirt on and buttoned it up on his way over to the bed. He sat facing her. "To what do I owe the honor of this visit?" he asked.

"This is very difficult for me," she said. "I have never defied the Order before. If I am caught, I shall be sacrificed to the Oracle."

"But you're the High Priestess," Jarrod objected.

She gave a wan little smile. "Wouldn't make a jot of difference. We are forbidden to meet alone with outsiders, most especially male ones. It is seen as a betrayal of our devotion to our Master. An example is always made." She placed a hand on her knee. "My legs are trembling," she said.

When she looked up at him Jarrod saw that her face was haggard. Her encounter with the Oracle had left lines etched around the mouth and there were dark smudges under her eyes.

"When I perform Magic," he said sympathetically, "it drains me completely and it makes me look decades older. It takes sennights to recover from really strong Magic."

"This morning's visitation was different from any I have experienced before," she said slowly. "I usually have to wait for Him to come to me through the smoke. I have to immerse myself in the petition and what I know of the petitioner before I can feel His presence and begin to know His will." Her voice was low and her delivery hesitant.

"This time it was as if He was there, waiting for me. I stood over the cleft and He was there in the devine vapor. He filled me with ecstasy." She looked directly at Jarrod. "It was joy such as I have never known." Her face softened in remembrance. "He was preparing me for His answers."

"We get our feeling of joy after the Magic is finished,"

Jarrod commented. "Did he answer my petition?" he added, unable to hold back.

"Yes, that too was different. There has never been more than one answer to a petition. There are times when I have not understood and sought to question, but the reply has always been the same, word for word. This time the answer was very simple, but I knew that it was not all. He did not leave me as He usually does. He whirled me away through visions." Her voice trailed off and the smile returned, a full smile this time: one that illuminated her face and made her suddenly beautiful in a haunted kind of way. Jarrod felt the tug of lust and hastily suppressed it.

"What was the answer?" he enquired.

She blinked rapidly and her eyes focussed on him again. "The first reply was, 'By leaving it.' "

"By leaving it? That's all?" His heart suddenly plummeted. How shall I best serve Strand? By leaving it. "You said there was a second answer."

"Not an answer really, more of a feeling and that's why I came to see you. When my Master left me, there remained a very strong impression that He wished you to have a great treasure, but I don't know what it is. I thought you might be able to help me."

"I will if I can," Jarrod said, preferring to concentrate on this aspect of the revelation, "but I know nothing about any treasure—unless . . ."

"Unless what?" She sat forward slightly.

"Well, no one has ever been able to create the spell that will banish the Outlanders." That's what the Archmage wants, he thought.

She sat back again, her disappointment showing in the way her shoulders sagged. "You're talking about the Great Spell, aren't you? You aren't the first to seek it here. Before I became High Priestess, I used to work in the library. We have records of all the petitions and the answers to them. We have no Great Spell and the Oracle has always declined to supply one.''

"What do you have that your master might consider a great treasure?" He tried for lightness, but he was beginning to consider the first answer. It made no sense.

"We have nothing of great value here," she replied seriously. "All the money we get is spent on maintaining the temple and feeding and clothing the Order. We lead simple, dedicated lives. We have no need of ornament or finery. I know that people think that we must possess great wealth, but it is not true. Sometimes a petitioner will send some jewelled object, hoping to impress the Oracle. We cannot sell them as they are, it would offend the petitioner, so we break them down and sell the jewels separately. We keep only the things that are useful.''

"There must be something," Jarrod said. "Why else would the feeling have been so strong?" He wanted there to be something else, something that would free him from the dilemma of the Oracle's answer.

"The only thing we have that is unusual is a very old book. It predates the foundation of the Order. It was one of our earliest gifts and was said to have been brought across the Inland Sea with the first settlers. The first Zena wrote that it was in an unknown language. Even your Errathuel could not decipher it, though he said that our book was a copy of the original.''

It didn't sound very promising, but if it could be translated somehow, it might contain something that would show him a way out of the enigma of the Oracle's response to his question. "Tell me about the book," he said.

"There isn't very much to tell. It was a gift from King Caer the First. He credited the Oracle's advice for gaining him the throne and he gave it as a thank-offering. The High Priestess wasn't entirely happy. She had been expecting something, er, more substantial. Still, Caer's insistence that the Oracle was responsible for the downfall of the Marden dynasty did a lot for the temple's popularity. The book was displayed in the Audience Chamber, the place where we first met, for a long time. We've tried to sell it, but no one's interested in old books, especially those that can't be read.''

''And there's nothing else you think the Oracle might have had in mind?''

''Nothing. Not that I can think of, anyway. Perhaps I should talk this over with the other two.''

''I put myself in your hands,'' he said helplessly.

''I shall give you the Oracle's answer in the Whispering Gallery tomorrow—we call it the Ceremony of Impartation— but I do not know what to do about the thing of value. I must consult with the other two, though I cannot tell them that I have spoken with you and you must not mention this visit to a living soul. It is my life that is in your hands,'' she said earnestly.

Jarrod was touched by her appeal. If this was another ploy, she was a superb actress, but his instincts denied that. ''Have no fear, lady. I shall not betray you. You have been very courageous in coming to tell me of these things and I am grateful.''

She uncurled and pushed herself reluctantly out of the chair. ''There is much that I should like to ask you,'' she said as he got to his feet. ''I want to know what the outside is like. I don't remember it and I shall probably never see it. I'd like to talk to you about Magic and the wonderful unicorn. But I must get back to my quarters before I am missed.''

''There is much that I would like to know about your life too,'' Jarrod said politely.

''It's probably just as well that we don't have the time. It might be dangerous for me to hear about life outside. I am happy in the service of my Master and I would not want to spoil that.'' She gave him a wistful smile.

Jarrod felt a surge of compassion. She looked so small, so vulnerable; more like a child with a strong face than a High Priestess. Whatever she said, it could not be an easy life, shut away from the sunshine. "I hope you'll get some rest," he said. "You must regain your strength. If there are things you want to ask me, you could do it in the Whispering Gallery. After all, I already know what the Oracle's answer is."

"You are a kind man, my Lord Mage." She smiled up at him. "Until tomorrow then." She pulled the cloak around her and raised the cowl. A final quick smile as she opened the door and she slipped out.

Jarrod closed the door behind her and went back and sat down on the bed. He was deeply troubled. 'By leaving it.' How could he leave Strand? He was no god to fly among the stars. No man left the world, save by dying. Did the Oracle mean that if he lived, he would do some damage to the cause of the Alliance? Was it because he wanted peace? How could peace be bad for Strand? Surely not. He got up and unbuttoned the shirt. No point in getting it wrinkled. He wanted to see Pellia. He needed the reassurance of that warm personality and she might be able to shed some light on the answer. He opened the door again and looked out. The corridor was deserted. He looked towards the mouth of the tunnel. Could he find his way back to the stables? Perhaps, but he didn't relish the thought of blundering down the wrong tunnel and getting lost.

He went back into the chamber and shut the door. Might as well go to bed, he thought, there's nothing else to do. He climbed out of his trousers and into the bed. There had to be another interpretation. Or perhaps the High Priestess had misheard the Oracle. She had said that it had been a visitation like no other. Perhaps there was some kind of explanation in the book—if he got the book. Perhaps . . . He lay awake a long time in the inextinguishable rocklight.

chapter 7

Morning began, as usual, with the Making of the Day. The exercises in concentration brought with them the comfort of the familiar, and the meditation relaxed him. It took his mind off the Oracle for a while, but his doubts returned as soon as the ritual was over. He brooded over breakfast and then sat impatiently waiting for a summons. The Ceremony of Impartation would change nothing, he knew that. If there was any change in the wording of the Oracle's reply, it would be the Cleantha's doing, not the Omen Maker's. Still, the Ceremony would give him something to do, something to stop the circling of unanswerable questions. Time dragged by and another meal came and went.

The day before, Jarrod would have been irritated and resentful, but thanks to Zena, he knew that they were not merely playing with him, but debating the nature of the gift. It was frustrating nevertheless. He found himself pacing like a caged warcat. This whole thing was bitterly ironic. It was also unfair. He hadn't petitioned out of need, not personal need at any rate, and he had given up one of his chances to consult the Oracle. Even the High Priestess had admired the question. What was his reward? Nonsense that hinted at death. By the time that the knock on the door came, self-pity was in full flower.

He followed the anonymous priestess, still trying to think his way out of his dilemma, and was surprised when she passed the opening that led to the Whispering Gallery. Instead, she took him back to the carved door of the first day and stood aside to let him enter.

The Audience Chamber, its proportions thrown off by the low ceiling, was almost as he remembered it. The braziers and the carpets lent it a welcome warmth. The three priestesses, who did not, were in their same positions. There was an addition, however, and a change. The addition was a carved, wooden lectern on which lay an open book. The change was in the High Priestess. The hair was dressed high again and she wore the collared cape that she had worn in the Whispering Gallery. Her eyes betrayed her lack of sleep.

He linked his hands in front of him and bowed deeply. The High Priestess inclined her head, but neither of the other women moved. Is that a sign? Jarrod wondered as he studied them covertly. Which one really holds the power? The Chrysippa's blunt features were unrevealing. The Cleantha's face was roundly innocent, but the eyes gleamed like holes where water sleeps at night. That one, Jarrod decided.

"We have granted you the privilege of a further interview." The High Priestess' voice brought his attention back to her. "We have approached our Master on your behalf and He has deigned to vouchsafe you an answer. You are fortunate among men, my Lord Mage." Jarrod bowed again and tried to look pleased.

"You shall receive the import of that answer at the proper time and in the proper place," she continued. "We have not bidden you hither for that. The Oracle, our Master, has seen fit to bestow upon you a further favor." She paused and her eyes slipped sideways to the Cleantha. "He has adjured us to give one of our most treasured posessions into your care."

Jarrod allowed his eyebrows to rise and his eyes to widen. He turned his head slightly as if to hear better what was to come. He dared not look at either the Chrysippa or the Cleantha. He tensed his muscles under the robe. There, he thought, if they are so skilled at observation, they will be aware that I am surprised.

"We shall render up to you a book that has been in our keeping since the days when our Master first communed with our race." She gestured towards the lectern and Jarrod followed the direction and discovered the book, as if for the first time.

"If I may be so bold, High Priestess?" he asked. She nodded.

Jarrod walked over to the lectern and looked down at the book. The pages were a dark yellow, the edges dark brown with age. It was obvious, even in this light, that it had been written with a brush. The characters were still glossy black after all this time. There was elaborate scrollwork in the margins and the righthand page began with a small jewel of a picture in vivid red and blue and gold: pattern rather than picture, for it adorned what he took to be a capital letter.

He peered more closely. The lettering was ornate, but there were shapes that he recognized. It was the Common alphabet, though highly stylized. Perhaps his salvation lay here after all, he thought, and he felt an excitement build. He concentrated on the curliqued line, seeking the basic pattern, and the words came clear—if you could call them that. The syllables made no sense at all. He reached out and stroked the page. It felt sleek and satiny.

"It belonged to a people long since vanished, my lord. It is old beyond the links of memory and is to be cherished for that alone." The High Priestess' voice cut into his speculations. "It is the only one of its kind in the world."

Jarrod turned slowly. If this was the Oracle's palliative, it was even more oblique that its prophesies. "Your Master does me great honor and I am unworthy of it," he said, masking his disappointment. "If this is indeed his will, I shall prize it above all things." He thought he detected the faintest of smiles.

"It is His will. We shall now proceed to the Whispering Gallery for the Ceremony of Impartation. When that is over, you will be taken back to your room. The book will be waiting for you. You will pack your things and ride from hence forthwith. Is that clear?'' The tone made it obvious that there could be no dissent.

''Quite clear, Sacerdotal Lady.''

''There is a priestess waiting outside. She will convey you to the Whispering Gallery and we shall see you there anon.'' She gave him an artificial smile.

''As the High Priestess desires,'' he said, using her formula and bowing.

The Whispering Gallery was as impressive as before. The assembled priestesses were already singing when Jarrod entered and he paced behind the acolyte through a basketweave of sound. He took his place before the stone chair and waited. This time it was not long before a portion of the wall slid back and the High Priestess entered. Once more she glided to the center of the gallery and bowed before retiring to the throne. The singing swelled and then stopped abruptly, leaving the echoes unsupported. They withered and faded into silence.

The High Priestess sat and Jarrod did likewise. He had no need of the acolyte this time to show him how to listen. He leaned back and turned his ear to the wall.

''Thank you, my friend,'' the soft voice said, ''you played your part well.''

''They agreed with you then.'' Jarrod felt awkward about this intimate conversation, across distance, in the presence of so many others.

''Let us say that they had no better ideas. The Cleantha wanted to attach terms to your receipt of the book, but the Chrysippa and I dissented. I because the Oracle gave no such instructions and the Chrysippa because she thought you would be likely to show more gratitude if the gift were unencumbered. The important thing is that you will get the book.''

''You are sure about it then?''

''I am the vessel of the Oracle,'' she said simply.

"Is the Oracle's answer to my petition still the same?" he asked, hoping that it would not be, knowing that it would.

"It is, Excellency." A note of humor crept in. "Not even the Cleantha could improve on it."

"I am grateful to the Oracle," Jarrod said, "though I confess that I am a little confused."

"That is to be expected, my lord. My Master's ways defy the logic of man."

"And what of you," he asked, "will you be all right?"

There was a long pause and Jarrod thought he had offended her. Then she said, "You are the first petitioner ever to ask me that, my lord, and I thank you for your concern. The Oracle is the one who does the prophesying, so I cannot tell what the outcome of your petition will be, but if my hopes and wishes mean anything, the words of my Master will prove a boon to you."

Jarrod could see no boon in them, but her sincerity touched him. "No more than do I, my lady, and I, in my turn, wish and hope that you find continued joy in your service."

"Selah to that. I shall miss you, Jarrod Courtak, as I shall miss the beauty of the unicorn. I am the happier for having met you both."

"You said there were questions that you wanted to ask."

"I did and I have, but I think it better if I did not voice them. I have been happy here and it is best that I do not tempt myself, lest I lose the savor of what I have; but, once again, I thank you. And now, I am sure you will want to be on your way. The only ones who want to linger are those whom my Master has refused to answer. In a moment, I shall stand. Do you do likewise. I'll come forward and bow to you and then I shall leave. Your acolyte will take you back to your room. We shall prepare the unicorn."

"I thank you, Lady, for presenting my petition. I shall take good care of the book. If it is possible, I should like you to convey my thanks to your master."

"Farewell, then, Jarrod Courtak, Mage of Paladine. May fortune attend you."

"Farewell, High Priestess of the Oracle, and farewell to the Zena who was my friend."

"You have yet to ask a heart's question. We may meet again." The sibilance died and there was silence.

The hymn welled up again and while the echoes made the words unintelligible, there was an unmistakable feeling of triumph to the music. A paen to the Oracle, Jarrod supposed. It had spoken. It had given the outsider his answer. It should be a time to rejoice and be thankful, but he didn't feel joyful: he didn't even feel particularly grateful. I'm not the first to feel baffled or upset, he told himself, and I doubt if they care. The important thing to them is that, once again, the Oracle has revealed itself to man.

He rose as the High Priestess advanced around the pricket. He wondered idly if she was wearing the scarlet robe beneath the enveloping cape. They bowed to each other and her lips framed some words that he could not decipher. He bowed again lest he offend her and when he looked up she was gliding away from him. The acolyte appeared at his elbow and he followed her out of the Whispering Gallery. The priestesses stayed and sang on.

He changed into his travelling clothes and packed his saddlebags. The book was there on his bed as promised. He assumed it was the same book that he had seen in the Audience Chamber. It was wrapped in oilcloth, tied securely with scarlet ribbon, and he didn't feel like taking the parcel apart. He folded it into one of the robes and jammed it unceremoniously into a bag and buckled the straps over it. It was as useless as the Oracle's answer. He hefted the bags onto his shoulder and looked around the room. He was not sorry to be leaving it.

He followed the young priestess back down the corridor and stopped in surprise at the entrance to the central cavern. It was full of black-robed women and in the center stood

Pellia. They were not there to see him off, he realized. They were there for one last glimpse of the unicorn. Well, he couldn't blame them. She looked magnificent as she stood all saddled up and waiting for him. The white and gold of mane and tail, the gloss of hide and nacreous whorl of horn all stood out in vivid contrast with the surroundings. She was beautiful and she knew it.

'You are a shameless hussy,' he thought as he walked up to her and rubbed the velvety muzzle. He moved back and strapped the saddlebags on behind the saddle.

'I do not understand the concept.'

'Never mind,' he thought back as he put his foot in the stirrup and swung up. *'If you can tear yourself away from all this admiration, I'd like to get out of here.'*

He looked around for the High Priestess, but if she was there he could not pick her out. He really could not blame his disappointment on her, though he had been tempted to. She had only performed her task and, by her lights, she had done it successfully. He waved to the priestesses as Pellia began to move forward, but none of them raised a hand in return. He half expected them to follow, at least as far as the entrance cave, but they did not.

'I think,' Pellia said as they emerged onto the bridge, *'that you should go back in your mind and show me what has upset you so badly.'*

'It's nothing. It's just that I don't understand the Oracle's message.'

'It seems to me that you are evading. It would be best if you would let me see for myself.'

Jarrod sighed, but he let her roam freely through his memories. They turned left off the bridge and rode back along the edge of the lake and still she made no comment. He found himself reliving his nocturnal conversation with the High Priestess as they climbed the hill towards the forest road. When they reached it, Pellia turned for a final look at the temple. The island was small below them and its stone guardians puny and featureless. Down in the valley to their right, a band of pilgrims could be seen riding towards the temple.

'They time things with great precision, those priestesses,' Pellia remarked as she resumed the journey.

'Is that all you're going to say?' he asked.

'I do not know what you would have me say. I do not pretend to understand your Oracle better than you do, but it is clear to me that, at some time in the future, you will have to give your life to preserve your way of life. What I do not understand is why that should trouble you.

'A noble sacrifice is the worthiest way of embracing death. To make a meaningful end is what every unicorn aspires to and yet the thought seems to fill you with dread. I find that strange. In truth, the more I know you, the less I understand you.'

He could not hide his disappointment. He was not looking for understanding, he was looking for a solution, and he had assumed that Pellia would be able to provide one.

'I have no wish to embrace death, at least not until I'm very old. I don't see what's so difficult to understand about that,' he retorted.

She was distressed at his reaction and, under that, irritated that he could not see such a fate as something for which to be profoundly grateful. He knew this as clearly as if they were his own feelings and it sparked resentment. They withdrew from each other, but there was no way to escape the mental link completely. Communion was a burden as well as a blessing.

The wind came up and set the canopy of new leaves to bouncing and roaring softly like a distant sea. Sunlight dappled them as they cantered down the road to Gwyndryth. Hedgehoppers chattered at them from the branches and small creatures racketed in the undergrowth. Greeningale was in full swing and his heart should have been high. Instead, this promised to be a long and uncomfortable ride.

chapter 8

Marianna was waiting for them at the gates of Gwyndryth, accompanied them to the stables and helped Jarrod wash down and blanket Pellia. The colt interrupted her conversation with her mother to bid Jarrod goodbye and the tone of her thoughts was affectionate. It made him feel a little better.

"And now, my friend, you're going to come upstairs with me and tell me all about it," Marianna said.

They sat in the withdrawing room and, over a mug of chai, Jarrod told his story. He had intended to be matter-of-fact, but under Marianna's sympathetic prompting, he found himself pouring out his frustrations.

She felt a little impatient with him. If he had asked a more intelligent, less self-centred, question, he probably wouldn't be in this quandary. Nor could she understand why he was so morbid about the interpretation. I keep forgetting that he's young, she thought. Boys his age are given to romantic melancholy. He was obviously upset, however, and she kept her thoughts to herself.

"Well," she said, when he was through, "I don't think we'll find any answers here. Loath though I am to leave home when everything is in bloom, I suggest that we go back to Celador. Perhaps the Archmage can solve the riddle."

Jarrod wasn't particularly anxious to face Ragnor, but he knew that she was right.

They emerged, frigidly unconscious, in the field to the east of the city. The grass had grown considerably and, by the hedgerow, was tall enough for the two unicorns to satisfy their hunger without unseating their riders. When the humans revived, they set off down the road to Celador.

Neither Jarrod nor Marianna had noticed anything untoward when they had ridden out of the capital. Marianna was eager to get home and Jarrod had been preoccupied with the question he would ask of the Oracle. Neither of them had thought to look back. Now, however, the handiwork of the Discipline was quite apparent. At the end of the road, where the city's walls should be, was a huge stretch of green. Jarrod glanced across at Marianna to see how she was reacting and saw, or thought he saw, apprehension. Quite natural, he thought. He concentrated on the trees ahead and saw that they were encrusted with moss and wreathed in vines. The forest looked as if it had been there longer than man. The Apprentices were certainly doing a fine job.

He allowed himself to merge into Pellia's perception and was startled to see the outer walls of the citadel. He pulled back and the forest reappeared. He rejoined the unicorn and it vanished.

No, I'm not doing anything special, the filly advised him. *The only reason that I know anything about a forest is the reflection of it in your mind.*

"Pellia can't see the illusion," he informed Marianna.

"Neither can Amarine," she replied, with only the slightest tremor in her voice. "If the Outlanders can't see it either," she added with her old swagger, "the whole thing's a colossal waste of time."

"Don't even think such a thing," Jarrod said tartly.

They were almost at the thickets that edged the woodland and Jarrod braced himself reflexively. The unicorns met no resistance and trotted forward without concern, though Jarrod continued to see trees and undergrowth all around. They appeared to be breasting through it. Jarrod's appreciation of the Collegium's work increased.

"I can hear people," Marianna said and Jarrod smiled to himself at the relief heard behind the words.

"So can I, and I think it's getting lighter up ahead. We'll soon be out of this."

As he said it, an arched space came clear with a court beyond it.

"The gates are open and I don't see any guards," she remarked.

"I suppose they feel they don't need them with the Cloak of Protection in place. You have to admit that it's a pretty good illusion."

They clattered in under the portcullis and met no challenge. The wardcorn, discouraged perhaps by the sheer number of arrivals in recent times, no longer sounded the traditional alarm. They did not get by unnoticed, however. The unicorns immediately attracted a crowd, but the party was allowed to pass through to the stables, albeit slowly. Once they were more or less alone, they saw to it that the unicorns were properly byred, and then they stood by their bags in the weak sunshine.

"It's incredible how behind everything is here," Marianna remarked. "I'm glad I've got gloves on."

"Yes I know. I suppose I ought to go and make a report to Ragnor," Jarrod said reluctantly.

"And I better see if the Chamberlain has a room he can assign me. I hope this one will have a fireplace. I don't know about you, but I'm going to leave my stuff here. I'm not up to carrying bags this soon after Interim."

"It bothers me less than it used to," Jarrod said, picking up his two saddlebags.

"Yes, I noticed. If it weren't for the extra clothes, I wouldn't know you'd made the trip. That reminds me, I'm hungry. D'you want me to get the Chamberlain to seat us together at Hall?"

"Better not for the time being. I expect that I'll have to

eat in Magicians' Hall and who knows what the old man has in store for me.''

"All right then," she said with no trace of disappointment. "If I need to get hold of you, I'll leave word with the Archmage's Duty Boy." She gave him a rather perfunctory smile and went on her way.

'I may not be able to get back today,' Jarrod thought out to the colts, 'but I'll see if we can't go for a gallop tomorrow.' He was wasting his time. The unicorns were attacking the hay singlemindedly.

His stomach twinged as he made his way through the milling people. Off the unicorn, he was just another Magician. The women doing laundry in a long trough didn't look up and neither did the groups of men playing knucklebones and quirt. He noticed grimy rings where campfires had burned, washing was strung between windows and some of the panes were broken. Celador was no longer the stately, elegant place he remembered from his days at the Collegium. Things had changed so fast of late. He had changed. He regarded his separation from Marianna with equanimity.

The same could not be said of the prospect of seeing the Archmage again. He felt distinctly uneasy as he approached the tower. Ragnor did not suffer fools gladly; his tongue-lashings were legendary. Jarrod was not looking forward to what would happen when the Archmage found out that he had wasted his question. He left his bags in the anteroom, straightened his clothes as best he could and followed the Duty Boy into the presence.

"Welcome, welcome, dear boy." Ragnor heaved himself out of his chair and crossed the room with palms out.

Jarrod touched hands and inclined his head. "It's good to be back, sir," he said with partial truth.

"Come on in, come on in: get yourself a cup of sack and come and sit by the fire. I remember that trips through Interval are excruciatingly cold."

Jarrod let the mistaken name go by. This was no time to

correct the old man. He poured himself a beaker and followed Ragnor to the fire.

"I've half a mind to let the season revert to normal," Ragnor said as he settled himself and pulled a laprobe over his knees, "but the Senechal won't hear of it, not while the rufugees are still here. Now then," the voice sharpened, "did you get to petition the Oracle?"

"Yes, sir." Jarrod took a sip of the fortified wine and coughed as it burned its way down. The afterglow felt fine and seemed to take the edge off his hunger. He took another sip.

"Well, tell me all about it."

Straight to the point; no sociable chat. "I did what you said, sir," Jarrod began nervously. "I kept the question simple and direct. I thought about it for a long time. I reckoned that someone must have asked the Oracle for the Final Spell before now and, since we don't have it, the Oracle must not know it. At least, that's what I thought." He came to an apologetic halt.

Ragnor grunted and looked across at the speaker. He stroked his beard. The young man was nervous. His hands were twisting in his lap. Can't be me, he concluded. He's always a bit tense, but not this bad. Must have asked for something damned stupid. He said nothing. Let him stew, he thought.

"There was a question that kept coming into my head," Jarrod took up again. "It seemed right somehow, so I submitted it to the High Priestess." He paused and looked at the Archmage, but saw nothing reassuring. He hurried on. "My petition was accepted and I rode one of the unicorns to the temple—lucky I did because the priestesses were expecting a gift and I hadn't brought anything."

"You didn't give them a unicorn?" Surprise made Ragnor sit up.

"No, sir, just the sight of a unicorn."

"Ah, I see." The Archmage settled back again. "Most appropriate. Go on."

"They put me in a rock chamber and left me there for a long time. It was quite comfortable, but the waiting was rather unnerving. Anyway, I was finally taken to be interviewed by the High Priestess. That's when the business of the gift came up." He was beginning to rattle and he knew it. "The High Priestess finally agreed to present my petition."

"And what was your question?"

Here it was. He had put it off as long as he could, but Ragnor had seen through him. "I asked how I might best serve Strand." It came out in a mumble.

"Speak up, lad. I can't hear you."

"I said I asked how I might best serve Strand."

"Did you indeed? That sounds very noble. And what, pray, did the Oracle answer?"

There was something that Jarrod took to be skepticism in the voice, but it was a far cry from the explosion he had been waiting for. "He said, 'By leaving it.' "

"By leaving it? That was the answer?" He looked sharply at Jarrod. The boy had calmed down. His hands were now caught between his knees and his shoulders looked tense. He's frightened of me, Ragnor thought. That makes a refreshing change.

"Yes, sir."

There was a silence as Ragnor took a pull at his tankard. Jarrod followed his lead. The old man didn't look angry, in fact he looked puzzled. Perhaps he was going to get away with it this time. He stared at the fire and hoped.

"Well," the Archmage said at length, "this isn't exactly what I'd anticipated. Whatever could it mean? Always supposing that there's a rationale behind the damned thing's pronouncements."

"I'm sorry, Archmage, I obviously asked the wrong question. I've let you and the Discipline down."

"Poppycock. Given what you've done so far, it's a perfectly respectable question. I'm just sorry that I sent you off into a blind maze. What do you think it meant?''

"The only way I can leave Strand is by dying," Jarrod said bitterly.

"Really?" Ragnor sounded unimpressed. "I'm not so sure about that. It rather depends on your definition of Strand, doesn't it?"

"I don't follow you, Archmage."

"What is Strand? We tend to think of it as being this continent and the Inland Sea, but we all know that we came from a southern continent beyond the sea. Does it include the territory of the Outlanders? I don't know. No, I feel that something's going on. There have been too many strange things recently. In one way I'm delighted, because it's continuing proof that my vision of the future has been superceded. That may be the only purpose, if there is a purpose to all this, but I have a feeling deep within that there is meant to be more. It's the same feeling that I had when I was hunting for the Cloak of Protection. The pieces were all there. I just couldn't see them. The unicorns may be the key. They seem too special to be merely Magical transportation and morale builders. Don't you feel that?"

"Yes, in a way, of course I do," Jarrod replied, "but it's a little more complicated than that." He took a careful drink. Why are we talking about unicorns? he thought. He set his beaker down. "I've known them, I mean really known them, since they were a few months old and in some ways they are very ordinary. This isn't easy to explain." He gathered his thoughts. "They can do extraordinary things, but most of the time they are interested in eating and having a good run. They are all very different when you get to know them, but they are basically peacable. They have helped me fight, but I can't see them delivering a deathblow to the Others. I'm not even certain that they think we're in the right."

That may all be true, but I still think they are central to something and that you are the probable key to the unicorns.

So anything that happens to you merits scrutiny. I don't want to take anything for granted. I keep trying to look with new eyes." He slouched back in his chair.

"You know, young fellow-me-lad, when you were describing the unicorns a moment ago as being able to do extraordinary things, but otherwise being quite ordinary, you could have been talking about yourself. This prophecy may be nothing more than mumbo-jumbo invented by the priestesses, but it may turn out to be important. You just have to go about your business as usual and wait and see what turns up."

Jarrod felt as if a dark cloud had blown away. Of course the Archmage was right. There were many things that the Oracle could have meant. "Oh, I almost forgot," he said suddenly. "There was one more thing and it's strange too."

"Ah yes?"

"Yes. The High Priestess came to my room in the middle of the night—she said it was against the rules—and told me that the Oracle wanted me to have a treasure. She wasn't sure exactly what and she wanted to ask me some questions."

"What kind of questions does a woman ask a young man in his bedchamber in the middle of the night, I wonder?" Ragnor was amused to see the young man in question blush.

"The temple doesn't have anything of value that she knew about. They sell all the gifts for food. The only thing that she could think of was a very old book that no one wanted to buy. The Oracle hadn't been specific and she had never had a communication like it before. She was looking for ammunition to convince the two chief priestesses. I think she needed convincing herself."

"Fascinating. And what was in the book?"

"That's the problem, sir. No one can read it."

Ragnor sat up and finished his flagon. "I'd be obliged if you could get me some more of this and what do you mean, no one can read it?"

Jarrod took the proffered vessel and made for the sideboard. "Apparently it's in a language that nobody knows.

The Zena said that Errathuel himself tried and failed.'' He spoke over his shoulder and then concentrated on pouring.

"D'you have it with you?"

"It's with my bags in the anteroom.'' Jarrod returned to the fireplace and handed the tankard over.

"Thank 'ee, lad. Well, what are you standing there for? Go and fetch it.''

Jarrod did as he was told and came back and laid the package in Ragnor's lap. The Archmage picked it up and turned it over.

"Have you opened this?''

"No, sir. I thought you ought to see it first.''

Ragnor raised his eyebrows, but made no comment. He tugged at the bow and the ribbon fell away. He unwrapped the book carefully. What emerged was a slim volume in a plain black leather binding. He opened it and rubbed a page between thumb and forefinger.

"Beautifully done,'' he commented, "but you're right, I've never seen a language like this. Here, take a look.'' He held the book out.

The ochre pages and the vivid writing were unmistakable. It was the same book that had been on the lectern. Jarrod read a few words, but they meant absolutely nothing to him. "It makes no sense to me,'' he said.

Ragnor rubbed the side of his nose and his eyes narrowed. "I've had a thought,'' he said. "I've been spending time, as I told you, in the Archives. One thing I noticed was that words change over time; both the meaning and the way they are pronounced. You've only to remember some of the strange rhymes in the old ballads to see what I mean. Spellings vary too and I found that it helped to read things out aloud. Sometimes the meaning becomes quite obvious if you do that. Why don't you take the unicorn off into the real forest and try reading the book aloud?''

"Yes, Archmage; I'll do that.'' He started to get to his feet, judging that the session was over.

"No need to rush off and do it right now. We've still got some catching up to do."

Jarrod subsided.

"Things have got worse since you left." Ragnor sniffed and rubbed his nose again.

"I thought the Cloak of Protection was working very well. The illusion of the forest was completely convincing—at least it was to me," he amended. "The unicorns couldn't see it at all."

"That so? Well, we'll just have to hope that the Outlanders see differently, won't we? They're still the cause of the trouble, of course. They're still coming east. It's beginning to affect the economy. With no planting being done in the Western Marches and precious little around here, we're headed for food shortages. Food shortages provoke civil unrest and the thought of civil unrest provokes great uneasiness in rulers. Do you follow my drift?"

"The priestesses have no record of the Great Spell," Jarrod said. "I asked the Zena."

"I know that, son. If they had it, they would have used it to bargain with long since. No, we're going to have to deal with this in some less spectacular manner. The army's under increasing pressure to achieve some results, but I can't see that happening. It looks as if we'll have to solve this problem on our own.

"Let it mull around in your mind for a bit and see what pops up. I shall be calling a meeting of our best people to try to come up with a solution and I'd like you there." Jarrod nodded. "Oh yes," Ragnor added, "that'll mean that Sumner will get the guestroom and that, in turn, will mean that you will be sleeping in my anteroom again."

"That's quite all right, sir."

"Good enough. Off with you then. Go and get yourself something to eat."

Jarrod took his cue and his leave, feeling enormously relieved. He wasn't going to die. And the Archmage hadn't been angry with him. The two fears had almost equal weight. He started humming as soon as the door was closed.

Ragnor sat on and drank his wine morosely. His suggestion about the book had been more for the boy's benefit than a conviction that it would do any good. First the unicorns, now a book that no one could read. Bloody marvellous. And the only connection between the two was the youth who had just left.

He got up stiffly and went to refill his tankard. It would be ironic, he thought, if the book contained the Great Spell. No point dwelling on that though. There were more pressing things to take care of. For a start there was the unenviable task of coaching the bunglebird that homed in on Fortress Talisman. The new Chief Warlock would not be pleased to be summoned to Celador so soon after his installation, but that couldn't be helped. He picked up the poker and stabbed the logs repeatedly with it, sending sparks cascading up the chimney.

"Bloody Outlanders!" he said.

chapter 9

Jarrod went down to Magicians' Court to Make the Day the next morning wearing his riding clothes. He cradled the temple's book in his lap as he went within himself in search of serenity and the sleeping sun. Awareness of the book was with him through the litany of relaxation and the meditative exercises, but it disappeared when he began to reach for the sun behind his back. All his energies were focussed to the east. All through the Magical Kingdoms, men and women sat as he did and concentrated on the creation of a new day. It was a compulsion in them, and an act of restoration.

Jarrod came back to himself as the stars began to fade. He got up and tucked the book into his belt. The bakers were already at work when he went into the kitchen looking for food. The ash boys were raking out the hearths and the first cooks were wandering in sleepily. It was warm and friendly and the ovens smelled wonderful. He was tempted to stay for a second mug of chai, but he wanted to be off before the place woke up.

The colts were ready and welcoming. There was no trace in Pellia's mind of the awkwardness that had marred the return trip to Gwyndryth and his own mood was very different on this morning.

'*Mam's coming with us,*' Pellia announced.

'Marianna isn't going to be very happy when she gets here and finds your mother gone,' Jarrod pointed out.

'*Can't be helped,*' Nastrus said as he submitted to saddling. '*Mam wants some exercise.*'

'We are going to get a good gallop in, aren't we?' Beldun asked.

'Of course we are,' Jarrod answered, *'although I'm going to have to do some reading at some point.'*

'After the gallop,' Beldun said decisively.

'Mam wants you to open the door.'

He did so and led Nastrus out to the mounting block. They rode out, threading a path between groups of sleeping people, until they came to the South Gate. The massive doors were still open, but now there were sentries dozing beside them like roosting watchbirds, and beyond them was dense forest. Jarrod glanced around for the Magician who was projecting the illusion, but could see no one. The colts saw a straight road running through grassland with trees emerging in the distance and trotted out onto it. Jarrod found it easier to see through their eyes as they broke into a canter.

The day was fair, cool and quiet. The trees in the Royal Forest were at the same stage as the ones at Gwyndryth had been when he first arrived there and he had the strange feeling of having gone back in time. The mood was underlined by the fact that the road was deserted. No Royal Messengers, no pack trains, no creaking coaches to mask the birdsong; they had the world to themselves. The colts were clearly enjoying it and their pleasure was his own.

They were cantering three abreast now, with Amarine bringing up the rear, and Nastrus was trying to keep a nose in front despite Jarrod's added weight. The other two knew it and the pace accelerated until they were galloping full tilt down the road. Jarrod found himself screaming encouragement to Nastrus, entirely caught up in the excitement of the race. When they finally pulled up, blowing, his legs were trembling.

They walked on until the sound of water caught their attention and then they swung off the road and trotted under the old roburs. The stream ran through a clearing and though it was empty there were signs that this was a popular watering place. Jarrod slipped off and loosened the girth strap. He gave the colt an amiable pat on the rump and watched him amble to the bank. He took the book out of his belt and felt, for the first time, the tenderness where it had chafed him during the gallop.

He wandered over and leaned back against the broad, smooth trunk of a soskia. The unicorns were standing splay-footed in the stream, their horns spearing the surface as they drank. The trees formed a canopy overhead, but since they were not yet fully leafed he could see the sky. Sunlight spangled the rough grasses and winked off the water. Mallowmere and idris bloomed along the banks and snowspots were bright stars underfoot.

He turned the book over in his hands. The leather looked almost new and there were traces of gold on the edges of the pages. He opened it carefully and ran his thumb over the vellum. It was slick, almost satiny. There were two words in the center of the page surrounded by bright, flowing lines. The title, he thought.

"Owra Sabachthan," he said slowly and clearly. It made no more sense spoken aloud than it did sitting on the page.

He leafed on, admiring the marching lines of black ink and the curling color of the decoration. It was a beautiful artifact, a testament to the skill of the copier, but, as a book, it was worthless. Still, he had told Ragnor that he would read it aloud. He turned back to the beginning. He read it as if it were Paladinian. The sounds were pleasant enough. His voice went on, birds called and trilled, the stream chattered and the wind whispered in the canopy.

He turned another page and began again. He stopped after the first line as a thrill of recognition ran through him. He tried it again to be sure, listening to himself critically, and then read on. There could be no doubt about it. This was the invocation that Greylock had used in the Place of Power. He stopped abruptly and licked his lips. His mouth was dry.

There was a nudge in his mind and he realized that he had blocked the colts out.

'Mam wants to know where you learned the language of the Guardian,' Nastrus said and Jarrod could feel the curiosity of the other two as if it were a touch.

'This is the language of the Place of Power,' he replied. *'You've heard me use it before and you've heard Greylock use it.'*

'We didn't recognise it,' from Pellia. *'Mam says your accent is atrocious,'* Beldun offered at the same moment.

All the unicorns were standing in front of the soskia now and Jarrod felt that he was on the verge of a great discovery. Everything around him was distinct and vivid. The play of sunlight across the unicorn's backs, the iridescent wings of the heron fly hovering over the surface of the stream and the heady scents of Greening combined into an epiphany.

'Does she understand it?' he asked.

'Not the way you pronounce it.'

'Who is this Guardian?' Jarrod enquired.

'He is in the Memory for as long as there has been a Memory,' Nastrus said. *'Without the Guardian there would be no unicorns,'* Pellia added. *'He commands the air, the water and the land,'* Beldun intoned.

'Where is he?'

'He rules from the Island at the Center where all the Lines of Force converge.' Nastrus' thought was accompanied by a picture of spokes radiating to infinity. *'He is the Lord of Interim. There is nothing that he does not know or cannot do.'*

It's almost as if he's reciting a litany, Jarrod thought and was instantly aware of the colt's disapproval. *'Well, you must admit that that is a little hard to accept.'*

'It is what is,' Pellia thought flatly.

'Then he could rid us of the Others and solve all my problems.' Jarrod couldn't quite keep a skeptical tinge out and

there was a break in the contact. He was afraid he had offended them but they were back almost instantly.

'*Mam says he could, but he won't. He doesn't interfere on other worlds.*' It was Beldun who transmitted the answer.

'*But he could?*' The excitement was rising again. '*If he controls the Lines of Force he could bring the Place of Power back again, couldn't he? You said it was a Force Point.*'

'*It is,*' Nastrus agreed.

'*If the Place of Power were to be restored, Greylock would be free. Yes, that's it. It all fits together. Could your mother find this Guardian again?*' He was trying to be calm and rational, but he knew that his heart was beating harder. There was amusement from the unicorns in his mind. He hadn't expected that.

'*Any of us can find him,*' from Nastrus; '*All we have to do is go home,*' from Pellia.

'*Home?*'

'*We were born here,*' Beldun explained patiently and Jarrod knew from the tone of his thoughts that he was getting bored with the discussion, '*but the Island at the Center is home for all unicorns. That is where we go to mate.*'

'*Then I can go with you.*' The statement popped out and it was the colts' turn to be surprised. They withdrew again.

Nastrus was the first back. '*Mam thinks it is a bad idea.*' It was obvious that he agreed with her. '*It is a long journey. Only Mam has been that far through Interim. You might not survive and even if you did, the Island is a dangerous place for any creature outside its territory. You have no territory and we could not protect you. I mean no discourtesy, but you must admit that human beings are poorly equipped to defend themselves.*'

'*I realize that there will be risks, but I have no choice. I have to go. Don't you see? This is what the Oracle meant. I can best serve Strand by leaving it and the only way I can leave this world is with you. That is why it directed the High Priestess to give me the book. It's so clear. Please explain things to your mother. It may even be the reason she came here to foal. Please talk to her, convince her.'* He was so close to the solution that it was unthinkable for him to fail now. It would be too cruel to provide him with the answer and then snatch it away.

This time the unicorns turned away physically. They ambled off in no seeming order. He was still part of their consciousness, but they were thinking too fast for him to know what was going on. He felt like the child that adults forget when the talk turns lively. The time stretched interminably. He hated this. He hated the not knowing, the inability to do anything that would sway the vote. He was too agitated to stay still and began to pace, the book held firmly in his hand.

If Amarine was dead set against me, he thought, they would have been back by now. He looked over at the far end of the clearing. They were grazing, ripping at the new grass with their blunt teeth. He probed and came up with a blurred jumble. Well at least they were still debating the issue. One of them must be arguing his case. Pellia? She was the most sympathetic of them. She was genuinely fond of him, he knew that. They were all fond of him, but she criticised him least. Perhaps, if Amarine said no, he could convince her to take him by herself? No, he thought, none of them would go against the family. The betrayal would be in the Memory for ever.

As if prompted by his thoughts, Pellia turned toward him. He reached out with his mind, half afraid to hear what he did not want to hear.

'Mam has agreed.' There were no feelings of pleasure or success behind the thought. *'She wishes you to be aware that there is no guarantee that you will meet the Guardian, or that you will be allowed to return to Strand if you do. The risks while you are there will be fearful.'*

'You don't approve, do you?' he asked.

'It is not for us to approve or disapprove what another creature considers to be its destiny. Unicorns have a high

regard for destiny and it was for that reason that Mam agreed. For myself, there is a bonding that exists between us that is unique in the Memory and I am loath to see you perish needlessly. Nevertheless, I am prepared to carry you when I return to mate.'

'I am deeply grateful,' Jarrod replied. *'You can tell that without my even having to think it, but I do want to emphasize it and to thank you all.'*

'It is accepted,' she returned gravely. *'How long do you need to prepare? Mam ways it will not be long before I go into my first season.'*

'Whenever you are ready.' A thought struck him. *'If I can get Ragnor to agree,'* he added. *'No, that's not true. I'll go anyway. It is, as you say, my destiny.'*

'I shall explain that. I should think that it will be in one of your sennights.'

'Are you all going?' he asked.

'Only Mam and I. The males do not reach rut until much later so they will stay here a while longer.'

'I am relieved to hear it. You are all much loved and greatly needed. Your leaving will affect Strand deeply. You have all become a sort of symbol of hope.'

'We are what we are, not what you make of us.' There was a touch of asperity in the delivery and then Pellia lowered her head and resumed grazing.

Jarrod was elated. This was what his whole life had been leading to. He felt a sense of certainty about it, a rightness to it, but then, he cautioned himself, he had had the same feelings when they had come upon the valley of the wild cloudsteeds and he had been wrong then. Yes, but he'd gone on to find the unicorns, hadn't he? And if anything ought to be infallible in this world, the combination of the Oracle and the unicorns should be it. The Oracle had ordered him to leave Strand and the unicorns believed it to be his destiny and were going to provide the means. There was no way that he could fail.

He became aware that the colts were getting restive so he went over and cinched Nastrus' girthstrap. He swung into the saddle and they set off back to Celador. The colts were too full to contemplate another gallop and Jarrod was content to let them trot. His initial bravado about Ragnor was beginning to fade. He couldn't just disappear with two of the unicorns. He might be sure of his feelings, but that didn't mean that he could convince the Archmage.

When they finally reached the stables, he spent a long time currying them. The colts enjoyed the extra attention, but they knew precisely why he was doing it. They twitted him gently about his relief in not finding Marianna waiting for them, but of the forthcoming trip they made no mention. When he had blanketed them all, there was no further excuse for delay and he took himself reluctantly back to the Archmage's anteroom to change out of his riding clothes.

He had just returned from the bathhouse in the corner of the court when the inner door opened and Ragnor came bustling out of his chamber.

"Ah, there you are. Just the man I'm looking for. Get your robe on and come on in." He turned and marched back inside.

Jarrod pulled his Magician's blue over his head and pushed his arms down the sleeves. He tugged the robe down and tied the rope belt around his waist. No time to bother with hose: he jammed his feet into his shoes. He ran his fingers through his hair and then abandoned the effort. He cursed under his breath and headed for the main room.

Ragnor was leaning against the mantlepiece cradling a goblet that Jarrod hadn't seen before. If I ever need to get him a present, he thought, I can always give him a drinking vessel.

"I've been giving a lot of thought to this invasion," Ragnor said as soon as Jarrod was across the threshold, "as you might expect. Summer won't get here for another sennight, but I'm anxious to get started. Anything pop into that head of yours yet?''

To Jarrod he looked like a raptor. The crooked elbows gave the outline wings, the nose sliced forward and the eyes, under the fierce tufts, seemed to see everything. He came to a halt in the middle of the room, not knowing what to do.

"Now I don't want you to be intimidated," the Archmage said, as if reading his thoughts. "What I'm looking for are new ideas. Your youth serves you there."

Jarrod scraped his courage together. "Well, Archmage, something has happened that might be important," he said hesitantly.

"The book; I'd forgotten about the book. You've deciphered it." Ragnor pushed away from the mantlepiece and took a step forward.

"Not exactly, sir."

"Not exactly? Not exactly? You trying to kill an old man with curiosity? Come and sit down and explain yourself."

Jarrod crossed the room and took the chair to the left of the fireplace. "Well, sir, I followed your suggestion and read the book aloud. Nothing made any sense until I came to a part that turned out to be the invocation that Greylock uses in the Place of Power. I don't know what the words mean, but I'm sure they're the same ones."

"So the only person who might know what it means is out of reach. Well, that's certainly interesting and I suppose in some ways it's a step forward, but I can't see that it's of much help at the moment. Anyway, I'm glad my suggestion proved helpful." His disappointment was evident.

"There's more, sir."

"More? Oh then, by all means . . ." Ragnor turned and plumped down into his armchair. He took a drink.

"Amarine recognized the language. She had never heard it used in the Place of Power, but she says that there is a being who rules the place where unicorns come from and controls all the Lines of Force and that the book is in his language." It came tumbling out. "The colts say that he can do anything, even rid us of the Outlanders if he wants to."

"Is that a fact? Well now, this is most interesting. A Magician even more powerful than Errathuel." Ragnor got out of the chair and put his goblet on the mantle. He retrieved the poker from its niche and chivvied the fire. It blazed obligingly. "And what do you make of it?" he asked.

"It's what the Oracle meant. To find him and get the Final Spell, I'll have to leave Strand."

"Oh ho, so that's the way of it, is it?" Ragnor straightened up and looked down at the young man. There was a part of him that was upset with the idea of the Final Spell being found by someone else. Work on it had always been the duty and the prerogative of the Archmage. He had been prepared to share the work with the others, an unprecedented gesture by an Archmage, and now the gesture and the work might be meaningless. The Final Spell was not going to be discovered, it was going to be borrowed, or perhaps stolen. It didn't sit right with him. He turned back to the fire and picked up the goblet again. He sipped. Jarrod watched him apprehensively. There was no way of telling what the man was thinking.

The fire and the wine warmed Ragnor's stomach. He must approach this unemotionally. He had told the boy that he was looking for new approaches; it would be foolish to dismiss the first one he came up with out of hand.

"This is very interesting, lad," he said, resuming his seat. "You mustn't mind my wool-gathering. There are a lot of implications here that have got to be worked through, so bear with me." He retired back into silence.

They needed an answer, that much was obvious, and this boy might be able to obtain it. Whatever the circumstances, the job was bound to require someone who was young and fit and could defend himself if need be. Courtak fitted those requirements. He had proved tractable. His recent fame didn't seem to have gone to his head. It might be possible to let him do the dangerous work and then take credit for the spell.

The boy was young and impressionable and a little afraid of him. Shouldn't be too difficult to persuade him that it would be for the good of the Discipline. Wait a minute, he told himself, you're getting ahead of yourself.

He looked across at Jarrod. "And where does this paragon of knowledge reside?" he asked.

"At a place where all the Lines of Force meet. Even for the unicorns it is a very long journey."

"And how do you propose getting there?"

"The only way I can is if one of the unicorns carries me. They have agreed because they see it as my destiny."

"I don't think it would be in the best interests of Strand to encourage them to leave at this juncture," Ragnor objected.

"They won't all go; just the females. They have to return to find a mate and when that time comes, they will leave whether we want them to or not. The two males will stay for a while longer."

"You wouldn't happen to know when this exodus is supposed to begin, would you?" It was not said altogether kindly.

"In about a sennight, sir."

"A sennight?" Ragnor sat up so sharply that a drop of wine flew out of the goblet. "And they've waited until now to tell us? That's a little casual, isn't it?"

"Today was the first time I heard about it. I think the colts just assumed that I would know. I can understand that," he added defensively. "When we are in each other's minds, it's as if we were all the same person, so you expect them to understand what you mean and know what you know. We forget that we're totally different species with completely different heritages and instincts. They simply took it for granted that I knew what their mating rituals were."

"I see, but that still doesn't leave us with much time. I think we'd better say that they've gone back to Paladine."

Jarrod felt a band across his chest relax. At least the Archmage believed him. "It would also explain my absence, not that anyone will notice that I'm gone."

"And what says the Lady Marianna to this plan?"

"She doesn't know yet, unless she's been to the stables since I left."

"Does she not? I wonder what she will have to say when she does?"

"I'd forgotten about that in all the excitement. All I was worried about is that she would give me a talking-to for taking Amarine for a gallop without her."

"And what will she say when she finds out that you intend to take Amarine clear away?" Ragnor permitted himself a slight smile.

"I'm not taking Amarine, she'll be taking me, but that won't make any difference. Marianna will say that she is the one who should be going, not me. She said it about my going to Fort Bandor."

"Well, we can't have that, but there are two females unicorns, are there not?"

"Yes, sir," Jarrod said with a sinking feeling. He knew what was coming.

"Perhaps it would be best if you sought her out and suggested that she join you," Ragnor said judiciously, tilting his head back.

"Oh no, sir. Do I have to?"

"I'm not entirely convinced that you should go at all. If the unicorns wish to leave us, there is nothing we can do to stop them. I would prefer if they stayed at least until this present crisis was behind us, but if not, not. You are an entirely different case. If I thought that you were expendable, I shouldn't hesitate to send you off, but you have come out of nowhere and in a scant two years you are the most talked-about Magician in the Kingdoms. For all I know, you may be the one who is capable of putting together the Final Spell. It would be a foolish and irresponsible of me to gamble with that possibility for the sake of a quick solution under the most improbable of conditions.''

This was as close to praise as he was going to get from the old man, but it made him feel miserable. "I've only been able to do what I have done because of the unicorns," he said. "Without them I am only a second-rate Apprentice who hasn't finished the Collegium.''

"Don't play me for sympathy, boy, it won't wash. What you say about the unicorns may be true, but Greylock spotted your potential early on.''

"But Archmage, it all fits together," Jarrod said desperately. "Can't you see that? The verse led to me, I led to the unicorns and now the unicorns are going to lead me to a solution. I really don't know if this Guardian knows the Final Spell, or if he'll give it to me if he does, but he does control the Lines of Force and the Place of Power is connected to them. The colts call it a 'Force Point.' Greylock used the language of the book to communicate with Those That Dwell in the Place of Power and Amarine says that it is the Guardian's native tongue. Surely he would be willing to restore the Place of Power and that would mean that Greylock would be free. I have to try this, Archmage. It fits in with what the Oracle said and it's the least I can do for Greylock.''

"I'll have to think about it. It is best to think things through before making decisions." Jarrod's intensity made Ragnor hedge.

"But we haven't got much time, Archmage. Pellia said that she would be ready in a sennight.''

Ragnor sat back again and took a deliberate pull on the wine. "Ah, the young," he said, "always in a hurry, and the irony of it is that you are the ones who can best afford the time." He smiled faintly at the saying. Jarrod did not. "You will have to be patient and, just as I have to trust you when it comes to the unicorns, you will have to trust that I am doing this because I have Strand's best interests to heart.'' He looked over at the waterclock. "Besides, it's time to go down to Hall. We shall talk about other things entirely and you will look as if you are enjoying the experience."

"Yes, Archmage."

"Tell you one thing though," Ragnor said maliciously as he got up, "if, as you say, the verse led to you, it also led to the Gwyndryth girl. Think on that. Now, let's go down and be jolly and do you proceed me. If I stumble on the stairs I should prefer to have something soft to land on."

chapter 10

"**T**here's been a lady here asking after you," the Duty Boy said from his place by the anteroom fire as Jarrod returned from Making the Day. It was clear from the whisper of envy in the voice and the look on his face that his opinion of Jarrod had jumped several rungs.

"At this hour of the morning?"

"The Lady Marianna, all dressed to go riding, she was. Said she'd meet you at the stables as soon as you could manage it."

"How long ago was this?"

"No more than a quarter, but I reckon you better hurry."

"Thank you. Is that water warm by any chance? And I'd like a cup of chai before I go." Yes, he thought as he sponged himself carefully over the pewter basin, that's Marianna all right. She obviously looked like a goddess to the boy and behaved like one too. He drank his chai while he donned his riding clothes and combed his hair in the spotted looking glass. He toyed with the idea of keeping her waiting, but did not entertain it long. She would be upset enough if she knew that Amarine was leaving soon.

"If the Archmage asks for me, tell him that I have gone to see the unicorns. I don't know how long I'll be, but I'll come right back here."

"Yes, Excellency." The boy was actually deferential.

Wonderful the way a pretty girl could affect a boy whose voice was cracking, Jarrod thought as he made his way down the stairs. You shouldn't make fun of the boy, he chided himself. You weren't exactly immune to her charms. The fact that he could phrase it in the past tense gave him great satisfaction. It did not, however, cancel the anxiety he felt in having to face her.

He was aware of the colts well before he reached the stable and knew instantly that Marianna was there. He could pick up nothing special. With luck that might mean that she was in a good mood, although why she should be was beyond him. Perhaps Amarine could shield certain things from her.

"Morning, Marianna," he said as cheerfully as he could.

"And may the best of the day be before you, Jarrod Courtak," she replied with a smile.

Not good, he thought. She's using a Formal greeting phrase. "The Duty Boy gave you my message . . . I mean gave me your message, and I came over as soon as I could." Why was he nervous? There was nothing to be nervous about. He would just have to explain things to her.

Marianna moved out from behind Amarine, smiling. She wore brown trews and boots, a leather jerkin and a man's shirt. The red hair was pulled back into a single plait and she had the healthy glow of someone who has just washed in icy water.

"Amarine tells me that you want to accompany her on her return to the Island at the Center. I think it's an exciting idea."

"You do? I mean I'm glad you do. So do I." He remembered the Archmage's words from the night before. "I would have told you before, but everything happened so fast and so unexpectedly and I didn't know where to get hold of you. I have to attend the Archmage while I'm here, so I couldn't just loiter around the stables on the off chance that you'd show up."

"Oh, I quite understand."

Jarrod smiled uneasily. Something was going on that he hadn't caught yet. She should be angry or upset, or both. He went over to Beldun and reached up to rub behind his ear. "You approve then?"

"Of course," she said, carefully casual. "It's about time we all did something together. You may not feel this, after all you've been off retaking forts, but I find palace life dull. All the other women can talk about are clothes, babies and husbands; all that the men want to talk about are hunting, battles and bed, not necessarily in that order."

"I see," Jarrod said, and indeed he did, all too clearly. "What's your father going to say?"

"Yes, poor Daddy. He won't know, I'm afraid; at least, not until after we're gone. Pellia comes into season in a few days and it's best for her not to be around her brothers at that time. There isn't time for a bunglebird to get to Stronta, let alone get back. Besides, he has so much to do, I doubt he'll miss me." The smile was back, but there was no warmth in it. "And what has Ragnor said?"

"Nothing really. He hasn't made up his mind and I'm not absolutely certain that he'll let me go."

"Oh, that would be a shame. I really would have liked you to come. Do try to convince him. It would be like old times again."

"Whoa. Hold on there. You're not suggesting that you would go off on your own, are you?"

"But Jarrod dear, what other choice is there? This opportunity isn't going to present itself again. One of us has to go and I'm not answerable to Ragnor."

"But you can't do that. I'm the one the Oracle directed."

"I don't know about that. I don't recall your telling me that at Gwyndryth, but it doesn't really make much difference. There's no reason why I shouldn't go and talk to this Guardian."

"It's far too risky," he said with a feeling that bordered on panic. "Amarine says that there's a possibility that I might not survive the trip and you know that Interim bothers you more than it does me."

The ambiguous smile was firmly in place. "You seem to forget that I have already been to the Island at the Center and back again."

"Yes, but that was different. If Amarine hadn't taken you away at that moment, you would both have died."

"Doesn't alter the fact that I've been there and you haven't." She was in control and relishing it. "And don't bring up the business of surviving in difficult and unknown terrain. Just remember who had to rescue whom the last time."

"But this is a Magical matter," Jarrod protested, all other arguments gone.

"Ah, yes, Magic," Marianna said dwelling on the final word. "Did Amarine tell you that your Magic wouldn't work on the Island? So that makes us equal. Well, let me put that another way: it removes any tiny advantage you may have had. Now, I don't know about you, but I'm going to saddle up Amarine and take her for a ride. You're welcome to come along, of course, but you'll probably have to do some more attending. If I were you, I wouldn't waste any time convincing Ragnor. The females and I will be gone before the sennight's out." The smile brightened and she swept past him on the way to the tack room.

The colts were aware of Jarrod's consternation and sent rumblings of support, though those from Nastrus were tinged with amusement. This was terrible. It was bad enough that he had to share his destiny with this impossible creature, but that she should take it away from him was intolerable. He couldn't stop her going, that he knew. The bond between Amarine and Marianna was far too strong for him to think of trying to interfere. Ragnor had to let him go, that was all. If he refused, he'd go anyway. He hurried out of the stable without even bidding the colts goodbye.

The Archmage was sitting on his bed, feet up with a rug over them and a hot brick wrapped in flannel beside them.

Cider was mulling by the hearth. He'd had a bad night. The cold and the damp made his joints ache. He'd been lucky, he reflected, to reach seventy with only occasional days like this, but that didn't make bearing the pain any easier. He'd been wrong to take it out on the Duty Boy, even though the child had been unbearably clumsy. He must remember to tip him well when his tour was over. Besides, the lost sleep hadn't been wasted. There was much to think about these days. He looked up at a tapping on the door.

"Enter," he growled, and the Duty Boy ushered Courtak in.

"I have to speak with you, Archmage. I'm sorry to interrupt you, but it's important."

"All right, all right; slow down. That's better. Now, there's some cider by the hearth. Pour us both some—there are cups on the sideboard—and then come and sit down and tell me all about it."

Jarrod poured a cup for the Archmage and carried it carefully over to the bed. He got an upright chair from against the wall and set it down at a respectful distance. There was a knot in his chest. He took a deep breath before he sat down.

"I've just come from the stables, sir," he said, plunging in. "The Lady Marianna was there. Amarine had told her of our plans and I expected her to be angry. She was delighted. She took it for granted that she would be going with me." He leaned forward in an unconcious attempt to get his words across more forcefully. "Worse! She said that if you don't let me go, she'll go alone."

Was I ever that earnest? Ragnor wondered. He looks like a praying mantis. Still, the boy was obviously upset. He'd have to handle him gently.

"The unicorn will take her, will it? Interesting," he said quietly. "In that case I don't see how we are going to stop her, short of locking her up, and I can't see the Princess Regnant acceding to that."

Ragnor paused and inhaled the aroma from the cider. He

sipped. He'd given the matter of this trip a lot of thought during the night, but he hadn't come to any firm conclusions. Events, however, seemed to be generating a momentum of their own.

"The Lady Marianna's father," he said, "is one of this country's more powerful vassals. He is also in charge of Paladine's armed forces and a hero to the Umbrians. The Lady Marianna is his sole heir. It would be unthinkable for me to allow her to go off on such a speculative and dangerous expedition, even though I did suggest it to you before."

"But you just said that we couldn't stop her," Jarrod pointed out.

"Precisely. I've been up half the night thinking about this trip. It's an appalling gamble whichever way you look at it. I had just about made up my mind not to let you risk it, but it seems that I have no choice now. If I cannot prevent her from leaving, I certainly cannot let her go unescorted.

"I shall have a bad enough time with Arabella and Holdmaster Gwyndryth as it is, but we do have a precedent for the two of you going off together. There has been nothing rational about this unicorn business from the beginning, so why start using logic at this late date? What d'you reckon you'll need in the way of equipment and provisions?"

Jarrod let his shoulders sag and a wide smile appeared on his face. He sat back up in the chair again. "I'll make up a list and give it to the Duty Boy," he said, surprised at the ease with which he had carried the day.

"Get on with it then," Ragnor replied in his best grumpy manner.

That's it, then, the Archmage thought when the young man was gone. The decision had been effectively taken out of his hands. None of the decisions about the unicorns had been truly his. Still, it proved one thing. He wasn't too old for the bold throw. No, not by a long chalk. Time to get up, he thought. He was feeling very much better.

* * *

Thereafter the days fled by. Ragnor's method for circumventing the expected opposition was to allow the bare facts that Jarrod and Marianna were making a special trip with two of the unicorns to become an open secret at Court. As a result, the two were bombarded with invitations. In a single day they both became adept at smiling evasion. Jarrod was further burdened by overseeing the collection of the gear they felt they needed. His meetings with Ragnor were rare and the Archmage seemed preoccupied during them.

The exception was the last evening when they were both summoned to his chamber. He fussed over them and poured the wine for them before settling into his chair.

"I'm not going to keep you," Ragnor said, "because I know you both have social engagements. I shall be coming to see you off in the morning, but I wanted to have a moment to thank you for taking this risk. You are doing Strandkind a great service." He paused and smiled. Jarrod felt slightly embarrassed.

"I want you to know," the Archmage continued, "that I shall see to it that your unicorn friends are well taken care of while you are gone."

"Excuse me, sir," Jarrod cut in. "I think I ought to warn you that they are liable to take trips of their own. They've promised to return here though."

"Well, I'm certainly glad you told me that. I hadn't thought of it before, but I'd appreciate it if the two of you would also try to return here."

"We'll do our best, Archmage," Marianna said.

"I'm afraid I haven't anything in the way of spells or potions to protect you, since Jarrod informs me that Magic is ineffective on this Island, but I do have something that might help."

He put his cup down, got out of the chair and went over to his chest. He came back with two suits of blue-black chain mail. He handed one to each.

"I hope they fit," he said. "One's mine and the other is

intended for Queen Naxania on her coronation. They are made of a special metal called Melzanite and, if it's at all possible, I'd like to have them back.''

"Thank you, sir," Jarrod said, "we'll be careful with them." He turned to Marianna. "I'll keep yours, if you like, and bring it to the stables in the morning." She smiled and handed the neatly folded package over.

"It's very light," she remarked.

"And amazingly strong," Ragnor said. "It doesn't rust either."

"I can see why you want it back," Marianna said with a smile.

Ragnor returned the smile. "You look after yourself, young lady. I'm going to have a difficult time explaining this to your father."

"Rather you than me, Archmage."

He turned to Jarrod. "I know you'll do a fine job, son, Greylock would be very proud of you." He looked from one to the other. "Well, I'll not keep you."

They rose and he went and put an arm round their shoulders as he escorted them to the door. He stopped at the threshold.

"I know this isn't going to make the slightest difference," he said with a twinkle, "but try not to overdo it, and get to bed as early as you can."

chapter 11

Jarrod resisted his body's prompting. It was black and cold outside and his mind felt blurry. His nose was clogged and his mouth was parched. Thirst was what finally drove him up, trailing the coarse blanket. The fire was down to the grey flutterings of ash and the Duty Boy was a cloak-covered lump on the pallet in the corner as Jarrod crossed the room on quick, cold feet. He lifted the ewer and felt the shards of skim ice on his top lip. He drank deeply and poured the remaining water into the basin. He splashed his face with it and the burning of his skin seemed to clear his head somewhat. Should have listened to the Archmage, he thought. He fetched his orel stick and worked it over his teeth and gums.

He filled the kettle from the bucket by the washstand and set it on a cooking ring over the embers before waking the boy. He dressed quickly, partly because of the cold and partly because he wanted to be out of the room before the boy was ready to Make the Day. He wanted to be alone for this one. It might, after all, be the last time he would perform the rite on Strand. His stomach growled. He'd have to cadge victuals out of the cooks. He was hungry now, but that wouldn't be a patch on the way he'd feel after a long trip through Interim. He let himself out quietly and made his way up the stairs to the workroom. When he came down again, the fire was burning brightly and there was a pot of chai on the hob. He glanced at his cot with the pile of clothes at its foot. Later, he thought.

He returned from the kitchens with loaves of bread and

half a wheel of cheese tied in a towel. He looked at his pack and the heap of things he intended to take. The food would have to be tied to the saddle as it was; there was no way he could fit it in. He put the bundle down on the cot. He should have packed last night. He ought to start packing now, but he felt a reluctance. He went, instead, to the fireplace and poured himself a mug of chai. It was hot and bitter and satisfying.

Jarrod looked round as the Duty Boy emerged from the Archmage's room carrying a tray. "How's the old man?" he asked.

"Bit subdued this morning. Something important must be going on today, though, he's ordered up the gold robe. He only wears that on special occasions. He gave me a message for you too. He said you were to go on ahead and he'd meet you at the stables." Unasked questions hovered in the air.

"Well, I suppose I ought to start packing then," Jarrod said, putting the mug down reluctantly.

"You're going off to fight the Outlanders, aren't you?" the boy said in an almost accusing tone.

"Now why would you think that?" Jarrod asked, picking up the pack and placing it on the cot.

"I'm not blind, you know. That's a military pack and you've got a sword and a bow and arrows. What else could you be doing?"

Jarrod smiled and wedged the cooking pot in sideways. He stuffed it with stockings, breachclouts and kerchiefs. The book, back in its oilcloth wrapping, went in next, followed by his best Magician's gown. If that wasn't respectable enough for the mythical Guardian, it was just too bad. His court clothes were too bulky.

"Well?" the boy persisted.

"What? Oh, good guess, but wrong." He continued packing methodically.

"This got anything to do with the gold gown?"

In went the tinderbox, the fishhooks and line. "It might."

He hesitated, then relented. "Oh, all right, but you must promise me that you won't breathe a word of this to anybody." The boy's eyes widened and he nodded emphatically.

"The Lady Marianna and I are going on a secret mission for the Archmage—the other suit of mail is hers. If you tell anybody about this, it might put her life in jeopardy." That ought to bridle his tongue, he thought. "And don't tell Ragnor that I told you. The only reason I have is that you've already seen all the gear and I don't want you blabbing your speculations all over Celador."

"You can trust me, sir." He licked his lips. "It must be very cold where you're going." He gestured to the pile of clothes. "Is it very far away?"

Jarrod smiled again. If he told the truth, the lad would think he was lying. "It's beyond the Unknown Lands," he said.

The Duty Boy whistled gratifyingly and then watched in puzzlement as Jarrod shrugged out of his robe and donned two pairs of woollen hose, two shirts, the mercifully lightweight mail, leather trousers and a jacket.

"Is there anything I can do, sir?" was all he asked.

"Yes. You can stop calling me sir. It makes me feel ancient. I'll be leaving that robe behind. I'd be grateful if you could have it washed and then keep it for me. If I don't get back by the time you make Magician, you can have it."

"Yes, sir. Sorry sir. Thank you."

"Just call me Jarrod." He swung round and took a look at himself in the glass. He looked surprisingly presentable; fat, but presentable. He checked his belt pouch and took out the coins; about half a royal in all. "Here," he said, tossing them to the boy, "You can have these. They won't be any use where I'm going."

With an enerring sense of value, the youngster caught the two silver and dropped the three bronze. "Thank you, Sir Jarrod."

Jarrod nodded and tucked his gloves into his belt. He

sheathed the dagger, slipped the baldrick over his head and set it at his hip before fitting his sword through. He buckled the pack and lifted it. They boy helped him get his arms through the straps and then adjusted the cloak over the whole. The figure in the looking glass was now an oval hunchback. He snorted at his reflection and retrieved his bow and quiver. There was scarcely room to sling them over his shoulders. He stooped awkwardly and picked up Marianna's mail. The boy handed him the bundle of food.

"You'll have to open the door for me," Jarrod said, "and then I suggest you get the Archmage's robe out. You know what he's like if he's kept waiting."

The boy made a face by way of acknowledgement and scurried for the door. "Goodbye, Sir Jarrod, and good luck."

"Thank you . . . I don't even know what your name is. What is your name?"

"Bromwyl, but everybody calls me Brom."

"You're a Marches lad, then."

"That I am. From the Holding next to Gwyndryth."

"Goodbye, Brom. Take care of yourself."

"Goodbye again, Sir Jarrod, and you take good care of the Lady Marianna." They grinned at each other and Jarrod plodded his laden way down the stairs.

The air was keen on his face, but he couldn't feel the cold. The puddles were white and his boots rang loudly in the silent court. A few women were astir in the next courtyard, fetching water and attending to fires, but they ignored him. The stables, by contrast, were unwontedly active for the time of day. The sun was still invisible, but there were half a dozen grooms bustling about in the grey light. They too ignored him, but the colts knew he was coming. Marianna's pack was propped against the wall beside their stable door and Jarrod's guess that she was already inside was confirmed by them.

"Morning, Jarrod," she said as he waddled in. "How did you sleep?"

"Like a rooster; dead to the world, but up before dawn." It was an ancient Collegium saying.

"I wish I could say the same. I only put in a token appearance at the party and my reward for virtue was to toss and turn all night."

She didn't look as if she had spent a sleepless night. Her color was high, her hair hidden under a velvet cap. She was wearing a leather jacket and trews that had seen better days and, as far as Jarrod could see, at least two shirts.

"I brought your suit of mail," he said. He put the food down and held it out.

"Thank you," she said, coming over and taking it. I left a space for it in my pack. I'll put it on when we get there."

"I'm wearing mine."

"Comfortable?"

"I can't even feel it. Mind you, with all this stuff on, I'm too uncomfortable to feel much of anything." He unslung bow and quiver and propped them against a bale of hay.

"I'll put this away," she said and strode out purposefully.

Jarrod concentrated on the colts. They were well aware of him, but were bound up in their own thoughts. He knew that they were involved in farewells, but could catch none of the individual details. It was as if they were conversing in a language that he had only just begun to learn.

His concentration was broken by the sound of hooves and the unmistakable scree of ironbound wheels on stone. He looked out of the doorway and saw a coach and four. Dark, gruff voices called. He couldn't see Marianna, but guessed that she had gone to the tack room for a saddle. He followed suit.

Ragnor was waiting for them when they returned, the gold robe gleaming quietly despite the lack of sunlight. The white hair and beard were still damp.

"Good morrow to you both," he said.

"Good morning, Excellency," Marianna replied. "I would

curtsey to your splendor, if I weren't so encumbered." Ragnor smiled at her.

All the Marches folk are free with their tongues, Jarrod thought.

"I want to show my appreciation to the unicorns, so I thought this would be appropriate," Ragnor said. "Are you two ready?"

"We'll saddle up the females and stow our gear," Jarrod said.

The colts were wide open to him as he turned to the door. There was excitement in their minds, but no sense of sadness. He walked over to Pellia and put the saddle on her back.

'Of course we shall miss them,' Nastrus answered the unposed question, *'but we shall surely see them again and, in the meanwhile, the Memory will let us know what has happened.'*

'This is a notable adventure,' Beldun added.

'Well, I shall certainly miss the two of you,' Jarrod thought as he ducked under for the girthstrap. He slipped thong through buckle and cinched it tight. *'I can't be so sure that I shall see the two of you again and I just want you to know . . . '*

'We know what you want us to know,' Nastrus said with uncharacteristic gentleness, *'and we are moved, you can tell that it is so. It has been, for us, a memorable experience.'*

Jarrod turned his head as if he could hide his emotion from them and let down the near stirrup. *'Are you coming to see us off?'* he asked as he went round to the other side and adjusted the strap.

'There is no need,' Beldun said. *'We shall know the instant that you have left us and we shall be with you until then. You will be in Pellia's mind and so shall we.'*

'You're right of course,' he said, his disappointment plain. They remained cheerful as he tied the bow and quiver behind the saddle. He tested the knots on the towel that held the food and lashed it to the saddlebow. There was nothing left

for him to do. He walked over and put his arms round Nastrus' neck.

'*Well, this is goodbye, then.*' The slightly spicy aroma of unicorn filled his nostrils and his eyes stung. '*Take good care of yourself and try not to get into trouble.*' He squeezed hard and backed away.

He repeated the gesture with Beldun. '*The Archmage will see to it that you get everything you need and he knows that you will be taking trips from time to time. Now I want you to be cautious around humans. . . .*'

'*We've already had this lecture from Mam,*' Nastrus cut in, the humor back in place.

Jarrod pushed off Beldun's neck and looked from one to the other fondly. '*There's nothing more to be said then.*' He mustered a smile and gave Beldun a last pat. He turned abruptly and Pellia followed him out of the stable.

Ragnor was already ensconced in the coach, the long reins gathered in the driver's hands. The only other attendant was an ostler, also sitting up front. Marianna was swinging up into the saddle. Jarrod waited until Amarine moved away from the mounting block and then stepped up and settled in the saddle. The coach pulled out first and the racket of the wheels on the flags brought the courtyard grumblingly awake. When they saw the unicorns, the grumbling turned to waving and an occasional squeal of excitement from the children.

'*I shall miss the affection of strangers,*' Pellia remarked with a touch of wistfulness.

'*If they knew you were leaving them, they would probably try to keep you here.*'

'*Kindly, but foolish,*' she replied.

The children scampered after them as far as the gate and the boldest of them ventured a little way into the forest of illusion. They were soon left behind, but the two male colts, true to their word, stayed with Jarrod and Pellia. They were unremittingly cheerful when they weren't being ribald to their sister, but even then they went slowly enough so that he was included. The meaning of some of the references still eluded him.

They trotted down the road behind the coach, past the lines of quandry trees. The sickle-shaped tops bobbed in the breeze, trying to solve the eternal question of which precise direction to choose. The coach swung off the road and into the meadow that had become the unicorns' reference point. When it came to a halt Jarrod and Marianna pulled up beside it. The driver jumped down and helped the Archmage out. He shook his robe and stood shimmering in the weak sunlight. He looked up at them.

"You needn't worry. I'm not going to make a speech. You are brave young people and I could do no better than to choose you as our representatives to another world. I wish you the best of fortune for a happy outcome and a speedy return. You are doing us a signal service by going, but remember that we need you here." He nodded as if to underline the point and smiled at them.

"Please convey my deep gratitude to the unicorns for the joy and hope they have brought to all who have seen them. It has been a privilege for us. Tell them that I hope that they and their offspring will visit us again." He bowed slowly, first to Amarine and then to Pellia. The unicorns dipped their horns in response.

"Goodbye, Archmage. Thank you for coming to see us off." Marianna was all aristocratic courtesy. "When you see my father, please tell him that I love him and that I'll be back in Stronta as soon as I can," she added.

Ragnor smiled up at her. "I'm not sure that your father will feel like speaking to me when he finds out what you've done, but I shall certainly see to it that he gets the message."

He turned to Jarrod. "I need you back here to help me, young man, so don't go taking any foolish risks." He spread his hands and gave a little grimace.

"I have every intention of returning in one piece, sir." Jarrod grinned unexpectedly. "Fortunately, I have the Lady

Marianna to protect me." It elicited a bark of surprised laughter from her. "And, of course, your splendid gift of mail," he added hastily.

"You are in good hands then," Ragnor said gallantly. He raised his right hand, palm out. "Go with my blessing, my children, and may the gods grant you a speedy and safe return."

The unicorns swung away and walked to the center of the lea. Jarrod pulled his gloves on and wished he'd thought to bring a cloudsteedsman's helmet. He leaned forward and buried his hands in Pellia's mane. The dagger pushed uncomfortably into his ribs, but before he could do anything about it, before he could even bid a proper farewell to Beldun and Nastrus, the grey and the cold took him. The fog seemed to leach all the heat from his body. His hands and feet felt brittle enough to break. He was afraid that his blood would freeze. He felt panic and then he felt nothing.

Ragnor gazed at where the unicorns had been. He had known what would happen, but the reality was still a shock. They had vanished, quite literally this time, from the face of Strand. He wanted, just this once, to believe what the Oracle had said.

He let his hand drop and sighed. Was he right to let them go? There was nothing he could have done to prevent the unicorns from leaving, but those children? No, he reminded himself, not children. Jarrod was a man and Marianna was very much a woman. They just looked so young and fresh-faced; so confident sitting up there on their unicorns. He shook his head and turned. The two attendants were rooted, one sitting up on the box, the other standing, both with staring eyes and mouths agape.

"We'll be going back now," Ragnor said loudly. "There's nothing more to see."

He allowed himself to be helped into the coach and sat quietly while the steps were folded in. The expedition had seemed almost inevitable such a short time ago; now it seemed foolhardy in the extreme. He reached over and pulled the fur rug over his knees. He was very cold.

chapter 12

There were shooting stars in the blackness that was Jarrod's mind. Oddly, he felt as well as saw them. It was, he decided, a feeling of intense cold lanced by heat, akin to the painful pleasure of blood returning to a deprived limb. If this is all there is to dying, he thought, a lot of people have been making a fuss over nothing. It was really rather pretty. He lay in the spangled dark and tried to stop his brain working. It would be easier to go back to sleep and extinguish the little hot needles.

Something nagged at him and the display of lights dimmed. He pushed it away, willing brightness back. It was persistent and he realized that his right side was throbbing. Must be the wound that had dispatched him. Funny thing, death: it let you remember the wound, but not the battle. Or had it been a fight? The nagging was back and it wasn't his side. It didn't matter. It would all be over soon.

'Wake up! We've been here for over one of your hours and you're getting heavy.'

Where had that thought come from? Were the Maternites right after all? Why would the Great Mother find him heavy?

There was an insistance now, a sort of mental shaking. *'Wake up!'*

He opened his eyes reluctantly. It didn't make much difference. There was something over his face. Graveclothes? Then knowledge flooded in and he raised his head and saw a long vista of grass framed by Pellia's ears. He pushed himself up, surprised at how little strength his arms seemed to have. The horizon swung and he grabbed Pellia's mane convulsively. The scenery steadied and he was able to take in a peacock-blue sky with puffy white clouds.

He disentangled his fingers and got himself back into the saddle. He poked gingerly at his side through the layers of clothing. It was tender, but nothing felt amiss. He decided that the bruise had been caused by the dagger and was decidedly relieved. He looked around slowly. They were in a shallow valley between sloping hills. This certainly wasn't the meadow outside Celador.

'Of course it isn't. This is home.' There was great pride behind Pellia's thought.

'We made it. We really made it!' He leaned forward to hug the unicorn's neck and his side twinged. He stroked the mane instead. *'You are a marvel,'* he said. Anxiety struck suddenly and he turned quickly in the saddle. Amarine was behind them, cropping sedately, and Marianna lay sprawled across her shoulders.

'Is she . . . ?'

'Mam says she'll be all right. Interim affects different creatures differently, it seems.'

Jarrod was feeling weak and hollow, but he knew what he ought to do. *'I think I'll go and check on her.'* He got his feet out of the stirrups, but it took three tries before he could swing his leg up and over. He slid off and his ankles buckled the moment he hit the ground. He sat up. Not a dignified arrival. He stayed where he was for a minute or so before attempting to stand up. He lurched to his feet and grabbed for the saddle to steady himself. The shooting pains were back.

'I feel as if I've been caught in a kina stampede,' he thought by way of explanation.

'It will pass,' Pellia replied, without the sympathy that she knew he had hoped for. *'You have travelled a very long way. We were in Interim for a long time. What you need to do now is eat.'*

The moment the thought was in his mind, he was famished. Hunger consumed him, clamored at him and he salivated in anticipation. There was no room for concern about Marianna now. His slow and stupid hands tore at the bindings of the bundle that contained the food. Guilt finally surfaced, but only after the gnawing emptiness had been filled. He had eaten almost half the bread and cheese. His jaws ached from the effort. He rewrapped the remainer and took a long drink from the flask hooked to the bottom of his pack. Then there was time for Marianna.

He made his way over to Amarine on legs that became more assured by the step. She raised her head when he reached her, looked at him and continued to chew. He took it as assent and dug into the mane to find Marianna's wrist. The pulse was strong. He withdrew his hand and shook her shoulder. He was rewarded with a moan. He shook her again.

"Not time to get up," Marianna mumbled. "Little longer, Mrs. Merieth."

"We're here, Marianna. We're on the Island at the Center."

The head shifted at the sound of his voice and bleary, green eyes looked at him through a tumble of red hair.

"Jarrod? What are you doing here?"

"Same thing as you are, visiting. The unicorns did it; they brought us through."

Marianna shook her head and pushed herself up slowly. She peered through her hair at the scenery. She pushed the hair away. "It's beautiful," she said, "but then I knew it would be." She put a hand up and explored the top of her head. "Didn't I have a cap when we started out?"

"Yes you did; a yellow velvet thing."

"Don't call if a 'thing.' It's, or rather it was, the very latest thing in men's fashions. I had it from none other than Lord Rossiter." She glanced at Jarrod, but he didn't seem to have heard. "Gods alive, but I feel terrible," she said.

"Eat something and you'll feel better."

"Food! Where's the food?" She started to get out of the saddle.

"Easy. Let me help you down. My legs didn't work at all at first." He put his arms up and his hands around her waist. He lifted her down and kept her upright as her legs behaved as predicted.

"Put me down. There's food in a bag on the other side of the saddle and hurry!"

He let go of her cautiously and fetched the bag for her. She snatched it out of his hands and tore it open. Jarrod turned away. He knew what she was feeling and had no wish to see her feeding like a starved animal.

"I'm going to walk around a bit and see if I can find a spring," he said, but she didn't react at all. He walked back to Pellia and began to take some of the clothing off.

'D'you know where I'd be most likely to find a spring?' he asked.

'The Memory indicates a small stream on the other side of those hills. The lake is in the valley beyond.'

'Keep an eye on Marianna until I get back.' He was rewarded by a snort of amusement that followed him up the hillside.

"How are you feeling?" he asked Marianna when he returned almost an hour later.

She was lying, sprawled comfortably on the grass. There was a neat pile of clothes next to the two saddles. The unicorns were on their sides in the shade of a copse halfway up the slope.

"Almost human," she replied. "Granted a human recovering from a fortnight of fever, but a human nevertheless."

"I'm glad you're feeling better," he said with a smile, noting the pallor of her face now that her hair had been tied back.

"I don't think I'm up to travelling just yet," she said, as

if in answer to his thought. "I feel washed out at the moment. Did you manage to find a spring?"

"I didn't think you'd heard that. Yes I did."

"Oh, I heard it all right. My mouth was too full to talk."

"I think we should take our time. We don't have to get back by a specific day. Besides, I don't know what kind of day and night they have. The sun is moving down towards those hills. It would make sense to get a good night's sleep and see how we feel in the morning." He looked around. "The unicorns don't seem to be concerned about our safety, but I'd feel better if we found some sort of cover. If there's no Magic here, the weather will probably be wild."

"Sounds sensible to me. I don't know how far I could carry my pack at this point, but I'm prepared to try in a while."

"Take all the time you want. If Amarine says it's safe, we can bed down here if you prefer."

Unspoken behind all their words was the admission that they were not ready to part from the unicorns. It hadn't occurred to Jarrod that it would be a problem, or rather he had not let it occur to him, but now that he was faced with it, he knew that the parting would leave a hole in his life. He had had so little intimacy in his life. At Dameschool he had been envious of the other children. They all had families. He had affected not to care, had ridiculed the ones who cried themselves to sleep for lack of a mother. He had envied, not knowing what it was he envied. It was different now. Nastrus and Beldun were worlds away and Pellia would soon be gone. He knew what would be missing. He would be alone again.

He sat and leaned against his saddle. "Did Amarine say anything about how we're supposed to find this Guardian?"

"Not much; he lives somewhere to the west on an island in the middle of a lake. Actually, she didn't say 'west,' she said 'in the direction the sun is travelling.' The border between her territory and the next one is just on the other side of those hills.'' She rolled her head in the direction of the unicorns.

''Perhaps we should try and make camp on the other side,'' he suggested. ''That way, if we felt up to it in the morning . . .''

''Slave driver.'' She sat up reluctantly. ''I don't know about you, but I'm going to ask Amarine if she wouldn't mind carrying my stuff. The hill doesn't look at all steep so I ought to be able to get myself up it, but that's about all I can do.''

They loaded up the unicorns and followed them up the slope. When they came to the crest they stopped and the unicorns eased to a halt below them. The view was nothing like it had been from the hilltop behind them. There Jarrod had seen a broad valley with a lake whose further end he could not see; opposite was another fold of hills. Here the grassland was abruptly terminated just after it had levelled off. A high wall of greenery cut straight across it, running north and south. The difference was made even more startling by the fact that it was raining over what he took to be a forest while cottonball clouds continued to sail over their heads. This was no wild weather, this was Weatherlore of the very highest caliber.

'That's the next territory,' Pellia informed him unnecessarily, 'and no, I don't know what kind of creatures live in it.'

''And we're supposed to go through that, are we?'' Marianna asked.

''That's the first one we have to get through,'' he reminded her.

''Well, there's one good thing at least. That grove down there will do to make camp in and, from the look of them, they're fruit trees. Amarine says that there's a pond in that dip over there. If there are some dead branches, that'll take care of all our needs.''

''I've some herbs in the pack. I'll make us a tisane. It'll help build up our strength.''

"I'll make the fire if you go and get the water," she said as she started down the hill, "though I certainly shan't need anything to help me sleep tonight."

They moved slowly through their chores while the unicorns gorged themselves on windfalls. Once the sun was down the light was quickly gone. There was no daymoon to provide the extra hour of rosy afterglow. The swift onset of night took them by surprise, but they were glad to turn in. The unicorns stood on the edge of the grove and watched their moon come up. The humans slept so soundly that they did not hear the bark and roar of predators across the border. Pellia shivered and moved closer to her mother.

The dawn came up cool and clear. Jarrod came awake with a start. The sun was in his eyes and he felt disoriented. Something was very wrong. He looked around but saw nothing amiss. Marianna was asleep beside the ashes, wrapped in her cloak, so that all he could see of her was her hair. The sun was barely clear of the hilltop and the tree trunks stood out black against it. Then he realized why his heart was pounding. That was not his sun. There had been no promptings to Make the Day. There was no Discipline here and yet the sun was up.

This was truly an alien land. It might look deceivingly like home, the hills and the grass could be the wool country south of Stronta and the jungle down there reminded him of the east bank of the Illushkardin just above Belengar, but it was not his world. The rules here were different. He got up and went to relieve himself and then to wash.

He didn't see the unicorns anywhere and that added to his edge of anxiety. He started back from the pond, towelling off his face with the end of his cloak. He was wondering if they would set off today when he felt Pellia in his mind again. She was cantering in from the far side of the grove and was in high spirits. Jarrod dropped the cloak and watched her come around the trees with the sun full on her.

She shone. Her hide was sleek and her mane and tail were

streaming. The sun picked out the flecks of gold and made the silver hooves flash. And the horn, the horn was like a slim spear of light. No minnesinger could do her justice and no painting could capture her. Her pleasure at being home and being alive on such a day was his as she slowed to a trot and came up the hill to meet him.

Her good humor blanketed but did not extinguish the pang he felt. He had watched her grow up from a shaggy-hided, round-sided colt to this powerful, sleek beauty. And it had happened so quickly, so impossibly fast. For the first time in his life, Jarrod glimpsed the true speed of time. He knew that Pellia was aware of all of it.

She kicked up her heels in a little burst of exuberance. *'Knowing is not understanding, you know,'* she said cheerfully. *'You can read me as easily as I can read you, but you don't really understand me, any more than I understand you.''* Her cast of mind turned quizzical. *'It's strange: I know that you are a different kind of creature, one look at you suffices for that, but I have known you almost all of my life and when we are in each other's minds, I think of you as unicorn.'*

'And I keep expecting you to react like a person,' Jarrod admitted. *'I always think of you as family,'* he added.

'I shall miss you once the rut is over.' Jarrod got a brief impression of the roilings that she was holding at bay and knew that she had been shielding him. *'I wish I could say that we shall meet again'*—her tone was entirely practical—*'but I do not know what will happen. I shall hope that we do. At the very least, I shall always be able to see you in the Memory.'*

'I envy you that.'

Her happiness bubbled up again, bewildering Jarrod until she said, *'You have given me the idea for a present to give you.'*

'You don't have to give me a present,' he protested. *'Besides, I don't have anything to give you.'*

'I know. It is something that I should like to do.'

'All right then,' he said, pleased and curious.

'First you have to go and lie down again and close your eyes.'

'Back in the grove?'

'That would be best; yes.'

They walked back down together, but she wouldn't tell him what she had in store. She stopped at the first of the trees.

'I'll stay here. I'm more comfortable in the open,' she said.

Jarrod patted her on the shoulder and went in under the trees. He picked a stretch of moss between two tree roots and lay down on it. He squirmed a little to get more comfortable and then he relaxed and shut his eyes.

'I thought you might like to see how you appear in the Memory. I want you to go back in your own mind to that first time that we met.'

'In the valley on top of the Anvil of the Gods?'

'Just so.'

He was back in the strange bowl with the black lake at the bottom. It had been raining. He could smell wet grass and feel the ground suck at the heels of his cold, sodden boots. He knew that something bad was going to happen and he knew simultaneously that he hadn't felt that way then. He didn't know what was going to happen and that in itself was frightening.

'Can't we start with another part of the Memory?' he asked.

'It is best if we begin at the beginning.'

His other self, Marianna beside him, slopped his way towards a belt of trees. He knew they would go into the trees, but his next memory was of waking up back at camp. They were in the break now. The wind was strong and the sound of it was loud in the treetops. The undergrowth was thicker at the far side, but he could see grass beyond the bushes. Marianna got caught on a bramble and cursed. He could feel the reaction of his younger self and smiled. She couldn't shock him any more. They were pushing through the foliage and then, there they were. He experienced the heart-stammering rush of elation. A full-grown unicorn and three fuzzy colts. The adult stood, head up, the tapering horn pointing at the valley's rim. Two of the colts were sparring and the third raced across the soggy meadow, tail streaming.

"Oh Jarrod, they're just beautiful," Marianna breathed in his ear.

Jarrod said nothing. It had finally happened. They had found the unicorn. Better yet, four unicorns. Greylock was going to be so proud of him. They looked just the way he had hoped they would, or at least the adult one did. The colts could be wild white ponies.

The adult's head came round and Jarrod stiffened. It quested the wind, its nostrils flaring. It's scented us, Jarrod thought. What do we do now? He realized that he had never thought of what he would do if he actually found the unicorn. The unicorn whinnied and then trotted straight toward them. Jarrod found that he was incapable of motion. He stared at the approaching animal. The horn was clearly no ornament. He couldn't take his eyes off it. There was no sound from his left, so Marianna must be equally rooted.

The mare pulled up, sliding a little in the muddy footing. Her head was no more than three feet away and her eyes were level with Jarrod's. They were large and violet, with clear whites. The lashes were black. She looked straight at him and a thrill ran through him that was partly fear, but only partly. She held his gaze and her nostrils widened and contracted; then she looked away and it was as if a spell had been broken. He turned his head to watch.

The unicorn was looking at Marianna now. She whickered softly and advanced a couple of paces. Marianna stepped forward and slowly raised her arm. She reached up and touched the muzzle. Her hand stopped and then stroked the top of the nose. The unicorn nudged upwards against her hand.

Jarrod looked away. The legend was true, then, unicorns did have an affinity for virgin girls. There had been no trickery. The unicorn had looked at them both and it had rejected him. Movement caught his eye and he saw that the three youngsters had followed and were standing, staring at him. Their heads were cocked at different angles and from time to time a tail would switch. Their rough coats were splattered with mud and he could see now that they had small lumps on their foreheads. They radiated curiosity.

They looked comical and he knew that he was smiling. He held out a hand, hoping they would come and investigate it. He swallowed, trying to clear his ears. He felt sudden pressure as if a storm was about to break. His head ached. There was a sudden release, as if a membrane had given.

'. . . *don't think it can be very intelligent all the more reason to be careful funny-looking creature.*'

His mind was full of overlapping thoughts and none of them were his. Fright bloomed and he was in his older mind again. He knew that he was lying under a tree, but his heart was beating fast.

'*There is no need to bring back the last little bit,*' Pellia said. '*The fault was ours and I wanted to make amends by restoring your first sight of us. Now, let us go forward.*'

She led him through the times they had spent together, seen, this time, through her eyes. He was by turns strange, foolish, unintelligible and impressive. Seeing himself practise Magic was a peculiar sensation. The scene of him, he could think of it in no other way, by the campfire outside Fort Bandor could only have been provided by Nastrus. His performance pleased him. More pleasing still was the deep fondness that permeated the viewpoint; as if he were the sometimes clownish, but always entertaining youngest brother.

He found it comforting, which was what she intended, and he settled a little deeper into the moss. Seeing it all at once like that, brought home what an extraordinary eighteen months this had been. It had been remarkable, too, to see all those familiar things in such an unfamiliar light. He had never thought of a castle as a prison before or a room as a confinement. They were right about a lot of things, his brothers and sister. It had been a wonderful gift. He reached out lazily to thank her, but the link was tenuous. He thought out more strongly. There was no one there to hear him. He opened his eyes and sat up. He looked through the trees to the spot where he had left her, but he couldn't see her. If she was lying down, he thought. He jumped to his feet and ran, though he knew it was futile. He stopped when he was clear of the trees. Pellia was nowhere in sight. He was alone again.

chapter 13

Marianna was still where Jarrod had last seen her. She sat by the remnants of the fire, head on knees and arms tightly wrapped around her legs. She made no sound, but Jarrod saw her shoulders moving and knew that she was crying. Tears welled up in his own eyes. Don't cry, he thought. She left you on a happy note, she would not have understood tears. He wanted to go over and hug Marianna, but held back. She had a right to her grief and he doubted that she would want him involved in it. He turned back and went for a long, wistful walk up and over the hill.

He had himself well in hand when he got back and he was relieved to see that Marianna was busy repacking. Her saddle sat on a pile of winter clothes.

"Good morning. I'm glad to see that you're feeling better," he said as he walked into the tiny clearing.

She looked up over her shoulder. "Morning. I wondered where you had got to." She had washed her face and combed her hair. The only trace of her weeping was a slight puffiness around the eyes.

"It was such a lovely day that I felt like walking," he lied. "Besides," he added, "I had some things to think over." It was a half invitation.

"It doesn't even seem to be raining over the forest," she agreed, ignoring the chance to talk about the unicorns. "I think we should get on with it, don't you? The sooner we find the man, the sooner we get home."

She's her old, assertive self again, Jarrod thought ruefully;

taking charge as usual. But she's right about one thing, we can't stay here. Better to keep occupied.

"We'd better stock up on fruit," he said. "There's no knowing what the game will be like in there. I'll string my bow just in case."

Marianna stood up and he saw that she was wearing her mail under her jacket. She had a sheathed dagger at her left hip. "That'll mean that we'll be eating meat again, won't it? I'm not sure that I'll like that after all this time."

"I brought a fishing line, but we might not find a lake or river for several days." He had been rather looking forward to the prospect of meat again after a year and a half of fish and vegetables. He bent down and got a bowstring out of his pack. He picked up the stave and began to flex it. "Might as well be prepared," he said. "We don't know what we'll be meeting. I doubt if all the creatures here are as friendly as the unicorns."

"That's why I brought the dagger," she said, levelly, "though, from the looks of that foliage, it'll come in handier for hacking a way through."

"How's your chain mail feel?"

"It's a lot more comfortable than the one I wore at Stronta. It's hard to believe it could stop a sword-cut. I just hope the Archmage was right about that."

"I hope we never have to find out." He held the bow close to his ear and plucked the string three or four times. Satisfied, he propped it against a tree and then set about folding his heavy clothes. He hesitated over the gloves and then tucked them into the pack.

"Why don't I fill the water flasks while you finish up?" Marianna said.

"Good idea. Catch." He threw the leather flask to her. He was all but finished with the packing, but knew that it would take Marianna a good quarter of the hour to fill the skins and get back. He wanted those minutes of solitude before he set off.

He lifted the pack off the ground and shook it gently to settle the contents. He really was on his own now. He'd always had something or someone to fall back on before. First it had been the Talent, then Greylock, more recently there had been his Staff and the unicorns. Now all he had were the scant aptitudes of his mind and body. There was destiny, of course; the unicorns had believed that their destiny was entwined with his and with Marianna's. That destiny had apparently been fulfilled. They would have to win through on their own merits from now on. Not the kind of odds I care for, he thought wryly. He itched to try a simple piece of Magic to see if he could, just in case, but he fought down the urge. It was harder than he expected. He was eager to be gone by the time that Marianna got back.

They walked the short distance to the border in silence and stopped a foot away from the wall of foliage. Marianna reached out and grasped a twig.

"Funny," she said, "I really expected it to be an illusion. I mean, it can't be real." She gestured from side to side. "It looks as if a squad of gardeners comes out every night and trims it."

Jarrod had his quiver over his right shoulder and his bow slung across his chest. He switched the quiver from the right shoulder to the left and drew his sword.

"We might as well see if we can get in here." He stepped back, raised his sword and slashed down. The sword passed through leaves, twigs and branches and bit into wood. Jarrod wrestled it free and swung again in a scything motion. Within minutes he was using both hands. The sweat ran down into his eyes and the salt stung. He plodded on, slashing away until the wall in front of him seemed less densely packed. He looked over his shoulder. Marianna was standing behind him in the green tunnel he had created. It was a depressingly short tunnel.

"I'll take a turn if you want," she said.

"I just want to catch my breath," he replied, wiping away the sweat with his sleeve, "but I hope this doesn't go on too much longer."

"Just let me know when you want me to spell you."

There was no trace of yesterday's weariness, but he doubted that she could do much in the way of a sustained effort. Not that she would ever admit that. He turned back and lifted the sword again. Slash and lift, chop and lift, swing and heft and swing again; trample forward on the uneven footing, the smell of sap and verdure heavy in his nostrils. Unseen birds shrilled their alarums and insects, attracted by his scent, swarmed for the sweat. The plants ahead grew pulpier, easier to cut and messier too. Then he was through and on clear ground.

He took a few paces forward and then stopped. Marianna came up beside him. The trees were well spaced and exceedingly tall. The branches didn't start for thirty feet and then radiated up to support thick crowns that blotted out the sun. A green dusk prevailed on the forest floor. Ferns that were either tall bushes or short trees grew in the leafmold. Vines looped from branch to branch, but little else flourished under that canopy, unless one counted the fungi blossoming along a fallen tree.

The contrast to the grassland they had left was pronounced, but what made it all the more unreal was the heat. They had gone from Greening to high summer in less than an hour.

"Gods but it's hot," he said, laying his sword down and taking his bow and pack off. He eased his quiver off and then shrugged out of the pack. He unbuttoned his jacket.

"And sticky." Marianna slapped at an insect. She took her own pack off and sat down by it.

Jarrod squatted down and started to wipe his sword on the ground. He looked critically at the blade. "Good thing I brought a whetstone."

"Good thing we don't have to cut our way across the territory, but I wouldn't be too quick to put it away if I were you. We don't know what lives here.''

"I could have gone all day without being reminded of that," he said in an attempt to lighten the mood.

"It's too bloody quiet."

"I expect we've frightened everything off."

"Everything except these motherless bugs." She slapped again.

"Perhaps it'll be better if we keep moving," he said, standing up. He sheathed his sword and began brushing pieces of plant off him.

"Here, stand still a minute," she said, getting to her feet. "I'll get some of the stuff out of your hair. You look like something left over after a wine festival."

"Oh, thanks a lot. I wage war against the god of greenery, taking the edge off a perfectly good sword and all I get is insults."

"Be quiet and bend down. I didn't bring a ladder with me. There, that's better." She stepped back and looked him over. "Are you trying to grow a beard, or did you just forget to wash your face this morning?"

He looked up quickly, knowing that he was starting to blush, and saw that she was teasing him. "I didn't feel like shaving in cold water," he mumbled.

"If it gets any hotter, cold water is going to feel wonderful."

"Yes, we'd best get going again before the sun gets too high, not that you can see the sun in this benighted place." Jarrod had recovered and busied himself with his pack. With his bow in his left hand, he practised a draw from the quiver. "Ready?" he asked.

Marianna nodded and adjusted the pack straps. They set off side by side and, as they did so, the forest noises seemed to resume. They could see no birds, but they could hear them again. A large, iridescent butterfly meandered by on their right.

"Look at the size of that thing," Jarrod said.

"Let's just hope that it isn't indicative of the size of the rest of the inhabitants."

A chattering from behind them made them turn quickly. Jarrod had an arrow in place before he had completed the turn. The noise came from above and he looked up anxiously. A small troupe of furry animals sat along the lowest branches and stared back. One of them began to hop about and scream and the others joined in. Jarrod sighted and drew the feathers back to his ear.

"Don't shoot. They're too far away to do us any harm."

Jarrod grunted and relaxed the bowstring.

"Besides," she continued, "it might be a good idea not to kill anything we don't have to. You never know what the Guardian might be fond of."

Jarrod slipped the arrow back into the quiver. "I hadn't thought of that. You're probably right, but if anything threatens us, I shan't hesitate to shoot it. I don't fancy ending up as a meal for one of his pets."

"Fair enough, but let's move before these little bloodsuckers sting me to death."

They moved out side by side and the long-haired, black and white animals followed them, running along branches and swinging from vine to branch and back. Now that they were in motion it was obvious that they had long, thin tails, which they used both for balance and to grip with. They chittered to each other, paused to peer down at the duo, leaped ahead to pause again. They were clearly curious, but they kept their distance.

"They don't look dangerous, do they?" Marianna remarked. "They remind me of hedgehoppers in a funny way."

"They don't look as if they've got much meat on them either."

She let that pass and they tramped on across the soggy ground in silence. They were soon sweating again. If there was a breeze, it did not penetrate the leaves. Their eyes were adjusted to the gloom and they kept a sharp watch to the sides, but their four-footed companions were the only things that moved. Jarrod had noticed that moss grew on the left-hand side of the trees and used that as a marker of direction.

They walked for what seemed like hours, but, without sight of the sun, it was difficult to tell. From time to time, flocks of gaudy, unfamiliar birds swooped down out of the canopy to feed on the clouds of gnats drifting towards the light, but otherwise the jungle was beginning to seem monotonous. They came across hollows where water had gathered. From the prints around them, it was obvious that there were other animals around, but they were nowhere to be seen.

They paused for half an hour at what they took to be midday. It was a relief to get out of the pack and use it as a seat. Jarrod took his jacket off and discovered that his chain mail was no protection against the insects. Every inch of exposed skin already itched. Marianna's face and neck were covered in red welts.

"I hate this place," Marianna said as she got some fruit out. "I don't even have a copper coin to rub on the bites." She sounded dejected.

"Well, look on the bright side," Jarrod said. "We're making pretty good time."

"I don't know how much longer I can keep the pace up. It's this sticky heat. It's debilitating."

"I know. We probably should have waited another day. Interim took a lot out of us. We can make camp any time you feel like it."

"Thanks, but I'd rather not spend a night here if I don't have to. It's spooky enough knowing that there are animals out there somewhere, hidden away. Has it occurred to you that one explanation for their absence is that the creatures in this area are nocturnal? Even the hairy little tree animals have disappeared."

"I expect they got bored," he said, trying to sound cheerful. "I mean all we've done is walk in a straight line and slap our faces."

She smiled in spite of herself. "What if they were scouts sent by the Guardian? Can you imagine the report they're taking back?"

"Large, hunchbacked, bipeds . . ."

"Much given to hitting themselves and quite probably insane."

"No wonder the other animals are staying away," Jarrod finished. They both smiled.

There was silence while they ate their fruit and took sparing drinks from their waterflasks. "We'll have to go on until we find a stream," he said as he tossed a core away. "I didn't fancy the look of any of the pools that we passed."

"And I'd like to find somewhere we can defend ourselves. I don't trust the trees. I have this vision of mammoth snakes coiling their way down the trunks."

"Those are the stems of the vine plants," Jarrod said.

"Aha. So I wasn't the only one who thought that."

"You're right," he admitted. "I suppose we had better be on our way again." He got up reluctantly and went over to help Marianna on with her pack.

They plodded on through the afternoon, enclosed in their own little worlds of weary discomfort, accompanied by the ache of the missing unicorns. Since the jungle floor looked the same in all directions, there was little sense of having made progress. At some point Jarrod's mind started to dwell on the life he had left behind. He thought of the boy who just the day before had envied him this glamorous adventure. If he could see him now, Bromwyl the Duty Boy would be well content with his spot by the anteroom fire.

Something intruded on his musing and it took him a moment to identify it.

"Stop a minute," he said, holding up his hand. "D'you hear that?"

"Wind in the treetops?"

"I don't think so. I think it's running water. Listen."

Marianna cocked her head and concentrated. "You may be right. It's coming from up ahead. Oh, Jarrod, just think of it; cool water all over your body."

"And flies can't bite you if you're submerged."

"If I had the energy, I'd run," she said.

Their pace wasn't noticeably faster, but their legs felt stronger. At least it was something tangible to aim for.

"There's something beyond those trees," Jarrod said after a while.

"Your eyes must be sharper than mine: all I can see are trees."

"There's something dark beyond them. I don't know; I could be wrong. It's difficult to tell in this light."

"Well, we'll find out before too long," Marianna said crisply. Her spirits had evidently recovered.

After another half mile of determined walking, the line had grown into a wall. Thereafter it emerged slowly in the green half-light and became a massive, variegated hedge. They stopped ten feet away from it and craned their necks to see the top. The sound of the water, loud now, came from the other side.

"What does this remind you of?" Marianna asked.

"The border we cut through this morning. You may get your wish about not sleeping here after all." He moved the quiver strap closer to his neck and then slung his bow over his head. He pushed it under the corner of the pack. It wasn't very comfortable and it stuck out from his left side, but at least it was secure and out of the way. He drew his sword.

"Here we go again," he said.

He clasped the grip in both hands and gave a practice swing. The sword weighed more than it had in the morning and the bow dug into his shoulder.

"D'you think you could manage my bow and quiver? They're getting in the way."

"What's a couple more things in this kind of heat?" she said sardonically.

Jarrod stuck his sword in the ground and transferred the quiver from his shoulder to hers.

"The damned thing weighs a ton," she complained.

"Yes, I know it does. If you want to use the sword, I'll carry them."

"Give me the bow and get to work," she said good-naturedly.

"One last favor."

"Now what?"

"Would you undo my flask? I need a drink before I tackle this." He turned around so that she could reach the bottom of the pack.

The flask was reattached and he pulled the sword out. He walked up to the greenery and started lopping off branches and creepers, clearing a space in front of him. He wanted to get a clean swing the first time so that he could establish a rhythm. He would have to conserve his energy. When he was satisfied, he let the point of his sword drop and shut his eyes. He collected himself as he would for the Making of the Day. He found a point of tranquility and focussed his will. Then he was ready.

He swung cleanly, down and back, pendulum fashion, and the bushes flew. He veered left to avoid a sturdy sapling and continued to clear a path. His breathing was becoming ragged and the sweat made his sight blurry. The swing was halted and he had to wrench the sword free. He chopped at the branch until it tore away. The edge was undoubtedly getting dull. He stopped to catch his breath and examine the blade. There were two notches on one side and one, near the point, on the other. Well, it couldn't be helped. Just as long as it held out until they were through this motherless thicket. He attacked again, arms aching, flailing at the endless green, hacking at stubborn vines. Abruptly there was nothing in front of him. The ground gave way and he was falling through the air. He was too surprised to yell and then the shock of hitting water knocked the wind out of him. That was followed immediately by the shock of cold. He came up whooping for air.

chapter 14

Jarrod was gasping. His left hand beat at the water as his right was dragged down by the sword. His hair was in his eyes and he could see very little, but he was out of his depth. that was clear enough. He coughed and pushed his hair aside. He was on the outside of a bend in what was clearly a river. From this viewpoint, it looked to be an alarmingly wide river. He tried to turn himself towards the near bank, but the sword and his pack hampered him. He heard screaming and turned his head as far as he could. Nothing but dense foliage. Had Marianna fallen in too? He tried to reverse direction so that he could see upstream, but the river had him in a silken grip and bore him away.

The yelling continued, but grew fainter. He felt surprisingly calm. There didn't seem much that he could do. He wasn't a strong swimmer at the best of times. There was one thing he should do and as soon as possible. He fought the current and brought the sword back under control. Sheathing it was another matter and it took four attempts before he got it back into the cover. Everything seemed to be happening in slow motion and it triggered the memory of a story he had heard about Robarth Strongsword.

The monarch had been confronted by an angry nobleman who accused him of forcing his daughter. The King had stared him down and demanded the man's sword and scabbard. He held out the scabbard and bade the nobleman draw. When the startled man complied, the King stepped back and, holding the scabbard by the tip, moved his wrist from side to side so that the mouth swung. He invited the irate father to resheath his sword and, when the man had tried a number of times without success, tossed the scabbard back to him.

"I believe, my lord, that you said your daughter had been forced?"

Old court gossip at a time like this, Jarrod marvelled. The river was making him numb, clouding his mind, taking his will away. He had to do something. He mustn't get too far separated from Marianna. He had a clear view of both banks now. The one to his right remained an unbroken wall of plant growth. He pushed himself up in the water. He was much closer to the center of the river and the point of the bend was coming up. He tried to crab sideways across the current. Things were moving faster now, as if time had reasserted itself. He lunged out diagonally, hands paddling beside his chest and legs kicking frantically.

His boots felt as if they were made of metal and his pack threatened to unbalance him. He could fee the power of the current against his side, pushing the sword across his belly. A wavelet slapped him in the face and he inhaled a breathful of water. He sputtered and swallowed more. He was going to drown. He had come all this way to die in a stupid, nameless river. His limbs redoubled their frenzy, fueled by his desire to live. He had come here to escape death, not to find it.

He thrashed on blindly until he felt the force of water lessen. He tried to see where he was, but only got a blurred impression. His legs were moving slowly now and the edge of the current had no trouble in swinging him into an eddy that skirted the bank. The river surrendered him with indifference and he bumped onto a gravel spit that ran towards the elbow of the bend. He felt the pebbles on his chin and under his hands. He got his knees under him somehow and crawled forward. It was a last effort and he collapsed with his feet still in the water. He retched feebly.

He lay there, incapable of movement. His body shivered violently as if to give that the lie. He was going to live, even if he didn't feel much like it at the moment. His muscles were as limp as boiled string and his joints ached. The river had taken the itch out of the insect bites, but the hitherto unnoticed blisters on his hands stung. He couldn't feel his feet at all. He dug his elbows in and tried to lever himself forward. His hold on conciousness wavered and then slipped.

There was fog and he was lost. He could see nothing but thick greyness all around. If he slid his foot forward, he lost it. He was completely cut off and yet there had been something that had given him hope. He recalled the flare of expectation, but he couldn't remember what had caused it. Then it came again; a faint halloo. He strained to locate the direction and heard it again, louder this time.

I'm here! Over here! he yelled, but the fog soaked up the words while they were still in his mouth. Anger and fear boiled up; anger at his impotence and fear of ending up like Greylock, entombed in this grey.

The cry came again and it was his name. A thought struck him. Pellia had said that the Guardian would probably find him. Could that be the Guardian? Fear gained the upper hand and he was glad now that he was mute.

"So there you are. Trust you to pick the last possible place."

The words were sudden and loud and came from above him. They startled him and he would have flinched if he could. It's only a dream, he told himself to combat the rising terror. Dreams can't hurt you.

Something behind him reached over his shoulder and a cold hand clamped on his throat. He screamed, but even his own ears did not register the sound. The pressure did not increase and after a short while the hand withdrew. Jarrod's heart was beating wildly. Surely it was making enough noise to wake him up. But no; instead, something was tugging at his right shoulder. He tried to turn his head to see what it was, but his head didn't move. He tried to strike out, but his arms wouldn't obey him. His right arm was obeying someone else though. It was being moved around.

There was a pause and then a scrunching of footsteps circling behind him. Then the pummeling and manipulation was repeated on his left side. Keep calm, he pleaded with himself. It's just a bad dream. It felt horrifyingly real, though. There was a grunt from above and a great burden was lifted from his back. He had been so afraid that he had forgotten the weight until it was gone. There was a scraping noise accompanied by vivid cursing. His assailant was human then.

He heard the crunch of returning footsteps. He knew what was coming. The night gods fed on the experiences of mortals, feasting on buried pain. It was surprising that they hadn't summoned up his treatment at the hands of the Umbrian press gang before. As strange as his being able to analyze a nightmare without being able to break out of it. It was no help to know that he was going to be flogged again. The footsteps stopped. His flesh cringed in anticipation.

"It's not fair, you know," a voice said from behind him. The voice was familiar, but he couldn't place it. It certainly wasn't Umbrian and it sounded more boy than man.

"Is it written in some celestial play," the voice continued, "that every time we go off on an adventure together, I have to rescue you and nurse you back to health? And why, you great, whoreson catastrophe, do you have to be so bloody big?"

Hands grabbed his left shoulder and rolled him over unceremoniously. His inner world sommersaulted. He had assumed that he had been standing. Hands were inserted under his armpits. There was a grunt and his body jerked. Another grunt and he slid backwards over stones. Another heave and slither; another and another. Then he was dropped.

There was hoarse panting that slowly modulated. "You're too thin to be this heavy," the voice complained.

The footsteps went past him and continued away. He was being abandoned, just when things were beginning to get better. There was a renewed flutter of panic and then the footsteps were returning, getting closer and closer. The impact of cold water on his face made him gasp. His eyelids flew open and light flooded in leaving him as blind as before. When the glare receded, Marianna was standing over him, dripping wet and red in the face.

"Sorry," she said shortly. "I couldn't think of anything else to do. Can you hear me? Don't move your head. You fell into the river and you may have hit it on a rock."

"Of course I can hear you," Jarrod said, relief flooding through him, but all that came out was a bleat.

"Good. I don't want to take any risks, so we'll go slowly. Can you move your feet?"

He moved them apart and tapped his boots together twice. He let his breath out in a long rush. He was awake.

"How about your right hand?"

He complied. He knew where he was and what had happened. The longer he was out of the water, the stronger he felt, but he went through Marianna's checklist obediently. There were branches above him, but these were covered by small, dark leaves and when the wind moved them, the sky was visible.

"Well, everything seems to be working," she said finally. "See if you can sit up, but don't make any sudden movements."

He sat up as smoothly as he could. "There," he said and his vocal chords produced the appropriate sound. "It doesn't look as if you'll have to nurse me back to health after all."

"Don't tell me you were pretending," she said dangerously.

"No, no." He held up a hand. "On my honor, I couldn't move. I couldn't even open my eyes. I didn't know what was happening or where I was. I think the river had something to do with it. Was I still in the water when you found me?"

"Only your feet. The rest of you was sprawled out like a beached lamprey."

Jarrod got slowly to his feet. "Well, whatever it was, I feel a lot better. I'm tired, of course, but no more than I would be after a long day's hunting."

"Speaking of a long day, we'd better find somewhere to make camp. We'll need a lot of wood. We'll have to keep a fire going all night. Everything's soaked."

"Where's my pack?" Jarrod asked with a sinking feeling.

"It's on the bank behind you."

Jarrod swung round and saw it. The straps were swollen and that made their unbuckling difficult, but eventually it was done. He started pulling clothing out. Wet; all wet.

"It would be better to build a fire first and then lay the clothes out," Marianna said.

"I'm looking for the book," Jarrod replied, putting more items on the short grass. "It's the only thing I have to offer the Guardian."

He reached the package and brought it out carefully. The oilcloth was damp. He laid it down and unwrapped the first layer gingerly. The second piece of wrapping wasn't even moist.

"May whoever invented oilcloth be remembered down to the last person left on Strand," he said fervently as he rewrapped the Oracle's gift.

"Now can we get going?" Marianna asked. "I'm freezing."

"I see you managed to save my bow and arrows," Jarrod said, noticing them for the first time. "Thank you."

"The bowstring broke and the arrows are probably all

warped by now. The quiver was full of water when I got ashore.''

"Well, thank you anyway." He climbed up onto the bank and turned to give her a hand up. His bow and quiver lay beside her pack at the base of the trees at whose branches Jarrod had gazed. He rebuckled his pack and then struggled into it. It was even heavier than it had been before. He adjusted his sword at his hip and went over to the tree. He started to bend and then checked himself.

"I'm afraid you're going to have to hand those to me. If I try to pick them up, I'll fall flat on my face."

Marianna smiled at his discomfort. "Must be like trying to walk around in a full suit of armor. Here." She handed him the quiver.

He opened the top, wrinkled his nose, refastened it and tucked it under his left arm. He took the bow and only then did he look around. They were in a forest, but this was much different than the jungle. Though the sun was below treetop level, there was more light than there had been on the other side of the river at midday.

Most of the big trees were what he would have called copper beeches at home. They had the same conformation and their leaves were the color of Marianna's hair now that it was wet, but these were far bigger than a beech's and the bark was a smooth and a shiny brown. There were groups of different deciduous trees and patches of high bushes. Short coarse grass covered most of the ground, though there were clumps of spear-leaved plants along the bank.

"Let's go back upriver a bit," he suggested, "and get closer to our original line."

"Why not. Let's just get moving. And keep your eyes peeled for dry wood."

They squelched along, leaving a trail of drops. A myriad of nut husks crackled under their feet. The air, even allowing for their wet clothes, was decidedly cool.

"Didn't the river affect you at all?" Jarrod asked, puzzled.

"Doesn't seem to have done," Marianna replied. "But then I'm a good swimmer and I didn't spend that long in it."

"Where did you come ashore?" Jarrod asked.

"About half a mile up. There was no way along the bank on the other side and I knew I wasn't going to catch up with you in the water, so I struck straight across. It wasn't too bad. The Lorin runs faster after snowmelt."

Jarrod's legs were getting tired and the pack straps were rubbing on his shoulders. "These dry pods, or whatever they are, should make good kindling, if we can get a spark out of the flint."

"Look over there," Marianna cut in. She pointed to the right. "Do those look like tree roots to you?"

Jarrod followed the indication and saw a tall, ragged circle of earth, with what looked like tentacles. There was a broad gap in the canopy about it. "Could be. Let's take a look."

They tramped on until they reached the bowl-shaped depression left by the tree when it was uprooted. With a fire in the middle it was as secure a spot as they could hope for. Jarrod walked around and looked down the tree itself. It ended in a tangle of dead branches about fifty feet away.

"This is the place," he called back. "There's more than enough wood."

He walked back and wriggled out of his pack. Marianna was already out of hers. He stretched and rubbed his shoulders.

"You go and get some branches and I'll gather kindling. Oh, get the flint out of your pack first. Might as well give it a chance to dry out."

He made five trips to the top of the tree before she was satisfied, and it took time to get the little pile of husks to catch. It would have been so much easier to use the Talent and think the fire alight, but he took the unicorns' warning seriously. The daylight was almost gone by the time the twigs were crackling.

"The first things we dry are our cloaks," Marianna said, laying hers out at the edge of the fire.

"Is there some kind of special order?" he asked, following suit.

"No. If you want to sleep naked, that's all right by me. I've seen you without your clothes on before. Personally, I think this climate is a little cool for that and I'd prefer to wrap up in a nice, warm, dry cloak while the rest of my clothes become habitable."

Jarrod felt himself blushing again and was grateful for the darkness. When had she seen him naked? He bent over his pack and began taking things out. He put the clothes out around his side of the fire, but the book was placed carefully against the wall of roots. The last thing out was the cooking pot. Jarrod looked at it sourly. So far it had been nothing but extra weight to lug around and there was certainly nothing to cook in it. The cheese and the last few pieces of fruit had survived, but the bread was a spongey mess. He picked the pot up. There was one thing it would be good for.

"I'm going over to the river to get some water," he said. "I brought a box of chai and I can't think of a better time for some."

"What a good idea. Hold on and I'll come with you."

"You don't have to. I'm not going to fall in again."

"I don't think it's a good idea for us to split up. We don't know anything about this stretch of country. Make sure you keep your dagger within easy reach."

"That's a cheery thought," Jarrod said, but he loosened his blade. "We'll have to do some serious hunting in the morning. We need to keep our strength up and we certainly can't afford to fall ill up here. Even if I could find the simples we needed, there's no way of knowing if they have the same properties as the ones at home."

"Now who's being cheerful. Let's fetch the water before we get too depressed."

They returned with the water without incident and put the pot on to boil. They turned their cloaks around and stayed near the fire for warmth. Their clothes, both on and off their bodies, steamed. Jarrod let the water boil awhile. If there was something in it that had caused his weakness, the cooking should nullify it. When he was satisfied, he added a handful of wet leaves to the simmering water and stirred it with a twig. He used the edge of his cloak to get the pot out of the fire and set it down to steep.

Marianna brought her mug over. "What do you plan on saying to this Guardian when we find him?" she asked as she settled down and dipped it into the pot.

"The first thing we'll have to do is find a way to talk to him. That's why the book's so important."

"But you can't read it."

"I know, but Amarine says that it's in his language and it's a starting place."

"He communicates with her mentally. He'll probably do the same with us."

"Not necessarily. We can do it with the unicorns, but we can't do it with each other."

"I think that's probably a very good thing," she said with an impish smile. "I mean, I love talking with Amarine, but having someone know absolutely everything about you takes some getting used to."

"I know what you mean," Jarrod said. "The wonderful thing with the colts was that they never made any judgments. Well, almost never," he added, remembering Pellia's attitude after the visit to the Oracle and some of Nastrus' remarks. "I miss it more than I thought I would. It's rather like being homesick."

"That's a good way of putting it," she said. She set her mug down and got to her feet. "My cloak should be dry by now. I'm going to get out of these damp clothes before I catch a cold and I suggest you do the same." She picked her cloak up and retreated out of the firelight.

Jarrod took her advice and came back with the cloak wrapped closely around him. He laid his clothes out where his cloak had been, feeling self-concious about wearing nothing under it. Marianna came back and took her place again. If she felt awkward, she gave no sign of it. They sat in a silence that became companionable and sipped their chai.

"This may be the best chai I've ever had," she said after a while. "Strange, but it brings back memories of Tryponthyd in winter. Sitting in Mrs. Merieth's kitchen on a snowy afternoon and watching her make mincemeat."

"I thought you only went there in the summer."

"We used to celebrate the Festival of the Moons there if the roads were passable. We'd get all wrapped up in sheepskins and we'd build a huge bonfire on the point. We used to scour the shoreline for days collecting driftwood and on Festal Eve we'd light the bonfire. We'd drink hot cider and watch the nightmoon rise out of the sea while the daymoon sank into it."

"Must have been beautiful," Jarrod said and yawned. "I don't know how much ground we covered, but it feels as if it's been a very long day."

"I should have preferred not to have swum over," Marianna replied, "but I'm glad we don't have to sleep in that jungle. I had a creeping sensation in the small of my back the whole time we were there."

"I suppose we ought to take watches," Jarrod said unenthusiastically, "but there's no way to tell how much time has passed."

"I'll take the first watch if you like. The river took more out of you than it did out of me. I'll stay awake as long as I can and then I'll wake you."

"That sounds very good to me. I'll help you build up the fire. There's enough wood to last the night. I didn't see anything that looked like a game trail, but I suppose animals might come down to the river to drink. Maybe not; I still think the river forms a barrier in more ways than one, though the chai tastes all right.''

He tossed the slops from his mug into the fire and got up to ferry wood from the pile he had made earlier. He had to do it one piece at a time because he needed the other hand to keep the cloak closed. That done, he went and curled up on the far side. He was asleep almost immediately.

chapter 15

Jarrod woke in darkness, as he usually did, but it was cold rather than any inner urging that roused him. He rolled over and was instantly reminded of his nakedness under the cloak. That in turn brought Marianna to mind. She should have been the one to wake him. The fire had burned down to the glow of ash-covered embers. He sat up and peered around, but there wasn't enough light to be certain about anything. He got to his feet and saw a darker mound on the other side of the fire. He felt a frisson of anxiety and padded around to investigate.

He squatted down and reached out a tentative hand. His fingers grazed cloth. Marianna's cloak in all probability and, presumably, she was underneath it. He squelched the urge to investigate further. She must have fallen asleep on her watch and it would be unkind to wake her now. In fact it was rather pleasing to have her fall short for once. He'd be able to rib her about it. Better yet, he'd make up the fire and not say a word about it unless she brought it up. If she did, he'd be all sweetness and understanding. She'd hate that. He smiled to himself as he stood up again.

He went to fetch wood, free to use both hands this time, and coaxed the fire back into life. He hunched over the young blaze until he was warm again and then investigated his clothing. He found a breechclout that was dry and a shirt that was bearable, but his trousers and boots were still coldly wet, as was his jacket. He girded his loins and donned the shirt, then put the suit of mail on. The rest would have to wait. He picked up the pot and set off for the river bank.

The husks that had crackled so satisfyingly underfoot the evening before were sharp and painful now. He gritted his teeth and concentrated on blocking out the pain, moving with the foot-shaking distaste of a kitten walking over wet ground.

The grass on the riverbank was a welcome relief and he set the pot down and wriggled his toes. He was tempted to sit on the edge and paddle his feet in the water, but his distrust of the river prevailed. He was probably being foolish, but he didn't feel like taking any chances. The water was obviously harmless once boiled since he felt no ill effects from the chai, but that was as far as he was prepared to trust it. He put the pot down and sat himself beside it.

There were no tree branches to shut out the stars and their light gave the water a sheen that made it look oily. He could not see the far bank, but sound carried and the barking roar, followed by a brief, high squeal of terror, were indication enough. If he hadn't fallen in, they would probably have made camp on the other side. His ducking was beginning to seem providential.

He leaned back on his elbows and looked up at the sky. There was a thick skein of stars and they seemed to be closer than they were at home. There were too many of them for any patterns to be apparent. The gods, in Old King Sig's story, had journeyed through the heavens in search of distraction and had lit these lamps. If there was anything to the legend, they must have spent a great deal of time on the Island at the Center. These lights were too thickly strewn to impose a Battleaxe or a Shield on them and it brought home to him just how far they had travelled. In that, they were a little like the gods.

He had smiled condescendingly when Ragnor's Duty Boy had assumed that they were going to the Unknown Lands, but the truth was that he had approached this trip in that very way. He had been going to a distant and unfamiliar place to be sure, but he had assumed that it would be a place where the rules, his rules, applied. This surfeit of stars mocked his parochial imaginings. He sat up abruptly and turned his back on the river. There was something that he had to try.

He knew that he had no natural connection to this sun. It did not reach out to him, asking for his help to raise it towards the new day, but perhaps he could seek it out and forge a link. It should be behind him somewhere, hidden below the rim of this world. There was no way of telling what o'clock it was, but if he could make the contact, it would leave him feeling less insignificant and alone. He cleared his mind and began the litany that sharpened his concentration and took him within himself. Tranquility came together with a measure of certainty, and he reached out for the sleeping orb. There was nothing there, nothing to anchor him, and he retreated back into himself again.

He roused himself with regret and retrieved the pot. He rinsed it in the river and refilled it. he climbed to his feet and looked up at the stars again. It might be his imagination, but the background seemed less intensely velvet. If he was right, it would be light within the hour. His stomach growled, reminding him how long it had been since he had had a substantial meal. He made his tenderfooted way back to the fire, added more branches and made a place for the kettle. Marianna hadn't moved.

He repositioned his belongings around the fire to help them dry out faster and sat and waited for the water to boil. He thought back over the events of the past couple of years and wondered anew at the changes they had wrought. He had certainly grown up in a hurry. He had never had a plan for his future. He had assumed that Greylock would decide what he was going to do in life, but if he'd had his druthers he would have been a Weatherward on a remote station. The solitary life had seemed romantic and satisfying, especially when the Collegium had proved to him that he had few, if any, natural aptitudes. Escape from the torments of his peers had seemed eminently desirable.

Come to think of it, he hadn't wanted Marianna along on this expedition, but now he was glad of her sleeping presence across the fire. Odd that he should value her more when she no longer disturbed him physically or invaded his dreams. It was one of the advantages of being an adult, he supposed.

He came out of his reverie and added chai leaves to the pot and then used a damp sock to grasp the handle and take it off the fire. Night had faded from black to grey and birds had begun to sing in anticipation of the sun. Some things at least stayed constant from world to world. The song did not bring on thoughts of beauty, but rather of food, and he dipped his mug hurriedly into the pot. With luck the chai would quiet his stomach. He sipped cautiously. When it was light he would restring his bow and go hunting. He cradled the mug and inhaled the steam.

Marianna stirred on the other side of the fire and sat up. She looked around blearily, as if trying to remember where she was, and then her eye fell on Jarrod.

"Oh gods, " she said, clearly disgusted with herself. "I went to sleep on my watch, didn't I?"

"No harm done," Jarrod said brightly. "We both got a good night's sleep. I've made some chai."

"Lovely, but first things first." She got to her feet, one hand holding her cloak closed.

"Put your boots on. Those casings are murder on the feet."

She gave him an ambiguous look, but did as he suggested before heading off for the river. Jarrod drank some more chai and then made the rounds of his clothes again. His trousers were still too wet to wear and he turned them once again. He contemplated his own boots and decided against them for the time being. When Marianna returned, he filled her mug.

"I thought we should do some hunting this morning," he said as he handed it back to her.

"I agree. I find my objections to meat have diminished considerably. In fact at this point I'd settle for Sandroz' infamous oat pudding."

"Now there's where I draw . . ." He stopped and looked up as a crashing sound interrupted him. It came from somewhere beyond the tree roots.

"What was that?"

"How should I know?" Jarrod replied. "It sounded awfully big, whatever it was."

They stood, frozen, listening intently.

"Perhaps it was another tree falling," Marianna ventured.

"You're probably right," Jarrod said and was instantly contradicted by renewed noise. "I'd get dressed if I were you. We may have visitors."

Marianna raced around the fire for her clothes and Jarrod struggled with his boots. He fetched his sword and dagger and walked around the roots to confront whatever was coming. There was nothing to see, but the sounds were coming closer. Whatever was making them was obviously confident enough not to need stealth.

"The larger they are, the more likely they are to be herbivorous." The tag from Dameschool popped into his head. Yes, he thought, but that was on Strand. He peered ahead. Thin rays of early sun slanted in from behind him, creating shadows. The great trees stood, solid and strange, all around. There was no undergrowth to block the view, but the crown of the fallen giant formed a screen ahead. Beyond it the source of the crashing ploughed forward. There was a pause in the advancing noise and he was suddenly aware that the birds had fallen silent.

"Can you see anything?" Marianna called.

"Not yet, and keep your voice down. We don't want to call attention to ourselves."

Why didn't I restring the bow when I had the chance? he

thought. Too late for that now. Build up the fire. That might keep whatever it was at a distance. He ran back, stuck his weapons in the ground and started piling on wood. Marianna finished putting on her mail and joined him.

"If we catch it, we can cook it," she said.

"And if we don't, the fire might stop it from catching us."

He looked around, thinking of the bow again, and his eye fell on the package that held the book. He strode over and scooped it up. He hoicked up the tunic part of his chainmail and tucked the parcel into the top of his breechclout. It was cold and felt awkward. He walked over and plucked up his sword, giving a practice swipe as he did so. The book was no hindrance. He stooped for the dagger. Not quite as easy, but no great problem. He looked round the campsite again. They could make a stand here if they had to. The roots would be at their back and the fire would provide partial protection.

"I'm going out again, but I think this is probably our best defensive position. Why don't you stay here for the time being."

"In a pig's eye I will. I'm the one who has ridden into battle, remember?"

He sighed. "Oh, all right," he said ungraciously. "But just remember that you don't have Amarine to get you out of trouble this time."

Marianna glared at him and he saw her knuckles whiten on the handle of her dagger.

"Perhaps we'd see better if we climbed up on the trunk," he suggested.

They trotted around the root wall and Jarrod went over to the base of the tree. He judged the top to be about fifteen feet off the ground. he put his weapons down and braced himself against it, arms extended over his head.

"If you can get up on my shoulders you ought to be able to hoist yourself up," he said.

Marianna needed no prompting. She used his back as a

ladder and she wasn't gentle about it. Once the weight of her was gone, Jarrod stepped back and looked up.

"Hand me your sword," she said, leaning down. "You'll have to put the dagger between your teeth and climb up the roots."

He did as bidden and scrambled up. The book was a nuisance and he wished he'd left it behind. He'd been stupid to try to carry it. Marianna was right, he was becoming obsessed with it. He moved sideways onto the trunk and then turned round. It was broad enough to make the footing easy, but the branches still obscured the view ahead. He took the knife from between his teeth and Marianna handed his sword back.

The crashings had stopped, but they had been replaced with regular thuddings.

"Sounds like one animal, but it must be bloody heavy," Marianna remarked. She sounded unconcerned and Jarrod envied her her composure. He was trying to keep his own breathing even.

"I expect it's coming down to the river to drink. It probably won't notice us if we keep still."

"Let's hope you're right. It's definitely coming this way."

Up ahead the twigs began to tremble. The pounding seemed very close. The agitation increased and Jarrod expected the wood beneath his feet to shudder. He leaned back against a root. Marianna crouched down. A whiff of stench redolent of old pond water reached them and, as it did, something clumped around the treetop.

It was very large. Jarrod glanced down at the ground for comparison and reckoned that, on all fours, it was at least twelve feet high. It could probably reach them if it wanted to. It stopped and sat down. A snout quested the air.

"I think it knows we're here," he whispered, but Marianna gave no indication that she'd heard. Jarrod concentrated on the apparition.

The top of the head was rounded and two tufted ears, set

too high, stuck out. It was covered with blotchy fur, except for the face which was a broad expanse of pallid, wrinkled skin. The eyes, set on either side of the snout, were large and dark. The maw opened and revealed two rows of pointed, yellow teeth. A fat, black tongue lolled out.

"What in the Mother's blood is that?" Marianna asked very quietly.

"Another of the Guardian's pets, I expect. Gods, but it's ugly."

The snout dropped and the head began to swivel away from them. It had no neck to speak of, but the shoulders were huge. It had a broad chest and the front legs were thick and bowed. There was no way of telling if the hairy feet concealed claws, but Jarrod would have wagered on it. He had no clear view of the hindquarters, but a long, thin, hairless tail was switching from side to side, scattering husks.

The pelt seemed to have a life of its own. Jarrod stared at it and realized that it was disintegrating. A couple of pieces came away and fell wetly to the ground. They lay there steaming. Marianna had her free hand to her mouth and Jarrod tasted the bile in his throat. It was sloughing off lumps of flesh, but what was worse was that the patches scabbed over and hair began to grow again.

The appearance of decay that the animal presented was reinforced by the smell. Rich, thick and fetid, it reached out and enveloped them. It brought images of sickness and mortality. It was cloying. Jarrod felt his stomach turn over and clenched his teeth. The muscles in his neck spasmed. The odor was ripe with the nuances of bodies left too long on the battlefield and the sweetness of drying blood. There were overtones of suppuration and the gas from drowned kina.

The head swung back and the dark eyes found them. The tail stopped its scything. The creature made a soft, pleased sound that devolved into a series of purling rumbles. The bald tail began to move again, slowly, almost metronomically, as if in anticipation.

"D'you get the feeling that it thinks it's found breakfast?" Jarrod asked in a stangled whisper.

"I'm too busy trying not to be sick to think," Marianna said between her teeth.

The sound grew louder and Jarrod realized, with horror, that he was beginning to be drawn by it. He fought an impulse to jump down and walk toward the beast. It was incredible that anything that hideous could have such an effect.

"Jarrod . . ."

"I know. I feel it. You've got to fight it. If that thing wants us, it's going to have to come and get us."

He tightened his grip on both sword and dagger. If it attacked, he meant to give a good account of himself. He pushed away from the root and braced himself. The parody of a purr stopped and the ratlike tail fell still. The sounds of the river reasserted themselves. The animal cocked its head to one side as if puzzled. It sat looking at them askance with the flesh peeling off its body and then it started to croon again. This time the pitch was higher and the message different. It was also harder to resist.

Jarrod hefted his sword and wished that he was more proficient with it. The creature certainly showed no signs of retreating and he wasn't at all certain that he could dispatch it. Perhaps he could outwit it somehow.

Attack, the beast counselled. You have nothing to fear from this rotting pile. Kill me, it urged. My suffering is terrible and it would be a mercy to end it.

It was a potent appeal and while Jarrod's intellect told him to ignore it, he knew that he was leaning forward. There was something familiar about the projection, but he couldn't pin down what it was. Marianna started to move and it triggered him into action. He swept her off the tree, away from the animal, and then jumped down on the other side. The head shifted, following him. The sound intensified and the message was encouraging.

Jarrod stood, legs apart, weapons at the ready, and stared at the creature. It was even bigger down here; half again his height. He found himself inching forward and forced himself to halt. He was shaking and, despite the early morning chill, sweating.

Well done, his instincts applauded. Take stock of it. Look for weaknesses so that you can kill it more humanely. He looked the beast over and experienced a wave of pity. It deserved to be dispatched. No animal should be allowed to suffer so. It would be an act of charity to put it down. If the Guardian really cared for his charges, he would not permit this hapless creature to linger thus. It was harmless enough. It was just sitting there hoping for release. He could walk up to it and make an end with a clean thrust through the chest.

Once the decision was made, he felt relief. He squared his shoulders and stepped forward. The animal did not move, though the pleading intensified. He advanced to within twenty-five feet of it and stopped again, this time to select a spot on the leprous chest. His nose had begun to discount the smell, but, closer in, there was nothing that could diminish the effect of the look of the thing. Pellia had said that the Guardian knew everything that went on in his demesne, so he should know about the pitiable condition of this animal. Perhaps he also knew about Jarrod's presence and was using him to put it out of its misery. Perhaps this was a test of some kind.

As he thought of it, he knew with certainty that it was not so. He was being lured to his death. This disgusting freak of nature was working on his emotions and doing it very skillfully. He had very nearly walked into the trap. Anger boiled up in him. A cry of rage escaped him as he hurled himself at the abomination. Compassion had been replaced by hatred, but his desire to kill it remained constant. He must have moved faster than the creature had anticipated, for it was slow to react.

Jarrod's swordarm slashed up as he closed. He was aiming for the throat, but the creature turned its shoulder to block him. The blade sheared through rotting flesh and another lump of carrion fell to the ground. He jumped back, sword at the ready again, nerves jangling and caution doing battle with the excitement stirred by combat. The tail lashed and the fearsome mouth opened. Rank breath misted him and made his eyes sting. He retreated another couple of paces and waited for the thing to make a move.

The raw patch at the shoulder clouded over and the blood ceased to ooze. The song rose once more, the tone one of heart-rending plaintiveness, and Jarrod felt a spurt of remorse for having attacked the creature so wantonly. It sat there, clearly inviting a quick death, and all he was doing was torturing it. He could do better than that. Where would be the best place to stab to find the heart?

Something nagged at the back of Jarrod's mind. There was something familiar with the pitch of the creature's entreaty. There was more than mere pleading, there was an element of compulsion. The moment the connection was made, the answer was obvious. It was using a form of the Voice to bring him within range of those massive front legs. He retreated further. He couldn't use Magic here, but the Voice wasn't Magic. The effect was achieved by pitch and practice and if it could work for this denizen, it might work for him. He calmed himself, trying to block out the sound and prepare his counter. He tried the command out in his head and then looked the beast in the eyes.

"Back! Get back! Begone!"

The words did not come out quite right because fear had dried his mouth, but it was enough to bring an abrupt end to the crooning. The creature pulled its head back and the tufted ears went flat. The compulsion was gone. Jarrod swallowed hastily, trying to moisten his mouth so that he could take advantage of the animal's surprise. He summoned up the image of it galloping back into the forest. Now for the snap of command.

"Back to your lair! Back! Run for your life!"

The creature stood and backed away, tail swishing furiously. It stopped and the head dropped slightly. It bared its teeth.

"Run!" Jarrod screamed, aiming the word with all the conviction he could muster. He brandished his sword.

Slowly, hesitantly, the animal turned and slunk a few paces away. The ears were flat and the tail drooped. It stopped and looked over its shoulder.

"Off with you! Begone!" Jarrod's control and pitch were perfect this time: the words were whips.

The beast shuddered and continued on its way, leaving pieces of itself in its wake.

Jarrod stood and watched it go, waiting for it to turn and come charging back. It kept on though and finally was lost among the trees. Only then did he relax. He leant on his sword in front of the twin heaps of meat that marked the place where the creature had sat. His stomach finally got the better of him and he heaved. It made no difference that he had nothing to bring up.

It was while he was in this undignified state that a new entity inserted itself into his awareness. *'Most interesting,'* a cool, detached voice said in his head. *'Not entirely fair, but most ingenious and unexpected. You are an intriguing surprise.'*

Jarrod ignored it. His physical distress claimed all his attention. When it was over, he wiped his mouth with his cloak and thought of Marianna. She must have been injured or she'd be here cursing him. He started for the campsite and had taken no more than ten paces when the hallucination reasserted itself.

'I think it's time that we met.' Jarrod's body jerked to an involuntary halt.

'Come to me now,' the voice said and everything wavered.

The air around him was flooded with a rosy, nacreous iridescence that thickened and closed him in. It invaded him, making him light, and then weightless and, finally, evanescent. He was whirled away.

chapter 16

he was sitting on a cold, hard, flat surface. That was all he was sure of. His sight was mewed in by the fog. It was baffling, but beautiful; the color on the unicorns' horns in the light of the setting daymoon. He ought to have been afraid, but he wasn't. The book was digging into him and that was reassuring. It meant that he was alive. His legs were stretched out trouserless in front of him and he patted them, just to be sure. They were solid. One other thing was clear to him without benefit of sight: there were machines in the vicinity. His body's reaction to them was unmistakable.

The iridescent mist began to thin and then evaporated, leaving him in the middle of what looked like a huge, black-and-white checkered gameboard. His fingers confirmed the slick coolness of marble. He looked around. The room was square and larger than the Great Hall at Celador. It was as light and airy as the other was dim and confining. The walls were white and arched effortlessly to a peak far above his head. There were tall, pointed windows down either side and the sun was flooding in. It would have been cheerful if it hadn't been so empty.

Empty. He looked round again quickly. Where was Marianna? Still lying on the forest floor? She would have no way of knowing what had happened to him. He groaned aloud. A fine protector he had been. He had to get back to find her. Slow down, he told himself sternly. Think. This was obviously the Guardian's doing and he was every bit as powerful as the colts had implied. He would have to wait until this

Guardian showed himself. He hoped it would be soon. He didn't like the idea of Marianna wandering around in the forest by herself.

He got to his feet and, in doing so, realized that his weapons were gone. Had he dropped them in the forest? He didn't remember. He turned around slowly. Two things stood out. There was a pair of wooden doors, surrounded by a riot of carved garlands, that all but filled the back wall: the other end was dominated by a throne that looked to be of a burled, honey-colored wood. The back curved up almost twelve feet and ended in a shell-shaped canopy.

As his eyes adjusted to the light, he noticed that the walls were decorated with raised panels, but, since they too were white, he could not make out the designs. He started off to his right to examine them, to see if they would yield some clues, and barked his shins. He stopped dead in his tracks and put out his hands, searching for the obstacle. His right hand encountered something. He peered hard and thought that he could discern an outline. He moved cautiously around it, tracing it with his hands. It was transparent, but solid, as if made out of the clearest glass he had ever seen.

There was what felt like a back and arms and a seat. He hesitated and then, overcome by curiosity, turned his back on it and lowered himself. His buttocks came in contact with it and, gradually, he allowed it to take his weight. It held. He put his hands on the invisible arms and gingerly slid himself backwards until his back touched its back. He relaxed and was held. He looked between his thighs and saw the floor. When he looked back up, the throne was occupied—almost.

Jarrod stiffened and stared. There was a head; that much was certain. It was hairless and looked as if it was made from very old vellum. There were two eyes, large, yellow and fiercely alive, made all the more startling by the lack of eyebrows and lashes. The nose was insignificant and the mouth little more than a straight line. The chin was pointed and the neck, what there was of it, marked by high-standing cords. The problem was that it petered out as it approached what should have been the shoulders. Where the body ought to have been there was a wavering like the air above a fire. The mouth opened.

"Welcome to my home, Jarrod Courtak of Strand," the head said, in accentless Common. The voice was as warm and mellow as an old viol. "I must apologize for the unorthodox way in which I summoned you, but it seemed the expedient thing to do."

The voice ceased and the bright eyes stared at him. Jarrod swallowed and his hands tightened on the insubstantial arms. He didn't know what to say. This was the Guardian and none of his preconceptions fitted. This, this thing spoke his language; so much for his careful husbanding of the book. He had brought a clean robe across who knew how many leagues of sky and here he was, sitting on an invisible chair, sweat-streaked and half naked. So much for the respectful attire. It also knew who he was; not a comforting thought.

"I see that you are uneasy," the apparition continued. "You have no need to be. Your presence on my island is far too interesting for me to wish you harm." There was a pause. "Ah, of course; I understand. Stupid of me."

Jarrod was shocked by a puff of smoke and when it cleared, the head was gone. The Guardian reappeared within seconds, giving fear no time to establish a hold. He was swathed in a dark blue cloak with a high, fan-shaped collar that framed the head. The lack of body was concealed, but Jarrod could not help noticing that there were no feet. The thin mouth curved into an alarming smile.

"That exit was a little melodramatic, but I couldn't resist it. I haven't had an opportunity to do that for centuries. I must confess that I had hoped for a livelier reaction, but no matter. You are obviously a brave and resourceful example of your species or you wouldn't be here."

Jarrod swallowed again and tried to gather his battered faculties. If he were to have any chance to succeed in this quest, he would have to make a good impression and he obviously hadn't done so. Nothing to lose then.

"Where is Marianna?" he said as forcefully as he could.

"A question?" There was no trace of the smile now. "You trespass upon my demesne and your first utterance is a question?" The rich voice seemed to roll around the room.

Jarrod swallowed. "Your pardon, August Majesty. I meant no disrespect. My companion and I have come a very long way together and I am concerned for her safety."

"You may be a poor guest," the Guardian remarked, "but you should not suppose that I am as inept a host as you are a guest." The words carried a sting, but the flare of anger seemed to have died out of the eyes. "I brought your companion here before I summoned you. She was unconscious. It was easier."

"Is she . . . ?" Jarrod began.

"She is slightly damaged, but it is not serious. She is asleep upstairs and when she wakes she will be whole. You need not concern yourself on her account."

"Would it be possible for me to see her, Majesty?" Jarrod asked.

"No it would not. And don't address me as Majesty. You make me sound like some impuissant planetbound satrap. I am the Guardian of the Lines of Force and in this universe there is none like unto me." The superbly modulated voice had risen again and the yellow eyes glittered.

Jarrod felt abashed and scrambled to make amends. "Your pardon, mighty Guardian," he said and bowed his head in a token of submission.

"That's better. You are a welcome distraction for me, but remember that I have lived a very long while without such distractions and shall continue to do so long after you are dead." The cloak billowed gently as if the Guardian had settled back in the throne.

Jarrod risked a look and found the unsettling smile back in place.

"You appear to be nervous," the Guardian continued. "It is to be expected, I suppose. However, if you behave yourself, you have nothing to fear from me. I have a long history of catering to my various pets, species that would have become extinct on their home worlds had I not rescued them."

"And was the creature we encountered in the forest one of your pets?" Jarrod enquired.

"The oblivore? Yes indeed. I admire the way you handled it. The poor thing must be very confused. I don't think it's ever lost a meal before, but I'm glad that you resisted the temptation to try to kill it. You would not have succeeded, of course, but you might have inflicted considerable damage. Oblivores, as you may imagine, have great difficulty in breeding."

At least I did one thing right, Jarrod thought. Nothing else was going well. He was out of his depth and, to make things worse, he could feel a headache coming on. The Guardian was staring at him and he couldn't think of anything to say.

"Do machines bother you?" the Guardian asked out of the blue.

"Sometimes," Jarrod admitted.

"That accounts for some of the tension then. I use a great many very sophisticated machines, but I had assumed that my shielding was perfect. You are more sensitive than I thought possible."

Jarrod was aware of a gentle intrusion into his consciousness and then the nagging disturbance he had felt was gone. It was as if someone had closed a heavy door. Now the fear came. This ancient Mage could manipulate him without moving a muscle. His mouth was dry again.

"Thank you, sir," he managed.

"I think you probably need some time to rest and recover," the Guardian said, "and I'm sure you could do with something to eat. Mind you, I have gleaned my knowledge of your eating habits from the unicorns. Unicorns are highly intelligent animals and they know you as well as anything can, but you are still very alien to them. I have done the best I can with the information they provided, but I should appreciate your comments. They will be helpful when it comes to feeding your companion.''

The Guardian blinked. Jarrod watched the eyelids move slowly down and up again and realized that it was the first time that he had seen it happen. And you, he thought, are far more alien to me than I am to the unicorns. He was aware of a faint creaking behind him. He wanted to turn and look, but was afraid that the Guardian's code of manners might be violated again if he did. He waited with what patience he could muster, ears straining. They were of no help. A bronze shape sailed past him without warning and came to a halt in front of the throne.

From the back he could see that it had arms and legs, a body and a head. It was obviously mobile, but Jarrod got no feel that it was truly alive. The object turned in place and faced him. Then it glided forward and stopped a scant yard from him. Jarrod stared up at it, at a loss. Close up, it was a caricature of a human being. The limbs were convincing, but the face was a mere sketch, with bulging, glassy eyes and a deeply etched line for a mouth. It floated above the floor, waiting.

''My servitor will escort you to your quarters,'' the Guardian's deeply musical voice said. ''If you have wants you may tell it what they are. I have programmed it to understand you. It will not, however, be able to respond verbally. Its circuitry is not sufficient for that. If you will follow it . . .''

Jarrod rose, not understanding half of what had just been said, but unwilling to give offense.

''Thank you for your kindness, Great One,'' he said, ''both to me and to the Lady Marianna.'' He bowed towards the throne.

''We shall meet again, Jarrod Courtak of Strand, and I

look forward to it. Go and rest now. You will need to be at your best.'' The yellow eyes glittered and then the throne was empty.

Jarrod stood looking at the empty chair, not knowing what to think or what to do. The metal man solved the latter problem by moving towards the doors. Jarrod had no choice but to follow. Out through the doors they went and down a long corridor until they came to a vestibule from which an ornate staircase rose. The metal manikin turned without hesitation and floated up the stairs. The legs, though separate, did not function separately. The whole rose smoothly and unarticulatedly, took the turns with ease, and left Jarrod in its wake. It waited on the landing for him to catch up.

It led the way past a series of solid-looking wooden doors, stopped in front of one, indistinguishable from the others, and reached out for the door handle. It opened the door and stood aside. Jarrod walked past it and into a lavishly furnished room. The mechanism followed and stood waiting.

The floor was of inlaid wood, warmed and partially covered by carpets whose main colors were deep reds and blues. The walls were covered in a burgundy silk with a lighter trefoil flag pattern. The ceiling was beamed and carved and picked out in gold leaf with accents of the same blues and reds that dominated the carpets. The overall effect was of a chamber of estate in the richest of palaces. There were doors to his right made, incredibly, of almost nothing but glass. He glimpsed a balcony beyond them. The house had obviously not been built with defense in mind. In front of the doors were four upholstered chairs arranged in a group around a low table. There was a small chandelier above it. There was a four-poster bed against the lefthand wall, replete with hangings. Very impressive, he thought.

Jarrod turned to ask about washing facilities, but the metal man was gone and the door was closed. He reopened the door and looked out into the corridor. Nothing. It's like the temple, he thought. He made a dissatisfied face. He was tired and hungry and worried about Marianna. He turned back into the room. She was somewhere in the building, presumably, but to go blundering about a strange mansion didn't seem very sensible.

He went over and opened the glass doors. He stepped out onto the balcony and leaned on the balustrade. There was a sloping lawn, perfect as a bowling green, that led down to a lake. He assumed it was a lake although he could not see the further shore. Waterfowl swam and dived and a large black bird, all long curving neck and immaculate feathers, moved across the surface with the same grace that Jarrod's recent escort had displayed. It was followed by a line of chicks struggling to match the parent's style. They brought a smile. It seemed to have been a long time since last he smiled.

A sound from the room made him turn. The servitor was putting covered dishes down on the table. Jarrod went back in and lifted one of the covers; heavy, silver. Steam and aroma greeted his nostrils; a bowl of meat and cubes of what he took to be vegetables in a dark gravy. A second cover concealed something that resembled rennet. There was a loaf of bread and a carafe of red liquid. He picked up the latter and sniffed. His nose told him that it was wine and he poured a glass. He sipped cautiously. It was mellow and pleasant, but not as sweet as he was accustomed to.

He lowered himself into one of the chairs, broke open the loaf and dipped the bread into the gravy. It was well-flavored, but it had an oily aftertaste. He washed it away with wine. He picked up a fork, which had three tines rather than the normal two, and speared a piece of the meat. It seemed to have no flavor of its own and the other cubes were similarly bland. He was too hungry for it to matter very much. He switched to the spoon and set to. When the stew was finished, it took the rest of the carafe to dispel the oily taste.

He pushed the chair back and went and tested the bed. The velvet curtains were tied back elegantly to the posts and the mattress was soft but resilient. He swivelled round so that he could lie back, and caught sight of another door that had been hidden by the hangings. He got up to investigate. The knob turned easily and when he pushed the door, it swung inwards. The moment it did so, a bright light sprang into life. Jarrod threw up his arm to shield his eyes and only gradually dropped it again. He squinted at the strange cabinet that was revealed.

It was white and shiny and bounced the light back at him. He moved forward cautiously. The whole room seemed to be made out of china and so did the furniture. There was a large trough, not unlike a bathtub, but apparently attached to the floor, with two miniature pump spouts, surmounted by small wheels. A gold chain ran down from them to a black bung. Next to it against the wall was a basin set on a pedestal. It too had pump spouts with wheels. In the corner was what he took to be the jaques. There was a gold handle in the wall behind it.

The light, he discovered, came from a long, blinding tube on the ceiling. There were white towels on a rack of pipes attached to the wall. The nap on them showed that they were newly woven. He walked to the basin and examined it. It had a hole in the bottom, ringed with gold. He turned one of the little wheels and water came out of the spout. He shut it quickly and tried the other. The result was the same and, reassured, he put his hand out for the water so that he could wash his mouth. He pulled it back immediately. The water was hot. He was about to explore further when his stomach rebelled.

The onset of nausea was swift and he was glad that it had taken him while he stood before the basin. His meal was washed smoothly away and he was able to rinse his mouth out when it was all over. He looked up into the looking glass set in the wall over the basin and winced. He was pale and dishevelled, with two days' growth of stubble. He took some deep breaths to steady himself and decided to risk trying the waters of the tub.

When he reemerged from the extraordinary washroom, he felt greatly restored and hungry again. There was the possibility that the Guardian had tried to poison him, but he doubted it. Other than the fruit from the unicorn's territory, he had eaten nothing from the Island. His system was probably not adjusted to the local victuals. He had heard Isphardi merchants complain of similar things on Strand. In any case, the tray was gone, though a clean glass and a new carafe of wine had been left in its place. New too, was the fur-trimmed robe laid out on the bed. There was a silk shirt beside it and hose that looked like trews with feet. A pair of shoes with jewelled buckles were tucked under the bedside table. The Guardian obviously had no intention of poisoning him.

He returned to the white room and retrieved his mail, the breechclout and the book. He draped the mail over one of the chairs, put the book on the table and poured himself a glass of wine. He carried it over to the bed and moved the new clothes aside. he went back for the book and tucked it under the bolster before climbing under the covers. A lot had happened and he had a lot to think about. He rolled on his side and got his wine. He ought to have a plan of action. He'd put it off by telling himself that it was fruitless to make specific plans until he had met the Guardian.

They had met and he still didn't know what to do. He was a supplicant here, that much was obvious. There was no way that he was going to compel the Guardian to do anything. He would have to plead his cause with as much eloquence as he could muster. He would have to go carefully. That flash of temper over a title was a warning. If he gave offense, he would be disposed of as easily as the Guardian had vanished and reappeared.

First, what should he ask for? The restoration of the Place of Power and with it, of Greylock. Yes, that would be first. A means to defeat the Outlanders; perhaps he should ask for their destruction? That didn't feel right. He wasn't sure that he wanted them totally destroyed. Marianna's arguments about their peaceable intentions had had some effect on him. What about the Final Spell, then? If anyone knew the answer to that conundrum, the Guardian would. He would have to explain the background and the reason for his great need. The background would have to include the history of the war, and there was the rub. He took another sip of the wine and shifted position.

How could he lay the history of Strand before a being on a different world when he didn't know it himself? Not much of it anyway. Jarrod sighed and finished the wine. He put the glass down and lay back, putting his hands behind his head. The roof of the four-poster, he now saw, was covered with a watered silk that matched the hangings. The markings seemed to form a pattern, but his eyes couldn't quite follow it through. The effort made them water and, without meaning to, he slipped off into sleep.

He was wakened by a soft, persistent chiming. He sat up and looked around for the source of the sound, but it stopped before he had a chance to locate it. There was a knock on the door instead.

"Come in," he said, making sure that he was decently covered.

The door opened and the servitor came gliding in. It came over to the bed and pointed to the clothes. Then it pointed at Jarrod. It repeated the gesture.

"You want me to put the clothes on?" Jarrod asked. The head inclined.

Jarrod waved his hand and the thing retreated several feet. Jarrod felt awkward about climbing out of bed naked. It was stupid, he knew. If it had been another man, it wouldn't bother him at all. He climbed out resolutely and began to dress himself. The robe was open down the front and was secured by widely spaced buttons that went snugly through thin loops of brocade. A belt of the same fur as the trim completed the costume. The fit was good. The hem barely touched the floor. The sleeves were long and wide and had pockets in them, one of which contained a kerchief. When he went into the washroom for a final check, he thought he looked stylish. He did the best he could with his hair, but, lacking a razor, there was nothing he could do about the stubble that darkened his jaw.

The Guardian was waiting for him in the wide white room, seated as before and wrapped in royal blue. Jarrod walked across the long reach of marble, new shoes clacking on the polished surface. He stopped twenty feet from the soaring chair and performed his best court bow. The Guardian was watching him as he came out of his reverence.

"I am sorry to have interrupted your rest," the mellifluous voice began and then broke off. The yellow eyes widened slightly and the mouth twitched. "Dear me: that's the second time in a single day that I've apologized. I can't think when it was that I last did it even once. How peculiar that something as ephemeral as etiquette should last so long. To think that my parents' tutelage still holds sway after millennia. Perhaps courtesy, like so much else, is a matter of genes. What think you?"

"Forgive me, Great One, but I do knot know what a genes is."

"No, no, you wouldn't. Stupid of me. No matter. I roused you because your companion has awakened and I wished to consult you before feeding her. How did you find the food?"

Jarrod hesitated, wary of giving offense, but realized that he didn't want to inflict the same malaise that he had suffered on Marianna.

"It did not agree with me, sir. I, er, lost the meal soon after I ate it."

"Pity. Still, it's not too surprising. This generation of servos has scant knowledge of foodstuffs. I have little need of, or interest in, food and they, of course, have no use for it at all. The longer you live, the less reward there is in the pleasures of the flesh."

Jarrod remembered the lack of body concealed by the cloak and repressed a shudder.

"What was wrong with the meal? Do you know what it was that upset you?"

"I can't be sure, sir, but everything tasted of oil."

"Ah, then I think I know what went wrong. We must try again. I want you to regain your full strength." The Guardian's eyes closed slowly and he appeared lost in thought. The eyelids slid back up. "There, that should do it. I thank you for your acuity. You have probably saved your friend—or is she your mate?—from discomfort, and me from having to apologize again."

"She's my friend. How is she, sir?"

"Well enough; a little disoriented, naturally. I reset her shoulder while she slept and bound it up. She will be sore for a couple of days, but otherwise she is hale."

"When may I see her, sir?"

"When I deem it appropriate." The tone was curt.

"But . . ."

"There are no buts with me, human," the Guardian cut in sharply. "Is that clear?"

"Yes, Excellency."

"That's better. Now, find yourself a chair. There will be another meal for you in a minute. I would not like to take advantage of physical weakness." The slash of a mouth stretched and the parchment skin around the eyes creased.

"I think I shall go and visit your companion. She should have an explanation of what has befallen her. What kind of clothing does she favor? Do male and female in your society dress alike?"

"No, sir. Women wear dresses. She likes rich fabrics and

bright colors. Oh, and thank you for my clothes, sir. They are very smart.''

''I am pleased with them. The fit seems good.''

The eyes flicked past Jarrod's head and he heard the creak of the door opening.

''Here comes your meal. I shall leave you to it. Some of my pets dislike being watched while they are feeding.''

The head inclined slightly and the Guardian faded away.

chapter 17

The new meal had been served and cleared. The dishes were the same as before, but the oily aftertaste was missing. Jarrod was feeling pleasantly full and a little tipsy as he sat waiting for the Guardian to reappear. How old must the creature be? he wondered. He used centuries and millennia as one would say months and years. Had he ever had a proper body? Perhaps it was there all the time and had been made invisible. Whatever the truth was, he wasn't likely to find out. It wasn't the sort of question one could ask.

The object of Jarrod's speculation was on the throne between one thought and another. There was no fanfare, no puff of smoke. One moment the throne was empty, the next the head and cloak were there. He had been expecting it, but it was a shock nevertheless.

"She sends greetings," the Guardian said. The mouth smiled; the eyes did not. "That's not entirely true. She demanded to be allowed to see you. She is a feist, that one, and does not seem to have your instinct for manners. As I said, genes."

"I must thank you for your kindness to her," Jarrod said, struggling to his feet. "She is very independent and"—Jarrod ventured a smile of his own—"her language tends to be on the salty side."

"So I observed. I put it down to shock. I gave her a mild sleeping dose with her wine. Enough of her. I am more interested in what you have to say. You have come a very long way to find me and I should like to hear why you risked such an undertaking.''

The moment was at hand and Jarrod still didn't know how to proceed.

"I'm not quite sure how to begin, sir," he said.

"No prepared speech? You surprise me. You can begin by sitting down. You will be more comfortable that way."

Jarrod complied gratefully. "There are two kinds of people on Strand," he began. "There are humans and what we call the Outlanders. They cannot live in our atmosphere, nor we in theirs, but in spite of that, there has been war between us since the beginning of time."

"Scarcely that," the Guardian intervened with a chuckle. "What started this war?"

"I don't really know, sir. Nobody does. There are legends of course, but I was made aware recently that many of the old ballads and legends embroider the truth somewhat. Our legend says that the Outlanders attacked and slew a harmless nobleman who was out hunting. I imagine that their legends say something quite different."

"I shouldn't be surprised. Go on."

"Well, over the centuries, we pushed them back little by little. We reclaimed the land and made it fertile. It is said that we drove them out of the land where first we grew and followed them across the Inland Sea to the land where we now live." He was reciting what he had learned in Dame-school.

"There came a time, however, hundreds of years ago, when they ceased to yield. They harassed us unmercifully and, to keep them at bay, we built an enormous wall clean across the Magical Kingdoms, all the way to the far borders of the Empire. The fighting didn't end, but the enemy was always stopped by the wall. Men and Outlanders still died, but things stayed the same for a very long time.

"Lately, however, everything has changed. The Outlanders have invented terrible new weapons. Worse, they have circumvented the Upper Causeway and they are rampaging freely, burning everything before them. We have no defense. The human race is faced with extinction and without your assistance, Great Guardian, we are doomed." He had laid it on a little thick, but he was pleased with his presentation.

"And you wish me to preserve you here, as I have preserved my pets?"

"Oh no, sir. I have come to ask, to beg you to restore the Place of Power to us and to reveal the secret of the Great Spell so we can save our land, our animals, ourselves, everything."

The Guardian smiled at Jarrod's earnestness. "The Place of Power? What is this Place of Power?" he asked.

"It is a place of great Magic and its Keeper has always been able to summon assistance from those who dwell there. They are the ancient spirits of the place; or so we believe. The colts call it a Force Point, a place where the Lines of Force converge. Once it was ringed by massive stones, but now all but one has faded away and those that dwell there have departed." Jarrod was startled out of his recitation by the harsh crackle of the Guardian's laughter.

"Wonderful, quite wonderful," the Guardian said when he had regained his composure. "What imaginations you primitive people have. Such superstitions."

Jarrod was nettled by the characterization, but held his tongue. He needed this creature's help, he reminded himself.

"The reason for my being here, my Lord Guardian, is that our armies are no longer capable of defeating the Outlanders. Our only hope lies in Magic. One of the sources of our power lies in your Force Point. It also holds one of our greatest Magicians prisoner. I have come here to plead with you to make things as they were. I have nothing to offer in return, or almost nothing. I have brought with me a very old book that Amarine says is written in your language. I cannot read it, but I do know that certain passages, when spoken aloud, summon those that dwell in the Place of Power.'' He came to a halt, feeling that he hadn't made himself clear after all.

"Fascinating, absolutely fascinating. I should very much like to see this book of yours. Amarine must have been using that ancestral memory of hers. My native tongue has not been spoken in this universe since the last of my kind left eons ago. I see that I shall have to investigate this Strand of yours more closely.

"As for the Force Point, it has obviously detected a threat to itself and activated its shielding. From what you have told me, the reason for that is obvious. Once the threat is removed, it will revert to its former function. It's all done automatically. The system was put in place when this universe was first forming and has worked well ever since. It is a living monument to the genius of my people." There was both pride and pomposity in the utterance.

"I fear, sir, that the danger it perceives is the same one that drove me here. When it's past, my people will be gone." He was urgent and there was passion in his voice. He had to make this creature understand.

"That is more than possible," the Guardian said evenly. "You cannot expect inanimate mechanisms on an interstellar grid to take sides in fleeting contests."

"But you, my Lord Guardian, you are in charge of all that. Surely you can command the mechanisms."

"Certainly I can. The maintainance of the grid is my unique responsibility."

"Well then, Great Lord, can you not see your way to use your great knowledge to save an entire world? I don't know how we could recompense you, but we could do our best to provide whatever it was you wanted."

The head tilted back, the mouth opened and the scratchy laugh came out. Jarrod sat there, bewildered by the reaction. This wasn't going well at all. He wasn't even being taken seriously.

"Forgive me," the Guardian said, "I found the idea of your buying my services amusing."

"I'm afraid I am not presenting our plight very well," Jarrod said stiffly.

"No, no; I am sure that your people feel a great sense of peril. Only desperation would drive someone to take the risks that you have taken. You must understand, however, that intervention in the affairs of a planet is an extraordinarily serious business. The smallest change can result in unforeseen repercussions far into the future. I am afraid that I cannot take your unsubstantiated word for the state of things. Besides, for me even to consider making an exception to my rule, you would have to prove yourself exceptionally deserving." The Guardian paused, letting the words sink in.

"I'll do anything you require," Jarrod said and meant it.

"Anything?" The mouth widened and the eyes glittered. "That is a very rash offer. You don't even know what my peccadillos are."

Jarrod kept his mouth shut. Nothing that he said seemed to be right.

"Yes," the Guardian continued, "there may yet be some diversion in you. After all, you are the first one of your species to discover my existence, you have the stamina to survive a trip along the Lines and you can communicate with my unicorns. I ought to be able to devise some interesting tests."

Jarrod risked a glance. The mouth curved up, but the eyes remained fixed, reminding him of a child's drawing of a smiling face. He felt chilled.

"First, though, you need to regain your strength. You must rest. You will need to be alert."

With those far from reassuring words, the Guardian closed his eyes and Jarrod knew that the metal majordomo was being summoned. He was to be given a chance, then. There was no knowing how he was to be tried, but whatever the test, he would have to pass. He knew with certainty that he would not be given another opportunity. When he heard the door opening, he rose and bowed. He waited until the servant was beside him and then turned and followed it out. It was the only way he could be sure he wouldn't bump into something.

Two long days intervened. Jarrod spent most of the first one in bed. He was more tired than he had realized and the interview with the Guardian had drained him. Food arrived at regular intervals, always the same food. He ignored the wine and drank water from the washroom instead. He slept between meals and if he dreamed, he did not remember his dreams on waking.

The second day was spent fretting. There was nothing to do. He sat out on the balcony a while and watched the birds, but he got bored of that. He would have liked to explore a little, but there was no knowing when the Guardian would call for him again. There was nothing to do but think and the thoughts were not comfortable. He had embarked on this expedition without fully realizing what was entailed. He had been impelled into it by the Oracle's prediction, by a misguided sense of his own importance in the scheme of things and a desire to do great deeds.

Well, he was here and that was something, a great deed if you will, but he saw now that his importance in the scheme of things was less than nothing. He was as likely to die here as he would have been had he stayed on Strand. If he could get the Guardian to restore the Place of Power, on the other hand, the balance of the war might shift again. What if that was not enough? Suppose the Outlanders triumphed anyway? All his efforts would be empty, his great deed meaningless. The Guardian had ignored his mention of the Great Spell, but he would have to push for it. He would have to pass the tests first, however, and he didn't know what they were. He wished the Guardian would hurry up and start.

The wish was granted on the morning of the third day. He was escorted down to the throne room. He had expected the Guardian to be there, but there was no sign of him. He stood and stared around. The weather had held and the sun was streaming through what he thought of as the eastern windows. It could have been the slant of the light, or perhaps familiarity had sharpened his sight, but he could see the ghostly outlines of the furniture. There were benches on either side of the doors and two groups of armchairs, each surrounding a low table. There were other tables spaced between the windows and in front and slightly to either side of the throne were two more of the armchairs. It was the right-hand one that Jarrod had bumped into on his first appearance in the room.

He walked confidently over to the side wall and saw that the raised panels between the windows were filled with carvings. He had been deceived by the uniformity of the color. The one directly in front of him was a forest scene. Slender white trees were embraced by white vines. Bleached flowers bloomed in exquisite detail, and silent, albino versions of the long-tailed creatures that had followed them through the jungle swung through the branches. He was reaching out to touch it when a streak of color caught the corner of his vision.

He turned and saw that the wall behind the throne was beginning to change. Color was flowing down from the top, spreading out as it went. There were blues and greens with a hint of the texture of shot silk. Purples paled to pink and then deepened into crimsons and magenta until the whole wall was an hypnotic exfoliation of pattern and color. It was an oasis of relief in the severity of the room.

"I'm glad you like it," the creamy voice said behind him.

Jarrod turned quickly. The Guardian was floating in the middle of the floor, the hem of the robe clear of the ground, Jarrod bowed. He was annoyed at being taken off-guard again.

"It is very beautiful, Excellency."

"It is, isn't it? I designed it myself. I used to spend hours watching it at first. I take your obvious enjoyment of it as a compliment, especially since you can never have seen anything like it before.''

Jarrod's mind brought back the cascade of flowering vines in the bowl on top of the Anvil of the Gods, but he kept silent.

''Are you ready to begin the tests?''

''I doubt it, sir, but I shall do my best.''

''I'm sure you will. I confess that I am looking forward to this. I hope you have the wits and resources to last for the full course. This is a rare and welcome interruption in my routine and I very much doubt if I shall ever have this kind of opportunity again.''

There was a pause and Jarrod began to feel uncomfortable under that unblinking stare.

''Since this will be, in some ways, a contest between us,'' the Guardian resumed, ''it would be ridiculous of me to pick a physical challenge.'' The cloak billowed suggestively. ''Besides, I could discontinue you at will. I think it might be amusing, however, to pit myself against an unfamiliar mind. On planet after planet, sophisticated cultures have fallen to barbarians. Let us see now how well the primitive mind can work.''

There was another pause. Smug bastard, Jarrod thought. I mustn't allow myself to be intimidated. I'm playing under enough disadvantages as it is.

''What are the rules of these contests?'' he asked.

''Rules? There are no rules. You may do whatever you think will serve you best. You already know that your Magic will not avail you, if you call that a rule.''

''Does the same thing apply to you, sir?'' Jarrod pressed.

''To me? What can you mean? I shall not be participating in these tests, I shall be setting them. As I said, the arena will be a cerebral one.''

Jarrod felt that his mind was working preternaturally fast. ''You can hear my thoughts if you want to, I know you can. It wouldn't be fair if you did.''

"It wouldn't be an unfamiliar mind if I did, would it?"

"No, but if I got lucky and won the first couple, you might be tempted."

The head tipped back and the ugly laugh came out. "What an admirably suspicious creature you are. I think this may be better sport than I anticipated." With his back to the light his eyes looked amber and they were sparkling.

"I shall 'play fair,' I think that would be your phrase for it. I have already determined the shape of the trials, based on what Amarine has told me and on my own observations. I know quite a lot about you without having to read your mind. And speaking of reading, please remember to bring your book with you the next time."

"Yes, sir. May I ask when these tests are going to begin?"

"I see no reason to delay. Just remember that you are your own worst enemy," the Guardian said and vanished before Jarrod had time to ask his next question.

He looked around quickly, half expecting him to be bobbing in a corner. He even looked up at the ceiling. There was no Guardian to be seen, but he noticed that the edges of the room were indistinct. The mother-of-pearl fog was thickening and closing in. He waited, not knowing what else to do. It cocooned him. There was no sound and nothing to see except the color of the mist. Soon there was the impression that it was thinning out again and then it was gone.

He was standing in a small octagonal room and there were men all around him. His hands clenched into fists and the gesture was echoed on all sides. He opened his hands again and his rueful little smile was reflected back at him. So this was what the old reprobate had meant. He approached himself and touched the mirror. It was cold and firm. Keeping his fingers on the surface, he circled the room until they found the overlap. He shuffled sideways through the gap.

He found himself in a passage filled with receding phalanxes of Jarrods. He edged forward along it, his hand questing out in front like a blind man's. The light was dimmer here. He looked up, trying to locate the source, and was surprised again by his own face. he dropped his eyes and resumed his sideways shuffle until he saw himself approaching. He was in another chamber.

Time to stop and think, he told himself, and sat down in the middle of the small looking-glass room. He peered around. It was odd to be alone in such a crowded place. His cross-legged self was everywhere. He turned his head from side to side, seeing himself from new angles. One profile convinced him that his nose was too long and the mouth dead ahead of him was on the large side. Many pairs of critical blue eyes confirmed the judgment. He stood up and turned slowly. Too thin, he decided, and his legs were too long for the rest of him. He contemplated taking his clothes off and completing the scrutiny, but the idea that the Guardian was probably watching daunted him.

Besides, he was wasting time. Here he was, in a crystal trap, and all he could think of was parading around as if he were getting ready for a ball. If anything was waiting for him at the end of the maze, it was more likely to be an oblivore than a pretty girl. He stretched his hand out again and walked to the wall. His fingertips touched their reflection and he began to move around to his right. He came to a narrow opening and continued past it. Within a few paces he had found another.

There were two exits and only one of them would be the right one. He'd been correct in thinking of the place as a maze, but this one wasn't going to unravel before him as Stronta's Great Maze had always done. He would have to solve this one as if he were Untalented. He had no string to unreel, no sack of flour to mark the path. The Guardian had said that this was a mental test, so breaking the mirrors and forcing a way out would be considered as cheating. He would have to think his way out.

'Look to your advantages,' is what Greylock would have said. Well, he was Talented and those of the Talent had always had an affinity for mazes. The Guardian might not know that. It was more a question of the way one looked at things than of magic. He had been taught to look for the underlying structure of things since Greylock first took him on. The Great Maze might have no perceptible pattern to it, but this construct assuredly did. He sat himself down again and closed his eyes to exclude the distraction of his reflections.

He slowed his breathing and concentrated. He brought back the shape of the first chamber, then the passage, then the present room: eight sides, two sides, twelve sides. One exit from the first and three from this one: one to go back, one to go on, one to go wrong. He probed at the seeming reality around him. Chambers and corridors everywhere; like being in the middle of a honeycomb. There must be a way through, he thought, or the game makes no sense. There was a pattern to all this; there had to be. He began to chant softly and the rhythm of the words lifted him. He tightened his concentration and pushed his imagination upward beyond the mirrored ceiling.

He looked down into the roofless comb. It was not as large as he had thought it would be. The looking-glass walls made it seem more complicated than it was. He traced a line through the mental image. It doubled back a number of times, but when all was said and done, it was nothing more than a circuitous, righthand maze. He came back into himself with a sense of triumph. If this was the best that the Guardian could do, he'd be back on Strand in no time.

The feeling dissipated rapidly. The Guardian, he reminded himself, was looking for distraction. Solving the puzzle too quickly might irritate their host, or lead him to make the next test far harder that he had originally planned. Better to play it slowly and pretend that blundering luck had brought him out. He opened his eyes and was back among the multiple images. He stood up and dusted himself off.

He made his way back to the narrow opening he had found first. If his vision was accurate, there would be no passageway this time. He stepped through and was in another faceted room. There should be only one other opening and there should be a passage beyond it. He fished a kerchief from his sleeve and dropped it. He trailed his hand across the cold surfaces until he found the gap, took off a shoe and left it there. There were no other interruptions until he got back to the kerchief. He collected it, crossed to the shoe, picked it up and stepped into the passage.

He proceeded cautiously, lopsidedly, through a number of rooms and connecting corridors until he was certain that his insight was correct, then allowed himself to take a wrong exit. He ended up, as he had expected, in a cul-de-sac and had to retrace his steps. He made two more detours after that, always returning to the line that he carried in his head, and felt that his performance was convincing. He had no sense of being watched by anybody but himselves, but he didn't want to take any chances. He approached the final room confidently. The next exit would take him out of the maze. He must be sure to look surprised.

The last chamber was another octagon, which added a nice symmetry to the whole. There was no way of telling how long the test had taken, but his instinct told him that it was more than an hour and less than two. He put his shoe down and, kerchief in hand, made his way around to the right. It was difficult to judge distances when one was inside a kaleidoscope, but it seemed to him that he should have come to the opening by now. When he got back to the shoe, he was certain of it. He set out again hoping that he had been careless and missed it. He had not.

He sank down and leaned back against the glass. He had been overconfident. He had taken a wrong turn somewhere and finished up in a dead end. He groaned quietly. Where had he gone wrong? He realised that he was tired. He had been walking for a long time and it had caught up with him. He pushed the thought away. He couldn't afford to be tired;

not until he was out. He closed his eyes and concentrated on his map. He had made no mistake.

Of course he'd made a mistake. He had missed an opening. He went back in his memory and compared the sequence of chambers to the pattern he had projected. It matched exactly. It couldn't be a coincidence and that meant that the map was wrong. He had worked his way to the center of the maze, not out of it. He reached out with all his senses save sight and began his chant. The overview returned and he traced paths through it with increasing anxiety. The route he had taken was the only one that crossed the entire space. He opened his eyes and let himself slump.

The Guardian had been right. He did have a provincial mind. He had used the abilities that had served him on Strand, but he wasn't on Strand. He had thought that he was being so clever in outwitting the Guardian, when all he was doing was walking into a trap. He shook his head and gathered himself. This was no way to think. This was only the first challenge. It was far too early to give up. The ancient creature wanted to pit itself against a primitive mind. Well, if stubbornness was a "primitive" characteristic, Jarrod could oblige. He summoned up the map once more and pored over it. The conclusion was inescapable: there was no way out.

Then the reason dawned on him. There was nothing wrong with his map. The place was exactly what it seemed to be, a closed maze. He had not wandered into this, it had been created round him. It was an illusion fabricated in the audience hall, just as the flowing wall had been. He felt the laughter build and his head tilted back to accommodate it. As he did so, the surrounding images faded and he was sitting in the middle of a black square.

The Guardian waited until the laughter had sputtered out. "I am glad that you enjoyed the first part of my little riddle." The tone was courtly. "I confess that I did not expect you back so soon."

"The first part?" Jarrod's laughter was quite gone.

"Dear me, yes. I did promise you that you would meet your own worst enemy, didn't I?" The lips thinned and turned up.

Jarrod was angry. He had solved the puzzle and ought to be credited with a win. It wasn't fair to set a test and then declare that it was only half a test. He looked up at the Guardian.

"Do you have something that you wish to say to me?"

Jarrod thought better of his impulse. "No, Great Lord," he said and knew that he sounded surly.

"In that case, you will have to excuse me. I have a number of things to attend to. This is not as easy a life as you might imagine." He inclined his head politely and faded gently from sight.

Jarrod stayed on the floor, fuming. The game was rigged, that much was obvious. He wasn't supposed to win. This whole charade was geared to give the Guardian some kind of millennial chuckle. He was like some celestial travelling player who had arrived without props or costumes and found himself acting out a part of his host's devising. He got to his feet feeling belligerent. The Guardian hadn't even had the grace to tell him what sort of play this was. He walked grumpily over to the righthand wall.

He did not mean to linger. He needed movement as an antidote to frustration, but the animals in the wall panel caught his attention. Seen this close, they were vivid and individual. Two steps back and they blended in with the background. That wasn't fair either. They should be scampering free, not fixed in place and out of time. He knew why the idea affected him so. He was not so different. They were all marooned. An unexpected wave of homesickness surged over him. He recognised it. He'd felt this way when he had first been sent to the Collegium.

Knowing what it was did not negate the effect. He felt unhappy. He ran his fingers over the smooth shapes. The sculptor had been marvellously exact. The jungle scene was as he remembered it. It reminded him of the jungle on the Umbrian bank of the Illushkardin and the homesickness intensified. He had no business being up here, wherever here was. He should have stayed on Strand.

The truth was that he had run away from Strand, from his failure to rouse Greylock and his inability to fill the vacuum that the Mage's absence had created. If he had really wanted to serve the Discipline, he would have stayed and fought Naxania over the Tithe. He was a failure and a coward on Strand and he was overmatched here. All in all, he was fulfilling Magister Handrom's assesment of him. He could still hear Greylock's voice reading the report. "A paradox: a boy who is overly bright and does not use his brain enough." Not quite; Handrom had been wrong about the first part. He pushed away from the panel. He ought to keep moving.

He went over to examine the doors on the back wall. He pushed at them, but they didn't move. He tried the doorknob, but it would not turn. He stood back and looked up. The doors were white like the rest of the room and they were a good eighteen feet tall, not counting the carved cornucopias at the corners. An orderly riot of white fruit, nuts and berries cascaded down the sides. Autumn overtaken by winter.

Jarrod's mood darkened and his mouth turned down. He moved away and ambled over to the throne. He climbed the two steps and ran his hands over the polished wood. The back rose straight up and curved over into the canopy. It had no joins that he could see. Even the best work at home was crude in comparison to the work in this room. Everything here was perfect and he was aware of himself as an esthetically jarring note. The unicorns found his body inadequate and the Guardian had no use for it at all.

It was a sad irony that he was being taken as a true representative of his race. He wasn't representative, he was a Magician, a freak who couldn't adequately explain the source of his difference. Marianna would be a better representative than he was. She would probably do better on the tests too.

He was here under false pretenses. He was no more than a mountebank whose tricks wouldn't work.

He sat down on the platform, leaned against the throne and drew his knees up. There were tears in his eyes and the muscles in his throat twitched. Bridle yourself, he thought. There's no need to cry. His lips compressed. Crying won't do a bit of good, he told himself. It's not going to impress the Guardian one bit. His mouth tightened and the tears rolled down. He cursed weakly and fished in his sleeve. No kerchief; he must have left it in the maze. He sniffed disconsolately.

Typical, he thought. You can't do anything right. Finding the unicorns had been a stroke of luck, no more. What was his record since then? He had asked the wrong question of the Oracle and his attempted defense of Stronta had resulted in the destruction of most of the Paladinian army, including the King, and in Greylock's . . . his mind shied away. He lowered his head to his knees and let the tears flow freely.

A small, submerged part of him knew that he should get up and move around, but that would require a decision and he didn't have the energy left for that. There was no point in it anyway: he had no future. He had managed to bamboozle the Guardian for a short while, but it was only a matter of time before he was unmasked. It was a mercy, really, that his parents had died without knowing him. He hugged his legs and his chest heaved spasmodically.

The light through the windows shifted and modulated from gold to rose. The huddled figure by the throne uncurled and looked around. His spirits were still at a low ebb, but he could cry no more and he was hungry. The room looked almost companionable in the waning light; a shame that it was so bleak the rest of the day. He wondered if the Guardian spent much time in the place now that he was bored with his wall of color. Poor Guardian, it couldn't be much of a life.

He had been abandoned by his kind. They had gone off, promising to return, no doubt, and left him to run things. He surely hoped to be relieved, but, after all this time, an un-imaginable amount of time, he must realize that no rescue would come. What had he done to deserve such a fate? What crime had he committed to merit such endless expiation? Nothing but beasts and mute servants to converse with; no company and no opportunity for love. The poor thing was condemned to days of iterated makework, all challenges and excitements rubbed smooth by familiarity. What a terrible life. Jarrod began to cry again, but this time it was not for himself.

Despair crushed down on him again. At least the Guardian wasn't a failure. He had stayed at his post and done his job, which was more than he could say for himself. It would be better if the Guardian disposed of him. He'd only botch the job if he tried to do it himself. He sighed and knuckled his eyes. Perhaps not, he thought, and sniffed. Perhaps he could muster the energy for that. One last effort and then peace. He looked around the room for some means of achieving it. Nothing presented itself.

The windows, he thought. If he could break a window, he'd be able to cut his wrists. It would make a mess of this nice, neat place, red running over the immaculate black and white—like the color wall. The idea produced a wan smile. It wouldn't matter. The Guardian had servants to scrub the floors. He wondered idly if the lifelike but mechanical things would be affected by the sight of human blood. He doubted it somehow.

The Guardian might be disappointed that his new toy had lasted such a short while. Then again, Marianna would still be there to take his place. She certainly wouldn't miss him. If she passed the tests and returned to Strand, she would have the glory all to herself and that was all that she was really interested in. Ragnor might be disappointed in him, but he'd be long dead by then. Tokamo might miss him, but he had his own life now and would quickly forget.

The first thing he would have to do was to stand up. Strange that it should seem such a major undertaking. First stand up, then deal with the window. He gathered his forces and hoisted himself to his feet, using the throne for support. There, that hadn't been so difficult. He shambled down the steps and over towards the windows. He was stiff from the long spell of sitting and his legs didn't feel as if they belonged to him. It was dreamlike and somehow fitting. This whole undertaking had been unreal.

He stopped and leaned his forehead against one of the long windows. The sun was down and the sky was orange and red; no moon to amplify the light. The trees were black silhouettes and they provided a sense of familiarity. Strange that he should think of it at this time. They took him back to Dameschool. Leafless trees outlined against just such a sky; it was the only painting he had ever done that had won praise. Stop maundering, he chided himself. Get on with it before you lose your nerve.

He turned sideways and positioned himself. He selected a point of impact and launched his right elbow at it with all the force he could muster. Contact was a jarring flash of pain dowsed by numbness. The glass winked at him serenely, mocking his impotence. Anger built in him; anger at the window, at himself and at the Guardian who had engineered all this humiliation.

Like most quickly kindled fires, this one burned out rapidly. Once the heat was gone he was left with an elbow that was starting to throb and a sense of shame that he had blamed the Guardian for his own shortcomings. Things might be bleak for him, but they were a good deal worse for the Guardian. He at least had known the warmth of friendship. Marianna might be irritatingly superior, but she was a friend. The Guardian had no one. The cold and lonely watches of the night must be terrible for him—and endlessly repeated. He sniffed as he felt the tears well.

"Stop that immediately! I will not have it!"

The voice boomed around him and the anger in it dwarfed

the feelings that had coursed through Jarrod scant minutes before. He turned swiftly, nursing his elbow in his left hand. The Guardian was sitting on his throne. He had not bothered with the cloak and the burled wood showed through him. The sight prompted another rush of pity.

"Stop it!" The lips were a harsh line and the eyes blazed through slitted lids.

The head bobbed slightly and the Guardian took a deep breath that passed from nothing into nothing.

"I do not tolerate that kind of attitude." The voice was back under control. "You are here at my pleasure and the operative word is pleasure."

He glared across at Jarrod and then the vagueness that might once have been a body seemed to shift. The mouth pursed and the nostrils flared.

"I cannot remember that last time that I was in the position of being a poor loser," he said, the voice a resonant legato once more. "I enjoyed the surge of feeling, negative though it was. I have been irritated from time to time, mostly by my own stupidity, but it has been eons since I last experienced real anger. Most gratifying." He was speaking more to himself than to Jarrod.

He looked up. "I must warn you, young human, that novelty is the most transitory of satisfactions. I would advise you against using that tactic again."

The Guardian looked at him, waiting. Jarrod knew that he was supposed to say something, but, even though the depression had evaporated, he was too tired and confused to think of anything. The pain in his elbow distracted him. He remained mute.

"Well," the Guardian said, breaking the silence, "you have passed the first test."

It took several moments to register. "Thank you, sir," Jarrod replied, sounding stupid in his own ears.

"I think you should have a good meal and a rest. It would scarcely be fair," the Guardian accented the word, "to take advantage of you in your current depleted condition. I look forward to our next encounter. You have surprised me and that is no mean feat.''

The massive head inclined towards him and Jarrod found himself standing by the four-poster bed. The curtains had been drawn across the windows and dishes of food steamed enticingly beneath the subdued glow of the chandelier. Jarrod took a deep breath. He had survived the first ordeal, though he knew now how close he had come to failure.

chapter 18

The Guardian was alone in his own quarters. He floated in front of the console that took up most of one wall and surveyed the hastily assembled additions with disfavor. Their temporary nature was esthetically offensive. They were not neat; they were not properly integrated. There was no help for it, however. He had been challenged. His whole stewardship had been called into question by this accidental human. He needed to know more, and that meant examination of its home planet in as close to real time as possible. The grid had not been designed for that.

His mind reached out and calibrated the makeshift instruments. He had already viewed the early history of the planet and had been struck anew by the ingenuity of his ancestors. The system that they had set up at the birth of this universe was an ongoing memorial to their expertise in astrophysical engineering. They had established termini in even the least promising gas clouds, anticipated supernovas and provided switching mechanisms that insulated the whole from damage.

A button clicked down and a bank of screens glowed into life. He activated retrieval for sector 309467. The Initiators had been brilliant, he thought, but they had not been able to think of everything. They had foreseen life, but not the emergence of cultures capable of destroying a planet. It had been his own vigilance that had detected that possibility and his own ingenuity that had perfected the failsafe mechanism that now protected the grid. It was he who had instituted the recorders that monitored higher life forms. It was axiomatic that the Caretaker did not interfere, but he felt justified with this slight bending of the rule. True, he had made an exception in the case of his pets, but never to the detriment of their homeworlds and only when they faced extinction. Now this Strandling had implied that his failsafe was going to cause the annihilation of a species.

A helmet floated up and settled on his head. He looked at the dial to his left and the pointer slid forward. As it did so, the space before his eyes blurred. He heard creaking and a subdued crackle. Static, he thought with a trace of annoyance. No, another part of his brain contradicted, wooden floorboards and a fire. A room appeared. It was low and dark and there was indeed an antique fossil-fuel fire. Quaint, he thought.

Three humans came clear. One, with a great deal of white hair, sat by the fire. The other two stood close. Their posture made it clear that they were in some way dependent on the seated figure. His makeshift adaptations were working well and the Guardian felt satisfaction. He had set them to home in on pivotal events, but it remained to be seen how accurately they would perform. He would need to know what these humans were thinking as well as what they said. He turned up the gain and the conflicting emotions in the room flooded out at him. He smiled and relaxed into symbiosis.

"Thank you both for attending my summons so promptly. I am aware that this is a busy time, but I needed the best brains in the Discipline. It's this blasted invasion of course. We're under a lot of pressure to come up with something and the army's at a complete loss. It doesn't necessarily have to be decisive, but it must be substantial. If we manage to turn the bastards back, so much the better."

The Guardian disengaged himself and ordered the helmet off. The tangle of unspoken thoughts was difficult to unravel. The two subsidiary characters were intensely ambitious and mutually distrustful. The old man's thoughts were a limpid stream compared to theirs. The Guardian made some adjustments. He had expected to see the Force Point, but it was too early to tell whether his assumption or the jerry-rigged equipment was at fault. Perhaps if he moved the time needle up a notch . . . the helmet floated back.

The picture materialized once more and, for an instant, the Guardian thought that his instruments had failed him. Then he realized that the old one was wearing a different robe. The selector was sticking with this trio. One of them must be central to developments on the planet. He began to experience what was going on.

"Back already?" Ragnor said, looking up from his reading. "I didn't expect to see you for at least another sennight." He peered up at them. "You're looking remarkably smug; like men with something in their sleevepockets. Out with it then. Curiosity is one of the things I don't intend to die of."

The two men exchanged looks. "Well, Archmage," Sumner said, "Handom and I have come up with something that we think might make a difference." He paused.

"Out with it, blast your eyes," Ragnor said irritably. The subtext showed that the old man was calm and alert. He was merely acting the way he was expected to act.

"Handrom, d'you want to explain?" Sumner asked, drawing things out deliberately.

"Oh, I think you'll do it well enough," the black-robed Dean replied with simulated comradeship.

"Gods of the odds! Get on with it. And after all this drama, it better be good." The Archmage was wary now. There was a thread of unease. They must feel very sure of themselves or they wouldn't dare to play with him like this.

"The idea actually came from one of the southern Weatherwards," Sumner began smoothly. "He's at the Collegium for a series of lectures. Handrom and I heard him discussing some of the problems encountered over the Inland Sea and among the problems were waterspouts."

"Waterspouts?"

"Whirligig vortices of water that look like giant funnels. They disrupt the air patterns and they flinder any ship that is unlucky enough to be in their path." Sumner sounded patient.

"I know what a waterspout is, Sumner, but what have they to do with the Outlanders? Are you suggesting that we decoy the enemy onto ships and launch them towards waterspouts?"

"Hardly, Archmage," Handrom rumbled, missing the humor, "but it occurred to us that if we could duplicate these spouts, using air instead of water, we might be able to disrupt their atmosphere. If we strip their atmosphere away, they'll perish." He spread his hands and his eyebrows arched a little.

Ragnor picked up a goblet from the table beside him and took a drink. Two could play at delaying games. "It's an interesting idea," he conceded.

"It's more than an idea, Archmage." Sumner's thin voice sounded annoyed. "It's a practical reality; a valuable new weapon in our arsenal."

"That a fact?"

"Yes, it is." Handrom's deep voice was final. "Sumner and I have put it to the test."

"Have you indeed?" Then why have I heard nothing about it? Ragnor thought.

"Yes, we have. The Chief Warlock and I have been conducting experiments beyond the Causeways."

"I see." His network had slipped badly.

"We were careful not to be observed," Sumner added, as if he had read the old man's mind. "We worked right at the edge of the new barrier lands." He smiled slyly. "Celador is a volatile place these days and we didn't want rumors starting."

"Most commendable," Ragnor pronounced. "You two are a credit to the Discipline." He watched the two middle-aged men bridle with pleasure.

He stroked his beard, weighing the possibilities. Magic needed another victory. Its reputation had suffered badly in the aftermath of the "victory" at Stronta Gate. If this worked, it would redress the balance, but a failure would be disastrous. The risks must be spread. He would need Arabella's support and that could no longer be taken for granted. Better bring the army in as well. If they did manage to strip away the poison and the enemy were in their suits, he'd need the army to dispose of them. He sat a little straighter in the chair.

"This has the potential, in my judgment, to be a major breakthrough," the Archmage said and lifted his goblet to them. "The thought of destroying the Outlanders single-handed, as it were, has enormous appeal, but, alas, there are political considerations." He gave them his man-of-the-world to men-of-the-world smile. "In this particular case I think we'll need the cooperation of General Nix."

"But Archmage . . ."

Ragnor held up a hand. The picture froze.

The Guardian, wise in the ways of viewing tapes, knew there would be an interlude while conferences were held and plans discussed. The threat to the civilization described by the young one upstairs appeared to be real, or at least the humans in the hologram seemed to think so. It was impossible, thus far, to determine what part, if any, the shielding of the Force Point had played. The selector did not seem to think that it was key and yet the level of technology on this world wasn't sufficient to cause a Force Point shutdown. Near-stellar reading gave no indications of a cosmic threat. There was no evidence of malfunction in the grid, but something had to have triggered the failsafe.

It was intriguing. It would be interesting to see how these primitives intended to control the weather. He knew from experience just how difficult it was to create a consistent climate and he had banks of sophisticated machines to help him. Still, that could wait. It was time to give the specimens a thorough physical examination. He had tested the sedative on the female and she had shown no ill effects. There was enough of it in the meal they had just been served to keep them under for a couple of days.

Perhaps it might reveal some physical anomaly that would account for the strange abilities he had seen demonstrated on some of the earlier tapes. It was a unique opportunity. Besides, he would enjoy the whole thing immensely.

The viewings were suspended for the duration of the examinations. They took longer than the Guardian had expected and by the time he found himself back in front of the temporary console, he was anxious to know what had transpired on Strand. He smiled to himself as he cued the tape. Humans were certainly taking up a lot of his time these days. The button depressed at his command and the picture began to build up. He glanced at the coordinates. They were the same. It was the scene that had changed.

It was night in the picture. They were outdoors. There was a fire with people sitting round it. The old one, the one they called Archmage, was standing a little way off. It was obvious now that he was tall and thin. There were no buildings visible, though the firelight did not carry very far. There was, moreover, a feeling of open spaces. The Guardian intensified the gain and was rewarded with a wash of emotions; anxiety, optimism, a hint of fear. He narrowed the band and began to pick up the old one's thoughts.

Tiredness, a hearty dislike of having to sleep on the ground, were a grumbling undercurrent, but there was satisfaction there too: the old warhorse testing the air on the morning of battle. The simile occurred to Ragnor and produced a wry twist to the lips. The plan had worked, even if it hadn't been the bloodless operation that he had hoped for. Nix had taken casualties, but the important thing was that the Outlanders had been maneuvered into position between the two folds of hills. That should be worth a handful of lives if the morning's venture proved successful.

He drew his cloak closer and moved to the fire. Four Weatherwards, Sumner, Handrom and three Apprentices to fetch and carry, ten of us in all, he thought as he looked down on them. A small enough band for such an undertaking.

"Those of you who are operating from the southern hill had better get going," he said. "It'll start to get light in about half an hour. That should give you plenty of time to get into position. Just be sure to give the bastards a wide berth. We don't want to wake them up."

Sumner and two of the Weatherwards rose and adjusted their cloaks. Everyone in the group wore the same lovat-colored cloak, designed to blend in with the heather. It was little enough protection, but it was all they had. Without surprise, there was no chance at all.

"Good luck," he said and waved in a vaguely benedictory fashion as they melted into the darkness.

He joined the remainder by the fire and sat down to wait for dawn. Handrom had his eyes closed, the remaining Weatherwards looked drawn and the Apprentices were yawning against sleep. It was difficult to think that the enemy was only the width of a hillside away. Not something one wanted to dwell on. He had done everything he could think of to ensure success and it was out of his hands now. The only thing he had left to do was to give the signal for the army to attack. He caught the eye of one of the Apprentices and beckoned him over.

"I want you to go down to the bottom of the hill and find General Nix. You are to tell him from me that he is to wait until he sees my arm drop. I'll be at the crest of the hill so I'll be easy enough to spot. When my arm goes down, and only then, he is to go in fast and get out fast. Got that?"

The boy nodded.

"Off with you then."

Ragnor watched him race away and then got to his feet. The others followed suit. "Let's douse the fire," he said.

They obeyed, stamping out the last embers. Ragnor nodded at Handrom and clapped him softly on the shoulder. The Dean gathered up his two Weatherwards and headed off uphill. Ragnor follow more slowly, trailed by the two Apprentices. There was a green glow on the horizon, but when he looked across at the hillside opposite he could see no trace of the others. As the sun sent warning of its approach, he felt the wind begin to pick up and knew that the spell was underway. First it blew from behind and the next minute it was in his face. It grew stronger and more contradictory as the light waxed. Ragnor's cloak flapped and fluttered.

He looked around and could not see the Apprentices. Then he glanced down and saw them lying in the grass staring down into the valley. He followed their gaze and saw the Outland atmosphere swirling below, filling the space between the hills. He shuddered. It looked substantial, as if it was made of more than corrosive smoke.

The air in front of him began to dance as crumbs of earth and bits of heather began to whirl upwards. Pebbles followed and splinters of shale. Ragnor put his hand in front of his eyes to shield them. His beard floated up around his ears. Through partially opened fingers he saw that the air was thickening at four distinct points. In the blink of an eye, the ghostly shapes of four rotating columns emerged.

He was distracted by a noise and then a tugging at his sleeve.

"What?" he shouted at the boy.

"Your arm, Archmage! Put up your arm!"

"Oh, yes, thank you, yes." He raised his arm, feeling slightly foolish.

The columns had gained in girth. They whirled faster and began to elongate, wider at the top than at the bottom. The weather spell was working. As they climbed, the funnels began to sway. Like four drunken fat men with tiny feet, Ragnor thought. Let them not stumble, not yet. His arm began to ache with the effort to stay upright, but the airspouts gathered speed and mass. He reached up to massage his shoulder and, as he did so, other hands took his arm and supported it.

The columns wobbled forward and converged on the Outland atmosphere. They struck almost as one, plowing into it, spinning out streamers of brown muck. The funnels bent gracefully as their narrow feet came out from under them and then went crashing down. The pocket of Outland air was shredded and spewed in all directions like dirty lint in a gale. There should be noise, Ragnor thought as he flinched; an explosion, a tearing, something. He felt a thousand tiny stings on his exposed hands and on his face. His eyes watered. His stomach churned with fear and revulsion, but he stood his ground.

A strong wind came hurtling out of the west, the last part of the special Weatherwarding. It scoured the valley, blowing the tatters of the alien air out to the east. Hundreds of little fires flared. Ragnor blinked rapidly to clear his sight. He dared not wipe his eyes with his cloak. He concentrated on the valley floor and saw some objects against the black of the abused earth. Some were the protective suits the Outlanders wore, others seemed to be weapons; nothing moved.

"Let it fall!" he yelled. "Let go of my arm!" He felt a sharp stab of pain as the boy complied.

There was a brief pause and then the air was filled with shouts, made staccato by the wind. He looked over his shoulder and saw the single-minded charge in progress. He looked around for an avenue of escape. He would never get out of the way in time and the only other possibility was down into the valley. Unthinkable. He turned back and began waving furiously at the onrushing troops. It was as futile as shouting into a gale. Why hadn't he foreseen this? Stupid! Stupid! Stupid!

His self-excoriation was abruptly terminated by a blow to the side that sent him sprawling. From the side? was his shocked thought. He tried to pull himself together in a ball and, as he did so, a weight decended on him, bringing darkness. He tried to move, but found that he could not. The weight above was yielding, but too heavy for him to budge. His mouth was filled with cloth and he could not cry out. Think! he told himself.

The Apprentice—the Apprentice must have knocked him to the ground. Yes, that was it. He struggled anew and was pressed more firmly into the hillside for his pains. The cloaks would serve them ill now, Ragnor thought. What to do? Shape-change? Not in the middle of a stampede. Besides, that wouldn't help the boy. He felt the ground shake and heard the pounding of boots. Too late.

It was galling that the Archmage of Strand was going to be trampled to death by the Arundelian army. It was such an ignominious end. One good thing, though. He wasn't particularly afraid. You never knew about those things. What he was was profoundly irritated, at himself mostly; no one else to blame. Calm, he told himself, calm and patience. There must be a humorous side to this somewhere. Breathing was becoming difficult. Some shed of dignity . . .

The point of view pulled back as direct contact with the human was lost. The Guardian seemed to be floating over the hills. He watched quaintly uniformed soldiers careen down into the stricken valley. The focus began to waver and he shook his head with annoyance. This shouldn't be happening. He'd have to check the circuitry. The helmet disengaged and floated silently to its niche. He himself floated away from the console.

An interesting culture, no doubt about it. This set of humans had cultivated their mental abilities to a remarkable degree, considering their circumstances. That business with the airspouts was a neat trick and he had no idea how it was done.

He dimmed the lights. Time to rest. His mind, however, was not ready to submit to sleep. Where, he wondered, did this "magic" come from? The old man in the tapes and the young one upstairs were obviously from the same subgroup, but brainscans had turned up nothing out of the ordinary. A mystery, but there was no rush. He had taken enough samples from both of them to clone them later on if he felt the need. Might as well let them wake up. He sent the necessary signal and, satisfied for the moment, drifted off to sleep.

chapter 19

In a bedchamber of the house that stood atop the Guardian's installations, Jarrod stirred. He came slowly and gummily awake. He turned his head from side to side. He was in bed, but he didn't remember undressing or lying down. He pushed himself up onto an elbow and looked out into the room. The chandelier was lit and the curtains drawn. He pushed back the covers and got out of bed. As he did so, his stomach grumbled and, as if in answer, the door opened and the Guardian's man-thing came in carrying a tray. Jarrod nodded with satisfaction and headed for the washroom.

When he came out, the meal was sitting on the table and the curtains had been drawn back. The sun was flooding in. Must have slept a long time, he thought as he poured himself a cup of hot black liquid. He sipped. It wasn't chai, but it wasn't bad. He started in on the bread only to be interrupted by a rapping. A knock on the door? The machine man didn't knock. Marianna? He hurried to the door and flung it open. His smile died. The Guardian, his nonexistent body swathed in a dark red cloak, hovered in the corridor.

"May I come in?"

"By all means, sir." Jarrod stood aside, masking his disappointment.

The Guardian moved in smoothly and came to a stop in the middle of the room. "I trust I am not disturbing you?"

Jarrod forced a polite smile. "Not at all. I was just having some breakfast and looking out of the window."

"I'm glad you like the view. I find it soothing. I change it

from time to time, but I always come back to this arrange-
ment. The lake is a constant, of course, and I've always found
waterfowl amusing.''

"It's very beautiful,'' Jarrod said. This was not the irri-
table autocrat of yesterday, but Jarrod's sense of danger bris-
tled.

The Guardian turned towards the glass doors, his cloak
following more slowly than it should. "I came to ask how
you were feeling,'' he remarked.

"I feel much better today, thank you, sir. I had a nice long
sleep.''

The Guardian's head turned in his direction. It was smiling. "No ill effects?'' he asked pleasantly.

"No. I am much refreshed.''

"Your elbow has stopped hurting?''

Jarrod's hand went instantly to the elbow and rubbed it.
"As a matter of fact it has. I didn't even remember it.''
That's not like me, he thought.

"I'm glad to hear it.''

"How's Marianna?'' Jarrod asked. "You said she'd been
hurt.''

"That has been taken care of,'' the Guardian said easily.
"She was sleeping soundly when last I saw her.'' The image
of her white body on the examining table returned briefly. "I
would say that she is in excellent health. However, I am aware
that she was not happy to be brought here.''

"You mustn't hold that against her, my lord,'' Jarrod said
quickly. "She was hurt and she was surprised.''

"Oh, I don't hold it against her. It was a perfectly natural
reaction, if somewhat pungently expressed. I merely thought
that she might be more comfortable elsewhere.''

"Elsewhere?'' Jarrod said, alarmed.

"Yes. I know that she has a very close bond with the unicorn called Amarine. I thought she might be happier there
for the time being. You and I have business together, but she
and I have none.''

Jarrod didn't like the sound of that. "Wouldn't it be rather dangerous for her there during the rut?"

"If Amarine were still in estrus," the Guardian agreed, "but she has mated. The season is almost over. Her stallion is very attentive to her, but a human female would pose no threat."

"We've been together for quite a long time," Jarrod countered, "and I don't think that she would want us to be separated."

"I shall ask her."

"In that case, there's one thing you should know," Jarrod said, tacitly admitting defeat. "Marianna seems to feel that I get all the interesting assignments and that she's always being left out. If she thought that she was being sent away and I was being kept here with you . . ." He let the sentence die off.

The Guardian's eerie laugh was his response. "So she speaks her mind to you as well, does she?"

"All the time," Jarrod replied with an answering rueful smile. "She's a remarkable woman and I'm very fond of her, but I wouldn't want you to think that she's typical of the women on Strand."

"What a shame. I take your point, however. I shall be diplomatic." The Guardian drifted closer to the doors and looked out. "If you would prefer to visit the unicorns, you are free to do so," he added.

Jarrod didn't know where his discussion was headed. "But I thought you wanted to test me," he said.

"So I do, but I have no intention of forcing you to it. If you wish to return to your world, that too can be arranged."

"But you would not help us if I did," Jarrod said flatly.

"I would not help you," the Guardian agreed.

"Then I shall be most happy to stay here."

The Guardian's head inclined slightly in acknowledgement. There was a pause and he seemed to ruminate, the chin sinking by infinitesimal degrees. Jarrod waited nervously. Something was going on and he still had no idea of what it was. The Guardian hadn't come to him for polite conversation.

The head came up again. "Since you humans seem to like choices, let me give you a couple of alternatives. We can continue with the mental tests until I find you worthy of what would be an unprecedented intervention, or until you fail, or we can put it all to one ultimate test."

"There's a catch in here somewhere," Jarrod said, very much on his guard.

"Not really. If you opted for the one final test, it would be tougher than any of the individual ones; that goes without saying." The Guardian paused again. A quick black tongue flicked across the straight lips.

"I think there should be a physical as well as an intellectual component." The words came out slowly.

"What kind of physical component?" Jarrod asked.

The stretched smile curved up. "I haven't decided yet. You have not made the choice."

"Can I have some time to think this over?"

The Guardian said nothing. He blinked and then the head turned slowly back to the view over the park.

I assume that means no, Jarrod thought. He turned away and paced toward the bed. Take your time, he said to himself. Think things through first, act later, was what Greylock would have said. He straightened his shoulders and breathed in, deeply and slowly. He had already passed two of the Guardian's mental tests. The next one would be harder, of course, but at least he would know what sort of thing to expect. Maybe. What did he have to gain by risking everything on a single throw? Time; time was what he would save. There was no knowing how long the series of trials would go on. It would be pointless to win here and find everything back on Strand lost. He turned and started back, head bowed.

When it came down to it, he really didn't have a choice at all. He wished he knew what kind of a physical challenge it would be. He wished he was more athletic. A little late for that now. He stopped and raised his head.

"All or nothing, then," he said.

"As you wish." The Guardian showed neither satisfaction nor disappointment. "You appear quite fit, but I think that you would benefit from some structured exercise."

"What about Marianna?" Jarrod demanded, ignoring the remark.

The Guardian abandoned the view and turned to face him. Once again, the swirl of the cloak took too long to catch up. "I shall take your advice and offer her a choice as well."

"You must agree to return her to Strand if I fail," Jarrod said firmly.

The Guardian raised an eyebrow. "A little late to be making conditions, don't you think?" He sounded entirely reasonable. "Besides, I have already said that I will not hold you here against your wills."

"Can I see her?" Jarrod asked, civil in his turn.

"It's a perfect day outside," the Guardian returned, "as it always is. It will take me some time to program one of the servos, so your exercises won't start before tomorrow at the earliest. I'd take advantage of the respite and get some fresh air if I were you. The gardens are quite lovely." The bloodless smile reappeared. "Bye the bye, I almost forgot what I came here for. I should like to see the book that you brought with you."

"Yes, of course, sir." Jarrod was caught off-balance. "I should have taken it down to you before." He hurried to the bed and withdrew the oilskin package from under the pillow. He came back to the Guardian and held it out.

"I'm afraid you'll have to unwrap it and show it to me."

"Stupid of me," Jarrod said with a little shake of the head. He unwrapped it carefully and held it up so that the Guardian could see it. Then he opened it at random so that the Guardian could examine the pages.

"And it is supposed to be in my language, is it?" the

Guardian enquired as he moved forward. He stopped abruptly two feet away and his eyes widened. The head moved lower and the eyes narrowed; the lips compressed.

"Turn the page." The beautiful voice was abrupt and harsh.

Jarrod complied.

"Again."

The Strandsman stared at his peculiar host, knowing that the Guardian did not see him. The eyes were totally concentrated. They did not move from line to line as Jarrod's would have done. They flicked up and caught Jarrod's scrutiny.

"Extraordinary," the Guardian said. "Show me the beginning."

Jarrod reversed the book and found the title page. He turned the book around again. "Do you recognize it, sir?" he asked.

"It is in our tongue, though the calligraphy is utterly alien. It makes it very difficult to read. The copyist has made some mistakes as well, but"—he nodded toward the open book—"the title is perfectly clear. It says, 'Force Point Manual with Magnetic Field Tables.' That it should have survived at all is remarkable and for it to turn up here is an uncomputable improbability." The eyes bored in. "What do you know of its history?"

"Not very much, I'm afraid. It is said to be a copy of a book that was found on the continent that gave birth to our people. I'm not even sure that that continent really exists. It was given to me by the High Priestess of a temple in the south. It must have been there for at least a thousand years."

The Guardian smiled inwardly at the way the human had said, "at least a thousand years" as if that were some unimaginably long time. Outwardly he said, "That book is a tangible link with my ancestors and, as such, it is infinitely precious to me. I thank you, Jarrod Courtak of Strand, for returning a piece of my heritage to me. I shall treasure it." The smile creased his face again. "If you would put it on the table, I shall have the servo bring it down so I can examine it at my leisure.''

He watched Jarrod go over to the table and put the book on it. His universe never ceased to amaze him. Once upon a time so far gone that even he could not grasp it properly, an Initiator, setting up the grid on a nascent world, misplaced his manual and now, eons later, copied who knew how many times, it was back in the hands of the only representative of his race left in that whole universe. It was gratifying and unsettling. He smiled at the young human. For an instant he really hoped that the creature would survive.

''Thank you, once again,'' he said and began to move to the door. He turned at the threshold. ''Don't forget my advice about a walk in the garden.'' He smiled again and sailed out into the corridor.

A most satisfactory encounter, he thought before dematerializing.

Jarrod walked back and closed the door. Well, he thought, at least the book had proved worth lugging from one world to another. He turned back into the room and uneasiness set in immediately. What had he agreed to? He didn't know what he would be facing and he didn't even know when. It had seemed so logical a few minutes ago, but now it seemed pure folly. The room was suddenly small and airless. He had to get out. He strode quickly to the wardrobe and pulled out a thin robe and a pair of sandals.

The house was empty as he made his way through it and when he found an outside door, he half expected it to be locked. It opened easily, however, and he found himself in sunshine. A gravel path ran right and left and disappeared around the corner. He was on the far side of the house from his chamber and the lake was nowhere in sight. A slope of lawn stretched invitingly ahead. He surrendered to it and walked across its springy turf until he found to his surprise that it dropped away into a series of hidden terraces.

The level immediately below him contained a formal knot

garden of great complexity and variety. A heady crossweave of scents rose from the hedgelets and teased the memory. The level below that was a carpet of color. Below that he could not see, but a weathered stone stair led down and he used it. Below the beds of flowers was a grassy terrace set about with evergreens. There was a pleasant, shaded formality here. Trees ringed pieces of stone carved into massive shapes or were set around basins into which jetting waters fell. Graceful benches were placed strategically. It looked inviting and he turned aside.

Marianna's voice halted him. His name came floating down the stairs and he turned and saw her skipping towards him. He opened his arms wide and she ran into them. They hugged fiercely and then she tipped her head back.

"I was afraid that thing had killed you," she said. "It said you were all right, but I didn't believe it."

"No, I'm solid enough. You look a sight better than the last time I saw you. Have you been well treated?"

"I suppose you could say so." She was grudging. "If you don't mind being locked up and fed disgusting food. I've been bored."

Jarrod chuckled. "Cruel and inhumane treatment if ever I heard it."

"Don't you start with me," she said, linking an arm through his. "We've got too much to talk about. Let's go and sit on a bench and watch a fountain while you tell me everything you've found out about this Guardian thing."

When they had seated themselves, Marianna gave Jarrod a careful and wordless looking over. "Except for that ridiculous fuzz on your face, you don't look too bad," was her final comment.

Jarrod ran the back of his hand down his cheek. "No razor," he explained. "I don't think the Guardian wants me to have anything too sharp. My weapons have disappeared—so's my chainmail for that matter."

"Mine too. Your friend Ragnor's going to be more than a little unhappy."

"If we don't get back, he's never going to know," Jarrod replied.

"True enough, but I don't care to dwell on that. Now, tell me, what have you been up to?"

He gave her a twisted little smile. "Quite a lot, actually. Settle back and I'll fill you in."

He told her about finding himself in the big white room and of the tests that followed. He told her of the morning's conversation and the choice the Guardian had given him. "If I fail," he concluded, "he'll send you home safely."

"No it bloody well won't. It's my country that's being invaded. They won't let me fight for it down there, but they can't stop me fighting for it here. You aren't going to fail, but you're not the only representative of Strand either."

"Do you think I made the right choice?" Jarrod asked.

"I don't know about the right choice, but it's the one I would have made. Anyway, I've got a choice of my own to make. The old horror offered to let me visit Amarine."

"What did you tell him?"

"I told him that I would have to talk it over with you, which, I may add, is something that doesn't seem to have occurred to you to do."

"You're right," he admitted. "I should have talked to you about it before I gave him an answer. I just didn't think that he was going to let me see you."

"All the more reason," she replied tartly, "for insisting, wouldn't you think?"

"I'm sorry. I didn't think things through. He took me by surprise."

"Well, what's done is done," she said briskly and to his relief. "We have to decide what we do now."

"The test won't take place for a while. The Guardian says that I need to do exercises first."

"Exercises? What sort of exercises?"

"I haven't the slightest idea."

Marianna shook her head. "I hate the not knowing," she said. "I hate having to wait around and react. I hate being held hostage to someone else's whim."

"I know, I know, but what can we do about it? We need the Guardian's help and he doesn't need us at all."

"I don't care. There must be something we can do."

"We have to pass whatever tests he sets us: we have to convince him to restore the Force Point so that the Place of Power can come back."

"I know all that," she said impatiently. "I just get so frustrated. I haven't even had a chance to convince that monster about anything."

"Well, whatever you do, try not to aggravate him. I prefer to have him in a good mood."

Marianna looked at him and grinned. "Too late for that, I'm afraid. The one time I did see it, I gave it a piece of my mind."

"Yes I know," Jarrod said drily. "He said as much."

"I'll try to behave." She didn't sound convincing.

"I think we'll have to go along with whatever he wants. We can't force him to help us and we'll never get another chance."

She sighed. "I suppose you're right. Maybe a visit to Amarine isn't such a bad idea, providing he brings me back before you have to take this test. I don't think I could stand being cooped up. Perhaps Amarine will have an idea."

"I'd worry less if I felt that you were safe with the unicorns. If I fail, it will be up to you. Work on his conscience, make him feel guilty, do whatever you have to do. We must get the secret of the Great Spell back to Ragnor. Failing that, we have to have the Place of Power and Greylock restored."

She patted his hand. "You're not going to fail. You're tougher than you think you are. If you could survive what that Umbrian press gang did to you, you can survive anything that truncated lizard can come up with."

As she finished speaking, the air around them thickened abruptly. That was the only way that Jarrod could describe it. At one instant he was looking at her and in the next there was an opaque mist between them.

"Marianna?" he said and reached out to touch her. There was nothing there.

"Marianna!"

He lunged forward, arms out, and found himself face down on the four-poster. He was back in his own room. He began to curse, starting with Marianna's habitual litany and then going on to ring his own changes, all of them directed at the Guardian.

chapter 20

The Guardian was blithely unaware of Jarrod's invective. He had changed his mind about letting the humans fraternize and implemented his decision. He was more interested in what was happening on Strand. He wanted to know what had happened to the old man and found that he hoped that the creature had survived. The helmet floated towards him.

The scene was familiar by now, cramped, panelled walls, tiny windows, open fire and all. He was pleased to see the old one sitting up in the big bed. A female was sitting on an upright chair beside him. About the same age as the one upstairs, but with yellow hair. She was elaborately gowned and wore a collar of pink stones. A person of some rank, he judged. She was speaking and the Guardian adjusted the fine tuning.

"A triumph, dearest Nuncle. A total victory with remarkably few casualties."

"Unless you count the enemy's losses." The Archmage sounded gruff, but he was manifestly pleased.

"And you were clever enough to let the army take most of the credit."

Ragnor had done no such thing. The plain truth was that Nix had beaten him to the punch, but he smiled at the Princess Regnant as if sharing in the joke. He pushed himself up a bit and reached for the cup on the bedside table.

"You mustn't give me too many kudos," he said. "Sumner and Handrom are the real heros of the piece. They did all the work. Your ancient and obedient servant was flat on his face with an overzealous Apprentice sitting on him.''

She laughed at his description. "In that case," she said, "I suppose I ought to decorate them."

"Well, I don't think that you need to go that far," Ragnor said quickly. "We all strive for the good of the Discipline and the Kingdom."

"The Princess Regnant's smile was disingenuous, but the sparkle in her eyes made it clear that she knew what was at the back of the Archmage's mind.

"Whatever you say, Nuncle," she declared innocently.

"In that case, you can do me a favor."

"Willingly; what?"

Ragnor took a swig from the cup. He made a wry and disgusted face as he put it back. "Gods, but that stuff is foul," he said. "Did the army find anything that could help us understand the enemy? I got carried off the field before I could hear anything useful."

Arabella lifted her head slightly and pursed her lips. "Nix's report listed a score of suits and half a hundred fire weapons."

"No machinery?"

"Not according to Nix's report. Why?"

"Oh, I just hoped for some answers, that's all. How they had survived that long without revictualing from a base somewhere. How they kept their atmosphere intact in the face of all our weather assaults; something that would tell us more than the nothing we know."

"There is one thing we learned," she said compassionately, sensing the disappointment behind the attempt at levity.

"I am all ears, Highness."

"We learned that they are not invincible."

"Yes, there is that, I suppose." Ragnor sounded disgruntled.

"I think it's time I let you rest," Arabella said, rising from the chair. "Now, you are to promise me to obey your Wise-woman. You know that I should be lost without you."

"Nonsense," he replied. "I brought you up better than that. You are going to be one of the best rulers that Arundel will ever have." He paused and added wickedly, "Provided, of course, that you marry the right man."

"Nuncle." There was warning in the word.

He looked up at her, cloaked and poised for departure. Nothing to lose, he thought. "You can't duck the question forever, you know. I don't have to tell you how the Council feels about this. Where they and I differ is that they think you need a husband to rule the country and I think you need one who will ensure the succession and keep out of the way."

"Need I remind you," she interrupted icily, "that both you and the Council are there to give advice; no more."

"Spoken like your father," Ragnor said, unabashed. "I hope you haven't inherited his stubborn streak. I'm not trying to suggest that you are not perfectly capable of running the Kingdom. What I am saying is that you need to produce an heir. The country can't afford a civil war if anything should happen to you."

"I am reminded," Arabella said, "that I have a judgment session in the Great Hall. I am also reminded that a certain Chief Justicar has been notable for his absence from the courtroom of late."

Ragnor leaned back against the bolsters and put his hands behind his head. He knew that he was on safe ground again—just so long as he did not mention the succession. "It is remarkable," he said pleasantly, "that tales of miscarriage of justice have not reached me."

"You are impossible," she said, turning on her heel.

That's my girl, he thought as he watched her straight, sen-sible, shoulders-back walk to the door. She turned at the lintel.

"You behave yourself," she said. "If I were your Wise-woman, I should poison you." She gave him a smile that was more practised than sincere and swirled out of the room, leaving a faint aroma of attar of lavender behind her.

Ragnor inhaled and settled back. Her mother had worn the same perfume. Now, there was a woman. . . . He drifted away into memory.

"Your pardon, my Lord Archmage." The Duty Boy's voice brought him back to the present.

Ragnor looked up, annoyed. "Yes, what is it?"

"His Excellency the Chief Warlock of Talisman craves admittance."

This one has a taste for titles, Ragnor thought and the innocent but earnest foible restored his spirits. "Show him in; by all means, show him in," he said with a flourish.

The boy bowed and then stood aside. Sumner's entrance was a considerable anticlimax.

"Give you goodday, Archmage, I trust that you are feeling better?"

"Fair to middlin', thank you, but I don't suppose you came here to discuss my health."

Sumner's distaste for Ragnor's circumvention of etiquette was patent and it bolstered Ragnor's good humor.

"In great part, Archmage, in great part. Your well-being is of concern to us all." This ritual insincerity was accompanied by little nods and hand gestures of indeterminate meaning.

Ragnor looked at him with a smile and a skeptical eye. What in the world is he after? Doesn't he know that he can't play suave? "What can I do for you?"

"Well, Archmage, I was just thinking that, with the Outland threat gone, there is no reason to keep the Cloak of Protection in place."

"Quite right, Sumner. As soon as the blasted Wisewoman gives the word, I'll take it down."

Sumner did a little shuffle worthy of a scholarship candidate. "Well, that's just the point, Archmage. I thought it would be good for morale if the Cloak came down as soon as possible—now that the danger has been banished. If you aren't up to it, I should be more than happy to . . .'' The words died away.

I'll wager you would, Ragnor thought. ''No need for you to worry yourself. Your point is well taken.''

''But, Archmage . . .''

Ragnor held up an imperious hand. ''We have taken up too much of your time for Arundel's sake. I know that the people of Talisman wait impatiently for your return. I do appreciate all you have done and I shall not forget it.'' He smiled and nodded enthusiastically at Sumner.

The Guardian willed the helmet away. He had learned all that he needed to know; besides, it had been all subtext and no action. But then, if he wanted action, he had only to watch his new guests. He would certainly keep his eye on the female. Her interaction with the unicorns should be interesting. As for the male, he would be put through his paces. He would be able to enjoy the creature's physicality at first hand, watch the play of muscles, the movement of the limbs. Yes, he was looking forward to that.

He was also aware of a sneaking desire to see the human fight. It was against all the ethics of his race, of course. It was one thing to allow a species to rise and fall in the natural order of things, but it was a very different matter to knowingly manipulate a sentient being into a position where it could hurt, even kill, or risk being hurt. It was the beauty and vitality of the movement that was so captivating. He wondered if this pair had any talent for dancing. He would enjoy seeing them dance—naked. Add the spice of danger and . . .

The Guardian stopped the thought. Concentrate instead on the exercises for the male. Human bodies needed exercise and in fact he was doing the creature a favor. No reason why it should not practise with the weapons used on its world. He would have to program a servo to help train it. An intriguing challenge. If he started on it now, he ought to have one by morning. First, though, he would have to do a little close research on some of the earlier tapes to find out just how the fighting was done. He smiled. Yes indeed, an interesting project.

Jarrod woke to the clatter of a tray being put down. Sunlight spilled into the room as the curtains were drawn back. He got out of bed and went to clean his mouth. He peered into the looking-glass and ran his fingers through the short silky beard. Given time, he thought, it could look rather dashing. Marianna's words the previous day still rankled.

When he was finished he went back into the room and tackled the breakfast. He was on his second mug of hot liquid when the door opened and the machine man returned. It stopped and pointed to the bed. Jarrod swivelled around to see what it was pointing at and spotted something on the bed. He got up and investigated. A breachclout and a pair of sandals. He shrugged out of his robe, put them on and then turned to go to the wardrobe. The servant stopped him and pointed to the door. Jarrod shrugged and went out into the corridor.

They left the house by the door that Jarrod had used the day before, but this time they stayed on the gravel path. The metal man accelerated smoothly away and Jarrod ran to catch up with it. They passed the massive flight of steps that led up to the front door, came back parallel with the lake and around the corner to the starting point. The metal man kept going and Jarrod settled into a steady pace behind it. The exercises had begun.

An hour of running, by Jarrod's estimate, half an hour of jumping, bending and stretching. His muscles ached and sweat was streaming off him. When the instructor pointed to the lake, he plunged in gratefully. He noticed that the instructor did not follow him. He turned on his back and kicked slowly to the middle. The birds kept out of his way, but they did not fly off. The sky was cloudless, the water cooling. He felt both invigorated and at peace.

He ate the midday meal in his room and was contemplating a nap when the mechanical man intruded. Jarrod followed him reluctantly. He had begun to stiffen up and another session of exercises held little appeal. He went through the routine anyway and felt better when it was over. A long hot bath and an early bed would provide the perfect coda to the day.

That hope was dashed when he returned to his room and saw that a suit of what he would call Court clothes was laid out on the bed. He went and took the long hot bath. The sun was setting when he emerged and he went and watched it for a bit. It was strange not to see a daymoon and he felt a twinge of homesickness. He turned resolutely away from the windows before it could take hold and went and got into the grand outfit. He hoped that the Guardian was going to provide dinner and provide it fairly soon. The exercise had stropped his appetite.

The silent servant led him down to a smaller room on the ground floor. The Guardian was seated at the head of a table and Jarrod was happy to see that food had been set out. He looked around for Marianna, but there was no sign of her.

"Ah, there you are. Come on in and sit down." The Guardian sounded jovial.

"Thank you, sir," Jarrod replied and pulled out the chair to the Guardian's left. There were forks and spoons in front of him, but none on the other side of the table.

"Will the Lady Marianna be joining us?" he asked, trying to keep the nervousness out of his voice.

"Alas no, but I am sure that she is much happier with her friend Amarine than she would be here."

"She accepted your offer then?"

"She did indeed, with the proviso that she return when you are ready for testing."

Jarrod had wanted her to go, but now that she had gone, he rather wished she hadn't. He composed his face into a smile. "I'm sure you are right. I'm just sorry she couldn't see me in my finery."

"I'm glad you like it. I noticed it when I was viewing tapes of Strand and I copied it."

The Guardian broke off as the servant placed a variety of dishes within Jarrod's reach. It provided a plate and a glass, which it filled with what turned out to be a very passable wine. As soon as it had withdrawn, the Guardian began to ask questions about Strand. He pressed Jarrod for his opinions on Ragnor, Sumner, Dean Handrom, even the Princess Regnant. His questions showed that he was frighteningly well informed.

When Jarrod's last plate had been cleared, a sweet-tasting, blue drink was served in a small glass. Jarrod sniffed it before he took his first sip. A slightly lickerish odor, not at all unpleasant. He put the glass down carefully. He was feeling sleepy again and he had no intentions of getting drunk. He wished that the Guardian would stop asking questions and let him go to bed.

"You are a very warlike race," the Guardian remarked. "Always fighting or training to fight."

"We have to be," Jarrod replied. "The Outlanders have seen to that."

"Do you blame them?"

"For what they've done to us over the centuries I do. Other than that, I really don't know what to think. One of the young unicorns thinks that they were there before we were. Is he right?"

"He is."

"I was afraid of that."

"Does it make any difference?" The voice was warm and melodic, inviting confidences.

"It ought to," Jarrod admitted, "but it doesn't change the fact that they are trying to wipe us out. It could become a moot point in the not too distant future."

"You are a highly adaptable species," the Guardian said. "You have overcome far greater hurdles in the past. In fact it could be argued that yours is the most successful species in my universe."

Jarrod had passed a point of tiredness and was beginning to feel wakeful again. "Your universe?" he said. "Did you create all this?"

"Create it?" The Guardian chuckled, a sound at odds with the musical voice. "Oh dear me no. It's just that I have been looking after things for so long that I've become a mite possessive. No, my race observed the creation and established the grid. There was much debate at the time as to whether the grid would attach itself to coalescing matter, or if the matter would condense around the grid. If the latter is true, we could be said to have formed this universe, although we did not create it."

"Who did then?"

"Ah, now we come to the mystery of the Primal Cause. There are almost as many theories about that as there are galactic systems."

Jarrod held up a hand. "Spare me, my lord. I don't know what a galactic system is, but I have enough trouble visualizing dozens of worlds scattered among the stars."

"I keep forgetting what a cultural shock this all must be to you. Your world is still one of superstition and face-to-face combat." He noticed that the human bridled slightly at the description. "Bye the bye," he said, "have you ever fought in a battle?"

"Not in the sense of wielding a sword, but I was involved in one battle and in the recapture of a fortress."

"But you were raised to be able to fight and, if necessary, to kill," the Guardian persisted.

What's he getting at? Jarrod wondered uneasily. "Not really," he replied, "but that was because I was Talented. Most boys, most boys of my class anyway, start learning how to handle a sword when they are about eight." He gave a puckered little smile. "At one point the King himself was going to give me lessons, but he was killed before they started."

"Perhaps I can remedy that for you," the Guardian interposed. "One of the servos could be adapted. It would help to build you up, and you might just as well learn something that will be of value to you later while you are preparing for the test."

Hope flared in Jarrod. It was the first indication that the Guardian was prepared to do anything helpful; and it seemed to assume that he would eventually be returned to Strand. "That's very kind of you, sir," he said.

"Not at all; you are a guest," the Guardian said knowingly. "And speaking of that, I should be remiss in my hostly duties if I prevented you from getting your rest."

Jarrod took a last sip from his glass and pushed his chair back. "Thank you for dinner, my Lord Guardian," he said politely.

"I have enjoyed our conversation. We must repeat the experience."

Jarrod bowed and made his way out of the room. He expected the metal man to be waiting outside the door for him, but the corridor was empty. He went back to his room wondering about the evening. The Guardian had made no mention of yesterday's forcible separation; but, on the other hand, he seemed to be genuinely interested in Strand. Jarrod had no clear sense that the Guardian had been won over, however. Oh well, he thought as he undressed, take it one day at a time.

Morning came in with the breakfast tray. Despite the big meal of the previous night, he was hungry. He ate first and washed afterwards and wasn't surprised to find the metal man in the room when he emerged. A new routine was beginning to form. The breachclout and sandals were back on the bed. He donned them and followed. The stairs brought out the soreness in his leg muscles, but a lap or two around the house dispelled the ache and by the time he had finished his swim he felt glowingly well.

He ate his lunch with gusto and had just gone to sit out on

the balcony when the bronze man reappeared. Jarrod felt lethargic after the meal, but he followed obediently. To his surprise, the figure turned right at the bottom of the stairs. They went a way down the corridor, turned right into another one and then took a flight of stairs down. The passageway was narrower at this level and the subtle odor of disuse was in the air. It was colder too. They took about twenty paces and the metal man stopped in front of a door, opened it and vanished inside. Jarrod followed and found himself standing on sawdust.

He was in a large circular chamber. It was windowless, but light came from the ceiling in a bright wash. There were no shadows. There was a long bench by the door and above it hung two swords and two small round shields. The metal man was standing by them. The Guardian had lost no time, Jarrod thought. It pointed to Jarrod's feet and mimed taking off the sandals. Jarrod took them off. It pointed to the breachclout and mimed again. Jarrod hesitated, then shrugged and unwrapped it. He went over and dropped it on the bench. He checked the room again, but there was no one to see them.

The metal man took down one of the shields and strapped it on the left arm. He took the other and handed it to Jarrod. He turned it over. It was made of thick leather stretched over a metal frame. There were metal studs around the rim and a stubby boss in the middle. Two leather straps crossed the inside and Jarrod slipped his arm through them. The shield stretched form elbow to wrist. The metal man reached for a sword and Jarrod followed suit.

He tested the balance and ran a thumb over the edges. They were dull. Not a killing weapon then. He made a couple of cuts through the air. The hilt was comfortable in his hand. The metal man moved past him and took up a stance in the center of the floor. It faced Jarrod, legs apart, in a slight crouch, sword and shield in front of it. Jarrod realized that this was the first time that he had seen those legs operate separately. He approached it and copied the pose.

They circled, feinting, probing, and then the instructor, as Jarrod was coming to think of him, attacked. Jarrod countered, but was forced to give ground. The sword came for his head and he threw up his left arm to block it. An instant later his right side was stinging from the slap of the blade and the instructor was back in its crouch. They circled again and the metal man did precisely what it had done before. Jarrod gritted his teeth as another red welt sprang up on his side. By the third time he had devised a counter and by the fifth time he had improved upon it. He was sweating hard.

The lesson went on until he was panting and his arms and legs were heavy. His hair was in his eyes and he didn't have a free hand to push it out of the way. His beard itched. The instructor's blade was landing less often, but it was ultimately a losing proposition. The bloody thing never got tired, never made a mistake. He took a deep breath, hefted his sword and brought his shield arm up a little higher. The metal man nodded, straightened up and dropped the point of its sword to the sawdust. Jarrod let his arms drop with relief. It was over, at least for today.

chapter 21

Jarrod woke up to the clatter of the tray. He rolled over and gave an indrawn hiss of pain and surprise. He was stiff and his sides hurt. He got out of bed awkwardly and shuffled wincingly over to the table. He felt like an old man. He lowered himself gingerly into the chair and then addressed the breakfast with a will. He felt better after that and better still after a soak in the tub. He was not particularly happy to see the metal man, but he donned the breachclout and sandals without a word.

In the afternoon he was led through the moves that he had mastered the day before. The pace was brisker and there were fewer repetitions. He was beginning to feel at his ease when his instructor introduced a variation and dumped him unceremoniously on his back. He was on the sawdust half a dozen times in the next hour, but he learned how to cope with that ploy. There was even one triumphant moment when his swordpoint rang against the metal chest before glancing away.

He was pleased when the session ended early and put it down to his improvement. He was disabused on returning to his room by the sight of the Court clothes waiting for him on the bed. He grimaced in annoyance and went to slake his thirst. He turned from side to side in front of the looking-glass, hoping to see some improvement in his physique, but his arms and legs still looked too thin and his chest had no definition to speak of. He made a face at himself and went and drew the bath.

The servant came for him and escorted him to the room

where he had dined before. The Guardian was waiting, as before, ensconced in an armchair at the head of the table. He was wearing black this time and Jarrod saw that it was decorated with a fall of glittering stars. He remarked on it as he took his place.

"It is attractive, isn't it?" The Guardian replied, clearly pleased by the compliment. "Another of the lagniappes of studying Strand. This, or something very like it, was worn by one of your Magicians a long time ago. I saw it when I was viewing one of the old tapes. An interesting character he was too. He seems to crop up on a number of them. If it really was the same person, he would have lived for about a thousand of your years, but I imagine that it is simply a case of a very strong family resemblance over the generations."

"Not necessarily," Jarrod said and took a spoonful of the soup that had been placed in front of him. "Errathuel, who is the father of Magic, was Archmage for centuries." The soup was a distinct improvement over the previous version.

"Is that so? It could be the same fellow, I suppose. The one I saw pops up within a couple of generations of the colony's foundation."

"Colony?" Jarrod enquired, looking up.

"Yes. Your remote ancestors came to the planet from another world. They were scientifically sophisticated, but not notably wise, and the culture regressed rapidly once the original settlers and their children were dead. One of the strange things about that Magician of yours, or whoever he was, was that he was so much taller than the rest. You may be taller than most of your compatriots, but he was a giant compared to the others. Given the circumstances, it is an unusual phenomenon."

"There are lots of stories about Errathuel," Jarrod said as his soup bowl was cleared and something resembling a meat and mangelwurzel stew was put in its place. "There are those who believe that he is still alive and will become Archmage again in times of peril." The Guardian nodded encouragingly. "I don't believe it myself," Jarrod added. "I mean, if he was going to reappear, now would certainly be the time." He felt rather pleased at the way he had managed to work the present danger into the conversation.

"Ah yes, the sleeping champion. It's a common myth among early societies. I'm not even sure if your world is unique in making him a Magician, but I think not. You are wise not to count on him."

There was a note of irony in the utterance, but Jarrod missed it. "We don't," he said. "That's why Marianna and I are here."

"That reminds me," the Guardian said, "she is riding around happily on Amarine and seems to be developing a fondness for swimming."

"She swims better than I do," Jarrod said, remembering the river crossing, "and riding when you are connected to the unicorn is one of the greatest experiences I've ever had. I rather envy her."

"Well, you are certainly getting enough exercise here. Tell me, how do you find your lessons?"

"Instructive and somewhat painful, sir."

The Guardian laughed. "Neatly put. I'm glad they are not too simple for you."

"Those are not the words that I would use to describe them."

"I must admit that I'm pleased with the outcome. It was a difficult program to write."

Jarrod didn't understand what he meant. "I'm grateful, of course," he said, "but I do have one question."

"By all means."

"Why do I have to practise naked?"

"Oh that," the Guardian said easily. "I feel that you will learn faster if you are, ah, exposed; especially the defensive moves." The unnerving smile was back.

"I see," Jarrod said, and it did make sense in a way. He glanced at his host. The Guardian seemed relaxed. The yellow eyes glittered, but that was because of the candles. He decided to risk another question. He drank some wine first.

"Have you decided when this final test is going to take place?" he asked as casually as he could.

"Quite soon; when I judge that you are ready."

"Am I to know what it is?" Jarrod ventured.

"I haven't made up my mind yet, but I shall let you know when I do." The smile reappeared.

"But will it be entirely physical?" Jarrod persisted.

"I am inclining that way," the Guardian returned.

"But I thought you said that physical tests were irrelevant since you, ah . . ." Jarrod gestured feebly with his right hand.

"Well, let us suppose that I have fathomed the extent of your mental capacity, found it wanting, and have decided to allow you to try to compensate on the physical side." The Guardian smiled enigmatically.

He was no wiser than before, but Jarrod knew that he would get no more, and concentrated on finishing the stew. The meal continued through another course and a glass of the blue liqueur. The talk picked up again, about Weatherwarding for the most part. The Guardian spoke of the machines he used to control what he called his climate zones and Jarrod tried to look interested and intelligent, but most of it went over his head. Dismissal came as a relief.

The routine of exercise and sword practice continued and, on most days, Jarrod felt that he had made an improvement. They were offset by the days on which his body seemed to forget everything that had been dinned into it. Overall, though, he was pleased. His speed and stamina had increased and, after a sennight, he was rarely disarmed by the instructor. He collected a few new bruises, but he managed to avoid being dumped on the floor. Better still, the finery did not reappear. He ate supper in his room and went to bed early, in part because he was tired and in part for want of anything better to do. He woke looking forward to the day's activities.

He woke one morning and found the Guardian in the room. The head and cloak turned toward him as if the Guardian had known the very instant he had come awake.

"Good morning, Jarrod."

"Give you good morning, my lord, and may the best of the day be before you," Jarrod replied formally.

"Forgive this intrusion, but I know that you are anxious to hear about the upcoming trial. I have thought long and hard about the matter and I have come to a decision."

Jarrod propped himself up and waited.

"You are fit, you are well coached and, as I have said before, you come from a naturally belligerent race. In fact, from my observation, your world prizes physical accomplishment over mental ability."

Jarrod felt a knot begin to form in his stomach. He knew what was coming.

"I have decided, therefore," the Guardian continued, "that this 'all or nothing' test will take the form of personal combat."

The knot consolidated and nervous skitters took place underneath his breastbone. "And what if I refuse?"

"I shall return you to your world."

"And if I win?"

"I shall return you to your world, but I shall also reactivate the Force Point and I shall give you a resonator to replace the one that your friend had."

"What about the Great Spell?" Jarrod asked, propelled by his anxiety.

"There is no Great Spell," the Guardian said flatly.

"What about Marianna?" Jarrod pressed.

"That is entirely up to her."

"And what happens if I lose?"

"You die." The Guardian was perfectly matter-of-fact.

"I see. And what happens to Marianna then?"

The bloodless smile appeared. "That is entirely up to her."

A sudden thought struck Jarrod. "I won't fight Marianna," he said firmly.

The Guardian chuckled. "I had not thought of that."

"I won't fight naked."

"A pity; but if you insist."

"I do insist," said Jarrod firmly. "And I want to know who I am going to fight."

"All in good time," the Guardian replied. "I can promise you that you will be most evenly matched."

"And when do you propose to stage this little bout?" Jarrod was relieved that his voice had remained under control.

"Tomorrow," the Guardian said briskly. "Do I take it that you accept?"

"I didn't realize that I had a choice," he said sarcastically.

"Of course you have a choice." The Guardian was urbane. "I have already told you that I would send you home if you did not care to compete." The words were carefully chosen.

The victim went willingly to his death, Jarrod thought bitterly. He could see through this scrim of considerateness. Not such a sophisticated being when you got down to it. "Of course I accept," he said. "I should have known what to expect when you arranged the course in swordsmanship."

The Guardian smiled his cryptic smile. "If you survive, the lessons should prove invaluable on your home world."

"Most thoughtful of you, my lord." The bitterness was overt. "May I ask again who, or what I shall be fighting?"

"The name is immaterial," the Guardian said. "You will be your opponent's equal in every way." The smile reappeared and this time it touched the eyes. "I think that I can assure you that this will be the 'fairest' match that has ever been arranged. Meanwhile, you shall have the day to yourself. If you feel like having one more session with the servo, it is at your disposal."

"Is Marianna back?" Jarrod asked.

"She will be here tomorrow."

"Shall I be able to talk to her?"

The Guardian thought about it. "Not before the fight," he pronounced. "I promise you, though, that you will have ample time to make your farewells, should that become necessary."

"Won't do me much good if I'm dead," Jarrod retorted.

"You will have ample time. You have my word on that. Please do not have any worry on that account. Now, I have taken up too much of your time. I shall leave you to your morning meal." The Guardian bowed his head and vanished.

Jarrod did not care to contemplate the implications about his having ample time for farewells should he be killed. He got out of bed and headed for the washroom. Well, now you know what the final test is, he told himself. Hand-to-hand combat. He would have done better to stick with the mental tests, but it was too late for that now. What an irony; that it should all come down to the one thing he was worst at. He wished that Marianna was around to talk to. It was going to be a very long day.

He woke to the familiar sounds of the breakfast arriving and rolled over when the sun burst in. Then it hit him: this was the day. No run, no exercises, no swim, just a fight to the death with a mystery opponent. There was a cold spider's web in his stomach. He swallowed to get the moisture back into his mouth, then he threw back the covers with a deliberate gesture and got out of bed.

He ate sparingly and then did his bending and stretching exercises. He sat cross-legged on the floor and went through his litany of concentration. He emerged calm. A kind of fatalism had come over him, but he knew what was at stake, what he was fighting for. This was how he could serve Strand best. Had the Oracle know of this when it prophesied?

The metal man interrupted him, carrying a sword and a shield. It put them on the bed and Jarrod went over to examine them. The shield was new, still had that distinctive leather smell, but otherwise it was the twin of the one he had used in practice. The sword was nicely balanced, the grip comfortable. He made a couple of passes through the air. It felt like an extension of his arm. It didn't take a thumb to tell that both edges were sharp or that the point was deadly. This, he thought, was when the Archmage's mail would have come in useful. Instead he took the breachclout that the servant had fetched. He tied it securely and then put the sandals on.

"Are we going to go straight down?" he asked.

The metal man turned towards the door and Jarrod strapped the shield onto his left forearm. He picked up the sword and walked over to the casement window. He looked at the trees and the water and the birds for a long moment and then turned and followed the bronze back out of the room.

He was led to a different door on the ground floor and once through it, found himself outside. He stopped, his feet on sand, and looked around in surprise. He had run around the house countless times in the last sennight, but he had never seen anything like this. A high wall, seemingly made of grey stone, stretched in a semicircle around him. The sandy area enclosed was about half the size of a tilting yard and parkland scents were wafting over it, born by a light breeze. Straight ahead of him, at the apex of the curve, was a slim shaft of white marble. There was a stone chair atop it.

Jarrod walked cautiously out into the middle and turned in a slow circle. None of this had been here before, he was certain of it. Not the wall, not the balcony with its wrought iron railings; he wouldn't have missed a balcony with no window or door behind it. There was a chair, however, a miniature copy of the throne in the white room. He looked for the door through which he had entered and could not find it. He walked back and forth studying the enclosure.

Other than the fact that it was empty, nothing seemed amiss, although Jarrod didn't care for the footing. He broke into a sudden run and then pulled up sharply. The sandals skidded and he had to use both sword and shield to keep his balance. He put them down and took the sandals off. He was straightening up when the sound of trumpets made him grab the sword. He looked around warily and saw that the Guardian now occupied the throne. Nothing else seemed to have changed.

"Give you goodday, Jarrod Courtak of Strand." The rich voice carried easily and Jarrod realized that the Guardian was using the Formal mode. He hadn't done that before.

"May the best of the day before us both, Great Lord," he replied carefully.

"I bring you greetings from the Lady Marianna."

The sound of her name triggered the anxiety that Jarrod had been holding at bay and his grip on the hilt tightened.

"If you turn around," the Guardian continued, "you will see that I keep my promises."

Jarrod turned and there was Marianna, sitting in the stone chair. She was wearing a long, white, pleated tunic and her hair was down around her shoulders. She did not acknowledge him in any way. He started towards her.

"She is perfectly well," the voice said. "She can see and hear everything, but I have taken the precaution of making her immobile. She is an impulsive creature and I do not want anything to disturb your concentration."

Jarrod stopped and swallowed. He stared up her, up there, above it all. Her face was in shadow and there was no way for him to guess what she was feeling. Affronted, if he knew her. He turned back reluctantly and went and retrieved the shield and his sandals. The latter he deposited by the wall, next to where he judged the door to have been. He strapped the shield back on his arm and then returned to the center of the enclosure.

"You know what is required," the Guardian said. "You will fight until one of you can fight no more."

"And where is my opponent?" Jarrod asked. His inner misgivings were meshing into quiet anger.

"Behold." The Guardian nodded towards the middle of the arena.

Jarrod shifted his stance and brought his swordpoint up. There was a shimmering, like the heat dance on a plain. A shape took on form within it and solidified into the figure of a tall man. The sun was behind it and Jarrod could make out no details. The man was broad-shouldered, but not notably muscular, with long curly hair. He was carrying a sword and the shield on his left arm was the same as the one that Jarrod had. The newcomer took a step forward and stared. Jarrod shifted slowly to his right and as his opponent turned to keep himself squared on, the sun found the left side of his face. The hair was dark brown, the eyes blue, the nose was strong and the mouth large. The man was clean-shaven, but Jarrod knew him, had seen hundreds of him in the Guardian's maze.

The Guardian's laugh brought both heads round.

"I told you that you would be evenly matched and you've both had the same series of lessons. Now, what could be fairer than that?" The laughter came again.

"Is he real?" Jarrod demanded.

"Every bit as real as you are."

"And you expect me to fight myself?"

"Only if you wish to help your kind, and if you want to live." He sounded urbane and sure.

"And what does he get if he wins?" Jarrod asked, pitching his voice so that it would reach the balcony.

"He gets his life. He remains real and that, believe you me, is a prize that he values above all else." The Guardian looked down at them and chuckled.

"This is ridiculous," Jarrod declared, irked.

"On the contrary. It is reasonable and eminently just. It is also extraordinarily ingenious." The Guardian was clearly pleased with himself.

"I can't go through with this," Jarrod said.

"I am afraid that your time for choice is past."

The Guardian shifted on his scaled-down throne and the sunlight made the cloak glow redly. It seemed to bulk out, the head to grow larger.

"Combatants!" The voice rang out. "This challenge is to the death. You both know what rewards victory will bring." There was a fractional pause, and then,

"You may engage at will."

Jarrod looked over at his rival, not knowing quite how to take the Guardian's performance. Seriously, he thought. The other man had already dropped into a fighting crouch. The shield was up, the sword ready. Jarrod assumed the identical stance with the feeling that he was caught in a bad dream. The figure facing him was grim and alert. I hope I look that formidable, Jarrod thought. If we're that much alike, perhaps . . . He reached out with his mind, but there was nothing there. Could this be another of the Guardian's machines?

They began to circle one another, swords darting briefly, retreating, shield arms moving from side to side. Twice they circled slowly, testing reflexes, assessing probable speed. If I close suddenly, Jarrod thought, and found himself bracing as the other charged. Swords clashed and shield met shield. They were breast to breast, no room to swing, shoving, breathing into one another's face, struggling for advantage.

"Who are you?" Jarrod hissed through bared teeth.

"Jarrod Courtak." Each word was clipped and accompanied by a shove.

"Where did you come from?"

"Came from the unicorns with Marianna."

"Liar!"

They sprang apart and began to circle again. Stay in control, Jarrod told himself. Think. He needed to know more and name-calling wasn't going to get it for him. He'd have to close again. He moved gradually closer until he knew he was in range. When his opponent thrust for him, Jarrod stepped inside and pinned the arm under his shield. They were chest to chest, beard rasping against smooth jaw, locked in an awkward, furious, dance.

"Before the unicorns. Where did you come from before the unicorns?" Jarrod said in his ear.

He felt a small hesitation and then his double resumed his effort to break the clinch. Jarrod held him.

"Before the Island at the Center," he insisted. He pulled his head back and looked the other in the eye. "Who was your mother?"

The lips drew apart into a snarl. "No before," the man said. "No before!" The words were shouted and accompanied by a massive, twisting heave that broke Jarrod's hold and sent him staggering back.

The man followed up with an overhand attack that had Jarrod backpedalling, blocking with the shield. Gradually the force of the blows lessened as the other man began to tire and Jarrod was able to stand his ground and parry the swings that were aimed at his body. He brought his breathing under control. No before. No memory of Strand, then. This daunting other self was a creation of the Guardian, but the Guardian could not know his past. There should be an advantage there. Superior experience—but not, he reminded himself, in hand to hand combat.

A quick thrust got past his guard and grazed Jarrod's ribs. A bright line of red sprang up and little individual drops of blood began to slide down. The thrust had been anything but half-hearted, a few inches to the left and the fight would have been over. Concentrate, he told himself, as they went back into their shuffling crouch. His determination hardened. He was no longer aware of the Guardian, or of Marianna. His world was confined to sand and sun and his other self.

Where were the weaknesses? They ought to have the same weaknesses and Jarrod knew that, on certain days, he responded a little slowly to a left-to-right attack. He moved in swiftly, blade swinging, checking and reversing. His opponent blocked the stroke neatly and then slashed for his legs. Not today, Jarrod thought as he danced out of range. He was panting again and sweat sheened his skin. The same was true of his opponent.

He launched out on a whim, trying to take the man by

surprise, but to no avail. They exchanged blows and retreated again. Very well, let him carry the pace for a while. Defense was less tiring than attack. What would I do? Go for the head and try and force me to look into the sun. No sooner thought than he was defending against it. His shield went up and metal crunched against it, jarring his whole arm. His counter was batted aside, making him stumble forward. Steel cracked against the shield again. He swung weakly, trying to regain his balance.

He saw the swordpoint coming for his left side as it had done before. The edge of his shield came up and deflected it, barely. He felt the sharp dart of pain in his shoulder and spun away. He turned back to fend off further assault, but there was no follow-up. He risked a look at his shoulder. A flap of skin was hanging and blood flowed. He moved the left arm. No pain; he had been lucky. He had also been careless. He had known that the lunge was coming.

He watched his rival closely. The man was tiring. The sweat was pouring down his face and his chest was working hard. Jarrod wasn't feeling any too fresh himself, but he judged that the other man had expended more effort. He attacked, striking low and then high before he thrust. The other gave ground and Jarrod harried him. The defense was marginally slower, but it sufficed. More was needed.

"Where were you born?" Jarrod taunted and was rewarded by a flicker of something in the eyes. Just what, he could not tell. He moved to the left and swung hard for the shield.

"Strand," he panted. "We were born on Strand. If I win, the Guardian will save our people; if I lose, they will be annihilated. Will the Guardian save them if you win?"

The opponent shook his head, as if in annoyance. "I do not know. I do not want to kill you, but I must. You have already lived a long time. I am just beginning."

The newcomer followed up his words with a slashing, wild attack. Jarrod gave ground, parrying and taking as much as he could on his shield. The blows continued. Jarrod's sword-arm ached. He wasn't aware of his shoulder, but the shield was getting very heavy. I can't keep this up much longer, he thought, and neither can he. Their swords crossed and Jarrod turned his wrist and leapt to the side. His enemy spun to follow him, but did not advance. They stood glaring at each other.

He's going to come in and try to finish me off, Jarrod thought, and came up onto the balls of his feet. I've got to get the upper hand. I've got to do something he doesn't expect. He's tired, his reactions will be slow. He saw the slight shift in his opponent's stance. The attack was coming. Jarrod turned and ran.

The twin hesitated and then, with a roar, gave chase. The advantage of surprise gave Jarrod a ten-pace start, but his lead began to erode. Jarrod saw the second shadow creep up, he could hear the rasping breath. The shadow sword came up past his shoulder. He swerved hard left and pulled up short. The other, at full tilt, dug in his heels, but his sandals lacked purchase on the sand. He skidded past and as he did, Jarrod's sword swept out and cut down across the back of his leg, hamstringing him. The man went down, blood spurting. Jarrod took two quick paces and placed his sword's point behind his double's ear.

"Well done."

Jarrod was only dimly aware of the melodious voice. He was staring down at his opponent. He could see the muscles of the jaw working and hear the stifled moan.

"What are you waiting for? Kill him."

Jarrod heard the voice this time and he shivered. There was a feral, needy sound to it. He threw the sword down and walked away. His breathing was coming back under control. He turned and looked up at the balcony.

"You created him. You kill him," he said. "That's not my responsibility."

"This is a fight to the death," the Guardian insisted coldly.

"It was a fight to the finish and it is finished," Jarrod said determinedly. He was suddenly tired and his legs were trembling. The smell of blood was in his nostrils, sweet, cloying. "Whoever, whatever, he is, he fought bravely. He doesn't deserve to die; not by my hand anyway."

There was silence. The Guardian's head did not move and Jarrod was too far away to see an expression. It didn't matter anyway. He might have won the fight, but he had lost all his chances. He turned back to the arena. His opponent was still lying in the sand. Perhaps he had fainted with the loss of blood. Marianna was still in the chair, unchanged, unmoving.

"Are you resolved to defy me?" The voice from behind him was silky and dangerous.

Jarrod faced the Guardian once more. "I am not trying to defy you," he said wearily. "I just can't kill him, that's all. I'm not clever enough to explain it any better."

The Guardian rose from the throne and one didn't have to be close to know that he was angry. The column of scarlet stood out against the honey-colored stone like a vivid gash.

"Mortal, you are without a doubt the most irritating creature I have ever encountered."

Jarrod waited for his sentence. He hoped it would be quick. His shoulder was beginning to throb. He hoped it would be painless. Something deep inside, something he had no name for, rebelled. He was tired of being manipulated, tired of doing his best and finding that it wasn't good enough. His chin came up.

"Kill me if you like," he said, projecting his voice, hoping that Marianna could hear it, "but that other man, if that's the right word, hasn't done anything wrong. I tricked him. He lost because he has no experience. Let him live, and give the poor bastard the rest of my memories."

He stood there in the silence, his own breathing loud in his ears. Would the Guardian remember his promise about time to say goodbye? He started to turn so that he could see

Marianna. They had come so far together. The Guardian's voice stopped him.

"An interesting thought." He sounded calm. "I can always decide what to do with you later."

Jarrod tried to complete the turn, but the arena had disappeared. Then everything went dark.

chapter 22

Jarrod woke. That in itself was remarkable. He opened his eyes slowly. He was looking at a bed canopy. He recognised the hangings: he was back in the room. He moved his right leg and it responded. He was definitely alive. He quickly moved his other limbs. No pain; no soreness. He looked at his left shoulder. No bandage; no scar. He sat up. The room was unchanged. The curtains had been opened, the inevitable sun bleaching the floor and the carpet. The breakfast tray sat on the table. Had he dreamed it? Was this the day?

He got up and went to the washroom. He checked himself carefully in the looking-glass. There was no sign that he had been in a fight, and yet his memories seemed too specific to be the invention of dreamtime. There were those at home who believed that dreams foretold the future. If it had been a dream and they were right, would he still refuse to kill his seeming self? Was a flesh-and-blood illusion worth the future of Strand? He sighed and rinsed out his mouth. He was terribly thirsty.

He went back to the bedroom and looked at the tray. He was hungry, but if he was going to fight, he ought not to do it on a full stomach. It might slow him down. He poured a mug of the liquid and sipped it. If I stay here much longer, he thought, I'll have to think up a name for this. He heard the door open and looked round. The metal man came in and went straight to the wardrobe. It selected a light gown and a pair of sandals and laid them out on the bed. Then it left. No fighting, Jarrod thought, not yet anyway. He sat down and took the covers off the dishes.

He got dressed after breakfast and went down to look for signs of the walled arena. No one challenged him and the door was open. He found no trace of what he was looking for on this side. He started off to the left and, as he rounded the corner of the house, he saw a figure down at the water's edge. He recognized the long white tunic instantly.

"Marianna!" he yelled and ran down the slope pellmell. She turned and a huge smile lit her face. They hugged for a long time and then she pushed him back.

"Let me breathe, you great lug, and let's have a look at you." She scrutinized him carefully. "You don't seem any the worse for wear," she said. "The beard's longer and none the better for that." She gave a choking little laugh and averted her head. Her hair swept forward and hid her face. "In fact you look remarkably well for a dead man." She took a breath and then lifted her head, tossed her hair back and looked at him. There were tears in her eyes and she swallowed.

"So it was you in that chair," Jarrod said, relief and affection flooding him. He hugged her again and let her go.

"I certainly was." She was in control of herself again. "It's not an experience I'd care to repeat. How's your shoulder, by the way."

"Good as new." He grinned. "So good, in fact, that I thought I had dreamed the whole thing. What happened at the end?"

"After you had shouted at the Guardian? I don't know. I got the everything-goes-grey-and-back-to-your-room treatment. I haven't seen anybody since, or at least nobody that can talk. The important thing is that we're both alive."

"What do you think is going to happen now?"

She laughed. "I doubt even the gods know." She tucked an arm through his and they began to walk along the lake shore.

"I ruined everything, didn't I?" Jarrod said. "I threw it all away. I'm sorry, Marianna, I really am."

"Nonsense." She was brisk and dismissive. "You did what you had to do. It was a bloody good fight. I never knew you could fight like that—either of you. You have nothing to blame yourself for." She looked up at him and studied his face as if for the first time. "Was he really as like you as he seemed to be? If it hadn't been for your baby beard, I wouldn't have been able to tell you apart."

"It was like fighting in a looking-glass," Jarrod replied.

"Where did he come from?" She shook her head. "Stupid question. I wonder if there is anything the Guardian can't do."

"Well, whoever my double is, he knows about you and he knows about the unicorns, but he knows nothing about Strand."

"Oh, so that's what you were shouting about. It made no sense to me at the time. I just thought you'd snapped."

"I think you were probably right," he said with a wry smile, "but what are we going to do now?"

"Nothing we can do, is there?" she said cheerfully. "We wait upon the Guardian's pleasure."

She looked up at him again and saw the worried cast of his features. She joggled his arm. "Brooding isn't going to do any good," she said, "and there's no point in trying to second guess the old monster. We might as well make the most of whatever time we've got here."

"I know, I know, but it galls me."

She lengthened her stride, forcing him to step out. "I haven't had a chance to tell you about Amarine and Pellia," she said and proceeded to give him a detailed account of her visit. This time there were no outside interruptions. It was hunger that finally drove them back to their rooms.

Jarrod was disappointed. The table by the casement doors was bare. Then he caught sight of the clothes. They were laid out on the bed, as the Court clothes had been, but these were infinitely grander. Brocade shimmered in the noonday light and jewels winked. He went over and picked up the jacket, holding it out. It was stiff and heavier than he had expected. The shoulders were broad and he could feel the padding beneath his fingers. The waist looked tiny, but that was mostly due to the embroidery, a triangle of rubies and garnets stitched in place with gold thread. The buttons were encrusted with diamonds. He whistled softly.

Pretty fancy, he thought. The egg-sized rubies at the cuffs were each worth Paladine's yearly Tithe. He put the jacket carefully back on the counterpane. There were trousers, long and slim, made of the same salmon-colored brocade. Not the color he would have chosen, but elegant nevertheless. The bottoms of the legs were ringed with large rubies. The shirt and hose were made of watered silk and there was a jabot of what looked like burgundy lace. If he was being dressed for the slaughter, he would go out in splendid style. He rubbed the fabric of the shirt between thumb and finger; soft and wondrously sleek.

"I trust that they are to your liking." The amused oboe-voice startled Jarrod and he whirled around. The Guardian floated in the middle of the room, swathed in blue.

"I did not mean to startle you. I came to invite you to join me for a meal. I thought it would be amusing to try to duplicate the formal pomp of one of your communal meals—on a much smaller scale, of course."

Jarrod was wary. He hadn't known what to expect when next he saw the Guardian, but courtly manners hadn't entered into any of his imaginings.

"Those clothes, for instance," the Guardian continued. "They are copied from an outfit worn by a long-dead emperor on your world. You are far taller than he was, but I think you'll find the fit acceptable."

"They are magnificent, my lord. I've never seen anything like them."

The Guardian smiled. "I am glad that you approve. The Lady Marianna seemed most pleased by hers."

"And my, er, my opponent, will he be there?"

The eyes in the smooth parchment face grew quizzical. "Would you want him there?"

Jarrod wasn't at all sure that he did. "Is he all right?" he asked, ducking the question.

"I have mended his wounds, as I have yours, and I would judge that he is happier to be alive than you seem to be. Oh, and apropos that other Jarrod Courtak, there was that, ah, suggestion that you made yesterday. 'Give the poor bastard the rest of my memories,' were your exact words as I recall. Do you still feel the same way?"

Did he? He had said it in the crucible of exhaustion and disgust, but he had to admit that the whole idea of a sudden twin was disturbing.

"Why doesn't he have my early memories, if he is exactly the same as I am?" he asked.

"Reconstructing memories for him of what you have done while you have been on the island was relatively simple," the Guardian replied. "After all, I have a complete record. To give him your early memories, I should have had to probe your mind and that, if you recall, I promised that I would not do."

"And what do you intend to do with him?"

"Do with him? I shall keep him here, of course. There will be useful work that he can do. My pets would benefit from some personal attention."

Jarrod felt relieved. He still didn't know what the Guardian intended to do with him, but if he was allowed to return to Strand he didn't fancy the idea of this other one tagging along.

"What would it entail—giving him my memories?" he asked.

"There is no pain," the Guardian said easily, "although there are some minor risks."

"Risks?"

"There really should be no problem where you are concerned. Your clone has a much greater chance of being damaged. There is precedent for activating and copying memories—the unicorns do it automatically—but I don't believe that anyone has tried to implant memories artificially. I find the possibility intriguing. That's why I spared your life." He was matter-of-fact.

"I'm not sure that I understand," Jarrod said.

"It's quite simple, really. I shall copy your memories and store them. Then, when I have worked out a method of introducing those memories into the brain of your clone, I shall attempt the transfer."

"But if you haven't worked that out yet," Jarrod objected, "how did you give him the memories he has now?"

"Oh, that was easy enough. I played the tapes of what you had done over and over until he absorbed them subliminally and assumed that the actions were his own."

"How long will this new transfer take?" Jarrod asked.

"For you? Not long at all."

"What happens if I don't agree?"

"Then I shall send you back to Strand. The Force Point will remain shielded until the mechanism determines that a reintegration into the grid is appropriate. Your clone will remain as he is, alive and incomplete."

I'm going to live, Jarrod thought. He's going to send me home. As a failure, an inner voice reminded him. "And if I say yes?"

"Then I am prepared to restore the Force Point. I have, as you can well imagine, taken innumerable readings of the site, and the instruments would seem to indicate that the human trapped there will survive the reintegration, but there can be no guarantee and no instrument can predict his psychological state once he emerges."

Jarrod didn't understand most of what had been said, any more than he knew what a clone was, but one thing was clear. Greylock would live. That made the choice simple. There was one more question that he wanted to ask though.

"Will I lose my memory?"

The Guardian's rasping laugh took him aback.

"No, no; I shan't steal your memories, I shall just copy them. You need have no fears on that account."

Could he trust the Guardian? Probably not, but what other course was there? "This other Jarrod," he said suddenly, "You're sure you won't send him to Strand?"

"The answer is no. I have no wish to create a paradox."

"Well then," Jarrod said, "it would seem that I have nothing to lose and everything to gain."

"I hoped that you would see it that way." The Guardian smiled his brief unsettling smile again. "I'll send the servo for you in about an hour and a half as you measure time. That should give you sufficient time to bathe and change."

He began to fade and Jarrod bowed. It seemed an appropriate gesture. As his head came back up it dawned on him that he had made the decision without consulting Marianna. That wouldn't sit well with her. He also realized that he had not asked what would happen to her. He had just assumed that she would be going home with him, but he had been here long enough to know that nothing could be taken for granted. He sighed. He'd get things right one of these days.

An hour and a half later Jarrod was being ushered into an unfamiliar room on the ground floor. His first thought, however, was how familiar it seemed. There was wooden panelling, a large stone fireplace with a log fire blazing, a lighted chandelier, human portraits on the walls and a hammerbeam roof. There were herbs and rushes on the floor, whose center was taken up by a table and four chairs. There were other tables around the sides of the room, darkly polished and laden with plate. There were Halls like this on Strand, through few would be as luxuriously appointed.

Marianna stood by the fire, as did the Guardian and the other Jarrod. They were facing the flames and he could hear

Marianna talking about the unicorns. She had a goblet in her hand and her face was flushed, or seemed so in the firelight. Her hair was swept up and held in place by knots of pearls, leaving her shoulders bare. The gown was full-skirted and made of a blue-black material that turned iridescent when she moved. A necklace of sapphires and emeralds curled around her neck. The combination was repeated in the earring that he could see and in the bracelet on her wrist.

The Guardian was covered by a deep green velvet cloak with a very high collar. A shower of bright stars started where the neck should be and cascaded to the hem. The other Jarrod, listening avidly to Marianna, was notable for the plainness of his attire. Brown jacket, darker trousers and brown boots; not a jewel to be seen. The Guardian looked towards the door and spotted Jarrod standing there.

"Come in, come in," he said.

A bronze man appeared at Jarrod's elbow with a goblet on a tray. Jarrod took it and moved forward. The jacket held his shoulders back. He felt taller somehow.

"Give you goodday, Lord Guardian," he said. He bowed to Marianna and nodded to his twin. The formality felt right in this room.

"Ooh, Jarrod, you do look grand," she said.

He looked her over appreciatively. The gown was cut low in front and he could see now that the necklace ended in an emerald pendant that nestled between her breasts.

"I must say that I have never seen you look so beautiful."

Marianna raised an eyebrow. "Don't overdo it," she said with a smile.

"If I may be permitted, Lady Marianna, your friend does not exaggerate." The Guardian was at his smoothest. "In fact the gown suits you far better than it did the woman for whom it was made and she was accounted a great beauty. I think her name was Janada."

Jarrod and Marianna exchanged a quick glance.

"That is a considerable compliment, Excellence," Marianna said.

Jarrod took a sip from his glass. It tasted like sherris, and very good sherris at that. He took a longer drink. "This is very good," he said.

"I am glad that you approve. I am aware that neither of you has a very high opinion of the food, but today I think I have a surprise for you. . . ."

A muted fanfare of horns sounded, right on cue.

"Ah, we are ready now. Lady Marianna, do you sit on my right and you, young man," he turned to the other Jarrod, "sit on her other side."

They moved away from the fire and Jarrod noticed that there was a bronze man behind every chair. He had never seen more than one of them at a time.

"Do either of you know anything about Clovis the Fourth?" the Guardian asked as the cloak floated down into his chair at the head of the table. It had been laid while they chatted at the fire and now the candles winked off crystal, gold and silver. "No? I find that rather surprising. He was a formidable warrior who extended the rule of the crown over the whole of—Arundel, I think it was. No matter; it is simply that this meal is my version of a feast that he gave."

As if conjured by his words, the servitors reappeared with platters of tiny roasted birds.

"I believe they are eaten with the fingers," the Guardian remarked. "There are bowls of warm water to your left."

Jarrod tried one gingerly while Marianna watched him. It was tasty, juicy and crunchy. He nodded encouragingly to Marianna and helped himself to another. His double watched intently and followed his lead. Wine was poured, which both Jarrod and Marianna drank, but the double did not. The birds disappeared rapidly and were replaced by bowls of steaming soup. Jarrod and Marianna washed their hands in the water bowls and the newcomer followed suit. Jarrod leaned forward and sniffed the aroma. He was amused to see the other copy him.

"Grampus soup," the Guardian declared proudly.

"Grampus?" From Marianna. "I remember hearing about them when I was a girl. I thought they had been extinct for ages."

"Precisely so. It was once a delicacy of your southern region."

Jarrod felt a flash of sympathy for his other self. None of this could have any meaning for him. He put the thought aside and sampled the soup.

"You have become quite an expert on Strand, my Lord Guardian," Marianna remarked. "Indeed you seem to know more about it than anyone now living."

"I don't doubt it," the Guardian said smugly. "I have given it considerable attention since your arrival."

"And have you studied our enemy as closely as you have studied us?"

"I have." The enigmatic smile curled up. "They are, in many respects, even more interesting than humans."

Marianna looked up, spoon suspended. She put on a little pout that Jarrod recognised. "That isn't very gallant of you, Lord Guardian," she said.

"Gallant?" The Guardian seemed nonplussed. "Ah, yes, a charming concept. My apologies, Lady Marianna, but the truth is no respecter of delicacy. The fact is that the species you call the Outlanders is more advanced in some ways than you are."

Condescending old bastard, Jarrod thought. "Advanced in what way?" he asked.

"Well, for one thing they have solved the problem of functioning in your atmosphere, while you have never penetrated theirs. It is all the more remarkable when you consider that they have to grow the shells that enable them to make weapons and to venture into your part of the planet. I'm not sure that I have come across a life form quite like them anywhere in this universe.''

Jarrod didn't like the sound of that. In fact he was beginning not to like this whole elaborate set-up with his lookalike sitting mutely across the table, stealing sidelong glances at Marianna whenever he could.

"Does that mean that we'll never beat them?" Marianna asked.

"Not necessarily. They are at an enormous disadvantage physically, and there are other factors besides war that cause populations to decline." He turned to Jarrod.

"I have yet to fathom the source of your so-called Magic, but it obviously centers around the manipulation of energy. From what I have seen, your Magicians ought to be able to summon up or divert enough energy to incinerate half the planet, but, fortunately, your bodies couldn't take it. They were not designed for that."

"Then we are doomed," Jarrod said bleakly.

"Oh, I doubt that," the Guardian replied easily. "You will industrialize eventually and you'll probably poison them all."

"I'm afraid I don't follow you," Marianna said, putting down her spoon and dabbing at her mouth.

"That's probably a very good thing." He looked over at Jarrod and then back to Marianna. "If it were in my power to grant you your nonexistent Great Spell, I would not do it. I will not help to destroy an entire species. If it happens naturally, I don't intervene, but I will not precipitate it."

"You will, however, allow us to be driven into the sea." Marianna said it sweetly, but her eyes were cold.

"Oh, I don't think it's that bad," the Guardian replied in an annoyingly reasonable tone. "Your friend the Archmage has solved the immediate problem that sent you here. It is true that there is another attack underway, but yours is a resourceful race. You may be on the retreat for a while, but plants are enormously tenacious once they are established and oxygen will rectify the balance over time. Your passion for cultivation should see to that.''

Jarrod was not comforted by this talk of plants. ''On the retreat for a while,'' the Guardian had said. That translated into the loss of Celador. It might even mean the fall of Stronta, the destruction of the Outpost, the loss of the Great Maze. What good would the Place of Power be then? And the Guardian had known that. Yet here they were, wearing a fortune in jewels, drinking wine and eating food that not even Varodias could command. It was all too much.

''In the matter of Strand, my lord. Is there anything you would advise us to do to avert this 'retreat'?''

''Details are not my affair. I shall fulfil my part of the bargain. The rest is up to you.''

''And what, pray, is this bargain?'' Marianna enquired. She was still using her social voice, but Jarrod caught the tension.

The Guardian turned to her. ''At the end of yesterday's contest,'' he explained, ''your friend demanded that I give this second Jarrod his early memories. I too would like him to be as close to the original as possible. I agreed that, if your friend went through with the procedure, I would restore the Force Point on Strand, despite his, ah, unorthodox performance in the arena.''

''Oh I see. I thought for a moment that it had something to do with me.''

''But of course it has something to do with you, Marianna,'' Jarrod protested.

''I can assure you,'' the Guardian interposed, ''that should anything happen to your friend, and I do not for a moment think that it will, I shall return you to your planet and I shall honor my word on the Force Point.''

''And what happens if I do not wish to return?''

''Marianna!''

''I had not considered that alternative,'' the Guardian said, ignoring him, "but you are welcome to stay here for as long as it pleases you."

"Marianna, what are you saying?" Jarrod was aghast.

"Stop looking at me that way. There's no reason that I can't stay for a while if I want to. I have no pressing reason to return. You're the one who's needed for the war effort, not me. Nastrus and Beldun are both at Celador and you can talk to them. Amarine is here." She paused and looked at the second Jarrod. He colored and looked away. She turned back to the Guardian.

"How long will this memory thing take?" she asked.

"With your friend? Not long at all; a day at the most. The trick is to transplant those memories and I shall need some time to work that out."

Marianna's smile came back, tinged with pure mischief. "So this Jarrod," she patted the sleeve next to her, "will be walking around for a while in blissful ignorance of what that other swine did back on Strand."

"That is true."

The smile broadened. "Would it not be an advantage, my Lord Guardian, if I prepared him for the inevitable shock?"

"But you can't do that," Jarrod broke in.

"I don't see why not, Jarrod dear."

"Then we can both stay," he said.

Her eyes widened. "But surely you remember Ragnor stressing the need to get back to Celador as soon as possible?"

"He meant both of us."

"We've just been through all that," she said and turned her attention back to the Guardian. "Would it be useful, my lord?"

"It might well ease the transition, help to socialize him," the Guardian allowed.

"There you are then." She was triumphant.

Jarrod threw his napkin down on the table. "And just what am I supposed to tell Ragnor? Let alone your father."

"Ragnor's your problem," Marianna replied, "though I can't see why he should mind. Daddy, on the other hand, is liable to be a mite put out."

She considered while the others watched her, one Jarrod with dread and the other with hope. The Guardian watched them all, delighting in the unpredictability of the creatures. Perhaps, when she was safely gone, he would clone the female too. He must make sure to record her memories before she left.

"If I were you," Marianna resumed, "I'd just tell him that I send my love, that I've decided to stay with Amarine a little while longer and that I'll be home soon."

"Oh, thank you very much," Jarrod said, sitting back in his chair. "That's a great help. The man will flay me alive for abandoning his daughter."

"Well, it's the truth," she retorted. "Tell him that you tried to convince me to come home, but I turned stubborn and dug my heels in. That's the truth too and he'll certainly believe that."

"I think you're being extremely irresponsible," Jarrod said angrily.

She tossed her head and her eyes snapped, but she bit her lip and held her comment in. She took a deep breath. "I don't think this is the time or place to discuss this," she said. "We are being very disrespectful to our host."

The Guardian looked from one to the other. "Are we still going to do the memory transfer?" he asked mildly.

"We are," Jarrod said. He was sitting very straight and his lips had become two thin lines. "And then I should like to go home as soon as I can."

"Well, I'm glad that's settled," the Guardian said. "Shall we proceed with the meal? I think you will enjoy the next dish—skywhale steak flamed in brandywine. . . ."

chapter 23

The following morning, Jarrod was taken deep below the house and into a long chamber filled with strange humming devices. He had still been angry with Marianna when he had woken up, but now he rather wished that she were with him. The couch at the far end of the room looked far from inviting, surrounded as it was by a spider's web of metal. He squared his shoulders and walked down the room towards the Guardian. The assurances that this would be safe and painless sounded hollow this time, but he nodded as if he were in agreement.

He allowed the servitors to shave his temples and to fasten little metal discs there. He lay on the couch and heard the humming, sinister now, increase in intensity. He had feared that his proximity to all this machinery would upset his system as it did on Strand, but whatever the Guardian had done to him when he had first arrived was working still. He felt no discomfort, but he was uncomfortable nevertheless.

The hum went up in pitch and began to pulse hypnotically. Jarrod closed his eyes and began his series of breathing exercises to maintain his fragile calm. He kept waiting for something unpleasant to happen, but somewhere along the way he must have slipped into sleep, unlikely as that was in a place like this. He dreamed: dreamed an inexplicable and unfocussed world, dreamed the incomprehensible absence of the body and the breast that were his security, dreamed childhood, boyhood, Dameschool and adolescence. The emotions were brief, but plangent, and Magic was an enduring thread.

He woke in his room, none the worse for wear, as far as he could tell. He bathed and washed his hair. When he was finished, he combed it forward to hide the unsightly white spots on his temples. When he came out of the washroom, he saw that the previous day's finery had been laid out on the bed. Of the valet there was no sign. He went over to the bed and looked down. He ran his fingers over the fabric. It was shallow of him, he knew, but he had enjoyed wearing the outfit. It had made him feel regal. The stiffness of the material and the encrustation of jewels had kept his posture perfect. The weight of the rubies at the bottom of the trousers had kept them absolutely straight. He began to dress with great care.

He was escorted downstairs, but to his surprise they ended up in the throne room. The Guardian was already in place, the wall behind him swirling silently with color. Marianna was there too, sitting, seemingly, on nothing. Jarrod could not see it from the doorway, but he knew that there must be another transparent chair to her right. What was visible was a small chest with a curved lid. It sat on the floor, close to where Jarrod thought the other chair would be. There was a scabbarded sword beside it.

"Well met for one final time, Jarrod Courtak of Strand." The mellow voice was relaxed to the point of a purr. Marianna turned to look.

Jarrod located the second chair and lowered himself into it. He sneaked a look at the things on the floor. The hilt of the sword was studded with topaz. The scabbard was covered in dark red velvet and banded with gold. The chest seemed to be made of painted leather.

"You will be happy to hear," the Guardian said, bringing Jarrod's head up, "that the recording of your memories went without a hitch. I now have them safely stored and, with the help of the Lady Marianna, I shall eventually transfer them to your clone.''

Jarrod turned to Marianna. ''You really mean to stay here?''

''For a while.'' She smiled at him. ''I'll be home soon enough, don't you worry.''

''How can I not worry? I don't feel right about this, Marianna. I really don't.''

''Poor old Jarrod,'' she said sympathetically. ''Am I such a trial to you? I'm not doing this to upset you, or to make your life more difficult. I'm doing it because I want to, I'll admit that, but I'm also doing it because I feel I'm needed. Can you understand that?

''Nobody's ever needed me, Jarrod. It's one of the reasons that I try to be self-sufficient. But he needs me. He's going to need a lot of help and there isn't another human being who could help him. I can't walk away from that. Is that so difficult to comprehend?''

''You're not making this any easier, you know,'' Jarrod said crossly.

''You must not quarrel,'' the Guardian chimed in. ''You have both made your choices. In a little while, I shall send you, Jarrod, back to your home world. I shall try to return you as close to the time that you left as I can. Your companion will join you when she has a mind to. If it will help, you have my assurance that no harm will come to her while she is here.''

He looked from one to the other and then his gaze returned to Jarrod. ''In the chest by your chair,'' he said, ''is the mail you brought with you. I have examined it thoroughly and I have taken the liberty of keeping a small sample. Beside it is the sword that you used in combat. I have had the edges rehoned and embellished it somewhat. I thought you might like to have it.''

''You are most generous, my Lord Guardian.''

The Guardian gave a little nod. ''There is more. The mail

was yours and you have certainly earned the sword. However, you also brought me a gift that I find infinitely precious. That, young human, is something that I thought was no longer possible. I intend to reward you.

"In the chest, you will find two resonators. I believe that they are of the same crystal that your colleague at the Force Point has set in a ring. My ancestors used them to excite magnetic fields. Your people have evidently found a new use for them."

The Ring of the Keepers, Jarrod thought. "My thanks again, Great Lord." He bowed his head.

"One final thing. The clothes you are wearing will go home with you." The cloak billowed slightly, as if the Guardian had settled back to look with satisfaction on Jarrod's stunned face.

Jarrod swallowed. He was suddenly very rich indeed; absurdly rich. His eyes focussed slowly on the ochre face. "I am overwhelmed, sir. I, er, I don't know what to say. 'Thank you' seems so inadequate."

"No thanks are needed. Now, I think it is time that you said your farewells. I imagine that you would prefer to be alone." He vanished.

"I wish he wouldn't do that," Marianna said, hand to her chest. "It's very disconcerting."

"I really do wish that you were coming with me," Jarrod said.

"I know you do, Jarrod dear, but I shall be perfectly all right." She cocked her head. "You mustn't forget," she said, "that Nastrus and Beldun are at Celador and Amarine is here." She shook her head and got out of the chair.

"I certainly hope that the Guardian sends me home with yesterday's evening-wear and I wouldn't mind having a sword like that either."

Jarrod smiled in spite of himself. How typical, he thought. Who else would want a ballgown and a sword. "Hurry back," he said. "We need you."

She grinned at him and then they were locked in a long, tight, hug. He kissed her hair. After a while she pushed him gently back.

"Take care of yourself," she said. Her voice was husky and she cleared her throat. "I don't want you taking any crazy risks," she continued, rallying, trying to lighten the atmosphere. "I don't want to get back home and find that you've gone out in a blaze of glory."

"Not much likelihood of that," he replied, matching her tone. "My first challenge will be to survive the meeting with your father."

"Send him a letter, and if he comes to Celador, wear the chainmail."

He smiled, leaned down and kissed her on the cheek.

"I think that we should begin, or rather end." The Guardian's voice startled them. He was back on the throne. "If you would both sit down again? I think, friend Jarrod, that it would be best if you held your gifts on your lap."

He waited until they had settled themselves. "I shall miss you, Jarrod Courtak. That's another thing I had not anticipated. It has been an extremely stimulating meeting. I wish you every good fortune." He paused and looked long and hard at the Strandsman. "Farewell, Jarrod Courtak of Strand. You have been a worthy representative of your race."

Marianna and the Guardian grew suddenly faint and Jarrod blinked to clear his sight. They grew fainter still and Marianna began to wave. He looked left and right and realized that the rest of the room was bleeding away. He clutched the leather chest, expecting and fearing the grey of Interim, but the light faded smoothly and he was left sitting in blackness.

A light bloomed somewhere below his feet. He stared at it. Not a light really, he amended, more of a glimmer. He had no idea how far away it was, let alone what was causing it. It was like a speck of phosphorous on the nightime sea.

He had seen something like it when he had sailed on the *Steady Wench*. As he watched, the speck became a patch and the patch resolved itself into a slowly turning cloud of luminescence. Tiny, but growing gradually larger and brighter.

He had expected to be cold, but he was quite comfortable. He groped with one hand for the contours of the chair, but could find nothing. He was in a sitting position with nothing to support him. His heart gave a quick lurch, but settled down almost immediately. There was no sensation of falling, no sensation of movement of any kind, just the ever-expanding pinwheel below him.

It was a brooch made of thousands of sapphires, laid on black velvet for the appraisal of some goddess. As it approached, the individual gems became distinct and the patterns changed. Jarrod was lost in the beauty of it as it swelled and engulfed him. The jewels changed hues as they swept up to and past him, blue before him, red behind. He turned slowly in a giant kaleidoscope and watched sapphires turn to rubies and dwindle back to diamonds.

He floated serenely in the midst of glory. Of all the Guardian's gifts, this one was the most spectacular. The Island at the Center seemed remote now; the events there might have happened to someone else. The details were clear enough, but it was as if he was remembering something he had been told rather than something he had lived through. It had been an extraordinary time, no denying that, and he was lucky to be out alive.

He realized that he was not afraid, that despite the fact that he was falling through a spangled void, he had no doubt that he would arrive safely on Strand. Such was the power of the Guardian. And because of it, the Guardian's existence would remain a secret. Who would believe him?

He looked between his feet and saw that the lights were moving faster. He hoped this latest experience would stay dazzlingly vivid, something he could call back when life seemed dull. Already the individual points were beginning to blur and he strained to catch as much as he could, turning to watch them flee away. When he looked down again, all he could see was a golden tunnel of almost unbearable light. He shut his eyes.

chapter 24

"Wake up, you recalcitrant young puppy!"

Jarrod heard the words through the haze of his dream. He was falling slowly through a jeweled tapestry and he was loath to leave it.

"Wake up, blast your eyes! We have work to do." The words were insistent, as was the pushing at his shoulder. Not the metal man's style at all. He opened his eyes reluctantly and blinked.

"Two days of sleep are enough," the voice continued. "The Wisewoman says there's nothing wrong with you. Up, you great malingering sluggard!"

"I'm awake. I'm awake," Jarrod mumbled.

The shaking stopped and the figure bending over him stood back. Ragnor, Jarrod thought. So the Guardian had kept his word. He swallowed to get some moisture into his mouth. "Where are we?" he asked.

"In Celador. Where else should we be?" The old man caught himself. "You do remember Celador, don't you?"

Jarrod smiled sleepily. "I remember. There's nothing wrong with my memory, I'm thankful to say." He shunted himself up in the bed and leaned back against the bolster. He was wearing a cotton smock.

"D'you know who I am?"

"You are Ragnor. You are the Archmage. And this," he looked around, "is your bedchamber."

"That's all right then." Ragnor turned away and picked

up a cup. "Here, drink this. It's a tisane with some fortifiers. It'll do you good."

"Thank you, sir," Jarrod said as he took the proffered cup. He sniffed at it; distinctly herbal. He sipped; warm and not unpleasant. He drank. He had said that there was nothing wrong with his memory, but he didn't know how he came to be in this bed.

"How did I get here?" he asked.

"How much do you remember?" Ragnor countered. He went and got an upright chair, brought it back to the bedside and sat down. "Well?"

"We got to the Island at the Center safely, we met the Guardian, I underwent a series of tests, the Guardian sent me home and here I am. That's a precis, but all the details are clear. I just don't remember arriving back on Strand. The last thing I can recall is being surrounded by light."

Ragnor gave a little snort. "You were found face-down in a field. A farmer bringing vegetables to market spotted you. I had men who were supposed to keep an eye open for you, but no one seems to have seen you arrive. Lucky for you the farmer was an honest man. He knew you for a Magician despite your fancy clothes. Frankly I'm surprised you weren't found stark naked with your throat slit. Are you aware that you were wearing a king's ransom in jewels?" Jarrod nodded and drank more of the tisane.

"Be that as it may, you made quite an entrance into the capital laid out on top of the swedes and onions. You collected quite a crowd. We had to turn out the Watch to restore order." He sat back, stroking his beard, to see what effect the story was having. Not much of one.

"We'll have to show you to the people as soon as possible," he continued. "The place has been a hive of rumor." He cocked an eyebrow. "You will no doubt be gratified to hear that news of your death brought on an outbreak of grief."

Jarrod grinned weakly. "I'm sorry that I shall have to disappoint them," he said.

"How d'you feel?" Ragnor asked.

"Well enough. A bit hungry, but otherwise all right. How long have I been taking up your bed?"

"You were brought here three days ago."

"No wonder I'm hungry."

"Well, you look hale enough. In fact you seem to have put on some weight."

Jarrod smiled. "I had some special training in swordsmanship on the Island." He was pleased that the exercise had finally made a visible difference.

"You seem to have had a lively time and we'll get to that. I've some questions first, if you feel up to it."

"I don't want to sound disrespectful, sir, but could you possibly ask the Duty Boy to get me something to eat?"

"Oh, very well." Ragnor turned and bellowed for the Duty Boy, gave him orders for food and wine and brought his attention back to Jarrod. "Now then, laddie," he said in a gentle voice, "what happened to the Lady Marianna and the unicorns? Take your time, I'm not going anywhere."

Jarrod finished off the tisane and then looked over at the Archmage. "I knew that you were going to ask that. Both unicorns are happy, pregnant and in good health. Marianna decided to stay with them a while longer." He put the cup back on the table so that he did not have to look at the Archmage any longer.

"She decided to stay?"

"Yes, sir."

Ragnor sat back in his chair and shook his head. "I was afraid that that would happen," he said. "I tried to guard against it, but I obviously failed." He looked up and caught Jarrod's eye. "Is she safe?"

"Oh, quite safe. She is the Guardian's honored guest."

"And do you think that she will come back? Can she get back by herself?"

Jarrod plumped the bolster and pushed back against it. "If

I came through all right, I'm sure she will; and she said that she intended to come back.''

"When?''

"When she's ready to, is what she said. It's possible that she may stay until Amarine drops her colts.'' He didn't feel like going into the business of his twin just yet.

"What in the world are we going to tell her father?'' Ragnor asked.

"I put that very question to her and she told me to tell him the truth. She also advised me to send the news in a letter.''

Ragnor snorted, "How long until Amarine foals?''

"She due at the beginning of the Season of the Moons I'd guess,'' Jarrod said, "but Marianna may be back before then even if she stays until the colts are born.''

Ragnor looked askance at him. "Here comes the boy with the food,'' he said. "Eat something; the hunger's got you lightheaded. You're not making any sense.''

"It's not that difficult,'' Jarrod said, taking a plate and a fork from the Duty Boy. "I don't know how long we were on the Island. It seemed to go on forever, but the Guardian said that he would return me as close to the time I had left as he could. Time may run at a different speed up there for all I know, but if the Guardian says that he can do something, I would tend to bet on it.''

"We can but hope,'' Ragnor said, accepting a cup of wine and drinking deeply. "Fill that up before you go.'' He held the cup out.

"By the way,'' Jarrod said, "where are my clothes?''

"Under lock and key. You can have them back any time you want to, though I doubt you'll get much use out of them. Monarchs tend to resent subjects who can dress more richly than they.''

"I'll remember that,'' Jarrod said with his mouth full. He swallowed. "Did I have a leather chest with me when I was brought in?'' he asked.

"Yes you did, and a rather fancy sword as well. The suits of mail were in the chest. I'm glad you brought them back."

Jarrod nodded and continued to eat. Ragnor sat and drank his wine and bided his time. When Jarrod had finished he said,

"All right. Now talk to me."

"Remarkable, quite remarkable," Ragnor said when Jarrod had come to the end of his narrative. "The gods of the odds have been kind to us. We have you back and, with just a little more luck, we'll have Greylock as well. Let's just hope that it isn't too late."

"Too late? How long have I been away?"

"You left just before Greeningale, didn't you? and it's midsummer now."

"What have I missed?" Jarrod asked.

"Quite a lot, most of it bad." The Archmage was succinct. "Are you capable of getting out of bed? Because this chair is getting very hard."

"Certainly. I need to get up anyway. I'll just go down the hallway while you get more comfortable."

Ragnor rose stiffly and went and sat in one of the armchairs by the fireplace. When Jarrod returned, he took the chair opposite.

"Where was I?" the Archmage asked rhetorically. "Ah yes. Things went well enough right after you left. Sumner and Handrom came up with a little twist in weather control that took care of the Outland invasion and I was able to dissolve the Cloak of Invisibility. The pictures came back, by the way, which rather surprised me, but they'll certainly come in useful next time. That's about it for the good news.

"About a sennight later the bastards were on the move again. We tried the new weather trick, but it doesn't do much good against the main body of their atmosphere. They're being very cagey; no feints, no skirmishes, they haven't even shown themselves. "Their atmosphere just creeps closer day by day."

He produced a twisted little grin. "I am told that the Chief Warlock is taking it badly. He considers it some kind of personal affront." He took a sip or two of his wine. "No matter, the cavalry gallops about, the warcat battalion struts and poses, volleys of arrows are loosed; it hasn't done a blind bit of good." Ragnor sighed and looked at Jarrod quizzically. "I kept hoping that you'd turn up with all the answers. Wishful thinking, of course." He slumped slightly in the chair and drank some more wine.

"The Guardian said that we had the power to defeat them," Jarrod reminded him.

"The power yes, the strength no, isn't that what he said?"

"More or less, but that doesn't mean that we can't find a way," Jarrod replied, trying to sound positive. It troubled him that Ragnor was so down in the mouth. Now that Greylock was out of commission, it was to the Archmage that he looked for certainty.

Ragnor stretched. "Well," he said, "we can but try. Now that I know that I shan't be the man to discover the Great Spell, I'm damned if I'm going to be known as the Archmage who lost Celador."

"How close are they?"

" 'Bout a league."

Jarrod whistled softly. "That close. Have you tried Greylock's shield?"

"We have. They just push it back. We've lost two Magicians so far."

"Perhaps if the colts and I . . ." Jarrod began. "Speaking of the colts, how are they?"

"Perfectly fine as far as I can tell. I've ridden with them in the Royal Forest a number of times. My old palfrey can't keep up with them, but they seem quite content to gallop off and circle back. They gave me no trouble."

"So they behaved themselves while I was gone?"

"They disappeared for just over a sennight, which gave me palpitations, but they popped up again."

"I'll have to go and see them," Jarrod said.

"After I present you to the Princess Regnant," the Archmage replied firmly. "Word of your resurrection will spread quickly."

Jarrod made a face. "Oh good; do I get to wear my new Court clothes?" The tone was openly sarcastic.

"If you insist," Ragnor said drily, "but I should wait until the mud and the odor of onions have been removed if I were you. There's a Magician's robe that you left behind. It's been washed and ironed. I'll order up some hot water and a razor."

Jarrod stroked his chin. "I thought the beard was beginning to look rather handsome."

"That Guardian feller may have found it acceptable, but I can assure you that the Princess will not." He grunted on the last word as he heaved himself up out of his chair.

Jarrod groaned softly and got up.

Ragnor smiled unsympathetically. "You're still an Acting Mage, son: you've got responsibilities. Welcome back to Strand."

"And just exactly what am I to say to the Princess Regnant?" Jarrod asked as he walked back to the bed.

Ragnor shrugged. "Tell her the truth: you've been away on a special mission for me. She won't probe."

"And how am I supposed to explain my arrival in the back of a vegetable cart?"

"Tell the truth: you don't remember a thing about it."

"You make it sound very simple."

"It is," Ragnor said. "If you tell the truth, you rarely get into trouble." He smiled. "Mind you, one has to be a trifle selective about the truth one tells."

Jarrod laughed, relieved that the Archmage was finding his old form.

"Do you have something in mind for me once this ordeal at the palace is over?"

"I've been thinking about it. The only trouble was that I didn't know when you were going to revive, or if your mind would be intact. Frankly, some parts of your story make me wonder." He held up a swift hand. "Not that I disbelieve you, not at all. What reason would you have for lying to me? You didn't represent yourself as a hero."

"You're disappointed in me, aren't you?" Jarrod said.

"Not in the least." Ragnor was emphatic. "Don't think that for an instant. To go there and return is a miracle in itself. On top of that, Greylock and the Place of Power will return to us. To say nothing of the fact that we now have not one, but two new Rings. These are considerable benefits."

He pursed his lips and his eyes narrowed. "It is true that I have absolutely no idea of what I am going to do with all these blessings, but that's not your fault. I've only just learned of them and I'll come up with something. A lot, of course, will depend on Greylock's condition."

And with that Jarrod had to be content.

chapter 25

Ragnor, true to his word, paraded Jarrod relentlessly around the Palace. First to the Presence Chamber for a hastily arranged meeting with the Princess Regnant and then up and down the galleries. Jarrod rapidly tired of smiling at strangers and dealing out half truths, but it was dusk before he managed to get away. He decided to skip Hall and see the colts.

He was out of sorts when he approached their stable and his feet hurt, but the warmth of their welcome and the stimulus of their unstinting curiosity overcame his weariness. His reentry into that special communion was like finding a missing piece of himself. He felt whole, he realized, for the first time since Pellia had galloped away.

He hugged each of them in turn, revelling in the unspoken communication. Home, he thought, this is home. Nastrus teased him gently, but Jarrod was too happy to rise to the bait.

'I must tell you all about your mother and sister,' he thought out to them. The statement was greeted with amusement and he realized that their Memory had kept them informed.

'You have been out of touch with them for quite a while,' Beldun pointed out.

'But we want to see your memories after you left them,' Nastrus added.

Jarrod dusted off his robe as best he could and went and sat on the edge of the water trough. He sent his mind back to the time when Marianna and he were hacking their way into the jungle and let his memories unroll from there.

'You had a difficult time,' Beldun commented when it was over.

'This is not the Guardian that my kind has known,' Nastrus agreed.

'You did very well, and yet you do not seem content,' Beldun said.

Jarrod's answering smile was wry. *'I'm not exactly happy about leaving Marianna behind,'* he admitted. *'Besides, today hasn't been the best of days.'*

'There is much anxiety in this place,' Beldun concurred.

'I know,' Jarrod agreed. *'Everybody I met at Court seemed to be very cheerful, but even I felt the tension.'*

'We assumed that it was caused by the proximity of your enemies,' Nastrus said, *'though I cannot understand why they should be that worried. After all, if you could deflect me from a Line of Force, you should be able to deal with mist creatures.'*

Jarrod initial elation had evaporated. *'Not according to the Guardian. Our bodies are too weak.'*

'There is one possible solution to that.' Beldun was pulling mouthfuls of hay out of a bale in the corner.

'What sort of solution?'

'It would require sacrifice.' There was an edge of excitement to Beldun's thought.

Jarrod felt Nastrus' curiosity stir. There was a rapid exchange between the brothers, an exchange too fast for Jarrod's comprehension, and when it was over, Beldun was still excited and there was an air of grudging admiration from Nastrus.

'What's going on? What's this all about?' Jarrod's interest was piqued.

'Can you recall an exchange we had at that funeral in the mountains? About our approaches to death?' It was Beldun who answered.

'*You were at the Burning Ground.*'

'*That was the name in your mind at the time. We told you then that we honored our dead. The voluntary submersion of ourselves for the good of the family is the best way to die.*'

'*What has that to do with the making of Magic?*' Jarrod asked shortly. He wasn't comfortable with this talk of death.

'*He isn't going to understand,*' Nastrus said and the tone made it clear that it wasn't the first time that he had said it.

'*We are taken into the Memory and we exist there for as long as the Memory survives,*' Beldun continued magisterially, ignoring all interruptions. '*A truly noble sacrifice is never forgotten. Dams search them out to show to their foals as examples.*'

'*I assume that there is a point to all this?*'

'*The point is that there may be an answer to your problem, but it would require a sacrifice.*'

'*I don't think I want to hear this,*' Jarrod said.

'*I told you he wouldn't understand,*' Nastrus chimed in. '*How can he? His ways are not our ways.*'

'*He is not like the others. He has spoken with the Guardian,*' Beldun replied.

'*I grant you that he has a special place in our affection,*' Nastrus persisted, '*but you cannot seriously think that he has the will for this.*'

It irked Jarrod that they should be discussing him as if he wasn't there, couldn't hear them.

'*He should know of the possibility.*' Beldun was firm. '*What he does with the knowledge is his affair.*'

'*What knowledge?*' Jarrod asked impatiently.

Beldun brought his head up, chewing still, and looked in Jarrod's direction. '*The Memory contains creatures who feed upon energy, but humans are not among them, nor are unicorns. Unicorns however do have one attribute that humans lack and that enables us to deal with energy, to travel the Lines of Force.*'

'*And what is that?*'

'*Our horns.*' It was a quiet statement of fact.

'*I see,*' Jarrod said. '*The horn protected me while I was in Interim and might protect me while I performed Magic. Is that it?*'

'*A horn would protect anyone capable of summoning energy.*'

'*So, if I were to ride one of you while performing a spell . . .*'

'*No, no.*' Beldun. '*It has to be absorbed.*' from Nastrus.

'*Please don't play with me. It's been a very long day.*'

'*To gain protection you would have to absorb a portion. I would suppose that ground into a powder would be the easiest way for you.*'

Jarrod recoiled mentally. He pushed away from the trough and took a couple of paces. '*I am not about to break off a piece of your horn and grind it up.*'

'*Not that simple,*' from Nastrus.

Jarrod stopped short as the thought formed. '*It's the whole horn, isn't it?*' He shook his head. '*The idea's obscene. There is absolutely no chance . . . I mean, I'm very grateful that you should even think to . . . but, ah, but . . .*

'*Told you so,*' Nastrus said to Beldun.

'*Wait a minute,*' Jarrod said. '*I'm missing something, aren't I?*' He looked from one dark shape to the other. '*Can you survive without your horn?*'

'*No.*'

The enormity of Beldun's innocence struck him along with the preposterousness of the suggestion. It restored his humor. '*It was kind of you to offer,*' he said, '*but I think we'll try to find another solution.*'

'*I mention it as a possibility,*' Beldun replied, unabashed. '*To press you on such a matter would be selfish.*'

'*Well, it's getting late and I should be getting back to the Archmage's tower. I'm sleeping in his anteroom. He was very complimentary about you, by the way.*' He was anxious now to be gone.

'*Will you take us for a gallop tomorrow?*' Nastrus asked.

'I shall make a point of it. I haven't had a good ride in a very long time.' Jarrod made his way over to the colts and embraced them again.

He left the stables and made his way through the sleeping courts. They were quiet and empty; no refugees sleeping on the grass, no babies crying. The night was warm and slightly damp after the croprain. He didn't really feel like turning in. He'd had a lot of sleep lately. Without any conscious thought he veered to the right. Familiar quadrangles took on disguises under the fleeting nightmoon. He stopped and inhaled, deeply savoring the mingled odors of stone and moss, wet grass and wood smoke.

He had left Strand and he had come back. He had fulfilled the Oracle's prophecy, if that was the word for it. He had served Strand by leaving it and he was still alive. He pushed his shoulders back and twisted his head slowly so that the bones in his neck made granular noises. He smiled at nothing in particular and resumed his walk.

He found himself looking through an archway at Fountain Court. The nightmoon had found a clear space for itself and the pale yellow limestone looked like silver gilt. The mullioned windows of the courtiers' rooms glinted and, in the middle of it all, the extravagant fountain gushed and glittered. Water slid from horns held by sea beasts, spouted from the mouths of great fish, collected in and spilled from innumerable scallop shells. Jarrod stared, his own mouth slightly agape, like any country bumpkin. He watched the nightmoon recreate itself in a million falling drops and was irresistably reminded of his journey back to Strand.

He walked forward into the court. He had never felt that those celestial gems were alive, but the sparkling fountain seemed to him to be pulsing with life. The Guardian would love this, he thought as he sat down on the rim of the basin and trailed his hand in the cool water. A fine mist drifted over him. Beldun's suggestion popped up in his mind and he pushed it resolutely away.

He looked around the tranquil enclosure. Vines were growing up the south-facing wall and the shadows of clouds hurried over the cobbles. The sounds of the water lapped and plashed around him. It was beautiful and it was peaceful. On the Island, waiting for the final test, he had told himself that if he made it back he would go away to some quiet place and leave the war to others, but he knew it was a dream. They would never let him go, not while the Outlanders persisted. "On the retreat for a while" the Guardian had said. For the rest of his, Jarrod's, life, probably.

The moonlight vanished and he looked up. There were no stars to be seen, just the muffling dark. He wondered if the old familiar patterns would look the same now that he knew that some of them might be worlds, homes to other living things. He smiled at his conceit. When the clouds cleared, the Sword, the Buckler and the Stallion would move across the skies as they always had. Everything had changed and everything was the same. There was probably something clever and profound to be made out of it, but he wasn't up to it now. It was late. It was time to turn in.

Jarrod was roused by a familiar prompting. It was dark in the anteroom, but the Duty Boy was already stirring, responding to the age-old call to Make the Day. It was a long time since Jarrod had felt it and he was glad to have it back. There might be suns galore, but this was his sun and it was demanding his assistance. He rose, dowsed his face and got silently into his robe while the Duty Boy shuffled around laying the fire for chai. He remembered all the times when he had done the very same thing for Greylock.

He gave the lad a small wave as he left and made his way down the stairs and out into the courtyard. The sky had cleared and the stars were in their proper places, reminding him of his night fancies. He smiled and went to find a quiet place for the ritual. He was looking forward to it.

The sense of belonging was reinforced when he went, ravenous for his missed meal, to Magicians' Hall for breakfast. No one paid him the slightest mind. He was just one more tall, blue-robed man among many. He would be an Acting Mage again soon enough, but for the moment he was just another Magician and the anonymity suited him. After breakfast he'd give the old man the slip and take the colts out for some exercise.

Ragnor cooperated by being away from his rooms, and an hour later they were riding through the gates, pursued by a cloud of children from the town. It's all a wonderful game for them, Jarrod thought. That combination of zest and innocence that the children and the unicorns shared was worth fighting for. He set his face into the steady breeze and they cantered away from their young escorts. He surrendered to the pure pleasure of the movement. There was no room for worry, or for thought of any kind. The colts accelerated smoothly and went galloping down the post road.

They pulled off the road eventually and the unicorns stood blowing under the trees. Jarrod slid off and loosened the girthstrap.

'I didn't realize how much I had missed that,' he said.

'It's good to run,' Beldun agreed, *'but now I need water. I smell some over in that direction.'* He tossed his head towards the southwest.

They walked between the trunks of trees that, by Jarrod's reckoning, must have been two hundred years old. The wind made the canopy sound like the sea, but all was calm below. Sunlight sifted down through the branches, wildflowers brightened the clearings. Nastrus, who was in the lead, turned onto a game trail and they followed it to a stream. The bank had been trampled down over the years and access was easy.

Jarrod wandered down the stream while the unicorns drank. Birds sang and butterflies looped their way from flower to flower. Celador might have been a hundred leagues away, the Outland curtain even further. Yet both were with him now, no sooner thought on than installed in his mind. There must be a way to push the curtain back, he thought. He'd tried it with Greylock and with the colts, he'd had the benefit of his Staff, but they hadn't been able to push the Outlanders back. They had held them though. He turned and made his way back up the bank.

'*Doesn't take you long to get down in the mouth these days,*' Nastrus remarked as Jarrod came up to them.

'*I know, I don't seem to be able to shake it off. I'm afraid we're going to have to go back to work.*'

'*You're thinking of the shield,*' Beldun. '*We tried that at Stronta,*' from Nastrus.

'*The Outlanders are much closer this time.*'

'*It will be a holding action at best,*' Beldun commented.

'*Better than nothing,*' Jarrod replied.

'*If . . .*' Beldun began.

'*Not again.*' Jarrod cut him off, knowing what was coming. '*I don't hesitate to ask for your help, but I have no intention of letting you get hurt. This is not your fight.*'

'*That's odd,*'' Nastrus commented. '*I was sure that you had spent a lot of time and effort in convincing us to stay here and help you against the Outlanders.*'

'*Help us, yes, die for us, no,*' Jarrod said flatly.

'*We can't force you,*' Beldun said, and Jarrod thought that he detected a trace of disappointment. '*You would have to perform the task willingly. Anything less would taint the death.*'

'*I would have to perform the task? You must have taken leave of your senses.*' Jarrod was horrified.

'*Naturally. You didn't imagine that the sacrifice would be entirely one-sided, did you? That there would be no payment?*' Beldun was unimpressed with Jarrod's squeamishness.

'*This conversation is absurd,*' Jarrod said, trying to stand on his dignity.

'*Let it drop, brother,*' Nastrus said placidly. '*You must*

*make allowances for him. He's not unicorn, he'll never be
unicorn. That isn't his fault.'*

'*I think it's time we were getting back,*' Jarrod said.

He went up to Nastrus and cinched the girthstrap tight
again. He swung up into the saddle and they walked back to
the road, keeping their thoughts scrupulously neutral. The
return gallop burned away the lingering discontents and they
arrived back at the stables tired but contented.

The ensuing days passed slowly for Jarrod. Ragnor was
busy with Palace matters and everybody else seemed to have
some kind of job. He visited the Upper Causeway and saw
the looming bank of Outland air, an unending smudge on the
horizon. He watched the Magicians from the Collegium
working on the shield and felt guilty that he had not participated. He intended to ask Ragnor for permission, but the old
man hadn't had time for him as yet.

He wandered around the old castle, doing the sightseeing
that he had always put off before. He went and saw the Bursar
and arranged to draw some money. Then he spent a whole
day in the town and emerged with riding clothes and boots,
a new cloak, three shirts and a quantity of hose. In short, he
kept himself busy with trifles, knowing that he was avoiding
the colts. He felt badly about not taking them out for exercise, but he preferred not to be around Beldun while the
unicorn was in the grip of his morbid fantasy. He wanted to
go back to Stronta and see if there was anything he could do
to speed Greylock's release, but he didn't dare do it without
Ragnor's approval and the Archmage remained inaccessible.

Jarrod continued to take his meals in Magicians' Hall, even
though he knew that it would be more politic if he dined in
the Great Hall. He enjoyed the comradely informality and the
occasional gossip that came his way and it was there that he
heard the rumors about the eerie non-battle that was in progress. The other Magicians didn't seem worried. The received
wisdom was that the Archmage was working on something

special. It was, finally, from the Magicians' Hall that he was summoned.

Ragnor was slumped in his favorite chair. A pair of oil lamps burned on the mantlepiece and there were lighted tapers on the sideboard.

"That you, Courtak?" The voice was tired.

"Yes, Archmage."

"Get yourself some wine and come and sit down."

Jarrod poured himself a cup and went and sat opposite him. The Archmage was wearing an old robe and slippers. He had a jug of wine on the table at his elbow. Jarrod thought that he looked all in. The light from the lamps accentuated the dark circles under the eyes and the white hair looked lank.

"People never cease to amaze me," Ragnor said, looking up. "Take Handrom; level-headed chap. Not very imaginative, but someone you can count on. Man's gone completely to pieces. Here we are in the middle of a full-blown crisis and all the man can think of is his blasted exams. He spent an hour today assaulting me verbally for insisting that the shield be kept in operation at all times. Accused me of ruining generations of Magicians to come. Doesn't he realize that without the shield, there may very well not be a Collegium?"

"I was going to volunteer to help out, sir."

"Think you can push 'em back?" Ragnor peered down his nose.

"I can try," Jarrod said. "The colts and I couldn't manage it at Stronta, but there's no reason we can't try again."

"Best not then. If people see the unicorns and you going up to the wall, they'll expect something spectacular. The last thing I need now is for people to lose faith. I'd rather hold the unicorns in reserve. I want them to stay here until the last possible moment. If they are perceived as abandoning the capital, all may well be lost."

Jarrod was shocked by the Archmage's comment. He had

not realized that the situation was that grave. "The talk at Hall was pretty gloomy," he said tentatively.

"They getting panicky?" Ragnor took a drink.

"I don't think panicky is the right word, sir," Jarrod said. He followed the Archmage's example and took a deep pull from his cup. "They're frustrated, but they think that you have something up your sleeve."

"Ha! Would that I did. They've pressed us too closely. There's almost no room left to maneuver." Ragnor took another long drink and then put his cup down. "If the Magicians aren't panicking, the same can't be said of the Council. They're behaving like a bunch of old women. There is, I regret to say, considerable sentiment for moving the Court south. Arabella is dead set against it, as am I, but if that kind of talk can start before anything that one could classify as a confrontation has taken place, you can see what kind of trouble we're in."

"Any news from Stronta?" Jarrod asked, aware as he did so that he had "forgotten" to write to Marianna's father.

"Gwyndryth's rebuilding the army, but they're nowhere near ready for battle," the Archmage replied. "I understand that there are mutterings against Naxania by the mossbacks who challenged her father, but the country is quiet enough."

And among the mossbacks, no doubt, is my uncle, Jarrod thought. "No change at the Place of Power?" he asked, hoping against hope that the Place of Power had returned.

"Not so far, but didn't the Guardian say that it would take some time?"

"Yes, he did, but I was hoping I might be able to hurry things along somehow."

"Better not meddle. Besides, I want you here. Now, if the worst comes to the worst, you're to take the unicorns back to Stronta. If Celador falls, you must try to preserve Stronta. If the Place of Power is returned to us, you are the only one trained to take advantage of it. Those that dwell there have already accepted you and that's where you can be of greatest use.''

"But what about you, sir? Where will you go?"

"I shan't go anywhere, son. If it comes down to it, the Outlanders will pay dearly for Celador. I shall delay them for as long as I possibly can. If I perish, Greylock is to succeed me and if he is unable to, the High Council of Magic will meet to pick my successor."

"But Archmage . . ."

"But me no buts, just do as you're told when the time comes."

Ragnor's tone was sharp and Jarrod took to sipping his wine rather than face that stare. "What would you like me to do in the meanwhile, sir?" he asked at length.

"You'll have to help me come up with something. This Guardian of yours said that we had the innate capability to destroy our enemies, so we have to protect ourselves better, strengthen ourselves somehow. I don't want to start tinkering with the rites of purification, so we'll have to start with the ingredients of the potion. There may be a missing ingredient that would make the difference." He helped himself to some more wine. "I hope your digestion is in good order," he said sardonically. "There's no reason why the ingredient should be palatable."

The Archmage's speculation was a little close for comfort, but there was no reason why there shouldn't be some other element that would do the trick as well. "When would you like to start?" Jarrod asked.

"Tomorrow will be soon enough. I've had a difficult day."

"Oh, well then, I'll be going," Jarrod said and drained his cup.

"Take your time, son. There's no tearing great hurry." Ragnor chuckled. "Sounds funny saying that when all I've been hearing these days are pleas to do something, anything, as soon as possible. Fill that cup and keep me company a while."

Jarrod went back to the sideboard. He was concerned about the Archmage. He seemed frailer than he had when he and Marianna had left for the Island. Jarrod glanced over his shoulder. Ragnor sat hunched in his chair, cradling his cup. He reminded Jarrod of a fallen leaf, curling at the edges, veins standing out. He sat up when Jarrod returned to his chair.

"What say we get some air?" the Archmage said. "This room gets stuffy in the summer. We'll go up to the balcony. The croprain's over and the air will be cooler. Give us a hand." He held out his left arm and Jarrod pulled him to his feet. "Bring the wine jug, will you? And you might as well fill it up while you're at it."

Ragnor made for the door while Jarrod collected the jug and replenished it at the sideboard. He followed the Archmage upstairs and found him already out on the balcony. He joined him and put the jug down on the balustrade where Ragnor could reach it. He craned his neck and looked up. The clouds were scudding north and the nightmoon came and went as they hurried past her. The Archmage had been right about the air. The rain had washed the dust away and the wind was pleasantly cool.

He turned his attention to the rooftops. Half of them hadn't been there the last time that he had been on this balcony. There were couples strolling on the leads now, lanterns flickered in the stone pavilions and laughter rose across the wind.

"I see that Lord Rossiter is maintaining his spirits," Ragnor observed drily. "That pavilion of his is over three hundred years old. See those chimneys over there?" He pointed. "The twisting ones? They're part of the original castle. No one's quite sure how long they've been there, but it's a very long time." He sighed. "I love the view from up here."

He turned slightly and, at that moment, the moon came out and Jarrod saw the faint smile.

"In a way, that's what I'm fighting for," the Archmage

continued. "This is my home and that is my view." The *my* was accented. "Most people at Court have homes elsewhere, but this is where I have lived for half a century. I came here as a boy of thirteen and I never left."

He completed the turn and the smile was broad and open. "Celador is a symbol of the realm and, to a lesser extent, of the Discipline, but to me it is the center of the world. It is also very beautiful."

"We'll come up with something, sir, don't you worry." Jarrod felt oddly protective.

Ragnor clapped him lightly on the shoulder. "Bravely said, young Jarrod, bravely said. And so we shall." The tone was brisker. "We'll begin after lunch—I've meetings in the morning. You got any ideas?"

"Not really. We need a lining of some sort so that the extra power won't scorch us."

"Yes, I know, but we must be careful what we try. Metals tend to be poisonous and certain substances simply can't be absorbed. Perhaps we should spend the first few days going through the books. We aren't the first to look for this, you know."

"Very good, sir. Then I'll come back tomorrow afternoon, shall I?"

"I think that would be best. Mind you get a good night's sleep and eat sparingly."

"Yes, sir; good night, sir." Jarrod was quick to pick up on his cue.

" 'Night, lad."

Ragnor watched him go, carrying his glass with him. Bet he washes it out and puts it back, he thought. One thing you had to say about the boy, he doesn't put on airs. You'd never think to look at him that he'd been to another world and returned with a fortune.

He refilled his cup and turned back to the rooftops. The trouble was that the young man kept on coming up with extraordinary things, but none of them seemed to make any difference. They changed nothing. The Outlanders were still firmly in control of the war. It was all very frustrating. He picked up the jug and moved back into his workroom. Maybe something would come of this latest venture. It would be nice to have Greylock back, but he wasn't counting on it. The new Keepers' rings were a wonderful acquisition but, without the Place of Power, they were useless.

It wasn't that he didn't believe the boy—nobody could make up a story like that. It was just that the Guardian's character, at least as revealed by Courtak's narrative, didn't seem terribly trustworthy. There was something fundamentally inimical about the creation of living doubles. He shook his head and began to douse the lights. Nothing to do but wait in any case. Who knew? Perhaps they would come up with something. Not too likely, but then nothing about this unicorn business had been rational.

chapter 26

Jarrod's morning began well. He Made the Day in the predawn cool and repaired to Hall for breakfast. He had a keen appetite and real food still tasted wonderful after the Island. He left feeling replete and energetic and decided to take the colts for a gallop. He was changing into his new riding clothes when a part of the previous night's conversation came back to him. "They've pressed us too closely," the Archmage had said. "There's no room to maneuver."

His thoughts moved on to the shield. If anyone could make it work offensively, he could. He had helped Greylock construct the first one, he had trained Magicians at the Outpost to operate it, indeed he had helped to formulate the guidelines that they were using here at Celador. He could not thrust the Outland atmosphere back by himself, he knew that, but with the colts' help . . . It was worth a try.

He understood Ragnor's reasons for not wanting to use the unicorns, but, if he was careful, there was no reason for Ragnor to know. If he wasn't making any headway, he'd pull out. People would be interested in the unicorns, of course, but with him in riding gear it would just look as if he was visiting the wall to see the enemy's position. If he did manage to move the shield forward, Ragnor wouldn't mind that he'd involved the colts. Besides, if he couldn't do anything about the Place of Power, he might as well try to be of use here.

Having made his decision, he took himself to the stables, saddled up Beldun and rode out with Nastrus following. The colts knew what he was planning and made no objection. He knew that Nastrus was skeptical and that both would prefer a long gallop through the forest, but he himself felt optimistic. They made their way through the town to the South Gate, attracting attention and children. The colts stepped high and dainty in response to the enthusiasm of the crowd, amused by Jarrod's foray into deception.

Once clear of the walls, they left the roadway and cut across open country in a wide curve to the north. Jarrod kept the colts to a rapid canter. He wanted them fresh when they got to the Upper Causeway and they humored him, settling into a comfortable stride. Despite their moderation, they were at the wall within the hour, walking up the ramp with quiet flanks.

Jarrod was surprised by the activity on the roadway. He hadn't expected to see anyone except the Magicians who were manning the shield this early in the morning, but there were military men everywhere. He rode down the Causeway, past the oblivious Magicians, and dismounted at an empty stretch of parapet. He looked out through the crenels and saw the dark line in the distance that marked the enemy. He looked down and saw the reason for the activity on the Upper Causeway.

The sun winked off metal, pennons fluttered, tent tops rippled and troopers rode past cookfires and picket lines; the cavalry were deployed in a broad band in front of the tumbled blocks of the Giants' Causeway. Patrols were setting out in the direction of the curtain. That complicated matters. He hadn't counted on there being so many people around. With the cavalry out on the plain, any mistake could cost lives, but with the cavalry out on the plain, there was an even greater need for the shield. He remembered the shield at Stronta bursting into color as it trapped the enemy fire.

He stood comfortably, weight evenly distributed, arms hanging by his sides. He controlled his breathing and went within himself, concentrating, blocking out his surroundings. He reached out directly to the shield. He knew what the pattern should be and where he could slip into it without disturbing the Magicians who were maintaining it. He probed delicately and found the opening. He joined the matrix and felt the pressure, the relentless weight, of the Outland. He added a little of his power to the net and was aware of an infinitessimal easing. He withdrew as stealthily as he had entered.

He opened his eyes and looked out. The patrols were fanning out, but seemed in no hurry to get to the boundary. Should he? He reached out to the colts. They were willing to join him. It was more interesting than standing and looking at humans who were too busy to pay attention to them. He went back into his contemplative state and linked himself once more to the pattern. He drew on the power that the colts fed him and made his presence known. He transmitted more energy into the structure and spread his control. He was matching the combined power of the five Magicians and one by one he felt them disengage, believing, presumably, that he had been sent to relieve them.

The burden wasn't particularly onerous, though he knew that it would wear him down over time. He allowed more power to flow through him and felt the opposition stiffen. He had suspected that he had gained in strength since he had last manned the shield and now he knew that he was right. Perhaps the trips through Interim had toughened him in some way; because if he could contain the enemy on this level, he could surely drive them back.

The colts knew his thoughts and obliged him. Power flowed out of them in a steady stream, lifting Jarrod's spirits and making the hair on the nape of his neck prickle. He directed his energies at pushing the fogbank back. It was like trying to budge a stone wall with his shoulder. He persevered, his breath coming a little faster. He took stock of himself and judged himself capable of greater effort. The colts answered his need at the instant that the desire manifested itself and the Outland atmosphere began to give, infinitessimally at first and then by fractions of an inch.

Jarrod consolidated his gain and made sure that the advance had been even all across the front. He opened his eyes as if he would be able to see the difference. He knew it was absurd, but he still felt enormously pleased with himself. He was holding easily and his body was feeling no strain. Movement caught the corner of his eye and he turned his gaze slightly to the right.

Spread across the sky were wave upon wave of cloudsteeds. It did Jarrod good to see them, reminding him of the long flight to Bandor and the cameraderie that had developed after the fort was recaptured. Now was not the time to think of them though. Time to concentrate again; time to drive the bastards further back. His eyes closed and he braced himself for the renewed effort.

The colts picked up their transfer of energy and Jarrod funnelled it into the shield, pressing forward with all of his will. The Outland atmosphere yielded grudgingly at first, giving up scant inches in a series of compressed shudders, and then more smoothly. Elation built and he opened the channel to the colts a little wider. Power surged into him, through him, out of him and into the shield. The opposition gave way and Jarrod pressed his advantage, gaining a foot, a yard, ten yards before his rush was slowed.

He felt the sting of the fire weapons high up on the edge of the shield. Color fountained across his awareness. His eyes snapped open as he increased the power. Red filaments bolted upwards. They were not firing at the shield. They were aiming above it. He saw the first cloudsteeds fall before he understood and then he was swamped by the revulsion and visceral disgust that surged from the unicorns. Their reaction was as strong as the first time that they had seen cloudsteeds killed. He fought to damp them out, to keep the shield going, to maintain his equilibrium, his command. He reached out to the other Magicians, summoning them. The shield was still holding when the colts lashed out and scattered his control.

He woke in Ragnor's bed. Past experience made him bring up a hand and examine it. It looked normal. He disentangled his other hand from the bedclothes and took a fold of skin between thumb and forefinger. He released it and the skin sank back.

"Remarkable, isn't it?" Ragnor's voice startled him.

He looked up and saw the Archmage sitting by the bed.

"This is getting to be a habit and each time I like it less." The Archmage's words were stern, but he didn't look particularly angry.

"What happened?" Jarrod asked.

"Suppose you tell me."

Jarrod pushed himself up and arranged the pillows behind him. "I took the colts out for some exercise and we decided to see how close the Others had got. When we got to the Causeway we found that the cavalry was out beyond the wall and I decided to see how firm the shield was." He looked over at Ragnor to see how he was taking it. The seamed face was impassive, but the eyes were lively and skeptical. Jarrod looked away again.

"Go on," the Archmage said.

"I thought that, since the colts and I were there, we might give the Magicians a bit of a rest," Jarrod said knowing that Ragnor saw through him. "I mean . . . If the cavalry patrols provoked the enemy, they would need all the strength they could muster later on." He paused and then plunged on. "Anyway, we took the shield over and let them disengage. Nobody but the Magicians knew that we had done it, no one could tell that the colts were involved. I remembered what you said about people being disappointed."

"Didn't pay it much heed though, did you?" Ragnor said. "What happened then?"

"Well, we sort of flexed our muscles. We weren't having any trouble holding the curtain back and we thought we'd see what would happen if we increased the thrust.'' Jarrod began to feel more confident. ''It worked. We moved the screen forward. Not very far at first, an inch or two at most, but we did advance. I felt perfectly capable of handling more energy and we tried that. We had started to make some real progress when the Outlanders fired on the shield.''

''On the shield, or at the cloudsteedsmen?''

''Oh, so you know about them.''

''Of course I know about them.'' Ragnor allowed himself a flash of irritation. ''I read the reports.''

''They were firing on the cloudsteeds and that's what triggered the colts. Cloudsteeds are particular favorites of theirs and they were very angry. I couldn't handle it. I called to the other Magicians, but I don't know if they heard me.'' Jarrod fell silent. It sounded pretty lame to him after all.

''You were very lucky,'' Ragnor said evenly, ''and in more ways than one, though I don't pretend to understand it.''

''What happened to the others?'' Jarrod asked anxiously.

''Nothing. They got your message and stepped in in time to keep the shield up. They even managed to preserve some of your gains. Didn't help the 'steedsmen though, we lost about two hundred of them.''

Jarrod winced. ''Are the colts all right?''

'' 'Far as I know. They waited around until you'd been carted off on a stretcher and then they trotted back to their stable as cool as you please. They've been there ever since and, according to the Master of the Stables, they're eating normally. All in all, things could have been worse.'' Jarrod relaxed and Ragnor caught the movement.

''That doesn't let you off the hook, however. You knew that I didn't want the unicorns involved in the shield and you chose to disobey me. Worse, you throw yourself into this endeavor without the slightest bit of preparation. You know better than that. That's the behavior of a callow Apprentice, not an acting Mage.''

"I'm sorry, Archmage," Jarrod said contritely. "I wasn't thinking straight. I got carried away. I meant no harm."

"I should hope you bloody well are sorry. Your behavior was inexcusable." Ragnor allowed anger to blaze out and then paused to let the silence build. "However," he said when he felt his point had been made, "there was no damage done. In fact we gained a little ground. It's a tragedy about the cloudsteeds, but that's not your fault. It would have happened whether you were there or not. What could have possessed the High Command to order a massive flyover like that?" He shook his head, then looked up at Jarrod. "In short, young man, I'm not going to take any action this time, but if you ever disobey me again, I'll make you a pot boy in our kitchens."

"Yes, Archmage; thank you. I promise I'll never do it again."

Scared the daylights out of him, Ragnor thought with satisfaction. "All right then," he said and leaned back in his chair, "we'll let bygones be bygones, but we ought to be able to learn something from this. The first thing I don't understand is why you don't look a thousand years old."

"I don't know, sir. The only things I can think of are that it happened so fast, or that all the trips through Interim have had some kind of effect. I mean, if you are travelling along a Line of Force, you must be exposed to a lot of energy."

"You still couldn't handle the power that the colts generated, could you?"

"No," Jarrod admitted, "but the colts and I did move the curtain back before it happened."

"Not good enough. You'll just create an enclave and when you get far enough in, it'll collapse around you, just as it did with the airspouts. We need something more and even you, with all your annealing in Interim, can't encompass the amount of power we need."

"What if I could persuade the unicorns to act directly?"

"Won't work," Ragnor said sadly. "That's another thing

we've learned. The unicorns did act directly against the Outlanders and that atmosphere is still out there. No, it'll have to be a combination, or some source other than the unicorns. I feel fairly certain about that. I'm also of the opinion that, when the time comes, you're the one that will have to perform the Magic. I wouldn't last a minute with that volume of energy. What we have to come up with is some way to prevent you from being incinerated. You were incredibly lucky yesterday, but you can't count on being that lucky again.''

"Yesterday?"

"Oh yes; you deprived me of my bed for the night. Again. It's time you got your own room.''

Jarrod started to get out of bed.

"I didn't mean right this very minute,'' Ragnor said.

"It isn't that, sir. I want to know if I can stand up.'' He pushed his legs over the side of the bed and stood up slowly. He took two slow paces forward and then walked over to the sideboard and poured himself a cup of water. "There don't seem to be any ill effects,'' he said after he had drunk.

"Well, that's a relief. In that case I propose that we get down to work first thing in the morning. In the meantime, get yourself dressed and out of here.''

Jarrod raided the kitchens for something to eat and came away with a couple of apples for the colts. They might be feeling awkward about blasting him and an unexpected treat would be a good way to reassure them. He sensed them as he approached Stable Court, but they did not seem to be concerned about him, indeed they were unaware of his presence. They were locked in debate and both were upset, that much was immediately apparent. The substance of the colloquy was a blur, even the subject matter eluded him, but he guessed that it would be about the cloudsteeds.

The unicorns paid him no heed when he walked into the loose box and he went and sat on the edge of the water trough, waiting for them to notice him. After five minutes Jarrod produced the mental equivalent of clearing his throat. He had to do it several times more before he caught their attention, but when he did, they turned to him both mentally and physically. They were apologetic when they realized how long he had been there, but they were far more involved in their own concern and there was anger not too far below the surface. They munched the apples with relish, but it was obvious that they were preoccupied.

'*Are you two going to let me in on the great debate?*' he asked with an attempt at jocularity and instantly wished he had not. The colts swept him into their recent memories and he saw what he had been spared before. Cloudsteed after cloudsteed fell out of the sky, their screams of fright and agony cleaving their way against the wind to curdle the guts. Blood and gobbets of flesh sprayed down. The fury and disgust that the colts had felt was all around him, as corrosive as anything the Outlanders had produced. His stomach heaved and the unicorns cancelled the vision instantly.

Jarrod was back in the stable, but he still felt shaky.

'*They must be punished this time.*' Beldun's thought was harsh and constricted. '*It was barbaric,*' Nastrus averred.

'*I agree,*' Jarrod thought weakly, recovering still from the unwelcome vision. '*The problem is that we can't get at them. They just hide in that cloud and creep up on us. At least we proved that we can push them back. If we do it properly, we ought to be able to drive them even farther back.*'

'*That's not good enough.*' Beldun was crisp. His nostrils were flared and he pawed the ground as if to emphasize his point.

Nastrus began to pace backwards and forwards as if motion would dispel his anger. '*It was wanton and unprovoked slaughter,*' he said. '*My brother is right: they must be punished.*'

I've never seen them like this, Jarrod thought, forgetting that they could hear him.

Nastrus rounded on him and Jarrod retreated. '*You humans are the ones who assume that we are always gentle and well-*

tempered,' he said. *'On other worlds we have the reputation of being considerable fighters when roused.'*

'And the two of you are certainly roused now,' Jarrod commented.

'And you, regrettably, are not,' Beldun put in coldly.

'Now wait a minute, that's not fair.'

'Fair?' Nastrus was caustic. *'Were the Outlanders fair when they burned down the cloudsteeds?'*

'Of course it wasn't fair,' Jarrod said. He didn't understand why he was being put on the defensive. *'Any more than it was fair when they killed peaceable Westerners and destroyed their farms. The Outlanders aren't interested in fair, all they're interested in is driving us back to the Inland Sea.'*

'It must stop,' Beldun said.

'I wish it would. Every year they attack us and every year we beat them back, but it gets harder all the time. Ragnor is already thinking in terms of what happens after Celador is lost.'

'Then it is time to do something about it,' Nastrus declared.

Hope kindled briefly in Jarrod and then he remembered that the colts hadn't been able to stop the killing of the cloudsteeds. The unicorns were not pleased with the reminder.

'You are correct,' Nastrus said coolly, *'we need the lens of your Magic.'*

'It keeps coming back to that,' Jarrod thought. *'Why does it always have to be me?'*

'You should be proud,' Beldun said critically. *'To hide from one's duty is cowardice.'*

'Now hold on,' Jarrod remonstrated, *'I didn't say that I wouldn't try to help. You two just don't understand what it's like. Two years ago I was an ordinary Apprentice at the Collegium, not a very good Apprentice either, and the next thing I know I'm scrambling half across Songuard looking for you lot. That turns out to be the easiest assignment I've had. I've*

been very lucky so far, but that can't last. One of these days I'm going to fail miserably.'

'If you do as we ask, you won't fail,' Beldun said confidently.

'And if you're talking about the horn, the answer is still no. The Archmage and I will start looking for an ingredient tomorrow. As soon as we find it, we'll join forces and inflict as much damage on the enemy as we can.

'There is no other substance on this world that will serve,' Nastrus said. *'We know that you wish it were otherwise, but that is the fact.'*

'How can you be so sure?'

'What he said is real,' Beldun confirmed.

'Then we'll just have to find some other way.' Jarrod was becoming angry in his turn.

'How disappointing,' Nastrus thought acidly. *'I had assumed that your species possessed a streak of nobility, or at the very least an appreciation of self-interest.'*

'You have no sense of justice,' Beldun pronounced and turned away. Nastrus followed suit.

'Oh come on,' Jarrod said, stung by the rejection that he could feel all too clearly. *'Is it so difficult to understand my not wanting to murder someone I love?'*

The unicorns were unmoved and unmoving.

'You're being completely unreasonable,' Jarrod thought out heatedly. *'You're not even trying to see things from my point of view. I resent that imputation of cowardice. I've risked my life on more than one occasion as you very well know and you can't consider my refusal to kill a friend in cold blood as cowardice.'*

The unicorns ignored him and this time they made it obvious that they were doing it intentionally.

'You're acting like children,' he said. They continued to shut him out. *'Very well then, have it your way.'* He started for the door. *'I'm sorry if I don't measure up to your high*

standards,' he said sarcastically, *'but I am, as you often remind me, merely human.'* He stamped out.

He was hurt and he was angry. How did I get to be the villain of the piece? he asked himself. They're being completely irrational. You'd think that being as close as we are, they'd be able to see that it's impossible. He strode through the archway, his face dark. A stablehand scuttled out of his path. Jarrod didn't even notice him. He was too caught up in his sense of grievance. They had no right to treat him this way. How could they turn against him after all this time? After all the kindnesses he had shown them? All the love that he had given them? They were unnatural.

He found himself back in the Archmage's anteroom. Habit had taken his feet there. He turned and was about to retreat when the inner door opened and Ragnor came out.

"Hello there," Ragnor said. "Seen the Duty Boy?"

Jarrod shook his head.

"Be a good chap then and put the kettle on."

He watched as Jarrod complied. "You feeling all right?" he asked.

"Yes, sir." Jarrod stirred the coals under the ring.

"Turn around and let's have a look at you." Jarrod straightened up and faced him. "You look as if you've just been jilted."

"It's nothing, sir. I've just had a fight with the colts, that's all."

"That's all? You haven't had a fight with them before, have you?"

"No, sir."

"Well then, it's very serious indeed. You must come in and have a cup of chai and tell me all about it." Ragnor was trying to sound comforting and he was aware that he wasn't very good at it. He was out of practice. It had been a long time since Arabella had needed comforting and what worked for a small girl probably wouldn't work for this boy. He had to try, though. If they were going to make any progress, the lad would have to concentrate.

"Thank you, sir," Jarrod said ungraciously, turning back to watch the pot. He didn't feel like talking with Ragnor, but an invitation from the Archmage wasn't something that one could turn down. He took a palmful of leaves from the little wooden chest and tossed them into the kettle, then moved it to the hob so that the brew could steep. He hunted up a couple of mugs and filled them with a dipper. The Archmage took one from him and they went into the chamber.

"Now then," Ragnor said when they were settled, "what's this all about?"

Jarrod sipped his chai, wondering how he was going to explain things. "The colts are very upset about the cloud-steeds," he began.

"I can't blame them."

"They want to punish the Outlanders."

"Do they indeed? Well, that's an advance. Any notion of how they intend to go about it?" Ragnor kept his voice light and his tone cheerfully inquisitive. He drank some of the chai to disguise the intensity of his interest. Would this be it? he wondered. Were the unicorns finally going to reveal their secret? What had that fool verse said? His memory was not what it used to be.

"No, I don't. Whatever it is, they need Magic to focus it."

"And by Magic you mean a Magician. I see. So we're back where we started. We all want to drive the bastards back, but we lack the means." Ragnor sat back in the chair, the excitement dying.

Jarrod was tempted to leave it at that, but his need for approbation, for someone to understand how shabbily he was being treated, prevailed.

"They have the means," he said. "That's what the fight was about."

Ragnor sat forward again and drank some more chai. "And what might the means be?" he asked as casually as he could.

Jarrod took a deep breath. "Beldun says that if I take his horn and grind it up and add it to a potion, it will make it possible for any Magician to contain enough power to drive the enemy back. There's a catch though."

Ragnor's spirits dipped. Why did there have to be a catch? They were so near.

"In order to get the horn, I have to kill Beldun."

Ragnor sat up straight. "Kill Beldun? Surely not." He was shocked. In his mind, the unicorns were sacrosanct.

"I knew you'd see it my way," Jarrod said, gratified. "I refused him point-blank, of course, and they both became totally unreasonable. They refuse to talk to me. They called me a coward. They said we lacked nobility and that we had no sense of justice." The words came rapidly and his eyes brimmed.

"Dear me yes. That was very strong and quite unfair. If anyone has shown courage, it's been you." Ragnor talked to calm him. His own brain was racing. Any Magician could control sufficient power to defeat the Outlanders? That was what every single one of his predecessors had tried to achieve and it was within his grasp.

"And Beldun was willing to let you do that, was he? I find that amazing."

"He's more than willing, he's obsessed with it." Bitterness surfaced. "It would give him a permanent place of honor in that Memory of theirs." Jarrod gestured with his hands to underline his disbelief and then, reminded of the mug, drank some chai.

Ragnor put his mug aside and forced himself to relax. Gently, he told himself. This is too important to muff. "How very difficult and unpleasant for you," he said sympathetically, "but one has to remember that they don't think the way we do. You mustn't be too hard on them."

"I suppose not," Jarrod said reluctantly, "but I don't see how we can be friends while they're feeling this way."

"You can't just take some shavings? Enough for one Magician one time?"

"Apparently not."

"And it has to be you, does it?"

"Oh yes. There was no other possibility in their minds."

Ragnor changed his position in the chair. "I wish I could talk with them. There are so many questions that I would like to ask. It's ironic, isn't it? Ever since you brought them back I've been waiting and hoping that they would turn out to be our salvation and now that they're willing, they set too high a price." He shook his head. "Dear me, but it is a tempting thought." He roused himself. "Still, the important thing is to get the three of you talking again. It does no one any good to have you at loggerheads." He looked over and smiled in what he hoped was a reassuring manner.

He looked over to the waterclock. "Well, time to start getting ready for Hall. I'd be grateful if you'd ask the Boy to bring me some fresh chai. Oh, by the way, you've got a room at the top of G Staircase, just across the Court. I think you'll like it, it's got a nice big window and it's comfortably furnished. I sent your clothes over, but I kept the finery here. It'll be safer." Ragnor wanted the youngster gone, wanted to be alone so that he could think this through.

"Thank you, sir. I appreciate it." Jarrod was puzzled by the swiftness of his dismissal.

"I'll see you tomorrow morning then."

"Oh, I forgot to tell you," Jarrod said. "The unicorns say that there isn't another substance. At least not on this world. They were quite emphatic about it."

"I see. Well that puts things in a different light, doesn't it." Ragnor said slowly. "In that case I'll send for you when I need you."

"Very good, sir."

Ragnor sat on, in a brown study. The Duty Boy came with

the chai and went again. So the unicorn's horn was the key to victory and any Magician could use it. The unicorns had proved to be the answer after all and the only one who could secure the horn was Courtak. Score two for Naxania's verse.

He wondered how much of the horn would be needed to defeat the Others once and for all and how many Magicians it would take. The fewer the better, he thought. If any of the powder was left over, how long would it retain its power? He sipped his chai and let his mind dwell on the things he could accomplish if he had the protection of the unicorn's horn. He could cleanse the land that the Outlanders had defiled. He could erect a new barrier to contain the defeated remnants far to the North. He could . . . The prospect was dazzling.

Was he going to order Courtak to kill the unicorn? Yes, if he had to; no doubt about that. He'd prefer the boy to do it of his own volition, but he'd use the Voice if he had to. The costs would be high, but the stakes were even higher. They would lose one unicorn and the other would almost certainly leave. That was no small thing. He might even lose the boy. Even if he wasn't hurt physically, the damage to his spirit would be great. Poor bastard. He liked the boy and he had proved valuable; he might have become Archmage one day. But put him against the lasting defeat of the Outlanders and he was expendable.

He finished his chai and got up and poured himself a drink. If he was in Courtak's position and the unicorn asked him to do the deed, would he? Of course he would, but that wasn't a fair comparison. He admired the unicorns, delighted in their beauty, but he didn't have the personal bond with them that Courtak had. Even without that, he had had a lifetime of making hard decisions. He prided himself that he had always put the good of the Kingdom, or of the Discipline, first. After thirty years in office he could still face his reflection in the morning with equanimity. This was going to be different. He wasn't going to like himself after this one.

chapter 27

Jarrod was in his new room waiting when the Duty Boy knocked.

"Not bad," the boy said, eying the premises.

"Glad you like it," Jarrod said caustically, but he looked around with a dispassionate eye. He hadn't been in the room long enough for it to have developed any kind of resonance. The proportions were good and one of its previous tenants must have been wealthy. He was sure that the panelling hadn't been a part of the original furnishings, nor the big bay window with its broad seat and lined velvet curtains. None of the furniture measured up to them.

"Have this all to yourself, do you?" the Boy asked.

Jarrod smiled, remembering the days when a room of one's own was the limit of ambition. "So far," he replied. "Did the Archmage send you over to do research on my room?"

" 'Course not. He wants to see you." The youngster was unfazed.

"What kind of mood is he in?"

The boy grinned, revealing uneven teeth. "He stayed in his room after you left. I had to bring him his supper. He was drinking hard. He needed cold wet towels for his head this morning."

"Do they work?"

"Depends how you look at it. He's in a foul temper before, but he doesn't say much, and he's in a foul temper afterwards, but his mouth works. I prefer before." It was delivered with all the man-of-the-world aplomb that a thirteen-year-old could hope for.

"That doesn't sound too encouraging," Jarrod said. He knotted his belt rope tighter. "Well, I don't suppose it'll get any better if I dawdle. Lead on: I might as well get it over with."

He played the role of the erring Collegiant about to be haled in front of the Dean, but the parallel was apt. He had had time to reflect on his confession. He had felt better for it at the time, but he regretted it now. Ragnor was going to browbeat him and Jarrod couldn't really blame him. He had tossed and turned for a good part of the night going through the arguments. He had tried to look at things objectively, the way that Greylock had taught him, and he had to admit that if he were Ragnor he would be planning to use the unicorn's horn.

He followed the Boy up to the workroom and waited while he was announced. He walked into the semicircular room with its arc of windows and saw the Archmage at work on the long table. Jarrod hoped for a moment that he had decided to try for an alternative, but then noticed that the Archmage was dressed in a loose shirt, stout cord pants and boots.

Ragnor turned from the table. "Come on in, lad. Come on in."

He didn't sound as if he'd had a rough night and he didn't look too bad. His eyes were puffy, but his hair and beard were newly washed and he seemed alert and lively.

"Good morning, Archmage."

"Can you ride in that robe?" Ragnor asked.

"I've done it before," Jarrod said, trying to fathom the direction the conversation was going to take, "but it isn't terribly comfortable."

"Think one of unicorns would let me ride him?"

"I expect so. Can you manage without reins? They won't take a bit."

Ragnor smiled. "My thigh muscles will probably outlast

the rest of me. My balance, however, is not always what it used to be.'' The eyes twinkled. "I shall hang onto the saddle for dear life. Why don't you go and change into something more suitable and join me at the stables?''

Half an hour later, Jarrod found the Archmage in the colts' loose box. He was patting Beldun's neck and looking pleased with himself. The colts were amused by him. There was no trace of the previous day's rancor.

'We like this one. He brings us sugar,' Nastrus explained.

'Would you let him ride you?' Jarrod asked.

'He doesn't look too heavy.'

'No tricks now.'

'Spoilsport.' Nastrus kicked up his heels in a miniature buck.

Jarrod turned to Ragnor. "Nastrus will be happy to let you ride him, Excellency,'' he said.

Ragnor had one eyebrow raised. "That is most kind of him,'' he said dubiously.

"It's only fair, sir,'' Jarrod said. "I understand that he has already been well bribed.''

The Archmage chuckled. "Couldn't resist it,'' he admitted. "They are ridiculously easy to spoil.'' The smile died and he became businesslike. "My saddle's just outside the door. I think it would be best if you saddled him, he's used to you.''

They rode out through busy courts, past the sentries at the gates, and into the countryside. Jarrod checked to see how the Archmage was doing and saw that, despite his protestations, the man had an excellent seat. His hands were resting lightly on the pommel and he showed every indication of enjoying himself. The colts moved into a canter and, unbidden, held it to a moderate pace.

"Wonderfully smooth gait,'' the Archmage called over. "D'you think they could manage a bit of a gallop?''

As soon as Jarrod had conveyed the request, the colts stretched out happily and raced, side by side, down the road.

He didn't abandon himself totally to the joy of the movement, he was too busy speculating on exactly how Ragnor was going to handle things once the galloping had stopped. The colts were aware of his thoughts, but concentrated on the running. Even so, Jarrod could detect a continuing anger at the fate of the cloudsteeds. Fifteen minutes later the colts slowed to a trot.

"Exhilarating," Ragnor said. "Now let's find a pond or a stream where our friends can get a drink."

As he said it, the colts came abreast a broad wedge of trees left as a windbreak for the adjoining fields, swerved off the road and under the branches. Jarrod knew that they were going to do it, but the move surprised Ragnor and he grabbed for the saddle.

"Sorry," Jarrod said, "I should have warned you."

"Knowing what your mount is thinking must be an enormous advantage," Ragnor said, ducking to avoid a low branch.

"Riding becomes unconscious," Jarrod conceded. "My body reacts as if it were part of the unicorn."

"And you can understand them perfectly clearly, can you?" Ragnor asked. "You don't have to translate or anything?"

"No, not really. It's as if I was thinking the thoughts, although there are times when they go too fast for me, and there are some concepts of ours, like lying, that they just can't comprehend."

"As there are concepts of theirs, like dying, that we do not comprehend," Ragnor added.

Here it comes, Jarrod thought. Part of him could stand back and assess what was happening and that part admired the ease with which Ragnor had turned the conversation.

"Like dying," Jarrod agreed.

Ragnor turned his head and regarded him steadily. Jarrod met the gaze.

"You know why I asked to ride a unicorn," the Archmage said.

"I didn't think that it was a sudden desire for exercise," Jarrod replied. "On the other hand, most people would pay to touch a unicorn and give their front teeth for the chance to ride on one."

"You're right on both counts, of course," Ragnor said. The boy was fencing with him; not a good sign. "My intention, however, was not to indulge an old man's whim, or, to be more honest, not simply to indulge my whim. I should like the four of us to have a conversation. Are our friends aware of what we say to each other?"

"They don't understand the sounds of the words, but they are very good at picking up on emotions. They know what you say because they see it in my mind."

"Very well. I think we should discuss the use of a unicorn's horn."

Jarrod could feel the colts' intense interest. They continued to amble forward, stopping every so often to forage, but their attention was clamped on the humans.

"Let us be clear that we are discussing the death of a unicorn," he said bluntly.

"I am aware of that, but I am right in saying, am I not, that the idea came from the unicorns themselves?"

"You are."

"Did the idea come from one colt in particular, or was it a joint notion?"

"The initial idea was Beldun's, but Nastrus thoroughly approves," Jarrod replied, echoing the colts' thoughts.

"Would you please ask them for me why they are prepared to die in our behalf." Ragnor sounded like the Justicer he was.

"I've told you that. . . ." Jarrod began.

Ragnor held up a hand and cut him off. "I know you have, son, but oblige me and ask them anyway." He was sitting very straight in the saddle and the sun shone through his windblown hair, turning it into a nimbus. If Nastrus hadn't had his head down cropping, it would have made for an impressive picture.

" 'Meaningful sacrifice is the noblest of ends,' is the way Beldun puts it," Jarrod said, "and Nastrus reminds me that the Outlanders need to be punished for the slaughter of the cloudsteeds. He further points out that I am not capable of doing the job properly without the horn." He gave the report flatly. He knew where this was leading and he was beginning to feel trapped. He didn't like the feeling.

"I cannot disagree with either statement," Ragnor said, "can you?"

Jarrod remembered Magister Handrom using logic this way to drive him into a corner. It had made him feel small and stupid. What Ragnor wouldn't understand was that this had nothing to do with logic and everything to do with how he felt about the unicorns.

"We may not have been able to destroy the Outlanders, but I did manage to drive them out of Fort Bandor and you scotched their invasion," he said stubbornly.

The colts came to rest in a grass-carpeted clearing caused by the death of some great tree. Ragnor made no move to dismount, but sat his unicorn comfortably, arms crossed.

"Quite true," the Archmage conceded, "but we had no luck when we tried it beyond the Causeways and I think you'll admit that your recent experience with the shield demonstrated our physical limitations."

"That's as may be," Jarrod began again, and again the imperious hand went up.

"I know, son, I know. Ask them if you are the only one who can perform the task, or if someone like myself could substitute for you?"

"They thank you for your offer," Jarrod relayed. "Beldun thinks that it displays largeness of spirit, but the meaning of the sacrifice would be diminished if someone else were to"—

he hesitated momentarily—"perform the act. There is a concept of beauty involved that I don't understand."

Ragnor smiled sadly across the intervening space. "I am sorry," he said. "I had hoped to spare you."

He's talking as if it was a foregone conclusion, Jarrod thought, but there has to be a way out of this somehow. Time, I need more time.

'No one is trying to stampede you,' Beldun interjected quietly.

Jarrod ignored him. "If the good of the realm required it, could you bring yourself to kill Arabella? With your own hand?" he asked the Archmage.

There was silence. Ragnor sat straighter and pulled his shoulders back. His eyes were wide open, but he had ceased to see Jarrod. Birds sang in the neighboring trees. A small animal bustled about in the undergrowth beyond the clearing and the sound of the unicorns' blunt teeth ripping at the grass was quite clear.

"That's a very good question," he acknowledged at length. "I could order her death, I'm pretty sure of that, but, in sober truth, I'm not convinced that I could do it directly."

"Well, there you are then." Relief flooded over Jarrod.

"However," Ragnor continued thoughtfully, reasonably, "if she wanted to die, demanded it of me, and if I believed that she was absolutely right in wanting it, I should have to do it. If I did not, my love for her would be based on selfishness."

The colts' approbation filled Jarrod's mind and his spirits plummeted. The empty feeling that is the amalgam of fear and anticipated pain was back.

'He is wise, your Archmage,' Beldun said.

'At last, a human who understands,' Nastrus remarked.

Jarrod did not find either statement helpful or sensitive. Beldun would not pressure him on this, he knew that, but he was also aware that both the colts would be deeply disappointed in him and, by extension, so would the rest of the family. They would love him still, of that he was certain, but things would never be quite the same. Human beings could mask their feelings from one another, but the colts could not and in that regard he was one of them. It was the blessing and the curse of their special communication.

'No matter what I decide, nothing's going to be the same again,' he thought angrily and the unicorns' wry agreement gave him no solace.

Ragnor sat waiting quietly. The tension seemed to have gone out of him and he swayed gently as Nastrus ate his way forward. He would be disappointed too, though he probably wouldn't stop trying, Jarrod thought. Would Greylock be saddened on his return to find that he had passed up a great opportunity? Jarrod wished that he were there. He would have known what to do. He had always known what Jarrod should do, but he was locked in the Place of Power. No need to wonder what Marianna would say. She'd think he was weak and vacillating. She'd be right, he thought, I lack the courage for this.

'We will give you strength.' The combined thought from the colts interrupted his self-scrutiny.

'What if I fail after all this?' he asked desperately. *'What if something goes wrong? I can't bring you back to life again.'*

'You are gifted in your Magic,' Nastrus said. *'We have seen that many times and I shall still be here with you.'*

'If your intentions and your heart are right, the death will not be sullied,' Beldun replied.

Their confidence buoyed him a little. Who knew him better than they did? And the unicorns could not lie. He lifted his head.

"I seem to have no choice," he said aloud.

There was bitterness in the strong young voice and Ragnor was glad that Nastrus was ahead. It was never pleasant to witness the loss of innocence. He bowed his head in acknowledgment. "In that case," he said, anticipating Jarrod, "I think perhaps we should head for home."

The unicorns came around as if he had commanded them. They enjoyed the canter back to Celador. The humans did not.

chapter 28

Jarrod sat on his new bed and stared at the panelling. Now that the unthinkable had become the imminent, he found that he had been expecting it all along. He didn't feel anything like he had thought he might on those fleeting occasions when he had allowed himself to wonder. He didn't feel devastated, it wasn't a shock, he just felt hollow and numb. His emotions seemed to have dried up, which was all to the good, but there was no telling how long the mood would last. He wanted to get things over with. He got up and tugged his jacket into order. No sense in waiting.

He walked briskly into Stable Court. Grooms and handlers went about their business in the hot sun. The courtyard was full of riding and carriage horses belonging to departing courtiers. There had been no sign of them when they had ridden in two hours earlier and Jarrod wondered if some new enemy offensive was causing the exodus. He threaded his way between animals to the unicorns' loosebox.

He pushed the half door open, knowing the mix of thoughts and feelings that the colts were experiencing. Their greeting had been warm but subdued. They too were feeling the aftermath of the decision. They evinced no surprise at seeing him again so soon and, if they were aware of the deadness at his center, it did not show in their minds.

'I think this should happen soon,' Jarrod said without preamble.

Beldun came over and rubbed his muzzle against Jarrod's shoulder. *'Whenever it suits you.'*

'*What, exactly, must I do?*' he asked.

'*You must get the sharpest knife that you can find,*' Beldun thought calmly, '*and we will go to a pleasant, secluded place. There is a large vein that runs down my neck. You will cut that. Then you must act quickly. Grasp my horn in both hands and break it in half.*'

The unicorn paused and waited for a comment or reaction, but there was none. Jarrod was simply accepting the information and storing it away.

'*At that point,*' Beldun continued, '*Nastrus, with my help and I hope with yours, will send me back along the Lines of Force to the Island. I mean no offense to your world, but I should like my remains to enrich the grasslands of our ancestors.*'

'*I see,*' Jarrod said dispassionately from within the crystal cage of not-feeling. '*And how long will your horn hold its power?*'

'*It begins to fade from the moment it is broken, but for your purposes, I think that it would be effective for one of your sennights.*'

'*And how much would I need, do you think, to inflict "a just retribution" on the Outlanders?*'

'*If you do it within a day, a piece about half the span of a hoof should suffice.*'

'*Very well then,*' Jarrod said, '*I shall be back tomorrow morning after the Making of the Day, providing I can find a suitable knife. It shouldn't be difficult in a place like Celador.*'

The thoughts he was forming, though concrete, seemed unreal, as if some play was being acted out for an unseen audience. He reached up and rubbed Beldun's muzzle. There ought to be something he should say at this point, but he could think of nothing. He patted the neck in an abstracted manner, turned and walked away. He detected the colts' unease as he left the loosebox, but it did not trouble him as it normally would. Time to talk to Ragnor, he thought.

The Archmage looked up from his work table as Jarrod came in unannounced.

"Hello," he said. "You look like a man who could use a drink."

Jarrod hesitated. Wine might make him feel better, but it might dissolve the intangible wall that mewed off his emotions and he could not afford that. "Thank you, sir, but I'll pass this time."

"Just as you like," the Archmage said pleasantly, trying to gauge Jarrod's mood. Had the lad changed his mind? He'd find out soon enough. "Let's sit down," he said, moving away from the work table and gesturing to the chairs by the hearth. "One of the nice things, among many, about this room is how cool it is in summer. It gets the sun, but up this high there's usually a breeze and with the doors and windows open, it really is most pleasant."

He was talking to put Jarrod at his ease and to give himself time to marshal his best arguments, though he doubted that Jarrod could be swayed again, short of using the Voice.

"Now, what can I do for you, young man?" he asked as he plopped himself down in the chair closer to the windows.

"I need a knife," Jarrod said. "It's got to be very sharp; very, very sharp."

Suicide? Ragnor thought with a start of alarm. "What do you need the knife for?" he asked as lightly as he could.

"Surely you can't have forgotten that I am supposed to commit a murder," Jarrod said acidly.

Ragnor winced inwardly at the choice of words. "Yes, of course," he said. "When d'you think you'll need it?" He gripped the arms of the chair a little too tightly and knew it. His sympathetic smile was mere show. The blood was beginning to hammer at the base of his throat.

"The sooner the better. I'd like to perform the rite as soon after the Making of the Day as I can. Beldun is willing."

Ragnor sat a little straighter and took a deep breath. Keep

calm, he told himself. Don't spook the boy whatever you do. "D'you want me to come with you?"

"No!" The monosyllable was a whipcrack and Jarrod knew that he had overreacted. "I should very much like to have your help with the preparations," he said more gently. "Everything must be done perfectly and I'm afraid I might make a mistake." It was part palliative, part truth.

"Of course, dear boy, of course. I should be honored. I'll take care of all the details."

"Just the purification tonight. I thought that tomorrow, after I've—after the ceremony has been performed, we could prepare the potions for the spell together. The sooner we blast the Outlanders the better. The horn loses its power. The quicker we use it, the less we'll need to use and I'd like to have enough left over so that we can try again if we have to. After a sennight, the potency's gone."

The gods of the odds be praised, Ragnor thought, he said "We." If the boy had insisted on going it alone, he would have acquiesced, what else could he do? But he was going to be a part of it. His whole life had been directed to this threshold, all his predecessors had striven to reach it, and now it was here. And suddenly there didn't seem to be any time left.

"Eminently sensible," he said and the smile that accompanied the words was broad and genuine.

"There are some other details."

"Name 'em, son, name 'em. I'll take care of them."

"Can you get the troops pulled back behind the Causeways?" Jarrod asked.

"I expect so. Crispus Nix owes us. When d'you want that to happen?"

"By sunset tomorrow."

Ragnor whistled softly. "Don't want much, do you?"

"If all goes well, I'd like to perform the spell tomorrow night."

"We'd better have a curfew after Hall then. I'll speak to

the Chamberlain and the Seneschal. I suppose we ought to consult the High Council, or as many of them as we can reach. It's an exercise in politics, I'm afraid, but they should at least know about it before we do it.''

"I'll leave all that to you.''

"Right you are,'' Ragnor said cheerfully. "I suggest you take it easy for the rest of the day. I'll send the Duty Boy over with your supper. I, unfortunately, have to preside at Magicians' Hall this evening, but I'll see you here directly afterwards.'' He looked over at Jarrod and smiled again. "It's going to be a busy couple of days.'' Jarrod did not return the smile.

The room gleamed softly in the light of the long tapers when Jarrod returned that evening. Flames danced in the windowpanes and all was black outside. He had eaten well and bathed carefully. He was wearing nothing but his robe and a pair of sandals, but the room felt hot and close. A small fire burned in the grate and three vessels sat on the hob. He'd be glad enough of the warmth sitting naked through the night.

The work table and the stools were gone and the two armchairs had been pushed back against the wall. Ragnor was sitting in one of them, waiting. He wore the embroidered robe he had put on for Hall.

"How are you feeling?'' he asked. He conned Jarrod quickly for signs, but the face was smooth and bland.

"Well, thank you, Archmage.''

It might have been the candlelight, but it seemed to Ragnor that the boy had regained his color. In fact he looked ridiculously young. From my senescent viewpoint, at least, he amended.

"Good; then let's get on with it, shall we?'' he said. "I laid out the pentacles myself, I'll have you know. I'll get the first potion.''

The Archmage nodded to himself, as if approving of his

decision. He moved over to the fireplace and retrieved one of the beakers from the hob. Jarrod looked at the two pentacles, one within the other, that occupied the center of the floor.

"I did a good job with them, though I say so as shouldn't." Ragnor was at his shoulder.

Jarrod accepted the beaker and drank. The liquid was thick and spicy. It felt as if it was coating his insides. As he finished, the Archmage made a small gesture. There was a faint pop and the lines of the pentacles took fire. The light was uniformly even, every line arrow-straight. The old boy has reason to be proud, he thought. They're flawless.

Ragnor fetched a second beaker and, hitching his robe clear of the floor, made his careful way across the lines. He set the vessel down slightly to the side of the center, turned and made his way back.

"You can adjust the placement when you get in there," he said. "I'll keep the fire going so that the last one will be warm when you emerge."

"Thank you, sir. I appreciate your keeping vigil with me." He went over to the side of the room and put the beaker down. He stepped back and pulled the robe off over his head, then he shucked the sandals.

"Well, here goes," he said with a tight little smile.

"May it be peaceful for you," Ragnor said and watched as Jarrod walked over the glowing lines and settled. He turned and busied himself tidying up the little fire. It was going to be a long night, but this close to winning he was prepared to lose a little sleep.

Jarrod sat, legs crossed, one hand resting on each knee. He stared at the wall of bookcases. The last time he had stared at that spot, it had been covered by the walls of Celador. His right arm drifted out and hovered by the beaker. His fingers felt the outline of the handle and then grasped it lightly. He let it go and moved the vessel slightly. He brought his arm back and then let it swing to the beaker again. Better.

He could feel the effects of the first potion. He felt very full and the persistent, dull pain along the tops of his shoulders had gone. He circled his head to the left and then back to the right. The tension in his neck had vanished. He was embarked. It ought to be an occasion for tears, but he was drained. Nothing mattered much. Better not to feel. It hadn't done him any good. Everyone he had ever cared about left him—his parents, Greylock, Marianna and now, soon, Beldun. Much better not to feel.

He drew in a breath and began the litany of concentration, welcoming the descent into himself. He heard the steady rhythms of his heart, saw his breath as it left his nostrils. He felt the quiet coursing of the potion through his blood. Let the potion work its will upon his flesh; let his mind become a willing blank. It would be a release.

Ragnor sat beside the fireplace. He extinguished the tapers with a blink of his mind. No point in wasting expensive wax. The room had enough light without them. It was bathed in the familiar greenish glow that, in better times, would have had couples gawping on the leads. Precious few left to see it now. The Magicians in their rooms below were inured to it, Arabella had sent her ladies-in-waiting to their homes, most of the men were gone; only the townspeople, unimpressible as always, had refused to budge. Just as well, Ragnor thought. Everything pointed to the unicorn's horn being the answer, but who could be certain about anything to do with unicorns?

Jarrod's eyes slowly came back into focus. He sat very still. Everything around him was pale green, as if he was sitting on the bottom of a pond on a sunny day. His eyes saw something that should not be there. He identified it as a curved dagger with a malachite handle. Ragnor must have put it there during the night. He knew where he was. He listened to his body. The potions had done their work. He glanced quickly at the beaker. It was empty, as he had expected it to be. He got awkwardly to his feet and stretched.

He felt none of the stabbings of returning circulation. He took a deep breath and looked around the room. The Archmage was sleeping in his chair, head lolled, mouth agape.

He smiled to himself and bent to retrieve the beaker. He picked up the dagger and then turned towards the hearth. He concentrated and the light went out. Darkness claimed the room only to relinquish it an instant later as the taper wicks lit up. Jarrod walked over to the fire and put the beaker on the mantlepiece. The last potion still sat inside the hearth, but the fire was long since dead. He picked it up and drank it slowly. He put the beaker down beside its twin and the dagger beside it. He went and got dressed, came back and got the dagger, looked round, dowsed the tapers and left the Archmage to his rest.

The morning air was fresh after the night's croprain. He pushed the dagger carefully between rope and robe and then hitched the skirt to avoid the puddles he knew would be lurking in the hollows of the old flagstones. He could feel the potions fermenting pleasantly inside him. He was calm and self-possessed, as if he had done all his grieving for Beldun in the night.

He hadn't come out with any particular destination in mind, but he knew now that he would Make the Day with the unicorns. It was fitting somehow. They had joined him in the ceremony before and they had always enjoyed it. The Guardian had made some comment about it, though he wasn't sure of the context. "A binding of the air before the sun's rays could distort it," that was it. No matter; this time the rite would be more for himself and the colts than for the sun.

The colts' greeting was no different than on other days. They seemed to have known that he would come to them early, but they were pleased with his decision to include them in the Making of the Day and they participated with gentle enthusiasm.

When it was over, Jarrod led Nastrus out to the mounting block and climbed up with great care. The unsheathed dagger was a nuisance. There was little chance of anyone seeing them at this hour, but if they were spotted it would look better if he wasn't carrying a naked weapon. The East Gate was open and the sentries did not challenge them. It was the same gate, Jarrod realized, that Marianna and he had ridden out of on the first leg of their hunt for the unicorns.

They rode towards the mountains of Talisman and the still buried sun. They crossed the clear ground that surrounded the walls and rode on between the quandry trees. Stirring birds began to twitter and Jarrod thought he detected an infinitessimal lessening of the dark. The colts were far more interested in the smell of things and their nostrils were flared wide. A skittish breeze ruffled their manes and anticipation and contentment were melded in their minds.

About half a league from Celador, Nastrus swung off the road and onto a track that wound south through hawthorn and highbush barberry. Wagons had come this way and the path was rutted, causing the colts to pick their way carefully. Jarrod could see nothing, but the colts were quite confident. He was aware when they abandoned the track because twigs whisked his sides. He kept his head down low, just in case.

The unicorns stopped when they reached a clearing. The sky, now that he could see it, had turned pale grey. The bright white of the flowers called ermine tails stood out from the gloomy ground. Everything else was obscure.

'I shall be happy here,' Beldun thought. 'This is a good place.'

Jarrod lifted his leg over Nastrus' shoulder and slid off. The colt moved on and began to crop.

'Don't you ever stop thinking about your stomach?' Jarrod asked him. There was no censure in the thought.

'It's good grass,' Nastrus replied, but Jarrod was pleased to detect an undertone of defensiveness.

'Are you ready?' Beldun asked quietly. 'It would be best for us both if it was swift.'

'I don't think I shall ever be ready for this,' Jarrod returned, *'but I am prepared to go through with it.'* He slid the dagger out of his belt and reflexively tested its edge.

'Then it is time for you to release me.'

Beldun lay down, back legs first, forelegs after, a neat, pale, symmetrical figure against the lingering darkness of the grass. The neck was arched and the head held high. The light was waxing and Jarrod saw that Nastrus had moved to the side of the clearing and was watching. Above them, the bellies of the clouds showed the first touches of rose. Jarrod looked down at the dagger and then back at Beldun.

'It is necessary and it will be glorious,' the colt assured him.

There was encouragement from Nastrus and Jarrod took two paces forward. He hesitated. He swallowed: his mouth was suddenly dry.

'Do not think of it as ending my life,' Beldun counselled. *'Think rather, that you will be ensuring the permanence of my existence.'*

Jarrod squared his shoulders and moved forward. He stopped by Beldun's side. The colt's head was level with his shoulder. The long spiral of the horn was pink in this earliest of lights and there was a blush on flank and shoulder.

'It's best to do it quickly,' Beldun said.

Jarrod leaned forward and draped his right arm over the neck; almost like an embrace. The handle of the dagger felt slick and unreliable in his hand, a hand that trembled as the blade came to rest against the throat. Then it was as if his arm acted of its own accord the way it had in the pentacle. This time it swept upwards and Jarrod felt the sharp edge bite. Blood fountained, unexpectedly vivid, impossibly red. It splashed on the grass, turning the ermine tails crimson. Blood was everywhere. He could smell it. He could taste it.

His mind was filled with a joy that was as irresistible as it was inappropriate. He staggered back and threw the dagger away. Radiant satisfaction poured through him, but the tears ran down his face nevertheless. The intensity of Beldun's sending lessened and he knew that the end was coming. The head drooped and then the neck sagged. Beldun rolled onto his side as the first rays of the infant sun came in below the treetops and illuminated him.

'*Quickly now.*' The thought was urgent. '*I must be gone.*'

Jarrod ran around and dropped to his knees on the blood-stained grass. He avoided the great blue eyes and grasped the horn with both hands. He braced himself and pushed out sharply with his thumbs. The nacre snapped cleanly and as it did, a rush of power from Nastrus whirled through Jarrod. Beldun's thoughts strengthened. There was a burst of energy like a shower of stars and Jarrod was alone in the middle of the clearing. There was a wand of unicorn horn in his right hand.

'*Now that was a good death.*' The unwanted thought intruded, filled with satisfaction and touched with envy. '*He's home now, but he is forever linked to you and to your people. You did exceeding well.*'

Jarrod did not respond. The numbness was back and his eyes, though dry, were hot. He stayed on his knees staring at the imprint of Beldun's body on the grass. His shadow stretched blackly across it. The bloodstains were already turning rusty and soon the template of the unicorn would be gone. I should be feeling horror, he thought. I should be feeling remorse. He felt nothing. He'd done what he'd been told to do. He always did what he was told to do.

'*It's time to go,*' Nastrus said walking over to him. '*You must take his horn back and use it.*'

Jarrod got slowly to his feet and looked at Nastrus. He was so like his brother in many ways, but he was not Beldun. There would never be another Beldun.

'*Shall I kneel down, or can you mount from there?*' Nastrus asked.

'*Don't kneel!*' Jarrod's mind played back Beldun setting down for death.

He pushed the memory away and launched himself at Nastrus in a wild scramble to get up on his back. He was hampered by the horn and his robe, but he made it. He pulled himself upright and got a leg across. He tugged at his robe with his left hand, first one side then the other, until it was high enough to let him straddle comfortably.

Nastrus moved out slowly, but Jarrod did not look back at the clearing with its stained blossoms and abandoned dagger. He had no need. The details were all there in his head and would be for as long as he lived. He moved automatically to avoid low branches, but he didn't really see them. They were soon back on the track and then on the road to Celador. He sat, grasping the half horn like a sceptre, and behind unseeing eyes blood fountained again and again.

chapter 29

Jarrod sat close to the cold fireplace, oblivious to the arguments that swirled around the room. He watched the familiar faces indifferently. The Princess Regnant was seated with a modicum of state on the Archmage's bed and the rest of them stood. Ragnor, Handrom and a Magister from the Collegium whose name he didn't know, all facing towards Arabella. They're afraid to come near me, Jarrod thought. They don't even look this way; they just talk about me as if I weren't here. Who could blame them? What did one say to a unicorn killer?

His arrival at the capital had been greeted with silence. The horn by that time had been hidden in his sleeve. The guard had been changed since they had ridden out and no one could have known that he had left with two unicorns and returned with one, but he read disgust and accusation in every face they passed. He had taken a long bath and had scrubbed his skin until it hurt, but he could still smell blood.

Ragnor had been kind, or at least he had tried to be. The old man couldn't understand how he felt, of course. How could he? A warcat warrior would know how it was to lose a part of oneself. They seldom survived the loss of a partner, but Jarrod would survive. He knew now, as the warriors had always known, that the aftermath of death was not pain, but an infinitely arid emptiness. He might be able to keep it at bay while he was awake, but sleeping would be unbearable. There was no refuge there from his memory, his relentless, infallible memory. Memory was Beldun's friend, but it was his enemy now.

"Jarrod." His shoulder was being shaken. "Come along, lad. We need you."

When had Ragnor come over to him? Why hadn't he noticed? He looked up enquiringly.

Ragnor smiled reassuringly and patted his shoulder. "Time for you to join in the debate," he said quietly, "but you don't have to worry; when all is said and done, you're the only one who will decide what you will do. I'll back you all the way."

He turned back towards the others. "Majesty, fellow colleagues," he said and the conversation around the bed died instantly. "The Acting Mage of Paladine has given us a priceless opportunity, dearly bought. He has shown a courage unmatched on any battlefield and the gift that he has won must be wisely used. We only have one chance."

"This is all so rushed," Handrom said petulantly. "It isn't fair to expect us to make a decision of this magnitude with so little warning and so little information."

"I can tell you from my own experience, Dean," Arabella said in a wry voice, "that there is never enough time or information for the really difficult decisions." Ragnor flashed her a look of gratitude.

"It is the spell that we must decide on," he said. "The Mage has earned the right to perform the Magic and the final choice will be his, but it is our duty to advise him." Ragnor's hand settled on Jarrod's shoulder and stayed there.

"I say that we should use the only proven method of success that the Discipline has come up with thus far." Handrom was irritated and didn't bother to hide it.

"You're talking about your airspouts, aren't you?" Ragnor said.

"Of course I am. We destroyed the Outlanders with them, didn't we?"

"We did indeed, Dean, but we must remember that they proved ineffective against the main body of their atmosphere." Typical, Ragnor thought. Academics are all the same. They inflate an insight into a theory and spend the rest of their lives defending it.

"But I doubt that that would have been the case if we had been possessed of the kind of power that we are talking about now," Handrom replied on cue.

"Perhaps something a little more traditional would suffice." Arabella's words were softly spoken, but they swung every head in her direction. "It would seem to me that the Spell of Dissolution would be a good candidate. Would you agree, my Lord Mage?"

It took Jarrod a beat to realize that the title was his. "I think not, Your Grace," he said. "Not that it isn't a very sound idea, but it requires great delicacy of control. The unicorns are certain that the horn will protect me, but they are not human and I have no idea how the potion will affect me physically. The potential for disaster with the Spell of Dissolution, or with the Spell of Unbinding, is very high and I shouldn't like to risk it."

He spoke calmly and rationally, with respect but without deference. Ragnor squeezed his shoulder gently.

"Do you have a suggestion, my lord?" the Princess Regnant asked.

Jarrod glanced up at Ragnor before he answered. "I thought that the Canticle of Dissipation would be best."

There was a squeak of disbelief from the nameless Magister.

Jarrod smiled. There was no warmth in it. "Yes I know," he said, "the lowly Canticle, used by Village Magicians to disperse fog. Dean Handrom was quite right when he said that it was the power that made the difference, only in this case it's the containment of the power that is the key. The power has been there all along."

"Then why not the airspouts?" Handrom ventured.

"Because I do not know the workings of that particular piece of Weatherwarding." The mirthless smile appeared again. "They didn't teach it at the Collegium in my day. Besides, the Canticle is, to my mind at least, peculiarly fitting."

Ragnor had his doubts, but he did not let them show. Something a little grander would have been more to his liking. Village Magic was somewhat anticlimactic after centuries of effort.

"Well, that's settled then," he said quickly. "Dean Handrom's suggestion of Weather Magic is most timely and Your Majesty's thought of the Spell of Dissolution would be ideal were it not for the frailties of the practitioners."

"When will the Canticle be performed?" Arabella asked as she rose from the bed.

"It will have to be tonight. Some time after the twenty-sixth hour," Jarrod said.

"I spoke yesterday with Your Majesty on the subject of recalling the troops," Ragnor interposed.

"And I have so instructed General Nix," Arabella replied.

"Your Majesty is most gracious. I also took the liberty of talking with the Chamberlain and your Seneschal," he continued.

"And there will be a curfew in both Palace and town from dusk to dawn," she finished for him.

Ragnor let go of Jarrod's shoulder and performed a bow. "One last thing," he said when he was upright again. "It should go without saying that word of this venture goes no farther than this room, but I have found that it is always wiser to say it. I thank you all for coming here and giving us the benefit of your counsel."

Jarrod rose from his chair and Ragnor went and escorted the Princess Regnant from the room. The rest followed them.

"A glass of sack is what's needed," the Archmage said as he returned. "Help yourself." He headed for the sideboard. "I'm sorry to have put you through that," he continued as Jarrod came up to him, "but I can assure you that it was most necessary." He poured a cup and handed it to Jarrod and then filled another for himself. "This way, if something goes wrong, they're implicated, and if we pull it off, they won't be nearly so jealous as they would be if they hadn't been consulted." He put an arm round Jarrod's shoulder and steered him back towards the fireplace and the chairs that flanked it.

"Even the death of a unicorn is a political event for you," Jarrod said with a tinge of bitterness.

"Life's a political event for me, son, and it's a damned good thing for the Discipline and for this Kingdom that it is," Ragnor replied, unperturbed. "Now then, the Canticle of Dissipation is it?"

"I've always thought of their atmosphere as a kind of fog," Jarrod said. "When I was a boy, I thought of the Great Maze as the good fog and the Outland atmosphere as the bad fog."

"Well, I suppose there's an irony about defeating them with the simplest of spells." He smiled slowly. "It might not be a bad thing to start history with an irony. I have a feeling that it will take itself far too seriously. The more I think about it, the better the notion seems." He sipped the wine. "You feeling all right? No regrets?"

"I don't know about regrets," Jarrod said. "I expect they'll come later no matter what happens tonight. If you mean, am I going to go through with it, you needn't worry. I'm going to find it hard enough to live with myself as it is. How could I possibly face myself if I didn't at least try to use the horn? No, no; we're going to prepare the potion and I'm going to perform the Canticle of Dissipation."

"We are going to perform the Canticle," Ragnor corrected quietly.

"Well, I was going to talk to you about that."

"Oh really?" There was a warning in the question.

Jarrod shrugged. "I have an affinity for unicorns. Nothing about them has ever harmed me, but I can't vouch for what would happen to you if you swallowed the horn powder."

"That's a risk that we'll just have to take," Ragnor said drily.

"But . . ." Jarrod began.

Ragnor cut him off. "There's something you better understand, young man. I am going to join you in the performance of this Magic. I do it partly for you and partly out of prudence. You will be venturing into unknown territory and to let you do it alone would be both heartless and stupid. If you lose control the—how did you put it?—the potential for disaster is high. If I am to be of any use at that point, I have to contain that kind of energy. Without the horn I cannot do that."

He settled back in his chair and cocked his head to one side. "Those are both compelling reasons," he said, "but if I left you with the impression that all my motives were altruistic, I should be lying by omission. Your life could be said to have been leading up to this point. The same is true of mine. My entire Archmageship will be judged by what we do tonight. Nothing else will be remembered, and if you think that I am going to step quietly aside, you're very much mistaken. I will not have it said that I had the chance to help deliver my people and shirked it."

"It's not that I don't want your help, Archmage, I welcome it. I simply thought that if I failed, I am expendable, whereas if we both failed it would be a huge victory for the enemy."

"That's another risk we have to take," Ragnor replied. "Now, what's the plan of action?" He took a long drink and Jarrod followed his lead.

"I thought that we would purify and fortify ourselves in the usual way, but we would add the powdered horn to the potions."

"Sounds sensible to me. You going to grind the horn down?"

"I thought I'd powder half of it this time. That, according to Beldun, should be enough for both of us. The horn loses power steadily, but there should be plenty left for someone to try again in a couple of days if we don't pull it off the first time.''

Ragnor nodded in agreement. ''How long before the horn is useless? he asked.

''About a sennight, why?''

''Good. It would be dangerous stuff to have around. Think of the potential for misuse; think of the temptation it would generate in the bosom of an ambitious Magician—and we do have one or two of them.''

''I see your point. I hadn't thought of that.''

''Where d'you figure on performing the Canticle?''

''I had thought about the Upper Causeway. It's the obvious place. On the other hand, the Outlanders are awfully close and whatever happens is bound to rile them. It's even possible that they can detect the presence of the horn and that they might try to stop us before we started. I think I'd rather be well out of range. The horn may protect us from the power of the Lines of Force, but I doubt it would do much good against fire weapons.''

''I'll go along with that. What about the balcony upstairs? It's high up, it's private and, since we are going to keep this quiet until after it's all over, the Duty Boy will find out bodies in the morning should the worst come to the worst. They won't have to drag us through the citadel to get us home.''

''I don't see why we shouldn't do it there,'' Jarrod said.

At any other time he would have been flattered that the Archmage was discussing this as equal to equal, but it didn't occur to him now. Discussing these matters as if they were planning a humdrum case of Magic making was bizarre enough.

''One last point,''Ragnor said. ''What are you planning to wear?''

Jarrod looked up and the corners of his lips curled slightly. ''I'll see if I have a clean robe; if not I'll have to borrow one.''

"Not this time, you don't," Ragnor said decisively. "We're going to dress up for this one."

"It isn't really necessary. . . ." Ragnor's waving hand stopped him.

"You have no sense of occasion, son, it's one of your biggest faults." He took a pull at the tankard and looked up with a wicked gleam in his eye. "If I'm to be found dead, I want to make a good impression."

"We're going to dress up for the Duty Boy?" Jarrod said incredulously.

"Absolutely. Duty Boys can be extremely useful creatures, but they lack imagination. That's usually all to the good since their chief talent seems to be for gossip, but on this particular occasion it would work against us. What you don't seem to realize is that a society that has been brought up to believe that it is to its advantage if the nobility keeps grand state will equate pomp with power."

"I could wear the clothes I brought back from the Island if you like."

"I think not, we want something that bespeaks the Discipline. You can wear one of my old gowns. They're too big for me, but I hate throwing things away. I think you should wear those rings you brought back though."

"Oh very well." Jarrod surrendered with a weak smile. "But first we should have the workroom prepared again. There's the horn to grind and the rest of the potions to prepare."

"All true," Ragnor said, "but the first thing we'll do is to have a good meal. I want something solid in my stomach before I season it with unicorn's horn and there won't be any time later. The Duty Boy should be bringing it in any time now. As I said, useful creatures, Duty Boys."

chapter 30

The workroom was swept and polished and bare. The chairs were gone and even the books and scrolls had been banished. A small fire burned pertly in the grate and six beakers sat on the hob in front of it. The Archmage, clad only in a loincloth, waited beside it. Out on the floor the lines of the pentacle looked pink in the light of the setting sun. Jarrod wasn't there. It was inconceivable, Ragnor told himself, that the boy would renege at this stage of the game, but the worm of unease kept on burrowing.

He had kept up a cheerful front, a deliberate nonchalance, while they had prepared the potions and laid out the pentacles, but he was aware of the risks, especially to himself. There was a good chance that his heart would be overwhelmed even if the unicorn's horn worked for him. He moved closer to the fire, though the evening was warm. If he died and the Canticle worked, there was a good chance that Courtak would end up as Archmage. His exploits had already made him famous in most countries, his face had been on broadsheets. A decisive victory over the Outlanders would make him the best-known Magician since Errathuel.

He heard steps on the stairs and looked up with a feeling of relief.

"Ah, there you are," he said expansively as Jarrod knocked on the open door. "I was beginning to worry. Everything's ready here. I've got a gown for you, rather a nice one as a matter of fact. Only wore it once as far as I can remember. It's over there on the floor with my stuff."

"Thank you, sir, I appreciate it," Jarrod said as he advanced into the room. He was wearing his blue robe and sandals.

"I suggest that we drink the first potion now. We'll wait a bit and see what kind of effect it has." He picked up a beaker from the hob and held it out to Jarrod.

Jarrod took it with a little smile of thanks and they toasted each other silently before they drank. He found the potion gritty, but he couldn't detect anything unusual in the taste.

"I don't much care for the consistency," Ragnor said, "but I thought it would taste different. I don't know what I was expecting, exactly, but this isn't it."

"I know what you mean, but I find that reassuring somehow." He gave a little smile. "I tend to like things that stay the way they are."

"That's an unusual position for a Magician. How old are you?"

"I'll be nineteen come harvest."

Ragnor shook his head. "That's depressing, but it's not your fault. However, you're the most conservative-minded nearly-nineteen-year-old I've ever come across. At that age, young men are usually fiercely against the existing order." He paused and looked quizzically at Jarrod. "Tell me," he said, "what would you like to do once this whole thing is over?"

"I haven't thought about it," Jarrod confessed.

"Well, think about it now. We've got nothing else to do." And it keeps the mind from worrying, he added to himself.

"I'd like to have a nice long holiday," Jarrod said without hesitation. "I haven't had one since I left the Collegium."

"That you shall have, I promise you." Ragnor grinned suddenly. "After the speeches and parades and investitures, of course. I remember how you love those."

Jarrod made a face.

"Where will you go?"

"The first place I'd go to is Belengar," Jarrod said. "I've got some unfinished business there."

"Some little whore, I'll be bound."

"No, as a matter of fact," Jarrod lied. "I've never seen the Exotic Bird Market and when I was on the Island I promised myself, if I got back alive, that I'd go and see the birds in Belengar."

"I haven't been to Belengar in, ooh, it must be thirty-five years. D'you know I can't remember when I last had a holiday? That's pathetic. If we come back from this alive, I've a mind to join you. D'you feel anything yet, by the way?"

"I can feel the potion working. I'm beginning to get that floating feeling."

"So am I. That's why I asked. I don't know how it normally affects you, but for me the onset seems to be a bit early."

"I agree. It usually takes about twenty minutes for me."

"Take a look at the waterclock, would you. My eyes aren't as good as they used to be and I'm too vain to wear spectacles."

"It's been ten minutes," Jarrod reported.

"I think we should put the second potion into the pentacle. I'll see to that. You go and put your robe over there."

Jarrod went over to the neat piles of clothing. Beside them, the Chain of the Archmages was a gleaming coil and the stones in the triple tiara glittered. What he could see of the gown he would wear later looked very grand. He pulled the blue robe off over his head, shucked his sandals and unknotted his breachclout. He kept the Guardian's rings, one on each hand. Ragnor joined him and added his loincloth to the collection. They both turned and faced the pentacles.

"Let's wait a little longer," Ragnor said. "No ill effects so far, but we can afford to be a little cautious. So, what would you like to do, if you had the choice, when your long, long holiday is over?"

Jarrod took so long to reply that Ragnor wondered if he'd heard the question.

"If I had my druthers," he said finally, "I'd give up Magic and go and live quietly somewhere. Do a little farming, maybe."

"Sorry, lad," Ragnor said sympathetically, "You can't walk away from Magic. It's in the blood; you're born with it."

"Then I'd like to be a Weatherward with a cabin by some mountain lake."

"A modest enough request," Ragnor said. Poor bastard, he thought. He doesn't realize what success would mean. People would make pilgrimages to his lake, there'd be souvenirs, likenesses of the great Mage. He shuddered at the prospect.

"Are you all right, Archmage?"

"What? Oh yes. That wasn't the potion."

"Perhaps we should start then?" Jarrod suggested.

"I don't see why not. Why don't you light the pentacles?"

Jarrod concentrated briefly and the lines flamed, then subsided into an even glow. They went forward side by side. Jarrod's skin tingled briefly as each line was crossed. They seated themselves in the middle, adjusted the positions of the beakers to their liking and began to submerge themselves.

The two Magicians emerged from their trances within an eyeblink of each other. The daymoon had set and the windows were black. The green werelight from the pentacles was reflected in them. Ragnor stretched and looked around.

"Blast!" he said. "I forgot to bring the candles back in. Better not extinguish the pentacles." He got up and examined himself. "How are you feeling?" he asked.

"Wonderful and a little bit nervous," Jarrod replied as he got to his feet.

"Perfectly natural. For myself, I feel as if I was forty again. I always enjoy this part of it. No aches, no pains and my knees work the way they did when I was twenty. The unicorn's horn seems to have enhanced things." He turned and made his way over to the clothes.

Jarrod stayed where he was. He could hear and feel Nastrus without the slightest effort. The colt was chewing hay and thinking of nothing in particular. In his mind, Beldun was back on the Island in exactly the same way that his mother and sister were back on the Island. Jarrod wondered if he was aware of the link.

'Of course I am. I can also see what you see. Beldun's horn has changed you. I don't have to slow down for you.'

'We're about to perform the spell,' Jarrod said silently.

'Yes, I know you are and I shall obviously be with you when you do. Don't worry, I'll only watch.'

'It'll be good to know you're there. Well, I suppose I better get dressed.'

'Typically human,' Nastrus remarked.

Jarrod joined Ragnor and put his breachclout back on. He picked up the gown and shook it out. It was black and shiny and slick to the touch. A band of stars in silver thread and diamonds ran diagonally from shoulder to hem, reminding him of the Guardian's cloak. He raised it above his head and wriggled into it. It seemed to take a long time before his head came out into the light again. He tugged it into place and moved his arms around. It was a fairly good fit. He slipped his feet into the sandals and turned to help the Archmage with the Chain. When it was set he bent down and picked up the tiara. Ragnor took it and set it firmly on his head.

"That does it, I think," the Archmage said. "One more beaker to go and then it's out onto the balcony."

They went over to the fireplace and retrieved the last two beakers.

"I wish we had something to stir them with, but here goes." Ragnor drank quickly and put the beaker down. Jarrod followed suit.

"What exactly are we going to do when we get out there?" Ragnor asked.

"We'll summon up all the power we can handle and then we'll translate it into the Canticle. We do it the way we always would."

"Quite, but do we do it linked?"

"What do you think?" Jarrod asked.

"Well, I would suggest that we be joined, but that I hold myself in reserve. If you need help or additional energy, call on me, but, if anything happens to me, you are to break contact immediately. You are not, I repeat not, to try to help me. It is the spell that is paramount. You are not to let yourself be distracted, no matter what. We shall never have this chance again. It doesn't matter what happens to me, you must complete the Canticle. Is that quite clear?"

"As water, Archmage," Jarrod said, mildly irked by the lecture. "I shall do my utmost, as much for Beldun as for us." He paused. "Of course the same warning applies equally to you. If anything starts to happen to me, save yourself. Strand can't afford to lose you."

The lined face with the bright eyes broke into a soft smile. "Thank you for that, son. I have a talent for surviving. Now, how are you feeling?"

"Marvellous. Very lightheaded, but absolutely clear. It's as if there were an extra reality. Things seem more vivid and more remote at the same time." He looked over at the Archmage. "Have you ever had the feeling that if you reached out to touch something it wouldn't be quite where you thought it was?"

"Frequently," Ragnor replied. "Every time I have a bad morning after."

"This must be the pleasant version."

"Let's not waste it then. Let's get out there and drive the bastards back so far that a cloudsteed couldn't find them in a sennight." At the mention of the cloudsteed Nastrus reacted, but it was over in an instant.

Ragnor put out the werelight with a wave of his hand and the room was dark. Jarrod waited while his eyes adjusted and then walked over to the glass doors and opened them. The moist, warm air of the night flooded around him. He stepped out onto the balcony. It was wet underfoot but Jarrod didn't notice. He was concentrating on the horizon. Somewhere out there, beyond the walls of Celador, beyond the Causeways, lay the enemy's atmosphere.

The Archmage came out and stood beside him at the balustrade. Thin clouds covered the nightmoon, but there was enough light to cast faint shadows. Jarrod leaned forward and looked down. The courts were empty and the windows were dark. If there were any daring couples hiding in the roof pavilions to watch, no candle flicker gave sign of their presence. No sounds came from the supposedly sleeping town behind. It was as if they were alone in the capital, lofty champions facing the foe with nothing intervening.

It was as it should be. Jarrod felt powerful and confident. There was a tingling in his belly and a pricking between his shoulderblades. He looked down at his hands resting on the top of the coping, half expecting them to be rimmed in light. They were not. Both the rings were dull.

"I'm going to try something," he said.

"Shall we join up?" Ragnor asked.

"Not yet. I'm going to see if I can bring the Rings of the Keeper to life."

Jarrod closed his eyes and concentrated on his memories of the Place of Power as it had been. The cromlechs stood in a circle around a bright patch of green and the three great stones rose like a giant's stepstool in their midst. Nastrus was a constant and interested presence in his mind as he began to intone the words that Greylock had taught him, words used, once upon an eternity, by the Guardian's people. They rolled out easily and he knew that the pitch was perfect, but there was no response, no acknowledgment. He opened his eyes and looked at the rings. They were unchanged.

"No good," he said in his normal voice. "The Place of Power may not have come back yet, or perhaps I'm too far away."

"I don't know about that," Ragnor said. "There's runelight on my gown and my hair's beginning to stand up on end."

Jarrod turned to see and it was true. Little blue sparks were playing in Ragnor's beard.

"Time then," he said and faced north again.

Jarrod stared out past gargoyles and roofpeaks, past spires and chimneystacks, out across ground trampled by armies for innumerable generations, out to the undulating curtain that blocked out the rest of the world. He raised his arms, impelled to the gesture by the occasion, and, as he did so, he felt Ragnor join him in a linkage of force that included the unicorn. Jarrod took a deep breath and sang out the first line of the Canticle. Fibrillations coursed through him immediately, rolling waves of sensate energy like nothing he had ever experienced, certainly not what something as humdrum as the Canticle of Dissipation should occasion.

There was a gathering, as of thunderheads before a storm, and, as the invocation proceeded, it built. It seemed to Jarrod that he grew taller, absorbing the burgeoning energy, and, as he expanded, he called on his companions for more. There seemed to be no limit to his capacity and the coruscation within made him feel more potent. Forces that he had not thought to dream of filled out the corners of his being, pushing him upwards and outwards. The turrets and steeples of Celador were below him now and becoming tinier by the moment.

The orison issued from his mouth with the force of a gale, booming out across the leagues, battering at the foulness that straddled the plain. He floated and watched the result. The lash of his words was absorbed by the sponge of darkness that was the Outland. Miserable spawn! More was needed.

No sooner thought than supplied. Energy flowed into him,

confidently from Nastrus, cautiously from Ragnor. It exalted him. He was the sky and lightning was his plaything. Beams of light flashed from his fingertips and with them he scythed along the leading edge of the enemy's front, boiling the murk away.

He felt a fierce pang of joy, echoed exultantly by Nastrus, and he surged forward. There was anger in him too. There had always been anger, anger at the Outlanders for killing his father before he could know him and for his mother's pining end. That anger grew as the verses of the Canticle, transformed beyond all imagining, sped away to wreak havoc. There were scores to settle. There were thousands of deaths to be repaid, human deaths and the slaughterings of cloud-steeds and warcats. Centuries of bereavement called out for vengeance and Jarrod was happy to oblige.

Images of the cloudsteeds as they tumbled from the skies came into his mind and he knew that Nastrus was reinforcing his will. There was anger in the unicorn as well and a cold purpose that Jarrod had never sensed before. It took hold and galvanized him, strengthening his voice and his will to destruction. Yes, indeed, he thought, unicorns could be implacable fighters. The images persisted and with them came power in surges that Jarrod could barely contain. He relished the moment, gravid with mastery, and then let it go in league-long sweeps. The fire that he directed and that was, somehow, a part of him, careened along the edges of the Outland fume and burned it away. There were no flames, no satisfying sizzle, at least none that reached his ears, but something visceral inside him, something deeply buried, responded with greedy elation.

He was opposed. It came as a shock, although he knew that it should not. It had just never crossed his mind, but there were pinpoints of red among the roilings nevertheless. They were a scattered handful at first and then clusters, like fireflies let out of jars. He expected to be hit, but he felt nothing. Laughter cascaded out of him. He was untouchable.

The unicorn was within him and they were entirely ineffective against it. Their dreaded weapons had been reduced to children's toys. They could not send him spilling from the skies as they had the cloudsteeds. He spread his arms wide and extinguished them.

The tide of energy drove him on. He looked, or pointed, or merely willed, and the poisonous covering writhed and bubbled, was sucked up into vapors and was gone. Where it had been, fungal forests burned. The continuation of the Meander River was revealed, unguessed-at hills and lakes came forth. Jarrod saw none of it. His vision was fixed on the endless undulation that had shielded the Others so efficiently for so long.

He pressed on single-mindedly, gliding west to east and back again. He rose on the spirals of heat that his own destructions had created and swooped down again, working in long, overlapping cuts reminiscent of the reapers he had watched when he was a boy. They had been harvesting. He was preparing the land for future crops.

It was an enormous task. He had not realized quite how large the Outland was. He had been well past Umbria's eastern edge and an equal distance beyond the Mountains of the Night that marked Arundel's Western border. The blanket of corruption had gone further still. He knew without looking back that the Causeways were out of sight. There was more of the darkness ahead. The Canticle was almost at an end, but there was still so much to do.

". . . That we may see clear," he said, completing the verse.

He hung there, adrift over a ghostly landscape. There was a spangled sky above him and the nightmoon. All else was unfamiliar. There was a mountain range ahead of him, toothy white peaks showing clear. Its flanks were shrouded in Outland fog. Should he recite the Canticle again? He thought not. It was plain to him now that the words were themselves a covering. Power was the only thing that mattered, that and his ability to control and direct it. The rest was irrelevant. He marvelled that he had not seen it before.

Enough of rest. He had a job to do. Both Nastrus and Ragnor were there to draw upon. He started off again and worked his way methodically towards the foothills. It was a monstrously long range, stretching from Arundel to Umbria, or so it seemed. There were no reference points. It was an endless and surreal undertaking. Constantly moving, constantly transforming energy into an instrument of cleansing and transmitting it out and down. He found it to be hard work. What he thought of as his body began to throb. Part of it was pleasure and part of it was pain and it was difficult to tell which was which.

Finally, it was done. The slopes were clear, the snow-covered shoulders of the peaks gleamed in the night. And still Jarrod wasn't satisfied. He had come a long way, but he would never be able to come this far again. The toll on his body was masked by the pulsing of the forces it harbored, but he knew that he would not recover from the night's work in time to use the rest of the powder. If the horn had to be used again, someone else would take his place.

He marshaled himself and rose up the face of the mountains. He would tackle the far side, but he would be sensible and pace himself. All that was needed was enough clear ground on the other side to make the mountains into a daunting obstacle for the enemy. He came level with the serrations and saw the nightmoon's reflection skittering out across water. He experienced an epiphany of relief. He had reached the end of the Outlands. It was over.

He turned then and knew, suddenly, that he was extremely tired. The Alien Plain was in front of him, looking like one of the relief maps he had seen in Fortress Talisman, though the geography was entirely unfamiliar. Strand seemed to have curved up under him and there was nothing on the horizon. That, in itself, was not too worrisome. He was, after all, no stranger to foreign terrains, and while he certainly felt fatigue, it was held in check by the continuing flow of energy. There was no reason why he should not make it back.

Jarrod looked out across the vast tract that he had just conquered and saw a barren, moonstruck landscape. There were no trees, no roads or buildings, no signs that intelligent, bellicose creatures had flourished there. He had wanted them destroyed, wanted no trace of them to remain, but the reality was sobering. We've defeated them once and for all, he told himself. It's a time for rejoicing. The power sang through him, but the thought rang hollow. Time to go back in any case. He launched himself south.

He was travelling against the wind now and he felt it. The energy was there for the extra effort if he cared to use it, but he knew that his protection against it had worn thin. He tried to gain height when there was the slightest updraft, but it was nighttime and the heat from his previous passage had dissipated. He skimmed along and his progress began to feel agonizingly slow. There was time now to take in the vast stretches of bare prairie, the uncountable small lakes and the huge expanse of water where the Meander ended. Long banks of hills lay outlined by their shadows. Other shadows cast by clouds raced under him.

He felt the euphoria that signalled the end of Magic-making creeping up on him. Not yet, he thought. There's still too far to go. Concentrate, he told himself, and concentrate he did, rolling forward on a wave of his own creating. Strand gradually turned under him and a tiny cluster of points on the horizon became the spires of Celador. They were heartening and daunting at the same time; daunting because they were still so very far away. This is not the reality, he told himself firmly, fighting the languor that threatened to engulf him. I am on the balcony with Ragnor.

But where was Ragnor? A dart of uneasiness sped through him. He couldn't feel Ragnor. He'd been so preoccupied that he hadn't felt him go. Nastrus was still there and that was reassuring. He could feel his presence, the only problem was that he could no longer tell what the unicorn was thinking. It was as if there was a pane of glass between them. I am on the balcony, Jarrod repeated. This is not reality.

'Real enough, wouldn't you say?' A familiar voice filled Jarrod's consciousness.

"Guardian?" It was more a gasp than a question.

'Who else could reach you now?' The tone was ironic. *'You know, for a moderately simple organism you cause a disproportionate amount of trouble. It was fortunate that I was monitoring this planet. In fact I should have caught it earlier, but who could have imagined that you could cause this amount of damage?'*

The tone had remained light, but Jarrod did not like the tenor. "You knew I would fight the Outlanders," he said. "You even gave me these rings."

'Yes, I know. I was prepared for your altering the course of the war, a little, delaying things, perhaps hastening your people's eventual victory. I rationalized. I never expected this kind of wholesale devastation.'

The voice had darkened and Jarrod felt a shiver of alarm.

'I could never condone the willful extermination of an entire sentient species. Species come and species go, I'm well aware of that. It is part of the natural progression. But now, because of you, I have precipitated the demise of an entire culture.'

"I don't know what you want, Lord Guardian," Jarrod said wearily. "Truth to tell, I don't even know if you're really here, or if you are a product of Beldun's horn. I simply did what everyone wanted me to do."

'Yes.' The word was drawn out. *'I can see that you did. Fortunately, you weren't too thorough. There are areas beyond your borders that remain untouched. The trouble is that you have destroyed the balance between the two atmospheres. It is just a matter of time before the rest are overwhelmed.'*

"Can you save them?" Jarrod asked, trying to keep aloft.

'It can be done. It will mean increasing the Island's size

and, that, in turn, means an infinite number of other adjustments.' He sounded quite happy at the prospect.

"I'm glad," Jarrod said.

'No thanks to you, though,' the Guardian retorted. *'It's not an ideal solution, I grant you, but at least something of their culture will be preserved.'*

"Are you going to let me live?" Jarrod asked and was surprised by his own temerity. He edged towards Celador.

The air around him was flooded with cynical humor.

'I should have killed you before, or kept you on the Island, but it's too late now. The damage has been done. In a perverse kind of way, I rather hope you survive.

'I do know one thing, though. You and your kind are addictive. I am glad that I shall have a lot to occupy me. I intend to have nothing more to do with this planet.'

Jarrod continued to inch south. In his present, supremely lightheaded state it seemed quite reasonable to be holding a conversation with the Guardian.

"What about the unicorns?" he asked.

There was silence, as if the Guardian had not expected another question. *'They can come and go as they please,'* he said finally. *'However, they will not be permitted to bring anything, or anybody, back to the Island.'*

"What about Marianna?" Jarrod pressed.

'Ah yes, the Lady Marianna. I shall miss her more than I miss you. She was good company towards the end and her interaction with your clone was fascinating. I don't think she wanted to leave, but I'm afraid I gave her no choice.'

The battlements of Celador were clearly visible and Jarrod bent his efforts towards them. There were questions still to be asked though, serious questions, but it was getting hard to concentrate.

"Where is she?"

'Close to a place called Stronta, I believe. She said her father was there.'

Stronta triggered the next question.

"Will you still let Greylock come back?"

'Your friend at the Force Point? Well, there's obviously no need for shielding now, so the Force Point should be back on line almost immediately. More than that I can't say.'

Jarrod couldn't think of anything else to ask. He was in sight of the tower and the desire to reach it was crowding out everything else. The Guardian's voice sounded again, faintly.

'I shall miss you, Jarrod Courtak. I shall cherish the clones, but they will never have your unpredictability.'

The Palace itself was below Jarrod now, the tower ahead and, beyond it, the town. There were no lights in the castle, but there were yellow windows here and there in the town. They'll wake up in the morning, he thought, and their whole world will be changed. It all happened here and they slept through it.

He was over the roof of the Great Hall and the tower with its balcony loomed. He could see two figures. One was sitting against the wall, tiara atilt, mouth agape, the other was slumped over the balustrade. Both had white hair. He reached out to the manikin draped over the stone coping. His sense of well-being was still intact, but he knew that the energy in him was fading rapidly. Probably just as well, he thought, most of his control was gone. There was enough left, though; there had to be enough left. . . .

Jarrod!

It was a trumpet blast to Jarrod's tired system, but it was indelibly Nastrus. The pane of glass had shattered and the colt was back in his mind.

'Not now,' he thought irritably. *'If I don't reach him, I'll die.'*

'You won't die,' Nastrus said calmly and Jarrod could tell that the unicorn was almost as weary as he was. *'We told you that the horn would protect you and it will.'*

'But it's almost gone. If I don't get back to my body in time, I'll die, horn or no horn.'

'You'll get back,' Nastrus assured him, *'and the moment*

*you do, you'll be unconscious for a good long time. There's
enough of Beldun's horn still inside you for you to be able to
listen and there's something you have to know before you slip
away.'*

There was a buoyancy to Nastrus' thoughts, a happiness
that matched any that Magic could produce and it was infec-
tious. Jarrod felt a little restored.

'Well, try not to be long-winded,' he said with a touch of
humor.

'Beldun was long-winded. I was never long-winded,' Nastrus replied, mock-serious. *'But what I want you to understand is how proud of you Beldun would be.'*

'I think I probably went too far,' Jarrod said.

'Nonsense.' Nastrus was all certainty. *'It had to be done.
You have no comprehension of what it is like to lose one's
original homeland, and without our work this night, you
would have lost yours. That doesn't matter, what is important
is that you succeeded and Beldun's place in the Memory has
been confirmed. Have you any idea what that means to the
family?'*

Nastrus was bubbling over with pride and glee. Jarrod's
own feelings were calm and elegiac by contrast, but the
unicorn's enthusiasm was a tonic.

'I'm glad that someone's happy,' he said. The pull of the
balcony was strong.

Nastrus knew it. *'We couldn't have done it without you,
you do know that,'* he said quickly. *'My brother could not
have asked for a better, more effective, friend. You, too, will
live in the Memory. "Jarrod-Human, without whom the sacrifice would have been incomplete." You will be famous down
all the Lines of Force.'*

Jarrod chuckled, but the idea warmed him. He looked down
and saw that he was directly over the decrepit body that he
knew to be himself. He didn't remember covering the distance between them, but it was only a matter of feet now.

'Will you be here when I, if I . . .'

'Of course I shall. You are a very important part of us now. There may be lots of us. Pellia will want to bring her foals here. How could she not? Beldun's blood will run in their blood, his memories with theirs. Many will be drawn here.' There was amusement. 'Our kinlines are spread wide.'

Can't last any longer, Jarrod thought and Nastrus knew that he was fading.

'Sleep well, Jarrod-friend, almost unicorn. You are a signal hero to our kind, and, when you wake, you will be a hero to yours.'

Jarrod did not hear him, but his final thought was that he was a hero.

The nightmoon had shed the last of her veils and was riding high. The walls and spires of Celador were bathed in silver, as was the balcony of the Archmage's Tower. The gowns glittered in the light and the tiara winked. People emerged slowly into the surrounding courts. Anxious groups gathered on the street corners and pointed to the sky, murmuring to one another, as if a raised voice might bring back the fires.

Jarrod had been wrong about them. They may have stayed indoors, constrained by the curfew, but few among them had slept. They could not know what had happened beyond the walls, but they were well aware that Magic had stalked abroad that night. Indeed, how could they not? Light had blazed from the Archmage's Tower, comets had been seen and there were some who said that great auroras had danced beyond the Causeways.

Stronta slept under that same moon, unaware of what had happened to the west. The Great Maze glimmered in front of it, as it had before Stronta was built. Then it had nothing to protect. Now it had nothing to protect the city from. Beyond it was another shimmering as, one by one, a ring of ancient dolmens wavered into solidity. The circle was broken at the top end and there a red-stained block began to bulk. Behind it, a white stele rose, taller, but not as tall as the great black monolith that had always been there. The shimmering ceased and the nightmoon's light held sway once more. Except over the black rock. It stood in the center and reflected nothing. It was not entirely lifeless, though. On its flat matte top a tiny figure stirred and groaned weakly. Greylock opened his eyes and wondered where he was.

The nightmoon sailed on uncaring, following her brother who followed the sun. If the conditions on Strand had changed on her watch, it was of no concern to her. They had changed before and doubtless would again, but her path would be the same for as long as there was a Strand to circle. She was waxing now. In a sennight she would begin to wane. That was enough change for a nightmoon.